Born in Liverpool in 198█ █████ █████ █ned at the
Liverpool Institute for Perf██████ █████ █, and worked
as an actress for more than ███ ████ █████ usical theatre and
new writing. She then went █████ ██ █nd work in Dubai,
where she founded Hayley's ██████et: a children's theatre
company specialising in musical theatre, acting and play-
writing. During her time in Dubai, she was also a regular
talk show host on Dubai Eye 103.8, the UAE's no.1 English
speaking talk radio station. Hayley currently lives in London
with her husband and their two children.

By the same author:

Never Saw You Coming

Love,
Almost

HAYLEY DOYLE

avon.

Published by AVON
A division of HarperCollins*Publishers* Ltd
1 London Bridge Street
London SE1 9GF

www.harpercollins.co.uk

HarperCollins*Publishers*
1st Floor, Watermarque Building, Ringsend Road
Dublin 4, Ireland

A Paperback Original 2021
1

First published in Great Britain by HarperCollins*Publishers* 2021

A catalogue copy of this book is available from the British Library.

ISBN: 978-0-00-836577-6

Typeset in Minion by Palimpsest Book Production Limited, Falkirk, Stirlingshire
Printed and bound in UK by CPI Group (UK) Ltd, Croydon CR0 4YY

MIX
Paper from
responsible sources
FSC™ C007454

This book is produced from independently certified FSC™ paper
to ensure responsible forest management.

For more information visit: www.harpercollins.co.uk/green

For Cheryl.

But of all these friends and lovers,
There is no one compares with you.
— *In My Life*, John Lennon & Paul McCartney

PROLOGUE

Three months earlier

'YES!' I say to Jack.

Perhaps too enthusiastically.

We're three days into our first holiday together. Beside a chaotic dual carriageway, an old lady lays out pop-up gift cards – intricately handmade and just thirty baht each – on the entrance steps to a modern shopping mall. The mall towers above us, LED-screen advertisements for international brands beckoning us to come inside. Jack and I gaze at one particular familiar logo. There we stand, stationary, as thousands move frantically around us. We're caught in a time lapse. The hot sun scorches through hazy white clouds. I haven't even held Jack's hand today; I'm just too hot and bloated. My pounding head and racing heart is a constant reminder that we hit it too hard, and now our bender is laughing back at us and yelling, 'I told you so!'

It's safe to say that Bangkok's intense speed has knocked us sideways.

'Yes,' I repeat. 'Please.'

'You sure?' Jack asks. 'I mean, we're on the other side of the world and I don't want you to think I'm not very cultured—'

'I'm sure,' I snap, before he talks us out of it.

'Really, Chloe?'

'YES!'

The golden arches lure us in. We order a feast. As we eat, we comment on how immaculate the restaurant is, how piping hot the fries are, how although it's McDonald's, it somehow just tastes better here than it does at home. Yeah, that's how hungover we are. I finish my meal by scooping up a fallen droplet of Big Mac sauce with my finger. Jack sips the dregs of his Coke like a child, releasing a burp for his grand finale.

'S'cuse me,' he says.

'We're disgusting,' I say.

He's laughing at me, and I know why; my Liverpool accent has come out in full force, as it does when I'm tired – or in this case, hanging. Mocking me, he scrunches up his face, and, making his voice high-pitched, repeats the word 'disgusting'.

It's a terrible – inaccurate – impression. I narrow my eyes.

'Feel better?' he asks, in his own voice. He calls it 'Home Counties'. I call it posh.

'So much better.'

Last night, in between haggling at Patpong night market for fake designer boxer shorts and swerving ping-pong shows, we had done shots in bars. Back at our hotel room, Jack had raided the minibar while I ran a bubble bath. We had had sex in the bath, followed by sex on the balcony.

Dressed in fluffy white robes, I had blended aquatic shades of blue onto Jack's eyelids with my eyeshadow palette and finished them off with a flick of black eyeliner. His tremendous bushy beard had made the overall look grotesque, but to me, he was beautiful. It must have been three in the morning, yet the moon shone on, so out we had wandered again, eating pad thai from a street food vendor who also happened to serve beer. I had bought (another) small wooden frog from a young boy loitering, selling a tray of trinkets.

'We've got about twenty minutes to get back to the hotel before the junk food crash hits us,' Jack says, his infectious smile creating a deep dimple in his left cheek. 'We need our bed.'

He leans across the table, reaches out his hand and tenderly wipes something from my chin. It might have been a dab of salt, or it could well have been a huge dollop of ketchup, but I don't care. The simple touch of his thick skin on mine makes me fuzzy, almost giddy. There's nothing more appealing than the thought of getting into bed with him right now, stripping off my dress – which is more of a loose cotton rag with holes cut out for my head and limbs – and pressing my body against his strong, sandy-haired chest, nuzzling into his neck.

'Come on, hun. Let's go,' I say.

Back outside, I rummage in the embroidered pouch slung across my bare shoulder on a long shoelace strap. It's from Patpong and the perfect size to carry around holiday cash and lip balm. I fish out one hundred baht, hand it to the lady selling cards, and pick out three designs. The lady throws in a fourth card and bows her head. I repeat her actions and thank her very much.

'Chloe, over here!' Jack calls.

A small crowd has gathered a few feet away. 'Look at this bloke,' he says.

Sitting inside a discarded supermarket trolley is a local man, unamused. His feet are bare, but his shirt and trousers suggest a blue uniform of some sort, perhaps for service at a hotel. Directly behind the man is a larger-than-life statue of Ronald McDonald with his giant yellow hands pressed together in the wai greeting, his red smile as bold as the food sitting heavily in my gut. The man seems to have found a perfect little spot to take a break, although he's interrupted by a couple of passers-by who ask if they can have a selfie with him. He nods repeatedly and they all pose tight, gesturing double peace signs.

'I've got to get a pic of this,' Jack says. He digs into his khaki canvas man-bag, another Patpong purchase and one that he has not stopped admiring, wondering why he's never bought anything like it before. I can already see it being slung into his wardrobe, never to be seen again; because believe me, he won't be using that commuting on the London Underground.

Jack ushers me to get into the picture.

'No way,' I cower behind his broad back. 'Leave him be.'

But raising his hands, Jack frames the picture in portrait and . . . *snap*! I glance over Jack's shoulder and he's nailed it. Clear, colourful and precise; not a photo bomber in sight. The man is looking directly into the lens. Ronald McDonald looms in the background, a God-like presence. Bangkok has been captured: a moment of honesty within the bizarre.

Jack shows the man, who gives a thumbs up, and then he shows it to me properly. It's a truly great photograph.

'That could win a prize,' I say.

'We should get it printed and hang it on our wall,' Jack says.

Stopping amidst the choppy sea of fast-paced pedestrians, he's head and shoulders above most, his thick sandy hair a foot above my recently bleached bob. He slaps his hands high onto an imaginary wall, pretending to see his photographic creation hung up there.

'*Our* wall?' I ask.

'Let's live together.'

In the short time I've known Jack, I'm used to his outspoken thoughts, his confident remarks. They're never arrogant, yet always strong, supported by his big physique and naturally bellowing voice. He's the big, friendly giant, and it seems like my innermost desire is coming true; he's *mine*.

'A couple of months ago we didn't even know each other,' I remind him, but there's a chuckle in my voice. I'm making him aware of what others might say, rather than airing my own concerns. To be honest, I don't have any.

'Move in with me, Chloe.'

'You want me to move to London?'

'We'll save a fortune on train fares.'

'How romantic.'

'And we'll see each other seven days a week.'

'Hmm. I might get sick of you, hun.'

'Doubt it. I'm far too adorable.' Oh, how true this is. 'I mean, what's the worst that could happen?' Jack booms, announcing this question to the whole of Bangkok, his arms outstretched like a preacher. I take the opportunity to cuddle into him, sliding my arms around his back as he wraps me up completely. We squeeze each other tight. It's a done deal.

Jack and I are going to move in together. This isn't a pair

of kids making an immature decision, swept up in the magic of youthful lust. We're in our mid – well, late – thirties. We know what we want.

'I reckon I love you, Chloe Roscoe,' he says, not for the first time.

'And I reckon I love you, too, Jack Carmichael.'

We meander back to the hotel, a mellow glow encasing us. We have absolutely nothing to do today. And there's nothing better than doing nothing with Jack.

Nothing at all.

1

I'm rinsing the shampoo out of my hair when I hear the front door slam.

'In the shower!' I yell, stating the obvious. Our flat is small and our shower is noisy. We don't have a bath. I have to brush my teeth sitting on the loo to avoid feeling claustrophobic: yeah, that's how small it is. But we have perks. Our fridge has an inbuilt ice machine and our kitchen door opens out onto the low-level shared patio, making ours the only flat in this redbrick Victorian house with direct garden access.

I don't know where Jack's been. He wasn't home when I got in from school a couple of hours ago and he'd left his phone by the blue Marrakech dish where we keep our keys on the bookshelf in the hall. Wherever he's been, I hope he's brought me a Kinder Bueno. Or a Magnum. Perfect weather for a Magnum.

I apply conditioner and leave it to work its magic while shaving my legs and under my arms. It's a lot of effort to look effortless when it's hot, but needs must. The whole country is experiencing a heatwave and we're heading out to uit in the basement of a pub in Greenwich, I can't imagine there'll be any air-conditioning and sweat will be dripping off the walls, so I need to wear next to nothing. We're going to a comedy night – one of the comedians on the bill is a best mate of Jack's. I've not met this mate before, but apparently he's close to the bone: you either find him hilarious or utterly offensive.

Through the transparent shower enclosure, I see the bathroom door open just a little.

'Where've you been?' I ask, making the mistake of rubbing my eyes with shaving gel on my fingertips and squirming at the sting. 'Jack?'

Jack doesn't respond.

I rinse my face, turn the water off and grab a towel. The bathroom door is slightly ajar.

'Jack?'

As I wrap the towel around myself, wet hair dripping onto my shoulders, the screech of a bar stool against the laminate floor tells me he's in the kitchen. Maybe I should drop the towel, give him a proper welcome home surprise: do a little shimmy-shake. But I expose myself involuntarily when I scream and the towel falls to the ground.

'Who are you?!' I hear from the man standing before me.

I scramble to cover myself, shaking.

'Who the hell are *you*?!' I manage.

He's about twice my age, edging on seventy, but in good shape and a little taller than me. Smart, silver-haired with an impressive hairline, cleanly shaven and wearing a light blue shirt with tailored shorts, he's pale, but doesn't look ill. His mouth is hanging open so wide that I can see his gold and silver fillings. I've seen his photo – it's on the fridge, beside where he's standing now, held up with a magnet of the Leaning Tower of Pisa – except he's decades older in real life. The shape of his green eyes behind his spectacles is eerily familiar. I know exactly who this man is. He's Jack's dad.

Gripping the towel around me with a tight fist, I wipe my free hand dry and offer it. 'I'm Chloe.'

John seems reluctant to accept at first, and we exchange the flimsiest of handshakes as he looks around the flat at anything other than my almost naked body. His focus falls upon last night's dirty dishes. Jack made bolognese. I'd made a lame attempt to start washing up, filling the saucepan with soapy water and letting it soak: remnants of minced beef and chopped onions float around like dead fish.

'Sorry, the place is usually a bit cleaner than this,' I say.

'It's not a problem,' he mumbles, a soft northern lilt in his voice, although I know he's lived the majority of his life down south. He removes his specs, rubbing his eyes with just his thumb and index finger. 'Uh – who did you say you were again?'

'Chloe . . .'

'Ah, yes. Chloe.'

'It's nice to finally meet you; although I wish I was more suitably dress—'

'Wait. I – I can't recall knowing about a – erm – Chloe.'

'Jack never mentioned me?'

'He . . . He – erm – never . . .'

'Are you okay? Mr Carmichael?'

'It's John. Call me John, please.'

I go to the sink, turn on the tap and fill a glass that's been draining on the side. 'Drink this,' I say.

He thanks me with a nod and drinks fast, dribbling onto his shirt. I pretend not to notice and turn around to look at the photo on the fridge: Jack on his dad's shoulders on a beach in Majorca.

'It's such a coincidence,' I say. 'I went to the same resort with me mum and dad when I was little, so I recognised that beach straight away. Jack said you stayed in a villa, but we were on a package holiday. Imagine if we were there at the same time, though. Wouldn't that be hilarious? It was 1989, I think. Can you remember when this was taken? Jack's rubbish with dates, isn't he?'

'Chloe,' John says, solemnly. 'Jack's dead.'

'Y'what?'

I'm still looking at the photo. An uncontrollable rush of giggles empties from within me. I don't know how to stop them spilling out of my mouth. Did he just say that Jack was dead? Dead? How is that even possible when his bolognese leftovers are still stuck to the plate by the sink?

'I'm sorry to break the news,' John says. 'I presume you were his – erm – girlfriend?'

'I am,' I catch my breath. 'I am his girlfriend. What's going on? And why don't you know who I am? Is this some sort of prank?'

'It'd be a pretty cruel prank, my dear.'

I must turn around. I must stop looking at this fucking photograph.

But when I do, I don't like what I see in John's face. It's broken. And this is nothing to do with age. Tears are streaming from beneath his specs, rolling down his cheeks. He dabs them with a white cotton handkerchief. I love how men from that generation always have a handkerchief.

'Jack's dead?' I ask.

John nods.

'I promise I didn't mean to laugh just then.'

John nods again. He knows.

A breeze floats in through the open window above the sink.

On a day as hot as today, it should be embraced, but I begin to shiver. John steps forward – perhaps to try and comfort me, or maybe he's decided to close the window – but his foot knocks one of the two bar stools. A stack of textbooks lying haphazardly on the seat falls to the ground between us, loose papers fluttering down in slow motion like white birds. I go to pick them up, but hesitate to ensure my dignity is intact. John gets to the books first. He lays them on the breakfast bar, one by one, reading the titles quietly aloud.

'*Macbeth, Blood Brothers, An Inspector Calls* . . .'

'They're mine,' I tell him. 'For work.'

'You're an actress?'

'No, a teacher.'

'Ah, English literature?'

'Drama,' I say, apologetically. I don't know why. 'I'm covering someone on mat leave.'

John puts the books into a neat pile and hands them over to me, but I don't accept them, keeping my hands tight onto my towel. He returns them to the stool. Every second that passes feels like an hour, a year.

'So, how did . . .' I attempt, but I can't find the words to continue.

'An accident. Hit by a van.'

'Oh!' I laugh again.

'It happened on this road, just a few yards from here.'

'But, how? I mean, Jack's unmissable. He's a massive, hairy bear.'

An almighty din startles me and I gasp, my heart now plunged into the pit of my stomach. My phone is ringing. It's on the breakfast bar, dancing to the vibration. John and I both stare at the device like an alien has invaded, the single word 'Mum' lighting up the screen. It rings and rings and rings, and then it stops. I release a sigh, as does John, who looks as if he's about to say something. Then a message alert interrupts him.

'Sorry, John,' I say, snatching my phone.

The message contains a photo of a wicker laundry basket lined with beige gingham cotton.

Isn't this lovely? Shall I get it for your new flat? Mum x

My flat isn't new. My mum hasn't been to visit yet because she lives in Liverpool and I only recently moved in. My suitcases aren't even fully unpacked yet: the Ikea drawers we purchased last weekend are still flat-packed. Jack, however, has been living here for three years. He has the laundry sorted. *Had* the laundry sorted. Fucking hell, must I resort to past tense already? Over a wicker basket?

I type back.

Thanks Mum but we've got one. Xx

She replies straight away.

It's only 8.99 you know.

Caught in a freakish crossover of past and present, I ignore my mum's persistence and notice that another message looms for me, unread, received at 11.33 this morning. It's from Jack.

Pizza at Dough-Re-Mi before the comedy? X

Yes, I want to reply. *Yeah, definitely.* But Jack's phone is on the bookshelf in the hall and he has no way of coming home to get it because he's been—

'Hit by a van?' I ask John. 'Seriously?'

'Shortly after lunchtime.'

'Why has nobody told me until now?' *Why does my voice sound so normal?*

'We didn't know about you.'

And yet I know about John. About how he grew up on a farm in Lancashire and moved to London when he was

12

twenty-two. He married his wife, Trish, and they settled in Berkshire, had three sons, Jack in the middle. I know that he's retired now, but he used to own a company that made stationery. He sold it for a good amount, but not as good as he'd hoped for. I know that he supports Manchester United, although, unlike Jack, he's never been to a game, and that he's a huge Barry Manilow fan – like, borderline obsessed.

But John – he didn't know about me. Seems Trish didn't – well, doesn't – either.

'Jack's driving licence still has our house as his permanent address,' John tells me. 'I was home today when the police came to inform us. He was killed on the scene.'

This can't be true. We're going to a comedy night.

'I'm here to find Jack's phone,' John continues. 'His work, his friends need to – erm – know.'

'I was hoping for a Kinder Bueno,' I think, perhaps aloud.

'Sorry?'

'Or a Magnum. Perfect weather for a Magnum.'

I stare at my phone, at the last communication I'll ever receive from Jack; except it's interrupted with another message from my mum, followed by another photo.

Chloe look! Cushion covers to match the wicker basket. Aren't they lovely?

My phone slips out of my hand and crashes to the floor. John's arms envelop my bare shoulders and I freeze, allowing this stranger's embrace to hold me together so I don't crack. I'm completely naked beneath this towel and I can hear Jack's king-size laugh bouncing off these basement walls at the sight of his dad and his girlfriend being pelted head-first into a top-notch awkward moment.

Except I can't hear Jack's laugh, can I?

2

I arrive at Beth's in a taxi.

It would've been much quicker to get to Islington on the Overground from Brockley, but that's far too much normality to follow the news I've been hit with. John has stayed behind in the flat, waiting for Trish. They want to spend the night there together, because apparently Trish doesn't like the idea of Jack's flat being left abandoned. I did remind John that I would be there – you know, because I live there – to which he said, 'Ah, that's right'. By the time I'd replaced the towel around my body with actual clothes, he told me that Trish was arriving in about twenty minutes. If that wasn't a cue to leave – well.

'Oh, go fuck yourself!' I overhear Beth scream.

I'm on the front step of her mid-terrace house, thirty quid down thanks to the rush hour surge, my finger hovering over the doorbell. We've known each other since high school and despite her living in London for the past decade, Beth hasn't lost a smidgeon of her Liverpool twang. A door inside slams and the front door swings open.

'Chloe?! Didn't know you were coming.'

Beth's husband Fergus is holding a large bin bag, bulging to match his muscles. Last month, when we went out for Beth's birthday, Jack described Fergus to me as Garfield on steroids. He had a point.

'Chloe?' Fergus asks again. 'You okay?'

I look to his grumpy face as he waits impatiently to lob the rubbish into the plastic bin beside me. I manage some sort of polite closed-mouth smile, confusing him further, and he sidles past to complete his chore.

'She's in the lounge,' he says, with a sharp flick of his neat, ginger hair.

I float through their hallway, not really present, yet somehow here. I pass by the brass-framed art deco mirror, the stylish coat rack, the three canvas prints of their wedding day. My worn-out Converse barely make a sound on the monochrome tiled floor. I linger by the wooden dining bench at the end of the knocked-through lounge-diner, carefully placing my second-hand leather satchel onto the table. It might as well be a used paper bag from a greasy bakery in these surroundings. Everything in Beth and Fergus Douglas's house is shiny and expensive, and although the house itself is small, it's got three bedrooms so worth a fortune in this neck of the woods.

As always beyond seven o'clock, Beth's in her pyjamas; she starts stripping off her corporate daywear before she gets her key in the door. Tonight, she's wearing little chequered shorts and a matching t-shirt. Her smooth, tanned legs are crossed over; she's slouching into the soft white leather sofa, surrounded by various metallic cushions, scrolling through her phone. Her caramel hair extensions are wound into a high bun sitting on the top of her head, her makeup still immaculate from the morning, a pedicure gleaming from her restless little toes.

'Hiya,' I say.

Beth performs a double take, then screams. 'Bloody hell, Chlo! What are you doing here?'

I shrug.

'I mean, is everything alright, babes?' Beth's hand grasps her chest. 'You didn't tell me you were coming . . . Or did you? Am I going mad? Did you message me? Did I tell you to come over?'

Beth scoops her phone off the sofa and taps the screen.

'No, I just decided to come,' I say.

'Y'what?!'

In my haste, I happened to forget how much of a modern-day sin it's become to show up at a friend's house unannounced. I even forgot to dry my hair and apply makeup, although the latter isn't much of a problem since I wear the bare minimum – a bright-red lip on a good day is my only major essential – but Beth doesn't hesitate to point out my state.

'Babes. You look. Like shit.'

'Cheers, pal.'

'And your roots need doing. Badly.'

Fergus returns from outside empty-handed, not acknowledging either me or Beth, and goes into the kitchen. He shouts, 'Brew?'

Beth rolls her eyes and falls back into the sofa, ignoring his question.

'Please,' I shout back.

Creeping towards Beth, I sit delicately on the bold, pink armchair, smoothing down the cotton floral dress I threw on before leaving my flat. Well, I say I sit delicately. What I mean is, I try. Unlike Beth, I'm not particularly delicate or graceful, and attempting to be either takes a lot of effort. I notice a button missing from my dress, right in the middle, exposing the milky-white flab around my belly button. I cross my arms and lean forward.

'Are you and Fergus alright?' I whisper.

'Oh, me and Fergie?' Beth responds, loud enough for the whole street to hear. 'Yeah. We're amazing. Fucking fabulous. Aren't we, Fergie babes?'

I hear a mug slam onto a marble work surface, followed by another.

'He's going on another "work" night out on Friday, aren't you, babes?' Beth goes on. 'This time, it's the casino. I mean, how exciting. How many times have you been the casino with your colleagues, *babes*? Once? Twice? Thirty-five thousand fucking times?'

'Give it a rest, Beth,' Fergus says, placing a mug of tea onto a coaster for me. I won't get offered a biscuit, though; they're both too health conscious to keep refined sugar in the house.

'Rest? Oh, why would I give it a rest?' Beth says, playing the innocent. 'It's so exciting. I mean, it just so happens that you wanna go out on the exact day I'll be ovulating. Isn't that a coincidence?'

I really should have rung her first. Or gone to my local pub.

Fergus takes a seat on the opposite end of the sofa to Beth and takes out his phone, scrolling and tapping. When he's not in his corporate suit, he always looks as though he's either about to hit the gym, or he's just been. Right now, I wish he'd go to the bloody gym. They have one in the spare room.

'Do you have to sit there?' I'm relieved to hear Beth ask.

'Yep,' he grunts. 'My sofa, too.'

17

I sip my tea, even though it's still too hot, and wonder how I'm going to break the news to them that my boyfriend died today. Beth's unfertilised eggs might not have any sympathy for me.

'You'd think he didn't wanna have kids,' she goes on, as if Fergus isn't there. 'And I mean, it's not me putting all the pressure on, is it? It's his bloody mother. The amount of times she's pestered me, asking me when I'll give her grand-kids so they can play in her massive garden-slash-field. I wouldn't mind, but every time we've been up to Scotland, it's pissed it down. I mean, I don't want any child of mine catching pneumonia.'

'She means well, Beth,' Fergus says, his eyes glued to his phone.

'So stay in this Friday.'

'No. Why don't you go out? You love going on the piss with your pals.'

'Not when I'm ovulating.'

'I told you. It's a work thing.'

'Does Jack devote his entire life to "work things", Chlo? Or is just my fella?'

I don't know how to answer these questions, but I also don't think Beth is expecting an answer. She might be talking to me, but everything she's saying is aimed at Fergus. She's so wound up that she's forgotten about being freaked out by my unexpected arrival.

'What's Jack's line of work again?' Fergus asks.

'For fuck's sake, Fergus. How can you not remember?' Beth snarls.

'I've only met the bloke once.'

'So've I.'

'Well forgive me for forgetting what he does.'

18

'He's a project manager, isn't he, Chlo?'

I open my mouth, but nothing comes out.

'What does that even mean? A project manager?' Fergus asks. 'What project does he manage?'

'Video games,' Beth huffs. 'I had a whole conversation with him about it.'

'And I suppose you're expecting a medal?'

'Fuck off, Fergus. Just because I take a genuine interest in people, especially important people, like the fella me best mate's falling in love with. Do you know how long it's been since Chloe said the "L" word to anyone? How long's it been, babes?'

I blow out my lips and shrug.

'Exactly. It's been a long, long time. And this fella, this Jack, he might be the one.'

'Steady on, Beth. She's only been with him for five minutes —'

'*Months*,' I blurt out, interrupting Fergus. 'Five months.'

'Oh my God, has it been that long?' Beth asks, her mouth hanging open. She does some calculations on her manicured fingers. 'Wow. Time flies. How come I've only met him once? Bloody hell, Chlo. Where've you been hiding him?'

This is stupid. Beth knows that I only moved in with Jack a few weeks ago. Before that, I was living in Liverpool and Jack was coming up to visit me at weekends, or I would come to London, or we would meet in the middle somewhere and stay in a hotel. We even managed a holiday in Thailand for two weeks. And anyway, if memory serves me, Beth kept Fergus a secret for a year before she introduced him to anybody. But none of this matters now. This whole conversation is moving at such a pace, it's like I'm on a train and completely missed the stop where I'm supposed to announce why I'm really here.

'Before you know it, twelve years'll go like that,' Beth clicks. 'Beware, babes. You might end up like me and soft lad.'

'Well, I won't get the chance to find out,' I say.

Beth's hand clasps her mouth and it dawns on her why I must look so dreadful.

'You split up?' she asks, high-pitched like a violin. 'Is that why you're here?'

I shake my head. Fergus finally sees this as a reason to leave the room and mutters something about leaving us 'ladies' to it, but Beth orders him to sit back down.

'You'll only ask me what happened later,' she says. 'Be supportive, Fergus.'

'I'm sure Chloe'd rather just talk to you.'

'You don't mind Fergus staying, do you, babes? I mean, he can give you the male perspective.'

I lean forward, rest my elbows on my knees. I guess now is the time to—

'Did he leave you?' Beth asks. 'Or was it your call? Was it just not working?'

Oh, it was working fine, wonderfully. But thanks to a spanner being thrown into the works – one the size of a delivery van going fifty-two on a road with a twenty-mile-an-hour speed limit – it had come to an abrupt end.

'No, it's none of those things,' I say, each word slow as I build myself up to *say it*.

'Shit, is he married?'

'Is he gay?' Fergus pipes up. Beth throws a metallic cushion at him.

I take a gulp of tea. I can't imagine telling Beth – or anyone, for that matter – that Jack Carmichael – the fella I met at the opening night of a terrible musical just five months ago, the man who turned on a light within me and made

20

me believe he's a species in his own right, a unique and brilliant individual with the ability to make me feel everything that is pure and good – is dead.

'We had breakfast together this morning,' I find myself saying. I'd last seen him sat at the breakfast bar, fixated on the canvas print hanging above the cooker, a photo from our holiday in Thailand; the man in the shopping trolley. As usual, Jack was pondering about what the man was *actually* doing there, as I half-listened before dashing out to work myself. 'We never have breakfast together during the week. He leaves for work so early . . .'

But he had a day in lieu.

Fuck.

Jack would still be alive if he'd just gone to work today. He would never have left our flat in the middle of the day, crossed the road and . . . oh. I think I know what happened now. Jack must've realised he'd left his phone behind, by the blue Marrakech dish. So he'd run back; crossed the road again without thinking.

'What a fucking idiot!' I say. Or perhaps yell.

'That's the spirit,' Beth says, standing up and cheering. 'Fuck him. If he can't see how fucking fabulous you are, you're better off without him. I mean, at least you only knew him for five minutes—'

'Months,' Fergus corrects her.

'Whatever. Fergie babes, go and make yourself useful and open a bottle of wine, will you?'

'I don't want wine,' I say.

'Whiskey then. Get Chloe a glass of that good stuff, the one your boss fobbed you off with after you thought you were getting a pay rise. Now, Chloe. Either tell me everything, or tell me nothing. If you don't wanna say the name "Jack" ever again, that's fine by me. I'll make sure you've forgotten he ever existed in no time.'

'No,' I protest. 'I'll never forget.'

'Oh babes, what the hell did he do? It's not like you to be so . . . crushed.'

I wince. I haven't had a chance to think about what physically happened to Jack yet, but oh God, what if he was crushed? Did every bone in his body break? Did he bleed to death?

'Did he hit you?' Fergus asks, his tone low and solemn.

'God, NO.' I stand, joining them.

'Because if he did, I'll kill him for you. I will, you know. I'll kill the bastard.'

Fergus clenches his fists.

'That's right, Fergie my love,' Beth whoops, giving her husband a supportive pat on the back. 'Let's kill him!'

'No, you don't understand.'

'I do. I do, babes.' She edges towards me, shooing Fergus away like a pigeon and reaching out to give me a hug. 'Ah, you really liked him, didn't you? You thought he might be the—'

'Beth, no, don't hug me!'

'Whoa. Okay,' she jumps back.

'I'm sorry,' I try again. 'He's . . .'

I'm trembling. I notice it in my knees, particularly the left one. God, it's trembling so hard that it's going to dislocate. I slap my hands down, trying to control it. My hands are clammy, yet cold. I might be sick.

'Can we get some air?' I ask.

Fergus has already started doing burpees in the back garden. I follow Beth out front and sit on the brick wall, staring at the grey pavement, and at Beth's dainty bare feet.

'We should be in Greenwich,' I say, catching my breath.

'So why are you here? In Islington?'

'It's that comedy night. You know, Jack's mate? The crass one?'

'I dunno . . .'

'Ross Robson?'

'Never heard of him.'

'No, you don't get it. He's, he's,' my breathing is shallow; my voice is cracking; 'he's dead . . .'

'Yep!' Beth goes in for the hug I told her not to do. She squeezes me and pulls my face down onto her shea-butter-scented shoulders. Like a mother consoling her child, she strokes my hair and kisses the top of my head, repeating her words as if whispering a lullaby, 'He's dead to you. Good. Good riddance. You said, it. He's dead. Dead to you—'

'NO,' I break away, my eyes heavy with tears. 'Beth. He's *dead*.'

Beth's eyes pop out; her complexion drains. Her sharp fingernails dig into my upper arms. Beth won't be grief-stricken. She won't even be sad, not really, because she didn't know Jack; not enough to grieve him in any way. She's simply in shock. Because things like this don't happen. Not in real life.

'Beth . . .' I say, desperate for the horror of this moment to pass.

Her nails dig deeper.

'Beth, you're hurting me.'

She pauses, then her thumb strokes my arm.

'What happened?' she asks, gently. 'When?'

'Oh God, I need to go, just be on me own.'

'Chlo—'

'No. I'm begging you, pal. I don't know anything other than . . .' and I clam up again.

23

No. I simply cannot say what happened to Jack today. This is all too surreal. Beth's road is spinning around us, the terraced houses dancing in zigzags around the parked cars, the evening breeze warm and sticky and making me gag. So, taking advantage of Beth not wearing any shoes, I break away from her, whisper something about being sorry, and run.

3

The day Jack gave me a key to his flat, I responded badly.

It wasn't in a little red box or tied to a fancy ribbon, but he did get down onto one knee and, throwing his arms to the gods, pretended he was in some sort of amateur dramatic Shakespeare production. He then took the key from his shirt pocket, held it up like a prized chalice and shouted, 'TA-DA!'

'Oh, I've already got one,' I said.

Back during one of my early visits, I'd nipped down the road to the Sainsbury's Local to buy some chocolate and Jack had given me the spare key to let myself back in. I'd just forgotten to give it back to him.

'Well, you could just play along,' Jack said quietly, gritting his teeth.

'Sorry, hun. I meant, OH YAY!'

Standing outside our flat now, that same key in my hand, I hesitate to open the door. Jack didn't own this flat; he rented it. From his parents. I was due to contribute to the rent and bills, starting from this month, and my landlords were to become the very people who are inside right now, perhaps watching the telly, taking a shower, making a coffee. The people who never knew I lived here.

A warm glow filters from the tall lamp in the lounge out onto the flower bed beside the driveway, yellow and purple petals highlighted like miniature stepping-stones. Our neighbours, the couple who live in the second-floor flat, are the keen gardeners, not me or Jack. They keep the front of the house looking delightful with hanging baskets and kindly mow the communal back lawn, too. I wonder if they know about Jack yet. There's no flicker from the telly or noise that I can make out, so John and Trish must be in bed. Our bed. *My* bed.

I check my phone is on silent and notice a reply from Beth. I'd sent her a message after subconsciously arriving at the tube station, telling her I was sorry for running off like that but that I just wasn't ready to talk about it yet.

I understand babes. I'm here for you whenever the time is right. Love you xxx

I slide my key into the door and open it with minimal disruption.

He's there; everywhere. Jack.

The musty smell of his parka. The dried mud from his giant wellies that he never cleaned after last year's Glastonbury. The hints of aftershave that always linger from his overspray in the morning, leaving me to get dressed within a cloud of manly spice. The lemongrass candle from Thailand that we only light on Friday nights when we're both home.

He's just *here*.

I tiptoe along the narrow hallway in the dark, cursing each creaky floorboard beneath the weathered Persian carpet runner. The bedroom door is closed, so I turn in to where the lamplight greets me. The small lounge and kitchen are

26

open-plan, separated by the breakfast bar. This room is one of the things I love about this cosy place. I throw my satchel onto the L-shaped sofa and notice an imprint in the seat belonging to Jack. It's too big to be John's and although I haven't met Trish, I know she's a petite woman. She happens to be a celebrity journalist and I've seen her on the telly, talking on panel shows.

'Where are you?' I whisper. 'I know you're here. You have to be here.'

I kick off my Converse. There's a chill in the room, a reminder that the heatwave is temporary and summer will be inconsistent as usual. I pour myself a glass of water. I drink it thirstily in one go and catch a glimpse of the canvas print hanging above the cooker; the man in the shopping trolley.

It seems mad that only this morning, Jack was staring at this man's nonchalant face as he ate Rice Krispies without milk. Neither of us remembered to buy milk yesterday. He was spouting off, delving into all kinds of deeper reasons why the man was sat there, refusing to believe he was just a fella sat in a trolley. He said how one day we'd go back there, find him and ask him. Of course, I was unaware that Jack's last words to me would be, 'What's behind the picture?' All I'd replied with was, 'Gotta dash. See ya later.'

I place my glass down and see the sink is clean and empty. The dishes have been done. They aren't even draining: they've been tidied away, meaning there isn't a trace of Jack's bolognese remaining.

'Agh.' A painful, single cry escapes me.

I clasp my hands across my mouth. The beat of my heart is heavy: a dull bassline, drowning out the natural rhythm of the night. My eyes are closed, fighting back tears. If I cry,

I'll be admitting defeat, buying into this ridiculous notion that Jack is no more. He's here. I can feel him.

I grip the edge of the sink; take a deep breath; turn around. And smile.

I can see Jack as clearly as I'd seen him this morning. He's wearing the shirt he wore the day he gave me a key. It's off-white and baggy, hanging out loose over jeans. His beard is wild, his hair in need of a trim; exactly how it was this morning. His presence in the kitchen is huge as usual, in this tiny flat. He looks at ease; at home.

'I knew you were here,' I mouth.

He points to the sofa and I nod. Taking the red bobbled throw, I wrap it around me like a giant shawl and curl up. I rest my head on the cushion shaped like the head of Rudolf the Red-nosed Reindeer. I know it's not Christmas, but this cushion is so soft, so dreamy, that Jack considered it a crime to keep it hidden for eleven months of the year.

Closing my eyes, I will Jack to lie here beside me: to smooth down my hair; to stroke my cheek. I'm expecting him to suggest we watch another episode of the true crime documentary we're currently bingeing on, although he'll fall asleep within the first ten minutes and I'll have to re-watch that ten minutes all over again at the next sitting. Unless we're at the pub, he can't keep his eyes open beyond nine-thirty. Rudolf always gets the blame.

'Jack?' I whisper.

I can feel him. He's here.

He's definitely still here.

4

I open one eye, and the wall clock above the telly tells me it's just after six.

The hissing chatter in the kitchen didn't wake me up, though. I never truly slept: the events of yesterday pressed hard into my subconscious and wouldn't let me drift off. But they think I'm asleep, John and Trish. They think I can't hear them.

'Did you know she was coming back?' Trish is saying. Even in a whisper I'd recognise that biting tongue; that clipped, over-articulated, media-trained voice. You can almost hear her saliva singing.

John is grumbling and inarticulate.

'Oh, Johnny, I can't deal with this right now. If she's got a key to let herself in whenever she fancies, how many more are there? How do we know Jack didn't dish out keys to all his friends? All his *girl*friends?'

I close my eyes tight like a child wishing to turn invisible.

'Jack wouldn't do that, love,' John says. 'Not in his nature.'

'What isn't? You're forgetting what happened with Florrie!'

I open my eyes. Who the fuck is Florrie?

'He was young,' I hear John saying.

'Don't make excuses. He knew how to control himself, Johnny.'

'Keep your voice down, love. She's asleep.'

'*She* has a name . . . What was it again?'

'I can't remember, love. Erm – Clare?'

'Well, how do we know that Clare was really his girlfriend? It can't have been serious, Johnny. Jack would've introduced us before shacking up with her.'

'Would he?'

'Don't act as if I don't know my own son, Johnny!'

Now this is great. Jack's parents don't want me here and I really need to wee. Obviously I'll have to get up at some point. I can't just stay on the sofa like a fat cat. But I don't know – should I wait until after I've used the toilet to tell them that my name isn't Clare? Or stand up and tell them right now that erm, sorry, but my name is not fucking Clare?

'Did you see the suitcase, Johnny?' Trish spits. 'Doesn't feel very serious, does it?'

She's upped the volume slightly because the kettle is boiling and it would be a travesty for John not to hear her every word. Wouldn't it?

'What are you suggesting, love?' John says. I imagine he's rubbing his eyes with his thumb and index finger, just how he did yesterday when we met.

'That we tell her – kindly – to leave. I'm sure she won't mind. We've got so much to do, so much to deal with, and I wouldn't be surprised if she wanted to get out of here faster than even we'd appreciate. She only needs to zip up her bags – there's nothing at all that suggests she's a permanent fixture around here. Jack was probably just casually shagging her.'

30

'Trish, please. Let's not discuss our dead son's sex life.'

I hear Trish gasp, and a long, sorrowful moan follows shortly after.

'Our *dead* son,' she says, muffled. John must be holding her close to him.

She's crying hard, uncontrollably, giving me no choice but to rise.

'Excuse me,' I say, and immediately wish I hadn't. 'Sorry.'

Darting into the bathroom, I lock the door and sit on the toilet, pushing the walls either side with my hands. Not a permanent fixture, Trish? Well, what about my electric toothbrush right there in the holder next to Jack's withered cheap one? Or the fact that the hanging caddy in the shower contains salon-recommended shampoo and conditioner for bleached hair? And coconut butter body scrub, mango shower gel and three used – yes, used – Venus disposable razors because, oops, I just forget to throw them away? Does (I'm sorry, did) Jack look as if he ever used a fucking razor in his life? Did he? And tampons. Yeah, there's a little box of opened tampons: clearly *mine*. Unless Jack went through a phase of using them for earplugs, or butt plugs, you know, something I wouldn't know about. Like Florrie.

Who the fuck is Florrie?

I wash my face, brush my teeth. I can see Jack in the mirror, grinning over my shoulder.

'It's not funny,' I say through a mouthful of toothpaste. 'You're not even there.'

Jack pretends to be offended, dropping his mouth open, splaying his hand across his heart.

'Well, for a start, if you were here you'd tell your mum that we aren't just shagging.'

Oh, he finds that hilarious. His jolly presence fills the

whole bathroom. I struggle to lean over and spit into the sink, banging my forehead on the mirror.

'*Ouch!*' I turn around.

He's gone.

I wipe my mouth on my arm and barge into the kitchen, annoyed at myself for . . .

I don't even know why. I'm just annoyed.

John and Trish are both sitting at the breakfast bar, staring into mugs of instant coffee. At least I'm dressed. Sort of. I'm still wearing the floral dress with the button missing, and although it shouldn't be an achievement, I'm wearing knickers, unlike yesterday's parental meet and greet. I took my bra off though, somewhere between sleep and disbelief. The underwiring was digging in and it now lies on the coffee table on top of last Sunday's *Observer Food Monthly*. I'd like to think that a pair of grieving parents wouldn't notice something like a discarded bra, but it's just the sort of thing Patricia Carmichael would spot and rant about, turning it into a political debate.

'Morning,' I manage.

John stands. He's still dressed in the same clothes as yesterday. His tailored shorts and light blue shirt are now creased, and everything about him is off-colour. Trish elongates her neck, straightens her posture. If I hadn't known that Jack's mum was Patricia Carmichael, I mightn't have recognised her. She isn't wearing any makeup and her short, spiky hair hasn't been styled. She's wearing an oversized t-shirt printed with a cassette tape across the chest. I know that t-shirt. It's Jack's. He bought it from Spitalfields market about a month ago. No – in fact, I bought it. The stall only accepted cash and he only had his card. I had a twenty quid note.

'I'm Chloe,' I say, avoiding eye contact with John and going straight for Trish.

Trish rolls her red, swollen eyes to John and raises one eyebrow. I give a little wave with my hand. Not intentionally, believe me. An abundance of questions dance around my mind, all of which John and Trish might have the answers to. Firstly: is this all real? Is Jack really dead? And how exactly did he die? What are the finer details, because are they sure, I mean absolutely *sure*, that he isn't perhaps *almost* dead? Did somebody get it wrong? And why did Jack never mention me to them? Or did he, and they've forgotten; in the same way that John forgot my name?

'We're leaving shortly,' Trish says.

'There's a lot to do,' John says.

'Help yourself to tea, coffee . . .' Trish tells me.

'Thanks,' I say.

I don't want to boil the kettle. It feels too much like intruding, pottering about behind them while they sip their own hot drinks. It'll give off the wrong impression entirely if I open the fridge and pick at the grapes, the first thing I usually do in the morning. And if I go back to the sofa, I can't go back to sleep or turn on the telly. So what should I do? Sit there with my hands on my lap awaiting instruction? In my own home?

The plays, now in a small pile beside the fruit bowl, are my saving grace. John knows they're mine. I lean across, slide them towards me and God, I'm relieved to have something in my hands. Shit. I have to teach practical drama to Year Nine in a few hours. Am I expected to go to work today? Even if my boyfriend died yesterday? Auditions for the school musical are tomorrow. I have to be there. But that's not right, is it? Or is it?

A breeze floats in from the back door, slightly ajar. Empty bottles of Peroni that need taking to the recycling bin shake, humming a gentle tune. They'll still have Jack's saliva around the rim.

'Have you finished with that, Johnny?' Trish asks.

John allows his wife to take his half-empty mug. She shuffles over to the sink.

'I can do that,' I say. 'The mugs. I know where they go.'

'It's no trouble,' Trish says, the water already running.

I exchange a look with John, which is both comfortable and embarrassing all at once. We give each other our gentlest smiles, laced with sadness. Trish is doing a good job with the mugs, scrubbing every tea stain clean, not a brown mark left in sight. She throws her head back and laughs: a hint of that wicked, infectious sound I've heard on the telly, only the cameras aren't rolling and she's got washing-up liquid on her hands.

'What's so funny, love?' John asks, twisting around on the bar stool.

'What do you think's funny?' she replies, her laugh on the verge of splitting into a cry. 'Jack, of course. Jack.'

'And what's triggered this?'

Trish steps back and theatrically, her short legs planted strong, she sticks out her chest and tilts her head upwards, throwing out words like, 'bonkers', 'brilliant', 'bizarre', in no order, repeating them over and over. She's looking at the man sat in the shopping trolley and John is nodding, his mouth curled. This is proving too much for him to cope with. He begins to cry, silently.

My throat tightens. Aches. But this is not my turn to cry.

'I got that printed for Jack,' I say. 'A moving-in present. Except I was the one moving in. So I guess it was a thank you present, for asking me; letting me. Anyway, it was something he really wanted.'

'Ah,' Trish catches her breath. 'But it's so . . . random.'

'Love . . .' John reaches his hand out to her.

'No, I know what you mean,' I say, a singsong in my voice that always pipes up when I'm trying to impress somebody. I definitely would've used it had I been given the chance to meet Jack's parents prior to yesterday. 'Out of context, it's a very bizarre – to use your word, Mrs Carmichael – photograph. I can see how you think it's random. But to Jack and to me, it represents a special moment, and also a boss holiday, and provides us with endless laughter, still.'

'You went to Thailand with Jack?' John asks.

'Yeah. In March.'

Trish swivels from left to right, her arms folded. She's still looking at the picture, but she isn't laughing any more.

'In fact,' I continue, no stopping me now. 'We always kind of joke about how one day we'll go back there, to that spot, and find that man. Or go to the place where he works, because can you see he's wearing a uniform and there's a badge, see? Top right of his shirt. We just wanna meet this fella – say a proper hello! Ask him what he was doing in the shopping trolley. Find out his name; shake his hand.'

I'm expecting some sort of response, but I get zilch. The thick silence sits in the triangle between us all. I realise I just talked at John and Trish using Jack in the present tense. I hadn't meant to do that, but they naturally picked up on it, loud and clear. I hug the paperback plays tight; feel them squash against my braless chest.

Trish stretches out her arm and taps the breakfast bar three times. This must be some sort of code for them to leave, because John stands up, puts his hand to the small of Trish's back and picks up her orange Michael Kors handbag, carrying it for her. They float past me like ghosts and disappear into the hallway.

'Look, I'm so sorry for your loss,' I call after them.

They pause by the bookshelf, a particularly creaky floorboard beneath their feet. John looks over his shoulder and gives me a pained, but kind, smile. Trish is frozen, the back of her head facing me.

'Take all the time you need, Chloe,' she says. 'We won't be coming back here today.'

And she opens the door and leads the way outside, John following, his head bent low. He closes the door behind him gently, but the flat seems to shudder, just as it does every time a double decker bus trundles past the road. Oh God. I want to run after them, ask them seriously, what the fuck happened? Who is to blame? There's always somebody to blame, isn't there? And how . . . how did he actually—

SLAM!

I run into the kitchen. *Jack?!*

5

I spin a full circle, expecting him to spring up from behind the breakfast bar and shout 'BOO!' – I know there's a good chance I'm losing the plot.

It's just the back door shutting, from the draught when Trish and John left.

'You never told them about me,' I say.

The silence pinches me, hard.

I go to the fridge and take out the plastic tray of grapes. I think I'm hungry. Or thirsty.

Neither.

Jack will never be hungry or thirsty again.

I have to get ready and go to school, but the sofa beckons and I flop down. I place the tray of grapes onto the carpet beside my feet and rock forward, my head falling into my hands. This has all happened so fast – too fast. I can't label how I'm feeling. Hollow? Sick? Grieving? Does grief happen straight away, or will it hit me tomorrow? Or the next day?

Is this grief? *This?*

'Jack?'

I stare beyond the windowsill, cluttered with burnt-out tealights. Some are in beaded holders, some not, and there's a ukulele that neither Jack nor I have ever played. My gaze burns past the frame, the window, the stone steps leading down from street level towards our front door. The remote is in my peripheral vision. I think about reaching for it. An ambulance siren sounds, gets louder, fades away. Footsteps from the ground-floor flat above pace about; a suitcase being wheeled. I've never met the fella who lives there. He travels a lot, according to Jack. A bird is chirping outside in the garden. I'm still pondering whether to reach for the remote.

I shake myself out, make a noise that resembles something like 'Wuoghhh.'

How long was I spaced out for? A minute? Five?

Fuck me, thirty-five?

I put the grapes back in the fridge, pausing as I close the door. The magnet of the Leaning Tower of Pisa draws me to the photo of Jack on his dad's shoulders in Majorca. A little lad, his whole life ahead of him . . .

No magnets on this fridge belong to me. I gave the one we bought in Thailand of a tuk-tuk to my nan. What *does* belong to me is confirmation for a ski lesson, printed off and Sellotaped up there by Jack on the chance I might 'accidentally' delete the email . . .

The flyer for Jack's mate's comedy gig is held up by a magnet I personally find very cute: a mini bowl of noodles. There are even teeny, tiny prawns inside the bowl. Jack got that in Vietnam, a place he was eager to revisit with me . . .

A flip-flop that doubles up as a bottle opener has a business card for Antonella tucked beneath it, the restaurant I've reserved a table at for Jack's birthday . . .

There's another business card popping out behind: some estate agent that Jack had been chatting to, keen for us to move out of this bunker flat to somewhere with a better view . . .

Beside that hangs the invite to my brother's wedding . . .

And tickets to *Mamma Mia!* Jack won at a raffle in work last month . . .

Oh my. This is our life. Right here, on the fridge.

Even the gas bill is there.

'I'm jealous you're off work tomoz,' I'd said, my head resting on Jack's chest as we lay in bed the other night. 'What you gonna do?'

'Pay the gas bill,' Jack said, his voice dry, lazy, already half asleep. 'And then, fuck all.'

But he didn't pay it. I know this because the gas bill wouldn't still be on the fridge. It would be ripped up and in the recycling; done and dusted. Jack was a total geek about things like that. He'd get angry if he found an out-of-date Sainsbury's Nectar coupon in his wallet.

I flatten the bill against the wall, iron out the creases with my fist, tickle the bold letters spelling 'Jack Carmichael'. This banal, boring piece of paper no longer belongs to the world I exist in. It's history. Yesterday morning, it had colour: it was presumed continuous. But today . . .

Today!

I have to phone the school. Tell them I won't be in. I'm sick. Very sick. Vomiting, diarrhoea; it's come on quickly. I'm sorry. I almost sob. I gather myself. Once again, I'm sorry. I know I'm new to the school. This isn't normal. It's odd. Very odd. They understand. I'll be in on Monday. I promise. I'm sure it's just a twenty-four-hour thing. It can't be permanent.

It can't be.

I pay the gas bill online. Then I slip back onto the sofa, my gaze fixed on a crack in the paintwork on the ceiling. Here I remain, all day.

6

I spend the weekend pretty low key, in my comfies. I listen to Jack's latest playlist on Spotify – some Beach Boys, Bowie, a lot of Creedence Clearwater Revival – his iPad is still connected to the speaker on the breakfast bar. Breakfast is skipped. Lunch is whatever I can find: toast; crisps; a tin of spaghetti hoops, cold. I order takeaway for my dinner, lots of it; a habit we'd gotten into. I don't eat a single bite. I just stare at the boxes. It's incomprehensible that I'll never do this with Jack again, ever.

I scroll through my phone's photos. 3,784 images. 23 images of Jack, 16 with his eyes closed, mid-blink. A grand total of five selfies with him, four of them pretty awful. The decent one, taken in the beer garden of our local pub on the May bank holiday, is my screensaver. So, word of warning to anybody who – like me – has fallen into the habit of taking photos of a rainbow salad; two wine glasses by candlelight; fucking feet on a fucking beach: don't. Take photos of people. You will never, ever, ever care about your toes painted neon pink on the sand, ever. But you'll wish you had more photos of the person you loved. Seriously, I've got a video of a plane taking off from Gatwick airport and I don't even know where that plane was heading. But the only video I have of Jack is a boomerang of him buying boxer shorts at Patpong market.

My phone pings.

You rang?

It's our Kit, my brother. He's noticed the missed call from me this morning. I start to type a reply along the lines of needing to speak to him, but the words fail me. I try again.

Kit, I've got some bad news . . . Nope. Delete.

I can't get into this on WhatsApp.

Ring me back when you get a mo ☺

I'm in Lisbon. You ok sis? X

Shit. I totally forgot. It's his stag weekend.

All good! Just wanted to tell you to HAVE A BALL. Love you.

Love you more. X

I down my glass of Shiraz and look at the spring rolls, seeping with grease in their plastic container. I should eat one, line my stomach. Biting it in half, the cold beansprouts and chicken spill into my mouth, making me gag. There's no taste, just mass. Chewing is a gigantic effort I can do without. I toss the uneaten half onto the floor. Then I grab the bag of prawn crackers and hurl it against the wall.

Agh, so what?

Nobody's here to stop me.

I'm new to London, aren't I, so unlike Jack or Beth, I don't have a circle of friends yet. Beth's in Liverpool for the weekend at a family do. She insisted that I tag along, but I was firm with my, 'no'. My mum's gone quiet – thank God, because I can't face giving her the news yet – and I presume it's because she's assigned herself a task for our Kit's wedding. He isn't getting married until August, but my mum's been collecting jam jars for years – you know, just in case. So either Kit's finally succumbed to her putting them to some decorative use, or my nan's sick. My mum only ever tells me that my nan's been sick once she's well again.

I open a second bottle of wine and make a start on the Ikea drawers. Jack's mum's words rattle around my head: 'there's nothing at all that suggests she's a permanent fixture around here', and I imagine her sat on a Channel 5 panel, discussing the headlines, daily politics, and *me*, her disgust at my existence clear to the nation.

Listen, Patricia. I'll give you permanent.

I drag the flat-pack box into the hallway, open it and browse the instruction pamphlet. I instantly feel tired and shiver, my sockless feet ice cold. Reaching up to the coat rack, I pull down Jack's parka, slip my arms into the heavy fabric and inhale deeply.

'Were you murdered?' I cry out. An Allen key drops, clattering louder than I expect. 'Like, were you involved in something – I dunno, like, illegal? I mean, maybe I've been naive. Maybe I don't know you as well as I thought I did. Maybe . . .'

I can picture Jack laughing at me, mockingly taking a stance like a tough guy, a drug dealer, a money launderer. But I'm only trying to rationalise the situation. In London, the traffic moves no faster than twenty miles an hour. There's speed cameras everywhere.

'How the fuck did a van hit you going more than fifty?' I yell. 'How? Why? I waited thirty-six years to meet you!'

Which isn't completely true. Yeah, I'm thirty-six, but I didn't grow up dreaming about Mr Right and weddings. No, that was my brother. It was cruel that he'd had to grow up in a world where although he wanted those things, some law told him they weren't for him. Honestly, I'd much preferred flatmates to boyfriends. Impromptu parties, hangovers with Domino's and marathons of *Friends*. Bingeing on *24* after work shat all over an awkward date with some guy I could only have sex with if I got bladdered.

But when I hit thirty, flatmates became engaged, or property owners, or parents. Some scored the treble. I progressed to my own flat, embracing the true value of space. I loved my framed posters of *The Sound of Music* and *Singin' in the Rain* hanging up in whatever room I desired, and my bulging mess of a wardrobe that no fucker was going to judge me for. Nobody was stealing my Brie. I only had myself to blame if I ran out of loo roll. Loneliness, however, creeps in when you least expect it. Everybody wants somebody, as the song goes. Dating seemed like a necessity, but a labouring chore. Until Jack. And it was easy. Easy like Sunday morning. Ye-ahh, ye-ahh . . .

I'm standing with two pieces of Ikea wood in my hands.

What the fuck am I doing?

Only a matter of weeks ago, I moved in with my new boyfriend. This fact cannot be suddenly wiped out. Nothing just stops, no matter how hard a van hits it. I found a pair of his dirty undies beneath one of my Converse today, for God's sake. Do I wash them? What the hell are you supposed to do with the dead's dirty undies?

The flat looks a mess.

The bins are overflowing, uneaten bananas are blackened and smelling, ripped cardboard and loose screws are taking over the hallway. The only corner of serenity is our bed. The pillows are plumped and the sheets are so straight – good enough for a hotel penthouse suite – that I've been wondering whether Trish (or John) ran the iron over them before they left. Needless to say, I haven't been sleeping in our bed, because I haven't really been sleeping. The sofa has more appeal: the red throw, the Rudolf cushion, the sense of never ending a day or starting a new one.

Right, where's that other screw?

Shit. I spill red wine onto the carpet. I'll never understand why anyone buys cream carpets, although I can imagine it looked lovely when John and Trish had this one fitted.

'I nearly died once, you know,' I say – to Jack, to nobody – tightening the screw. 'I was only little, about three or four. Me dad was making tea and toast before bedtime. He likes it burnt, black, except I have a theory that he can't make it any other way. God, I wish you'd met him, had the chance to go for a pint with him. Anyway. As me dad was buttering the toast, me grandad came rushing in, panic stricken, and he said, "Chloe's choking". Me dad dropped the butter knife and ran upstairs, burst into me room. He found me red-faced, eyes watering and struggling to breathe. He dangled me upside down by me feet and shook me, whacking me back – not the most elegant or correct manoeuvre. Whatever he did, though, it worked. And do you know what it was? A Polly Pocket. I'd taken the toy to bed and God knows why, I'd put one of those teeny, tiny plastic dolls into me mouth. Me grandad's warning saved me life that night . . . Except me grandad died before I was born.'

I said that last part pretty loud – you know, in case the ghost of Jack needed me to speak up a little in order to appear. If my dad saw my grandad, why can't I see Jack? Come on. Appear. APPEAR!

The doorbell is ringing.

Did I order anything from Amazon? Did Jack?

Stepping over the unscrewed parts of drawers, I grab the toothpaste from the bathroom and squirt a blob into my mouth. Blue stains of red wine sit on my bottom lip.

The doorbell rings again.

Please, please, please don't be Trish and John.

'Hello!' a couple sing in chorus as I open the door.

God, they look so freshly scrubbed. Their cheeks are rosy. It's the couple who live in the second-floor flat. They've been out walking, and they're wearing matching hiking boots and designer raincoats. They must have driven out to Kent this morning at the crack of dawn. They make me feel revolting. I don't even know what time it is.

'How are you settling in?' the fella, Giles, asks.

'Good,' I say. Well, what else can I say? 'Manic.'

'I bet,' Ingrid says. She's Norwegian and her skin is so flawless I can't imagine she's ever ingested anything processed. Ever. 'Is Jack home?'

They don't know.

Okay, I should've known they didn't know by the tone of their arrival, asking how I'm settling in, but it's only just dawned on me. They don't know. And it's going to be up to me to tell them.

'Building a chest of drawers,' I lie.

Giles and Ingrid cock their heads to the side and look past me into the hallway, at the obvious chaos of weekend DIY. I point at Ingrid and release some sort of weird grunt.

'Ikea,' I say.

'That is Swedish,' Ingrid reminds me.

Giles waves his hands. 'No need to bother Jack – we just wanted to let you both know that we're getting our bathroom refitted next week so it might be a bit noisy. The builders will need to go around the back of the house to check some plumbing so if you see any strangers in the garden, don't be alarmed.'

He finds this really amusing. Maybe I would too, on another day, in a previous life. Giles looks so together; so clean; so innocent: I can't imagine anything could get near him to break him. He's probably got some sort of sensible insurance policy to protect himself from anything bad ever happening.

'No probs,' I say.

'Anyway, we must have you both over for a cuppa some time,' Giles says. 'Or perhaps something a little stronger?'

'Or pasta?' Ingrid says.

'Or pasta,' I repeat.

'We bought a new hanging basket, by the way,' Giles adds. 'For the front of the house.'

'Lovely,' I say. 'Thanks.'

'Oh, it's no trouble. No trouble at all. Shame the weather's taken a turn for the worse, eh?'

'Has it?' I look upwards to the thick, white sky.

'Been chilly again, like spring for the past couple of days,' Giles tuts.

'He is so obsessed with the weather,' Ingrid says.

'Aren't we all?' I say, aware of my massive contradiction.

And fuck me. I'm still wearing Jack's giant bloody parka.

I bid them goodbye, mimicking their pure politeness. When I close the door, I touch the blue stain on my lower lip. Ingrid's natural blonde locks have also reminded me of my roots, all dark and mousey and threatening.

Why didn't I tell them?

Because it didn't seem appropriate. Like I'd be interfering.

I close the curtains to stop the outside glare reflecting on the telly, and I have a long, long flick through everything

47

Netflix has to offer. There's still two more drawers to build, but I imagine Jack lying beside me. We watch a film about a high school misfit with the ability to move mountains, literally. We drift in and out of some sort of drunken sleep.

A message alert shakes me awake.

Dear Chloe, I hope you're keeping well. I got your number from Jack's phone. The funeral is taking place next Friday. Regards, Trish Carmichael.

I wonder if she's read the exchanges between him and me over the past few months. As perverse as this might sound, I hope so. It'll prove we weren't 'just shagging', as she so bluntly put it.

7

On Monday, I go to see my department head and ask for compassionate leave for the funeral. When she asks me who passed away, I tell her a friend. She says sorry, and I'm granted time off. I suppose you're wondering why I never told her it was my boyfriend, but come on – she would've questioned how, why and when, and I don't have concrete answers. Unless I've missed it, the local news has reported nothing and I can't bring myself to call Jack's family. They might call me Clare. Besides, I lied about being sick last week when it happened. I'm new to this school, remember. I don't want to be thought of as a liability.

Except I am.

Year Ten are preparing for their mocks and all I can do is put them into groups, telling them to devise 'whatever they like'. I spend the double period going back and forth to the staff toilets trying to pull myself together. Luckily, the kids don't seem to notice.

At lunchtime, I'm cornered entering the drama hall.

'Miss, Miss, can I audition for the musical?' asks the lad,

confident. Perhaps Year Eight. He flashes a brace-dressed smile and despite a baby-soft jawline, he reeks of aftershave.

'What's your name?' I ask.

'Jonah Matthews, Miss.'

'You know today's the recalls, Jonah. The main auditions were last week.'

'Please, Miss. Please?'

'Fine. Grab your lunch and come back in ten minutes.'

'AH, FANKS, MISS!'

'Pronounce your "TH", Jonah. You can't be an actor if you don't work hard on your articulation.'

'Sure fing, Miss,' he winks at me. He actually winks at me. 'Fank you. I mean, TH-ank you. Can I bring my girlfriend, Miss?'

'No.'

'Why not?'

'We've got too many girls already.'

'That's sexist. Give her a chance.'

'It's not sexist, Jonah – your girlfriend missed out.'

'Well, I fink it's sexist, Miss. Unless you fancy me, Miss. Are you jealous?'

'Jonah Matthews get your lunch now before I put you on detention.'

God, that's exhausted me. I ache.

Gathering the recalled students into a circle, I assign Layla Birch to lead a warm-up game of Zip, Zap, Boing. This means I can sit in the corner on a plastic chair drawing doodles, pretending to be doing something important like marking essays or counting names on a register. I let the game go on much longer than necessary, telling myself that it's cool because I'm still waiting for Si – Mr Sullivan, the music teacher and brainchild behind this musical – to show up.

I say 'brainchild'; I jest.

He's written this musical himself, a story of a starlet arriving in the big city without a dime (yep, a dime) in her pocket but a heart full of dreams. I know, I know. The music will be mashups of famous show tunes and obscure songs that only true fans of Broadway will know, mixed in with some current music – you know, to 'keep it real'.

Layla Birch is politely calling my name.

'Are we going to start soon?' she asks.

I look up from my impressively shaded biro drawing of a Venus fly trap and see that Layla has ended the warmup game and got everybody to sit cross-legged in the circle: focused, ready. They even have their eyes closed.

'It's the breathing techniques Mr Sullivan teaches,' Layla assures me. 'They help with nerves and anxiety.'

She's brilliant, Layla Birch. I've only been at this school a few weeks, covering for a teacher on maternity leave, and admittedly I'm not great with names, but Layla Birch stood out to me from the word go. Attentive, keen and passionate about drama, she's dyslexic but is determined to excel. And she will. She's got that spark – one that can't be taught.

'Sorry, sorry, sorry,' Si Sullivan runs into the drama hall, flapping.

He heads straight for the piano, making an absolute meal of laying out his sheet music.

'Thank goodness the show isn't until October,' he reassures us all; but frankly, he lost the room on his first 'sorry'. Breathing techniques ended with a group sigh, and heightened chatter has since broken out.

I leave it in Si's flappy hands to regain control. I'm fixating on the word 'October'. *October. Oct . . .*

Thank goodness the show isn't until . . .

October.

That's one, two, three . . . four months away. Half term.

'It'll fly by,' Jack had said to me, recently. A week ago, maybe. 'Vietnam. October.'

'Seems a shame we can't go this summer though,' I'd said. 'I've got six weeks off.'

The true crime documentary was on pause while I made a cuppa and Jack laid his wet socks on the radiator in the lounge. The heating wasn't on – it wasn't cold enough – but it's how he hung his washing out to dry regardless, whenever it was raining.

'I can't take time off during this project,' Jack went on. 'It's our biggest client and the deadline is end of August. I'll get bank holiday off, though. We could go camping. Dorset, maybe?'

'So I've got to wait 'til almost the end of the school hols to go camping? In this country?' I'd glanced towards the garden, to the rain lashing down outside.

'Not necessarily, darlin'. You can still go abroad if you want, just without me.'

I'd squeezed the teabag against the side of the mug with a spoon, turning the milky tea orange. If this were some other early relationship, I would've been cautious of seeming needy; worried about giving off the air that I couldn't possibly have a life beyond my fella. But not with Jack. We hadn't played any mind games or stuck to the sweepingly generic rules to keep each other keen. We *were* keen. And not ashamed to show it.

'No, I'll save me money,' I'd said, tossing the teaspoon into the sink.

'For Vietnam? In October? *Avec moi*?'

'Yes, yes, and *oui*.'

'Trust me. It'll fly by,' Jack had said again, and I believed him.

'What did you say, Miss Roscoe?' Si asks me, lifting his chin above the piano.

The drama hall is in silence and when I look up from my doodles, all eyes are on me.

I smile. We must be ready to start. A few sniggers waft over and some kids give me *that look*, as if I've just started dad-dancing in the nude. My smile remains fixed, but I'm confused.

'You said something,' Si says, and he cups his ear with his hand.

'I didn't,' I tell him.

'You did.'

'No, I didn't—'

'You did, Miss,' Layla says, her frustration apparent. 'You said, "It'll fly by".'

'I did?' I ask.

Layla nods, as do some others.

Oh, God.

I try to wrench myself back to the present, but I can't stop thinking about Jack. I realise how right he had been. Okay, we weren't going on a big holiday for four months. But so what? In that time I'd be settling into the flat, exploring London, making dinner, going out for dinner, drinking in pub beer gardens, hitting a few festivals at the weekends, meeting old friends, making new friends, and of course, going to our Kit's wedding, *all* with Jack. I think of the fridge. Our plans. Jack wanted to teach me how to ski. Me! Ski! Of course the time would fly by. Everything I've just listed sounds like pure heaven – the best four months I could possibly imagine. And fuck me, forgive me for using a big old cliché, but time flies when you're having fun, doesn't it?

Si and the students are still looking at me, waiting for an explanation.

'I was just warning you all,' I say, forced authority in my voice. 'Mr Sullivan mentioned that the show isn't until October, but don't be fooled. It'll fly by.'

Layla closes her eyes, dramatically taking my words fully on board. Si slams the piano with his elbow and grabs his throat with one hand, pretending to be strangled.

'Aggghh! You've scared me to death, Miss Roscoe!' he screeches.

One kid, a little Year Seven girl, finds this funny. But it's her and her alone, and when she realises, she slaps her hands across her mouth, mortified.

A restless energy has returned.

'FOCUS,' I yell, 'or there won't be any auditions and I'll allocate parts willy-nilly.'

Shit. Can't believe I just said 'willy-nilly'.

I don't want to be here. I shouldn't be here. Why the hell am I here? Why?

I take a deep breath.

When I arrive home, Jack's smell will hit me. His fat thumbprint on the bathroom mirror will take me by surprise. His drawer will invite me to choose a t-shirt I can wear to sleep in on the sofa. That's why I'm here – to have those precious snippets to look forward to.

Jonah Matthews appears with his whole crew. 'Are we on time, Miss?'

He's brought his girlfriend regardless of what I said, presuming his girlfriend is the one almost twice his height with an intimidating stare and a lip piercing.

'Right, let's get started,' I say.

Si bashes out a chirpy eight bars of generic cheesy musical theatre. I'm not sure I have the energy to see this through – even walking towards the piano makes my legs ache.

'Everything okay, Miss Roscoe?' Si asks, a rhetorical question if ever there was one.

I give one, bold nod.

'Layla Birch,' I say, returning to my Venus fly trap doodle. 'You're up first.'

*

After school, I pick up a decent bottle of wine from the Sainsbury's Local. The auditions went well. A few dodgy performances and, unexpectedly, Layla Birch messed up her lyrics, but on the whole, I was impressed.

As I open the front door, I stumble upon a package.

It's soft, small enough to get through the letterbox.

I pick it up and read who it's addressed to.

Miss Chloe Roscoe (and Jack!)

I recognise the writing.

Fishing out the contents, I feel the soft cotton between my thumb and fingers. It's the beige gingham cushion covers, two of them, all ready to slip onto plain square cushions and add a bit of home from home. If Jack were here, oh how we'd laugh. I'd insist we didn't use them, but Jack would disagree. He'd love how much I hate them. He'd make poor Rudolf redundant just to revel in this moment for as long as possible, winding me up to the point of me admitting that, fine, I can learn to like them. I slump against the radiator and squeeze the gingham so hard that I wouldn't be surprised if it bled. The handwritten note accompanying the package has fallen beside me on the floor.

Congratulations on your new home! We hope you're both really happy there.

Love Mum and Dad xxx

8

It takes me another two days to ring my mum.

'Did the parcel arrive?' she asks, screeching panic.

'It did. Thanks Mum.'

'I'm not cramping your style, am I?'

'No, Mum. I'm not fourteen.'

I'm waiting for the bus home from school after staying behind with Si to compare audition notes from Monday. A handful of pupils meander to the bus stop, either from detention or athletics training. Traffic is bumper-to-bumper on this road, horns honking up by the William Hill. It's either a seven-minute bus ride (without traffic) or a twenty-five-minute walk. I know, I got lucky landing a job in Lewisham so close to Jack's flat, relieving me of the dreaded commute.

Lucky.

I think I'll walk.

'Been busy then? How's the new job going?'

'Yeah, it's okay.'

'You don't like it, do you?'

'It's fine.'

'I've never liked my job, Chloe. But that's life. You just get on with it.'

She works for the Inland Revenue and loves it. Always taking charge of the collection for office birthdays.

'Chloe, I just saw Pam Gillespie in Matalan. She hasn't half aged, my God. Told me about how her Jason's living in Canada now. Remember him? From school? Wouldn't say boo to a goose, would he? And now he's living in Canada. God knows what he's doing there – I didn't pry. Told her you're a fully qualified teacher and she thinks that's marvellous. Told her how you're living down in London now and she said, "Oh isn't that fantastic!" She wondered if you've been to see *The Lion King* yet? I told her I wasn't sure. Have you?'

I take a short cut through a residential street, although it's not quiet. A woman pushing a pram is dragging a screaming toddler along and a group of workmen are taking a raucous cigarette break outside a grand terraced house top-to-toe in scaffolding.

'Mum, I need to tell you something,' I say. 'Something . . . sad.'

'Oh no,' she starts, and I know she's taken the landline phone in her hands to sit down on the bottom stair, bracing herself. 'Oh, God. Please, don't tell me. Oh no. What is it?'

'Jack.' I clear my throat. 'Died.'

'What?' she asks, as if she's part deaf.

'Don't make me say it again, Mum.'

'He *died*?'

'Yeah.'

'Ah,' she sighs. Then she repeats this sound in various tones and pitches.

'Mum? Are you okay?'

'Ah, love. Ah, I can't believe it. I'm shocked, I'm really, really shocked. I mean, I thought you were going to say that he left you, or that you had cancer or something. I never expected this, Chloe love. Ah. What was it? Was it suicide?'

'No, Mum – I'd rather not discuss the det—'

'Drink driving? Did he have a problem that you weren't aware of, you know, because let's face it, you hardly knew the lad, did you?'

'Mum!'

'Or was he ill? Oh, God. Had he been ill this whole time and not told you?'

'Mum, it was an accident. Simple as that.'

'Oh, love. Oh, Chloe love. My heart breaks for you, it does. It really does.' She sounds like she's in pain, her voice thin, sliding along ice. 'Just devastating, isn't it? His poor mother, oh she must be in pieces. And you thought this was it, didn't you? Our Kit said as much, said you thought you'd found The One. And after all these years, there's me thinking you never believed in The One—'

'Mum, please don't cry.'

'We never even met him, Chloe.'

'I know.'

'Oh, my God, who will you bring to our Kit's wedding now? You can't come on your own.'

'Yeah. God forbid.'

'I mean, you're thirty-six, Chloe. I thought you'd—'

'Mum, I know what you thought.'

'Don't snap at me, love. I'm very upset for you, I am. I really am.'

'I'm gonna be fine,' I say, convincingly, although not at all convinced.

She sighs loudly down the phone. I come to the end of

the residential street and walk along the main road, passing a pub, a pharmacy, a florist, another pub. She's still sighing, I think; a fire engine's siren is drowning her out.

Once it passes, I realise she's talking to someone, not me, relaying this new information about Jack in a loud whisper, as if I can't hear her.

'Is Dad home from work?' I ask.

'What's that, Chloe love?'

'I can hear you talking to Dad.'

'Oh, no. Your dad's still out; had to take someone *all* the way to Manchester today. Carol's here. Her daughter's pregnant again, you know. What's that, Carol? Oh, a girl? She's having a girl, is she? Ah, one of each. Oh, isn't that just perfect. I bet you're over the moon, Carol. Did you hear that, Chloe?'

'That's nice, Mum.'

'Yeah. It's nice to hear nice things at a time like this . . .'

I can picture her sitting on the stairs, catching a glimpse of herself in the hall mirror and using her fingertips to create a temporary facelift.

'You sure you're alright, Mum?'

'I'm fine, love. I am. I just thank God that you barely knew the lad. Thank. God. He really does work in mysterious ways, doesn't He?'

'This wasn't an act of God, Mum.'

'Oh, Chloe. Imagine if you'd been with Jack for years. Imagine if you were married, had children. This would be an absolute tragedy. Christmas doesn't seem like five minutes ago and you didn't even know he was walking on God's green earth. You were still knocking about with that fella you went to youth theatre with.'

'Mum, this *is* a tragedy.'

'Yes. I know. It is for all who knew him, but Chloe my love, you didn't. I mean, you never really know someone until you've lived with them.'

'I DO live with Jack. DID live with him.'

'Oh, love. Your suitcase isn't even unpacked yet.'

'How do you know?!'

'Because I know you!'

I want to hang up, but I know better than to hang up on my mum. I did that once. Twenty years ago, from a phone box outside Central Station in Liverpool. I can't even begin to explain the guilt ingrained within me that's lingered ever since, all stemming from her deep hurt at being hung up on by her own flesh and blood. For a whole week, she laid the table for three instead of four, refusing to feed me. My dad took pity once and saved me half of his cottage pie, but I survived the rest of the week on cereal, going to the chippy on my way home from sixth form or eating at Beth's, although her family was experimenting with vegetarianism in the nineties. My taste buds weren't accustomed to couscous and hummus back then.

'Hold on a sec, Chloe . . . What was that, Carol?'

I hear Carol's raspy rattle in the background. She's still on forty a day.

'Chloe,' my mum comes back to me. 'Carol's asking when you're coming home.'

'Dunno.'

'What do you mean, you "dunno"?'

'I haven't made any plans.'

'Well, you better hurry up.'

'Why?'

I'm walking through a park now, along the footpath, dodging small kids on scooters. All hints of sadness have evaporated from my mum's voice and she's annoyed. Plain annoyed.

'Chloe, I've got a wedding to organise,' she reminds me.

'Well, *Kit* has a wedding to—'

'Don't talk about something you don't know anything about, love. You've never come close to organising a wedding in your life. There's so much to do, and I'm gonna need to know when you're coming home so I can get your room ready.'

'I'm not coming home.'

'What?!' my Mum shrieks, then lowers her voice for Carol. 'She says she's not coming home.'

'Mum, I live in London now. I've got a job, a flat—'

'Oh, you can't be serious?'

'Why is that so hard to believe?'

'Because you've only been there two minutes. You've got to come home.'

'I haven't got to do anything.'

'But it's too busy down there; it's too bloody expensive.'

'Well, Pam Gillespie seems to think it's fantastic.'

'Oh, get your head out the clouds, love. You can't survive down there on your own.'

I think of all the gingham disguising what used to be my childhood bedroom.

'Doubt I'd survive much better at home with you.'

She gasps.

'Where's the Chloe I know, eh? That London's gone to your head.'

'Look, I'm sorry, Mum. I just haven't had time to process everything yet.'

'You will,' she says, softer now. 'It'll all come clear, love.'

'I know.'

'Everything happens for a reason. You mark my words. You'll look back on today soon enough and think, wow, this all happened for a reason.'

Okay, it's time to wrap things up.

'Please don't worry about me, Mum,' I say, honestly not wanting her to hang up and start fretting. You see, she'll be fine while Carol's there – she'll nick one of Carol's ciggies (even though she 'quit' in 1988) and together they can chew the fat – but once she's on her own she'll overthink my whole situation and get herself into a right state. 'I'm fine.'

'But you're all on your own, love.'

'That's not the tragedy here, Mum.'

'What do you mean?'

'Never mind. Besides, I'm not on me own, I've got Beth . . . work . . . you know.'

'You're single, though,' she says, sobbing.

I hear Carol ask if she'd like a gin and tonic.

'Slimline tonic,' my mum tells her. 'Open a new one. On the left in the pantry.'

'Mum, I've got to go. I've got a hairdresser's appointment soon.'

'Oh, no love. How do you know you can trust this hairdresser?'

I'm losing the will. Let's be honest, unless she's referring to Sweeney Todd, I'm not sure anyone'd be able to give a logical response. My brain hurts and I grind my teeth.

'Are you still there, love?'

'Yes, Mum. Still here.'

'Chloe, wouldn't you rather wait 'til you're home, go to the place you like in town? The one with the purple chaise longue in the window?'

'I can't go the funeral with these roots, Mum.'

I can hear Carol suggesting I wear a hat.

'Did you hear that, love? Carol said—'

'I heard her.'

'You don't half suit hats.'

She's genuinely concerned about this. I know she'll play with her tea tonight now, unable to focus on *Corrie*, worrying how my hair will turn out. She's never forgiven me for going full-on bleached blonde, forever suggesting I grow it out to my mousey brown and get some highlights with the cap. The cap!

'I'll speak to you soon, Mum. Love you millions.'

'Love you more.'

9

On Friday morning, I arrive at All Saints Church in a Berkshire village, and spot a wooden bench beneath the shade of an oak tree. The scene is picture perfect. A small medieval stone building with a steeple, a weathercock proud at its tip; a quaint path leading from the wooden double doors to a pretty floral arch. Nothing like the church I got dragged to for Sunday morning mass growing up. Even the sky is an idyllic blue. For a moment, I feel like I'm starring in a nineties Britflick.

That moment passes in a flash.

I feel nervous. I feel jittery. I feel numb and I feel pain. I feel such a cocktail of contradicting emotions that I'm dizzy, I'm heavy-headed, I'm scared. I'm not wearing a hat – my roots are now a silvery blonde – but I'm wearing a black cardigan, and black tights beneath my black shift dress. So I'm hot. I'm sweaty. I'm wishing I hadn't worn shoes with a heel because they're already hurting, but nothing else I own would've been smart enough.

I'm also early.

65

Well, I'd got myself into a right panic about being late. I mean, I had to take the tube to Paddington, a train to Reading and then a slow train seven stops, followed by a fifteen-minute walk following Google Maps. The conductor on the Reading train had caught my eye and told me to have a nice day. It made me wonder how often people have said this to me on a daily basis and how often I've taken all those nice days for granted. I'm not going to have a nice day today.

I sit myself down on the bench, slip my heels off and crack my toes, waiting for Jack's mourners to arrive. I didn't even know the location of this place until last night. When Jack's mum sent that text, I'd replied saying, *Thank you, Cx* and forgot to ask where the funeral would be. I couldn't bother her again, could I?

So I turned to Facebook.

I've been avoiding social media, knowing I'd lose days trawling through Jack's online life, specifically his life before me. He was more of a Twitter user, really, following the football, his fave comedians, a few prolific scientists and activists. Personally, I use Instagram. My settings are private and my name is an alias because I'm a teacher. I nose often and rarely post. But I had to find out about the funeral – I had to *go there* – and wow, there's nothing like a Facebook page to hammer home a tragedy, is there? Jack's profile was plastered with tributes: lyrics to songs, emojis of broken hearts, photographs – some recent, many old, going back to his uni days and beyond, that moonfaced blur of retro snaps retaken on a smart phone – and – thank God – the details about his funeral, posted by his older brother, Alex.

But there was nothing from me.

And of course. I never digitally professed my love, and so neither have I declared how his death has shattered my world.

There isn't a single photo of us together posted. Not a mention of my name within the long lists of those tagged, those who will remain in people's thoughts and prayers during this sad, sad time. Everybody on the list is a stranger to me, other than Patricia Carmichael and John Carmichael and Freddie Carmichael, Jack's younger brother who I met briefly at a pub a couple of months ago. I never got the chance to meet his older brother, Alex, a tech whizz who lives in Seattle with his wife and kids. I recognised the name Ross Robson, the comedian we were supposed to go and see in Greenwich the evening I found out Jack died. I don't know him, though.

And this is why I didn't want to expose myself to Facebook. This.

As I scrolled through every public message to Jack, I found her. Florrie.

Florrie Ellen Tewkesbury. I mean, it's hard not to ignore a name like that, eh?

*We strive to find great love in life. **Jack Carmichael**, thank you for being my friend, my stormtrooper, my bud. Thank you for being one of my life's great loves. Heaven celebrates what we commiserate. Boogie on up there and we'll catch up again one fine day. I knows it. You know I knows it. You knows it. Haha xxx*

Stormtrooper??
I had to click on her profile. (Wouldn't you?!)
Her privacy settings are tight but her profile pic told me enough. Sipping an oversized cup of hot chocolate loaded with floating marshmallows, her pinky out; a severe eyeliner flick; cherry-red dyed hair. I hated that I was peeking, presuming, imagining them together.

'So don't look,' is what Jack would've said. 'Simple.'

'But I had to find out where your fucking funeral is!' I yelled at the wall. 'And thanks to that, not only have I been reminded hundreds and hundreds and hundreds of times that you're dead and with the angels and never to be forgotten and taken too soon, but I'm wondering why Florrie called you her fucking Stormtrooper? Since when were you into Star Wars? What the actual . . . Jack?!'

I wished for him to be checking the spice rack for paprika, or singing the wrong words to Elton John songs from the bathroom.

I opened Facebook again. Not to read any more tributes, though. I wanted to see him; Jack. I tapped on his photos, something I hadn't done since our earliest days – when I found them, to be honest, uninteresting. His profile pic was simply his bushy beard and his teeth grinning. His last upload had been in March this year, and, typical Jack, it wasn't a photo of him. It was a photo of a different person altogether. The man sat in the shopping trolley.

The last morning we spent together floated into my mind: him pondering the meaning of what could be behind the picture. I wished I hadn't rushed off to work, wished I'd been given the gift of hindsight so I could have called in sick, spent the day with him. Oh, how we could've pondered such notions all bloody day! I looked up from my laptop, over towards the cooker where the picture hangs, and saw Jack, arms folded across his chest, a smile – a little smug – stretching across his face.

'I reckon I love you, Chloe Roscoe,' I imagined him saying.

'And I reckon I love you, too, Jack Carmichael,' I said.

And now, today, it's his funeral.

I squeeze my feet back into my heels. A couple of people

have arrived, a few cars parking on the quiet country road. I stand; not sure why. It's not like I'm looking out for a mate or hoping to be noticed. So I sit back down again and wait, watch; some women my age, linking each other; another with a baby in a sling, bouncing. Four fellas get out of one car, a variety of beards, all suited and booted. None of them are wearing black. In fact, their attire is more in line for a wedding. They all know each other. The fellas kiss the women on the cheek; coo at the baby.

More people filter into the old graveyard, tombstones so ancient that the writing is too weathered to make out. And more, and more. A scattered few in black: the older generation.

I spot Florrie running towards the group with the baby, hugging each one individually and swaying from side to side mid embrace. She's got a peach fascinator on her head.

I want to mingle, and yet I don't. I really, really don't. I want to make sure everybody knows who I am, that I'm Jack's girlfriend; but I also don't want be here at all, because quite frankly, who wants to be at a funeral? I want two weeks ago; I want a month ago; I want anything that isn't this. But I want to be involved.

Because I *am*. Involved.

As I make my way from the bench beneath the tree towards the crowd, I wonder when everybody here saw Jack last. He'd spent the majority of the past few months with me, or at work. I bet some of these people haven't seen him in years. I had sex with him the morning before he—

A hand touches my shoulder.

'Hey . . . Chloe, right?'

I nearly scream.

'Sorry, didn't mean to frighten you!' It's Badge.

He's slight and holds his suit jacket by the collar, resting it upon his shoulder casually, pushing his square-framed specs further up his nose. I think his full name is Paul Badger, a colleague of Jack's. I went to his house for drinks and nibbles one Sunday last month, something Jack thought would be a good laugh, except there were lots of small children. The majority of adults were bent at the waist chasing their offspring around in a tizz. When Jack had gone to the loo, I'd got stuck talking to a couple about potty training and catchment areas. We didn't stay long.

'Nice to see you again,' I say, like an idiot.

'Terrible, isn't it?' Badge says, clearly bewildered.

I nod.

'We just can't believe it,' he shakes his head. 'The whole team, we're just, you know.'

'Yeah.'

Then Badge holds up one hand and crosses his fingers.

'So were you and Jack an item?' he asks.

'I'd just moved in with him.'

'So that was you! I presumed so. Jack mentioned he was living with a lady.'

I'm grateful for this information and although I don't say anything, I hope others heard it.

'Such a horrid tragedy though,' Badge says, swallowing. 'And the driver—'

He stops abruptly as we notice the hush descending amongst us. An almost-silence falls. The only sounds creeping in are the leaves on the trees rustling in a soft breeze. The cars are here. They move so slowly that they don't make a sound. Around me, people gently edge towards the church entrance. I can't see anything. No coffin, no wreath that spells out Jack. I just see the black roofs of cars and allow the crowds to pass me by, my heels sinking into the soft, grassy earth. Badge is no longer beside me; he's nowhere to be seen. There's crying. Hefty, meaty sobs. The noise triggers my throat to tighten, to hurt. I watch everybody filter inside.

The pallbearers surround the hearse. Jack's brothers, both with kind faces.

I can't look.

I won't look.

I turn around, my back facing what's supposed to be Jack inside a box. My God, from what I see of the box before I turn it doesn't even look big enough for him to fit inside. I don't want to gawp, check, or think that thought ever, ever, ever again. I gaze out past the gate; the stone wall dotted with moss; the horses in the distance across a field.

And when I turn back, the hearse is empty.

The girl with the baby in a sling waits by the church door, jigging in and out of the entrance, her spot for the ceremony. I walk forward, give her and her baby a gentle smile and slip into the back row pew.

The vicar begins. Jack's brother Alex delivers a few anecdotes about Jack as a kid, 'Always collecting things; ladybirds in matchboxes, football stickers, rings from Coke cans . . .' Sweet; I never knew that. Alex reminds us all that Jack liked to own a room; to be heard. Laughter drops the tension of many shoulders and a few people clap. It's more of a best man's speech than a eulogy and Alex invites some of Jack's friends to say a few words, too.

They talk of terrible chat-up lines and something they got up to as students called 'naked stair diving'. There's much appreciation for the latter – it's something a good chunk of the congregation seems to know about. We're invited to look up to the white screen set up on the altar. A video montage begins, with 'Don't Stop Me Now' by Queen as the soundtrack. People whoop and cheer at various moments – Jack downing a shot or bombing into a swimming pool – and there's a group 'ah' for old clips of him as a kid with a dog or pecking his mum on the cheek. A short video game animation slots into the mix, made by work colleagues: 'Jack' the avatar running through a desert with a machine gun. As Freddie Mercury finishes up with the slowed-down 'da's of his song, the montage goes into slow motion too, ending with a familiar face, crossing his eyes and sticking out his tongue, raising a pint of Guinness . . .

Familiar to everybody in this church bar one.

Me.

I barely recognise him. Of course, it *looks* like Jack. But it's not Jack. A lad who was apparently into Moby and The Mighty Boosh? I mean, Jack? *My* Jack? Never in a million years. And as for the choice of song for the montage – well.

As the vicar rounds up the service, Trish gets to her feet. A ripple of applause begins, more and more people standing, until I have to follow suit or I'll be the only one sitting down. As the coffin is carried past me, I look at the mahogany wood and think, 'You're not in there – you're not.' Because if Jack's in there, I won't be able to cope. I'll die right here on the spot from pain. Instead, I'm just going to feel ashamed that I've just crashed some fella's funeral.

I'm an intruder.

Outside, I stand beside Florrie as the coffin is placed back into the hearse. It's off to the crematorium where, the vicar had informed the congregation, only immediate family could attend. Florrie is wailing, as is the pal she's arm in arm with. The girl with the baby in the sling says she has to nip off, pick up her other kid from preschool. They air kiss.

'Pub?' Florrie asks around to nobody specific, but her eyes find mine.

I don't know.

Should I go?

I suppose Trish and John will be expecting to see me there later.

'I've got space in my car,' a fella says, and another says, 'Me, too.'

One of them is Ross Robson. Here we are, finally meeting. He's the tallest of the men here; a fifty-fifty mix of smart and scruffy, with wild curly hair and a sweet baby face for a fella in his late thirties.

'Ross?' I say. 'I'm Chloe.'

He looks at me, blank. He's not being rude though – I can sense his embarrassment, his panicked search around his mind. *Who is Chloe? Did I sleep with her once? Is she a crazy fan? Was she the fat girl in school?*

'Jack's girlfriend,' I help him out.

'Chloe!' he sings. 'Ah, mate. We finally meet.'

'My thoughts exactly,' I say, sadly.

Florrie muscles in. She's got that whole *look* going on: the forties dress, the victory roll. Up close, the fascinator is more of a pillbox hat, with a peachy net veil covering half of her face.

'Flo, this is Chloe,' Ross says, introducing me.

'Oh, hi,' Florrie says, and meekly shakes my hand with the tips of her fingers, all decorated in an assortment of silver rings.

'As in *Chloe*,' Ross tries to spell it out. 'The girl Jack was dating.'

'Ohhhh, hiiiiiiiiii.'

Another fella joins, skinny-fat with enormous teeth.

73

'I didn't know Jack was dating someone,' he snorts, but kindly. 'What a dark horse!'

'Actually, we were living together,' I say.

Ross slaps his hands to his face.

'Ah, mate,' he says. 'I didn't know it was *that* serious.'

'You mustn't have been together long,' Florrie suggests.

I shrug. 'Almost half a year.'

'Oh, you poor thing,' Florrie cries. 'That's hardly any time at all.'

Fuck. I'd meant for that to sound like a long time.

The skinny-fat fella reiterates. 'I had *no idea*.'

'I better dash,' Florrie taps my arm, then everybody else's individually, as if she's playing bongos. 'I promised Trish I'd check on the caterers.'

Ross puts his arm around Florrie – little willowy Florrie – and gives her a shake. Well done to her, helping Jack's mum out. That should be my job. The skinny-fat fella is rounding up the troops, sorting out lifts.

'You coming to the pub, Chloe?' he asks.

'I'll follow on.'

And I watch them all leave the churchyard, down the path towards various parked cars. Their spirits are higher than they were before the service, an obvious warmth of friends being reunited, although for a most dreadful reason. I'm not one of them – it's likely I'm already forgotten.

I'll swerve the whole pub ordeal. The wake. The one with in-jokes about naked stair diving and Jack's ex. *Fucking Florrie*. I need to get back to my flat; my Jack.

Because, you see, my Jack can't be dead yet.

We only just got started.

As I start my walk down the country lane, barefoot, carrying my heels in my hand, I hear my name being called, as clear as the church bells striking one. It's a sound full of love and warmth, and most importantly, familiarity. A white Audi waits outside the church, its driver door open. The driver is standing and waving me over.

'Chloe babes!'

It's Beth.

10

We hit the pub.

Not the one where the wake is happening – we're in the next village; long, winding roads apart. It's a posh one with an outdoor decking area overlooking the Thames, framed by weeping willows. A couple of barges are moored up across the river; the expensive sort. There are a few old age pensioners inside, enjoying a leisurely lunch of fish and chips; the waft of vinegar is strong. I imagine this sort of place only ever gets busy on Sundays. I take a seat outside and Beth goes to the bar, returning with a bottle of Sauvignon in an ice bucket and two glasses.

'Who's driving us home?' I ask.

'We'll worry about that later, babes.'

We clink. My first sip is large, satisfying, and goes straight to my head. I haven't eaten all day and probably didn't eat anything last night, either. I can't remember. This is just what I need.

'Your mum rang me,' Beth says.

'Was she dramatic?'

'So-so. She wants you to go home.'

I roll my eyes and Beth grins. She gets it.

'I found an article online,' she says, 'about the accident.'

'Beth, don't—'

'Such a tragedy. And the driver—'

'Can we not go there? Please?'

Beth massages her temples with her fingertips, releasing a sigh.

'I'm sorry,' she mutters.

'Look, you didn't have to come. You've wasted a day's holiday.'

'Your Kit's beside himself, you know. Said he's been trying to ring you all week.'

'I can't . . . I don't know how to talk about it.'

Beth is dressed down today. Minimal makeup; her lips are soft and unpainted. She's wearing jeans, neat white trainers and a grey t-shirt with a simple left breast pocket. Large sunglasses sit on top of her caramel locks. She had no intention of attending the funeral. She's one hundred per cent here for me.

'You look weird in black,' she says, scrunching up her cute little nose.

'I feel weird in black. I never got the memo.'

'What do you mean?'

'It was like I was just there to pay me respects.'

'I'm confused. Isn't that what funerals are for?'

'Well, yeah, any funeral I've been to before. Like me Aunty Dot; or remember that nice dinner lady, Mrs O'Leary? But this one was different.'

'How?'

'I wasn't a part of it. And I should've been.'

A cloud has shifted, and Beth puts her sunglasses on. I know she's glaring at me though.

'Don't say it,' I say, my mouth draped over the side of my glass. 'Don't say how I hardly knew him. I haven't been living in cloud cuckoo land since January, Beth, I've been *living*. And so had Jack. We'd been actually living *for* each other, *with* each other, everything was about each other. I knew him better than anyone. But I feel like I've just paid me respects to a bloody stranger.'

'So, come on. Tell me.'

'Tell you what?'

'About Jack. Pretend it's the funeral again; pretend you're getting a chance to speak about him. And I'll listen.'

'No.'

'Why?'

'This isn't role play, Beth. This isn't one of me GCSE Drama classes.'

'No, but it might make you feel better, babes.'

'It won't.'

Beth stands and holds one finger up, indicating she won't be a minute. I down the wine in my glass and top it up, returning a wave to a couple of fellas cruising past on a rowing boat. Beth returns with three bags of posh crisps, mature cheddar flavour, and opens them out as if she's demonstrating origami.

'Eat,' she orders.

To be fair, I already feel as though I might be swaying.

'I've ordered some sweet potato fries and halloumi sticks, too. Now, listen babes. Remember when you were obsessed with Robbie Williams?'

I nod and dig into the delicious crisps: so cheesy they could be actual cheese.

'And remember how you framed that A4 poster from

78

Smash Hits,' Beth continues, 'and stuck it to your bedroom ceiling—'

'Yeah, so he was the first face I saw in the morning and the last I saw at night.'

'And yet you stuck the bloody frame to the ceiling with what exactly?'

'Blu-tack.'

'And what happened to you, babes?'

I stuff my mouth with more crisps, speaking with my mouth full.

'The frame fell off and split me head open. Four stitches!'

Beth clinks my empty wine glass and sips, giggling at the story she's heard and told endlessly since we were twelve years old.

'Did you ever tell Jack about that, babes? Show him the scar on your scalp?'

'No way,' I say. 'I'd feel ashamed!'

'Did he know about the time you got sacked from that call centre job?'

'I never got sacked,' I remind her. 'I was on a zero-hour contract.'

'Yeah and they specifically said they wouldn't give you a single hour again, ever.'

'It was a blessing in disguise. I'd probably still be there today.'

'Did you tell Jack about it?'

'Dunno. Maybe?'

'Or what about how we used to gatecrash those late-night parties above the video shop with those potheads? Does Jack know about how you'd sneak—'

'Okay, stop. I know what you're trying to do.'

Beth removes her sunglasses and reaches out for my hand. I snatch it away and sit on it.

'Babes, we've got history. Jack has the right to have history, too.'

Our fries and sticks arrive but Beth shakes her head.

'We need more wine,' she says, and hands the ice bucket with the empty bottle to the waitress. 'Please.'

'I did,' I say, burning the roof of my mouth on a fry. 'I definitely told him about the call centre. He thought it was a brilliant story.'

'That's great.'

'No, it's not. 'Cause it's not a brilliant story. It's a self-deprecating anecdote. I mean, you've hit an all-time low when you get booted out of a job you hate that pays minimum wage, haven't you? A job where you weren't even worthy of being officially sacked. Yeah, I became a teacher. Whoop, whoop, good for me. But, Beth – I'm an absolutely shit teacher. I don't change the lives of the kids. I do the bare minimum and tick the boxes and for God's sake, I teach them fucking drama.'

'Okay, you're really spiralling into the dark place, babes.'

'You came to meet me at a funeral. What did you expect?'

And for some reason, we laugh. Cackle. Like a pair of old witches.

The second bottle arrives and I do the honours.

'Sometimes I think I'm going mad, though,' I say. 'Like, I feel like he's still close to me. And no, I'm not into ghosts. I just . . . feel him. I mean, it's impossible not to. I paid his gas bill last week. It's like me relationship's still happening.'

'I know you're trying to make sense, but—'

'How can anyone make sense of death?'

'So you're still in a relationship? With a dead lad?'

I wince. She makes it sound so—

'Sorry, babes. That was harsh.'

80

'The fridge in the flat, Beth – it's like a bloody to-do list. And I have to look at it every day, this massive reminder that me and Jack had started a real life together. And I need to finish off what we started.'

'How can you possibly do that, Chlo?'

I shrug and allow my gaze to wander up the river.

'That's what I've got to figure out.'

We drink in a semi-comfortable silence for a while, nibbling snacks. A knot sits in my stomach and it's nothing to do with the amount of salt I've consumed in the past hour. It's Florrie. All-important Florrie. Helping Trish; checking on the caterers. God, if she's so important, why didn't Jack ever mention her?

Beth is on her phone, tapping away.

'Everything okay?' I ask.

'Fergus wanting to know when I'll be home. It's fine. Honest, babes.'

She doesn't sound fine.

'I'm still not pregnant,' she says, and gulps her wine. 'Clearly.'

'Ah shit. And I guess I'm stopping you and him from—'

'Nope. Got me period yesterday. Super early this month, for fuck's sake.'

'What a bitch.'

'I know, right. Let's get another bottle, babes. I'm halfway hammered, and you know how I hate doing things by halves.'

'On one condition,' I say, standing up too quickly and steadying myself on the table. 'That you don't mention me "not knowing" Jack, or the relationship being "too short", or any of that bullshitty bollocks the world's harping on about.'

'So long as you don't mention Fergus. Or me ovaries.'

Another bottle of wine later and we're desperate to crash.

We find a twin room above a different pub in the same village and Beth makes the most of it, running a hot bubble bath for herself, nipping downstairs for a cappuccino. Not wanting to prolong today any longer than necessary, I dive under the covers of one of the beds, not even attempting to remove my black clothes or put the telly on. I pretend to be asleep when I hear Beth pottering about, and somehow it works. I sleep.

11

As we drive back to London the next morning, we listen to Graham Norton on Radio Two. Beth doesn't pry or poke me into talking much and I'm glad. My whole body aches from a pain I can't pinpoint.

There's a bouquet of flowers waiting for me on the doorstep.

Wildflowers: beautiful; not your average online purchase. These were either bought in a specialist local shop or hand-picked from some glorious field. A small card sits amongst the lilacs and yellows. *To Chloe.* It's with love from Giles and Ingrid, the couple on the second floor. They know.

How do they know?

Trish and John must've told them.

They'll be looking for a new tenant. It's only polite to inform the neighbours.

I stand in the hallway, chuck my keys into the blue Marrakech dish, miss, and watch them fall to the carpet. I drop my cardigan; my heels; the flowers, too. I walk through our flat, brushing my middle fingers along each wall. A pair of Jack's trainers obstructs the small space between the coffee table and the telly. How have I only just noticed that?

I open the fridge and stare at the sparse shelves: butter, an old onion, a splash of tonic water that's gone flat. No grapes. The funeral plays over in my mind. I fast forward the worst parts, rewind the lighter moments. During the video montage, the volume of the (inappropriate) Queen song had dipped so the mourners could endure Jack's Ali G impression, caught on an old camcorder. How I'd cringed in that back pew.

Sorry, Jack.

'Who was that guy?' I ask the ceiling, as you do. 'Because he wasn't you.'

And Florrie. That hat.

I'd been open with Jack about my previous relationships; trial and error, I'd liked to call it. I'm no hopeless romantic but in the last few years, I'd started to become intent on finding a partner in crime. Maybe it was seeing my brother happy, his wishes coming true. Maybe it was biology. I dated. Lots. Even at work, I'd engage in a staffroom flirt over instant coffee. Last year, chaperoning a Duke of Edinburgh trip, I snogged my colleague – a Geography teacher – once torches were out and teens were (apparently) asleep. My mind and heart were open to finding love; any time, any place. I had no experience of heartbreak, only disappointment. And a fair few dry, lonely spells. Jack knew all this: I hid nothing from him. Well, I had nothing to hide.

And Jack?

'Plenty of flings,' he'd said. 'But I've never been in love.'

When I asked him if there were any skeletons in his closet, he told me about a girl he fingered in an actual closet, dressed as a skeleton. He was sixteen: a Halloween party at his mate's house. We rolled about laughing, exchanging horror stories of our youth. We didn't backtrack.

But Jack and Florrie – what happened between them?

'I guess we were only five months in,' I say, matter-of-factly, leaning back against the sink. 'We still had plenty to discover.'

The fridge door looks back at me, a glorious mishmash of memories and plans. It's so alive. To my left, I can see Jack popping his head out of the kitchen door, checking to see if it's warm enough to have a beer outside. To my right, he's there again, hanging his wet socks on the radiator.

'Who was that man whose funeral I attended yesterday?' I cry. 'Who? He made people cry and cheer and laugh and applaud and hug and unite and I don't know him. I'll never know him. Because I know you! And you're not here anymore!'

I check my phone for distraction, slumping down onto the kitchen floor.

There are two messages from Gareth, our Kit's fiancé. One is just checking in, sending his love. The second is a YouTube link to some political satire. He sends these often. I've got a message from Beth, too.

My sis just announced baby number 2's on the way. I'm happy for her. I don't want her baby. I want mine. But still. FFS. Xxx

I send back a crying face and string of red hearts.

I never asked Jack outright if he wanted kids. I didn't need to. We were always playing the name game; it was a habit that developed quite early on. Even when he was cooking the bolognese, the night before he died, he said, 'I like Lily for a girl. Not Lilian. Just Lily.' It was a breath of fresh air, since he'd recently declared our son would be called Wild. Now, I'm all for alternative names, but *Wild*? Nope. My argument was that we can control our kid's name, but not their personality. What if he was naturally tame? At least a Joe or a James can be anything they want without judgement . . .

Hold on.

Could it be possible? Could I . . .

I scroll through my phone; look at the calendar. I've never been one to chart, keep up with dates about what's going on with my body. I've been on the pill for years. But I read a negative article a couple of months ago and decided to stop taking it. Jack and I were careful, most of the time.

I count the days.

And count again.

So I won't know for sure until next week, when my period is due.

But, oh my God. I might be pregnant.

12

'Miss Roscoe?' Si Sullivan calls. 'A word, please.'

The bell has shaken us out of our first lunchtime rehearsal. I didn't have to do much – Si was the one on the piano and teaching the song. Layla Birch didn't show up. I wonder if she's rebelling because she didn't get the lead.

Si reaches into his anorak pocket and pulls out two West End theatre tickets.

'Say, whaaaat?' He attempts a terrible American accent.

'Surprise!' I say.

I had been supposed to be going to see *Mamma Mia!* tonight with Jack, who, to my ultimate shock, had been keen on going. He said his boss raved about it and his mum hated it, so he was interested to see whose team he'd bat for. This morning, I'd left the tickets in Si's pigeonhole with a note saying *Yours if you want them*. It seemed a shame to leave them stuck to the fridge, going to waste.

Anyone would think I'd just handed him a cheque for a million quid.

'They were a raffle prize,' I tell him.

'And you chose me to accompany you?' I think he might cry.

'Oh no. I can't—'

'But you're my partner in showbiz crime, Chloe! Please say yes, please,' he begs, fluttering his eyelids. He's not pretty; rather he's petite and, well, *pointy*. His nose, his cheekbones, his chin are all at a sharp angle, matching the pointed quiff in his hair. There's always a twinkle in his eye though, a live wire keeping him buzzy. Very, very buzzy.

I look at the ticket.

'Erm . . .' I say.

'Oh, it's not a date or anything! I'm not – er – you know, I mean, I wouldn't—'

I smile. I know it's not a date.

'Have you already seen it?' Si asks, deflated.

'No . . . It's just . . .' I can't seem to express myself. 'Perhaps I'm a little more suited to *Les Misérables* right now.'

Si shoves his musical score into his smart rucksack, not hiding his disappointment.

'Why don't you ask your pal who teaches English?' I suggest. 'What's his name? Mr Belling?'

'For starters,' Si holds up one hand in my face, 'Drew Belling is not my pal. And secondly, he'll think it's a date. And it's not.'

'Right . . .'

'And I'll be honest. I called my sister before lunch. And my mum. They're both busy.'

'Wow. So I'm your last resort, eh?'

Si folds his arms and purses his lips, making them so thin they disappear.

'Whatever. Forget it,' he sulks. 'Thanks for the tickets, Chloe. I mean *ticket*. Singular.'

Well, he's made me feel awful. And perhaps that was his intention, because I tell him fine, fine, fine, I'll go with him to see *Mamma* bloody *Mia!* And he breaks out into a bouncy routine – something which I expect is along the lines of what I'll witness on stage tonight – and tells me he knew I wouldn't let him down. Which is kind, if inaccurate. I'd had every intention of letting him down. I wanted to stay in tonight, terrified that tomorrow might be the day a member of the Carmichael family shows up and boots me out. You see, it's been two weeks since the funeral. I'm floating through each day, waiting for something to happen; wanting nothing to happen. I just want to stay in the flat and imagine Jack's just late home from work.

I arrive at the theatre ten minutes before showtime, still in my school clothes: a maxidress and baggy cardigan. I haven't seen a West End show for years, something I used to get as an annual birthday treat, with a hotel deal and open-top bus tour of London. Now I live here, I'm already taking it for granted.

'This is my fourth time,' Si tells me, brimming with pride, as we bustle through the busy foyer, up the lavish staircase towards the dress circle. 'Thank you, again.'

'You've seen *Mamma Mia!* four times?'

'It's ALL about the second half,' he says, giddy. 'Well, the second half of the second half. But I won't spoil it for you. Unless you've seen the film?'

'No, haven't seen either,' I say, settling into my seat, miffed at how Si has completely undersold the majority of what I'm about to endure.

The overture kicks in, almost knocking me out with its powerful beat. It's so dynamic, so alive that my eyes water. I get that old tingle from my youth, the smell of the greasepaint, and I'm not even on stage. I calm down once the acting begins: it's upbeat and perky, and I don't pay much attention to what's going on. I just revel in the dark at not having to speak.

During the interval, Si buys himself an overpriced bag of Minstrels and asks if I fancy a wine. I decline and sip a plastic glass of free tap water from the end of the bar: my period hasn't made an appearance yet. He bops over to me, loving every second of being here. I miss having that abundance of enthusiasm: I'm here merely to pass time, to continue breathing, to keep going.

'What's your favourite bit so far?' he asks. 'Mine had to be "Dancing Queen". You?'

'Same.'

'So, did you ever see yourself up there, treading the boards?'

'Didn't we all?'

'Not everybody, surely?'

'Ah, come on, Si. It's a pretty common dream to be a star,' I say, realising that I'm behaving like a right bitch, raining on his parade – no theatrical pun intended. I soften my tone. 'I loved it as a kid. I used to dance in the local pantomime every Christmas. One year I even got a speaking role, but I fucked it up.'

'No!'

'Yep. You know when Cinderella shows up to the ball and nobody knows who she is?'

'Incognito. The best part, of course. Go on . . .'

'Well, it was my line to introduce her as a mysterious princess from a faraway land, and as I opened me mouth, I somehow – well – breathed wrong.'

Si chokes on a Minstrel. 'How do you breathe wrong?!'

'I dunno! I kind of breathed in when I should've breathed

out – or the other way round – and ended up coughing uncontrollably. Some other kid jumped in like a trouper and said me line for me, but it was drowned out by the fit I was having. Seriously, Si, I sounded like I was on me last legs. The show couldn't continue until I stopped.'

'I can't bear it!' Si shrieks, and covers his face with the Minstrels bag. 'I can't even look at you! This is mortifying.'

'I know, right? So there you have it. My glittering career as an actress. I joined the youth theatre in the backstage department once I was old enough. I used to paint the sets, did a bit of wardrobe.'

'Ooh, I can totally see you as a wardrobe mistress.'

'Ha, well. When the girl playing Elizabeth Proctor fell ill the night before we opened *The Crucible*, I knew exactly who'd fit into her costume.'

'You?'

'Yep. Easy as that, I was back in the game.'

Si gives a neat round of applause. 'And were you marvellous?'

'Nah. I was a total flop. And so what? I just liked the whole world of it, you know. That feeling of being part of a big, weird family. On the stage, off the stage, the after-show parties—'

'Oh, I loooove an after-show.'

'That's probably where I was going wrong. I preferred that to putting in the graft. I ended up doing a piss-poor drama degree at a poly nobody's ever heard of; but God, we had a good laugh. Used to put on terrible sketch shows in the student union – we thought we were hilarious. Loads of Blair jokes.'

'*Cringe!*'

Over the tannoy, we're instructed to take our seats as the

performance will recommence in three minutes. I'm a little lightheaded from talking so freely about something that's nothing to do with Jack or my life with him. A shard of guilt stabs me and I grab onto the bar, willing that freedom to return. But no. It's gone. I should be here with Jack, not Si.

'Chloe?' Si asks, clearly wondering why I'm not following him into the dress circle.

'Sorry. Coming.'

Settling back in our seats, I just want the second half to start. Now.

'Chloe, can I ask you something?'

I want to say no.

'Just something that's been playing on my mind this evening,' he goes on.

I look at him, waiting.

'Why didn't you want to come tonight? Is it because I'm a bit of a – well, er – a dweeb?'

'A dweeb?' I laugh, taken by surprise. 'What is this? *Grease*?'

'It's just you really, really didn't wanna come, and—'

'Me boyfriend died. Recently. This is me first trip to the theatre without him.'

Si grabs me and hugs me tight. I don't reciprocate because of his haste, and I let him hold me as if I'm a wooden plank. He releases me as quickly as he grabbed me and apologises for being unprofessional.

'It's fine,' I tell him. 'We're not at work now.'

'Did you both go to the theatre often?' he asks, tentative.

I shake my head. 'Just the once. It's how we met. At the opening night of a new musical in Liverpool. A friend of mine was playing one of the leads.'

'Oh, marvellous. What musical?'

My face scrunches up as I admit, '*The Book of Brexit*.'

For a second, I think Si is going to vomit.

'I heard that was atrocious,' he says.

'It was.'

The chatter surrounding us is quite loud, the audience having enjoyed a swift drink or two at the bar, now eager for the second half to begin. A group of women sitting behind us have started singing the title song, each making up their own version of the words and the tune. Si unsubtly sticks a finger in his ear and scratches until it squeaks, making me chuckle.

'Chloe,' he says. 'I'm sorry for your loss. I wish I'd known.'

'Please, it's fine.'

'No, it's not. I never would've guilt-tripped you into coming. The firsts are the worst.'

'The what?'

'The firsts.'

I'm lost.

'My dad passed away two years ago,' he says, edging closer to me so he can lower his voice. 'After the funeral, that's when it began. The *firsts*. The first birthdays we'd all have to celebrate without him; the first Christmas; the first flipping Wimbledon. And sometimes you're just not ready to face them, and nobody should force you. We ignored Christmas that first year.'

An almighty bang of drums throws us upright in our seats and the band blasts the audience with the entr'acte as our attention is thrust towards the stage. I listen to the mashup of Abba songs half-heartedly, waiting for the curtain to rise, thinking about what Si has just told me. The firsts. Jack and I never got the chance to make enough memories to warrant a whole year of firsts. We never made it to my birthday. Is this a good thing? Because it sure doesn't feel

93

good. When *Mamma Mia!* finishes tonight and I tick the theatre box, what's next? A restaurant? A holiday? Fuck me, I've already done the first pub and the first overnight stay, both with Beth last Friday. And I've been to the Sainsbury's Local without him almost every other day. What happens when I've completed all the firsts? Am I forced to move on? Like an expired parking ticket?

I rest my hand on my belly.

Yesterday, in the Sainsbury's Local, I stared at the home pregnancy tests on the shelf. All I had to do was take one. But I reached left, added a tube of toothpaste to my basket instead. It's always good to have extra toothpaste. And it won't give a negative result.

Don't be over. Please, *please*. Don't.

I'm sucked into the performance. The mother, the daughter. Si was right. It's all about the second half, and I listen to the songs and the words and the winner taking it all, the loser having to fall, and oh, I sob. I'm not alone, of course. Tears stream down Si's pointed little face. When the happy ending inevitably comes, the whole audience jump to their feet to boogie to 'Waterloo' and it unnerves me. I preferred wallowing in my safe, dark haven, but Si won't let me get away with it and I'm yanked up, pressured into dancing like a middle-aged woman around her handbag. I even sing along, shocked that I know the bloody words.

'Thanks again, Chloe,' Si says as we follow the exit signs along with hundreds of others, many of whom are still singing Abba songs. 'You could've ripped up these tickets and who could blame you?'

'No, thank *you*. It was a good "first". I have to admit I enjoyed it. And Jack, well – he would've hated it.'

Si beams.

'Well done, you,' he says.

We edge towards the street, stuck between a hen party and a group of Japanese tourists.

'We've talked a lot about me tonight,' I say, 'but I'm intrigued. What's going on between you and Mr Belling? Drew?'

'Nothing.'

'Doesn't sound like nothing.'

'He thinks I'm gay.'

'Oh.' I'm stumped. And embarrassed for presuming.

'And, I'm not.' Si folds his arms, his lips disappearing into his mouth again. 'And I'm not straight, either. I don't know what I am, okay?'

'Okay,' I tell him, gently. 'That's totally okay, Si.'

'Is it?'

We stand there as the crowds disperse into old pubs and late-night coffee shops, or hop aboard rickshaws heading across the West End. I don't know if I should return the hug Si gave me before the second half began; whether we've crossed the line from being colleagues to mates. But he's started to unravel his headphones and places them into his ears.

'Got the soundtrack all ready for my tube ride,' he grins, although a little awkwardly.

'You're going to listen to *Mamma Mia!* now?' I laugh.

'Nobody's gonna stop me.'

I give him a wave which he mirrors before heading towards Holborn to catch the Central line and I back off in the direction of Charing Cross for the Northern line southbound. It's a beautiful night, the perfect temperature for a night-time city walk. I turn before reaching the station's entrance and keep walking towards the river, stopping once I reach the front of Embankment. My head turns right, up at the Golden Jubilee pedestrian bridge.

But I can't go there, can't walk across it.

That would be another first.

The evening of the day I moved to London, Jack had brought me here. We took the tube to Waterloo, walking from the South Bank, opposite where I'm standing now. I remember the sky was orange, with dashes of cloud like tiger stripes. Once we reached the middle of the bridge, Jack told me to look out beyond the National Theatre. Buses, already lit up, crossed Waterloo Bridge ahead; iconic buildings – St Paul's and the Oxo Tower – stood proud, pleased to be watched. Jack stood behind me, his arms around my waist, and he kissed my neck, my cheek.

'I love this spot,' he said. 'But it's also overwhelming.'

'Why?'

'It's London in all its glory. I feel like if you can make it here, you can make it—'

'Erm, isn't that New York?'

'Meh. New York, Shmew Shmork! This city is glorious. Tough. Awesome.'

I swivelled around so we were face-to-face. In the near distance, the London Eye and Big Ben framed Jack's head. Friends, couples, families were passing by, or stopping to take selfies.

'And have you?' I asked. 'Made it?'

'Darlin', we're making it.'

As I remember what came next – a kiss; soft and long and unashamedly public – I rock against the station wall in pain. It's not painful pain – not the kind you can take a pill for or wince through the ache – but a grand itch, a restless shake, a feeling that's too much and never enough all at once.

The air is calm, the vibe low-key.

I breathe.

Bangkok is the only other capital city I'd had the chance to visit with Jack. If I were there now, overlooking the Chao Phraya instead of the Thames, I'm not sure I'd have time to reflect. The place moves by so quickly, even late at night. From my experience, anyway. Oh, how we'd wanted to return there one day; find the man sat in the shopping trolley. We'd invented a Saturday night drinking game, coming up with the reasons he might've been there – in protest; to sunbathe; waiting for a Big Mac; posing for art students – and the lamest guess had to be drink. I start wondering, again, what really is behind that picture – just as Jack wondered before he died – what that man is doing right now. Alone in the big city, perhaps. Like me. Like Si.

I check my phone, mindful of not ignoring Beth if she's messaged.

My mum's been texting again.

I have a job for you. It requires your crafting skills!

Well, I do excel with a needle and thread. Or a glue stick. I click on the next text.

It's for the wedding. Come home and I'll explain. Love you. Mum x

Forty minutes later I arrive at the flat. On the fridge, there's a space where the *Mamma Mia!* tickets had been. The magnet – a Man United shirt – has nothing to hold up any more. One of our plans is done and dusted. The gas bill was paid weeks ago, too. I take it down, rip it in half, chuck it into the recycling.

'So, what next?' I cry.

Skiing lessons, holidays, birthday celebrations . . .

'I can't . . . I can't do anything else without you, Jack.'

I go to the bedroom. The moonlight filters through the open blinds, shedding a low glow onto the king-size bed, which takes up the majority of this room. I want to see Jack in his boxers, sitting up against the pillows on his iPad with his bare feet crossed, wriggling his chunky toes. I want to see him tucked up and flicking through a paperback filled with scientific facts about what makes humans behave in certain ways. I want to see him crashed out; or fuck it, I want to see him passed out drunk, stinking of ale and snoring so loud I have to wallop him on the back just to get a minute's peace.

'Jack?' I whisper.

I step away, back to the lounge, and curl up on the sofa. I stay exactly where I am, my head upon Rudolf, where it's been every night since Jack died.

Si was right. Nobody should force those firsts.

13

It's Saturday and I'm a week late. I'm going to nip out to buy a pregnancy test. Today could be the day when that something I've been waiting for happens.

Would I have left it this long to take a test if Jack had been alive? Or would I have told him immediately, as soon as my period didn't show up? It would be sudden to hit this milestone, but it's one I don't doubt we were heading towards. I'm thirty-six – time's not on my side. So the serious baby chat would've taken place next year, for sure. What a luxury that seems like now; *next year* with Jack. Confidently expected; nailed-down impossible.

I shower, pull on a tight black t-shirt and throw the cotton rag I refer to as my 'holiday' dress – the one I'd worn endlessly in Thailand – over my head. I finish off my summer look with some chunky beads and a hint of bright-red lipstick. I'm ready. And what's more, I'm motivated.

The flat's a mess, though. An empty pizza box is tossed on the kitchen floor, too big to fit into the recycling bin. I imagine Jack in the kitchen, sulking that the only pieces of bread left by the toaster are the crusts. I make a mental note to grab a loaf while I'm out, too. I grab my keys from the blue Marrakech dish, and the doorbell rings.

'Chloe,' Trish Carmichael says, elongating the second half of my name and flashing her teeth into a plastic smile. 'Nice to see you again.'

She looks like Patricia from the telly today: pastel makeup; dangly earrings; hair spiked, ready for business. She's not wearing one of her panel-show suit jackets, though – they always look a size too big – but rather she's in her casual wear, a pashmina draped with finesse around her small frame, her specs on a gold chain. John's not with her.

'Wow, Mrs – erm – Trish. Hi.'

'I was going to call,' she tells me. 'But I thought, well—'

'You have a key, so what's the point?'

Trish clicks, points at me and winks. 'Exactly.'

I hold the door open and she walks straight into the kitchen and tosses her orange Michael Kors handbag onto the breakfast bar. She slowly twirls around, taking it all in, her fingers re-spiking her hair.

'Thanks for keeping an eye on this place,' she says.

'Sorry about the pizza box,' I say, pointing it out.

'Oh, we all have to eat, Chloe, don't we?' Trish laughs, a punchline to a joke I misheard.

If Jack could just show up, you know, in an alternate universe from the one Trish and I are enduring, then I wouldn't be the Chloe who Trish has convinced herself I am. I'd be more important.

'How are you?' I ask, instantly wondering if I've said the wrong thing.

Trish folds her arms, a stance that reminds me of Jack. Arm-folding isn't uncommon – I mean, we all do it. But it's

100

the way she taps the fingers of her left hand on her inner arm. Physically, Jack was larger, broader, taller than his mum, their size difference so extreme that if he ate her whole, he wouldn't look like he'd put on any weight. And yet, here, there's a distinct similarity, which I love and hate all at once.

'I'm sad, Chloe,' Trish sighs, looking directly at me. 'I don't think I'll ever not be sad.'

'Me too,' I admit.

Her reply is silent: a subtle narrowing of her eyes.

God, I'd love to tell her that she's going to be a grandma. A nan.

'I'm sorry I never came to the wake,' I say.

'Oh. Didn't you?'

'No . . . I . . .' . . . have no idea how to respond.

Trish takes the wall calendar down from the side of the fridge. It's mine, one of the only household accessories I've contributed that's in use. The themed photographs are of cats snapped in unusual objects; a novelty Christmas present from our Kit.

'You are aware that it's July?' Trish asks.

I nod, puzzled, and follow Trish's gaze downwards.

'Oops.' The current page is still on June.

With an unsubtle tut, Trish flicks to August. Her finger taps along the boxes and stops at the last weekend, pressing hard into the paper. She reaches into her handbag and takes out a pen – the sort nicked from a hotel room – then, adjusting her specs to dip to the end of her small nose, she peers at me with her naked eye.

'My son, Freddie, is moving into this flat,' she tells me, circling the date. 'Then.'

'Got it,' I say, having got nothing at all.

Trish stands upright and holds out her arms as if to say

well then. Or perhaps she wants me to give her a hug? Luckily, I don't have to decide. I'm saved by the doorbell again. Giles or Ingrid inviting me upstairs for pasta, hopefully. I think. I leave the eerie silence between Jack's mother and me, head to the front door and open it.

'Chloe love! Whack the kettle on, will you?'

'Mum?!'

'Well, you wouldn't come to me, so I've come to you.'

And now it's my mum's turn to barge past, stopping halfway down the narrow hallway.

'Where's your loo, love?' she asks. 'I'm desperate.'

Gobsmacked, I direct her to the bathroom. Attempting to process this unexpected arrival, I turn around to close the door.

'Steady on, Tilly Mint! Don't leave me hanging on the doorstep.'

'Dad?!'

'I tried to tell your mum you'd get a fright,' he says, apologetically.

He takes my face in his hands and kisses the top of my head before pulling me into a hug. He's boiling. God knows why, but he's wearing his smartest winter coat. And the checked shirt beneath is fastened up to the top button. Little beads of sweat sit beneath his dark grey hairline – the neatest hairline you'll ever see on a man of sixty-three; it's not receding a jot. We're the same height when I wear shoes, something he's never come to terms with since I hit fifteen, remarking often, 'God knows where we got this one from'. Although there's no denying he's my dad. We have the same wide grin, the same piercing blue eyes. The same patience with my mother.

A flush rattles through the flat and she emerges from the bathroom, her lipstick reapplied.

'Bloody hell, Chloe, you couldn't swing a cat in there,' she says.

My mum combs through her auburn bob – highlighted with the cap – with her hands before dabbing her forehead and above her upper lip with her middle fingers. Then she shakes out her loose navy-blue shirt, which is hanging on her small curves.

'I'm sweating cobs here,' she says, stating the obvious. 'I thought you lived in London, love, not halfway to bloody Kent. Them tubes! Jesus!'

My dad lifts up two matching overnight holdalls; grey and pink polka-dot from Matalan that they've had ever since I can remember.

'Eh, Tilly Mint? Where shall I pop these?' he asks.

I have no words.

What I do have, surprisingly, is energy, and I manage to make it into the kitchen area just before my mum invites herself in. A part of me wants to double-check that Trish is still there, that this isn't a bonkers dream, or even whether luck is on my side and she's decided to do one out the back door. But, no. She's there, hands on hips, poised like a waxwork of herself.

'You better have a teapot,' my mum's saying, her eyebrows instructing my dad to follow her through. 'I never had a cuppa on the train; they leave the teabag in the plazzy cup. It's just not proper, is it? I can't tell you how much I'm gasping for a—*Jesus Christ*! Oh! Hiya Patricia. What the hell are you doing here?!'

Trish Carmichael – for once, in my experience of knowing her from the telly – joins me in being lost for words, her slim lips open. I need to intervene, to explain (although I'm not sure what I should be explaining) – except I'm far too slow on the ball.

'Bernie, love,' my mum says, punching my dad, her teeth clenched. 'Say hiya.'

'Hiya, love,' my dad sings. 'Y'alright?'

Trish blinks frantically. 'I'm quite alright. Yes.'

'Oh, I'm a massive fan of yours, Patricia,' my mum says; the words I was dreading she'd say, told myself she'd never dream of saying, and yet, there you go, she's said them. 'You know, I don't work full-time anymore, not since I turned sixty, so Monday, Tuesday, Friday I never miss you on the telly. And you know what? I always agree with everything you say. I do, you know. I get on the phone to me mum – she's eighty-seven but mind as sharp as a knife – and I say *that Patricia Carmichael's hit the nail on the head again.* And I have to be honest with meself, Trish, I don't usually agree with a Tory.'

'I'd never have guessed,' Trish says, now poised.

'What's the model like in real life, the one who keeps getting the surgery?' my mum goes on. 'Because I worry for that poor girl, you know, I do. One of these days her face's gonna pop and she'll never get another husband again. And the fella, the washed-up pop star from when our Chloe was little, he's clever isn't he? You wouldn't have guessed it. But he's very bright, always says the right thing when you're all debating the headlines. A good family man, too.'

Trish nods slowly.

'Look at me,' my mum says, slapping her cheeks, her sweaty, heavily made-up face now melting into her palms. 'Gabbing away to none other than Patricia Carmichael. Anyone'd think we were mates. Ignore me, just pretend I'm not here, ignore everything I said.'

'I'll try,' Trish says.

'Oh, bloody hell,' my dad pipes up and snaps his fingers.

104

'I've just cottoned on to who you are. The pleasure's all mine, Patricia, all mine, my love. Weren't you in the jungle last year?'

Trish sighs. 'No.'

I jump in.

'Trish,' I say. 'This is Sue, and this is Bernie; me mum and me dad.'

'Again,' Trish says, reaching for her Michael Kors handbag. 'I'd never have guessed.'

I laugh, because that was a joke, right? She was being funny, yeah?

My mum laughs with me, my dad joining in a slow moment later.

'She'd never've guessed,' he jokes.

'Do you live around here, Trish?' my mum asks. 'Is that how you know our Chloe? 'Cause I don't know how you do it, how anyone does it. Them tubes. All the people. Some bloody big fella was effing and blinding at me and Bernie 'cause we were minding our own business, weren't we, love? Just standing still on them escalators.'

'"Keep right! Keep right!" he was yelling,' my dad calls out, his hand cupping the side of his mouth. 'Like he had this almighty power over us. Bloody Londoners.'

'We stood our ground, didn't we, Bernie love?'

'Mum,' I stop her. 'Trish is Jack's mum.'

'Oh!' she squeaks. 'Oh! Oh!'

I look to my dad for help. He gives a dainty shrug and tenses his jaw; his brow. He's not going to help. He's helpless.

I stand like piggy in the middle between my mum and Trish, there to stop any forward advances my mum is likely to make. Only, she knows me too well. She guesses my tactic, and like a top-scoring Premiership striker, slips past me the opposite way from my block, and her hands grip Trish's forearms.

'Of course,' my mum says. 'I can see the resemblance now. He was the image of you.'

Hmm. He wasn't, but—

'Did you meet him?' Trish asks, quite genuinely.

My mum shakes her head. 'Our Chloe sent me photos on that WhatsApp.'

Trish never got a photo of me, did she? Of course not. Jack never sent one. Not that I asked him to, or expected him to; it's just that right now, I wish he had. My mum's talking to Trish about God now, saying how she'll be remembering Jack in her prayers. My dad's removed his coat and is hovering, looking for somewhere to hang it.

'I'm speechless,' my mum says, vomiting words. 'Just speechless.'

If I turn right, I could snatch my keys and leg it to the Sainsbury's Local as planned.

Or, if I turn left, I can hide in the bathroom. That old trick.

I go for the latter.

Letting the cold water run, I dab the back of my neck with a few splashes, not wanting to smudge my red lipstick. I've made an effort today, and believe me, that really puts the word *effort* to its full use. And I mean, fuck. My mum and dad are here, in my new flat, which isn't new and isn't mine. Not for much longer anyway. I'm being evicted, which was to be expected, but once again, the decision about when to end the special entity of me and Jack is being taken away ruthlessly. I need a steady pace; I need to let our story play out, please.

I look up, hopeful of seeing Jack in the mirror. Nothing. So I reach into the shower and take hold of his shower gel. Opening the lid, I inhale the aroma of bergamot and try to feel him; find him. And shit! I drop the bottle. An ache engulfs me.

No, please, please, no. *No.*

I bend, pull down my knickers and sit on the toilet.

Another first.

I reach down to the little box beside the spare loo roll and unwrap a tampon. Never before has this simple act symbolised so fucking much. Any chance of having Jack's child has gone, wiped out as quickly as a man gets hit by a van. Is it stupid that I'd been banking on a part of Jack living within me? It seemed like the fairest outcome of a most horridly unfair situation, right? Doesn't every cloud have a silver fucking lining?

I guess not.

Oh, God. I'm empty.

I breathe slowly, in and out. I bite my fist.

Making my way back to the kitchen, willing Trish to be gone, I'm also hoping my mum and dad have made a snap decision to get out of the London they hate so much. But no. My mum's talking about our Kit's wedding and my dad's still holding his coat.

'He's having a portable photo booth which's costing a fortune,' she's telling Trish. 'I don't know why. I mean, can you name one person who likes the look of themselves on a passport photo? Bernie looks like a bloody serial killer on his, don't you, love? But our Kit knows what's trendy, I'll give him that. He's wearing Paul Smith, you know.'

Trish catches my eye.

'I need to get going, Chloe,' she says. 'I've marked the calendar for you. You've got my number if you're able to get out sooner. Okay?'

I say nothing and my mum widens her eyes at me, telepathically spelling out how my silence is embarrassing her and my dad. But I don't care. I'm sick of the overwhelming sense that the last few months of my life are being belittled wherever I turn. I'm invisible to all who knew Jack, and my own family are jumping on that bandwagon, too. This is wrong, and I have to prove it. It happened. Jack and me, it fucking happened. It was sexy, it was annoying, it was frustrating, it was perfect, it was mediocre, it was shocking, it was hilarious, it was real. *It happened*.

'Bye bye Trish.' My mum sees her out and my dad plays follow-the-leader, trailing behind, carrying his coat. 'It's an absolute pleasure to have met you.'

I think I hear Trish say, 'Likewise.'

'And if you ever find yourself in our neck of the woods,' my dad's saying, 'here's me card; Bernie Roscoe Taxis. We've only got a handful of cars but we're the most reliable in Liverpool.'

They're waving Trish off like the Beverly bloody Hillbillies. I can't see them, but I know they'll continue to wave until Trish's car is out of sight.

'How could you forget to tell me who Jack's mother is?' my mum cries once she's back in the room, making her way to the kettle knowing full well I won't be making tea anytime soon. 'And where's your teapot, Chloe?'

'What are you doing here?' I ask. 'Dad?'

'We're just worried about you, love,' he tells me. His coat has disappeared and I imagine he's hung it on the rack beside Jack's parka. 'I told your mum you just needed some time, but let's face it, it's already been a month and we get the feeling you aren't coping.'

'How?' I squeal, aware of how similar I sound to my mum, who's looking through all the cupboards for a bloody teapot.

'Beth said she's hardly seen you,' she says, impatience oozing out of her.

'She lives in Islington and it's a hike to get there from Lewisham after work,' I say.

'She also said you're full of excuses. Wanting to spend time with *Jack*. Chloe, love. He's in Heaven.'

I need them to get out.

My dad is inspecting the lounge with a childish grin, as if he's just arrived at a self-catering holiday apartment on the Med. He tests out the sofa with a buoyant bounce, then gets up and tests the other side by lying down with his hands behind his head, putting his feet up but letting them hover without touching the cushions. He twists around to look out of the window.

'Shame about the view, eh?' he remarks, referring to the stone stairs and the gravel.

'You sound like Jack,' I say.

'We really are very sorry, love,' my dad says, sitting and patting the seat beside him.

I take it, my head falling naturally into his shoulder. I want to be ten again, sad that my bike got a puncture and I had to push the damn thing all the way home from the park. Or sad because I got the knock-back from the pub when I was sixteen and my dad had to come and pick me up, all dressed up and nowhere to go.

'Yesss!' Mum shouts from the kitchen. Miraculously, she's found a teapot. 'Now come on, Chloe. Give us a smile, will you?'

'I thought I was pregnant,' I say. My dad's arm tenses around me and I panic that my mum might drop and smash the teapot. 'It's alright, it's alright – I'm not. Pregnant.'

'Oh thank God,' my dad says and buries his face in his hands. He thinks he's saying the right thing, bless him.

'Actually, I'm . . .' I search for the correct word, 'disappointed.' Except that doesn't give weight to the truth. I'd be disappointed if I failed my driving test.

'But you've got your whole life ahead of you, Tilly Mint,' my dad says. I don't need to remind him that I'm thirty-six. He'll forever see me in my purple shell suit and Pony trainers, attempting *Dirty Dancing* routines in the back garden. 'Tell her, Sue.'

My mum is cradling the teapot, rubbing it absent-mindedly with a tea towel. Oh, what I'd give for a genie to appear and give me three wishes so I could vanish. Or send them back up north on the bloody train.

'Oh, Chloe love,' my mum whimpers, 'you've no idea how happy this makes me.'

I shift beside my dad. He chokes on thin air.

'I never thought you wanted children,' she goes on, 'but you do, and that makes me and your dad so happy, love. Isn't that right, Bernie? I'd honestly given up. Honestly thought, *nope. She's one of them. Not interested.* I mean, it's always baffled me, you know, the fact that you're not very career-driven either, but—'

'Whoa. Mum. Stop. And I'll say it again, I'm *not* pregnant.'

'But you want to be! And now's your chance. You're gonna meet a fabulous fella, love. I can feel it in me water. He might be just around the corner. Or better still, in Liverpool. A nice Liverpool lad, Chloe. Wouldn't that be marvellous? And you'll get your baby. You will.'

I stand, to enforce an end to this conversation.

'Mum, have some respect. Please. You're in Jack's flat. Amongst Jack's things.'

'Exactly. Jack's! Not yours!'

My dad jumps up and rubs his hands together with vigour. He's got an idea.

'Who fancies a Chinese tonight, ladies? Any good chippies around here, Tilly Mint?'

My phone starts ringing and I practically do the splits leaping across the room to answer it.

'Hello!' I sing, paying no attention to the caller or number.

'Hi, this is Gianna. I'm calling from Antonella,' says the melodic Italian accent. 'Is this Chloe Roscoe?'

'Speaking.'

'Just calling to confirm your reservation for this evening at 8 p.m.?'

'Oh . . .' Jack's birthday treat. I'd genuinely forgotten.

He turned thirty-eight the week before he died. I couldn't get a table for his actual birthday weekend; the earliest possible night was, well, tonight. I glance at the business card for Antonella on the fridge, the words embossed in gold scroll. I'd been meaning to cancel. Seems dialling a number to cancel a reservation for your dead boyfriend's bucket-list restaurant isn't the easiest task to complete.

'Hello, Chloe? Are you still there?' Gianna asks.

I clear my throat. 'Yeah, sorry.'

'Wonderful. See you tonight then?'

I hear my mum tell my dad there's a red wine stain on the carpet.

'Yeah . . .' I panic.

'Great! So that's a table for two at 8 p.m.—'

'Wait! I – erm—'

'Oh, do you need an extra seat? Is there another person joining you?'

Is there another person joining me?

'No. Thanks.'

'Okay, see you later, Chloe. Have a great day!'

And Gianna hangs up. Guess I'll be seeing her later, then.

14

Antonella is near London Bridge.

Through the main entrance is a grand silk curtain. I peek around, like I'm spying on the audience from the wings. I'm greeted by a striking woman dressed in black standing behind a high table, 'Gianna' embroidered onto her shirt with golden thread. Another theatrical curtain is draped behind her. The space we're standing in is cramped and circular; we're like two kids hiding in a tall, pink tent. I give her my name and she looks past my shoulder, asking, 'Do you prefer to wait here?'

'Actually, it's just me tonight.' I widen my eyes, grow an inch.

Gianna is thrown. This doesn't happen often, clearly.

'Just you?'

I give my best breezy shoulder-shrug.

'So . . .' Gianna says, as if she's trying to remember where she left her keys, 'a table for one?'

It's the upward inflection on *one* that does it; the absolute disbelief that anybody in their right mind would show up to Antonella alone. To eat; to drink; to party alone. I return to my standard hunched pose, squeeze out a laugh and say, 'No! Only kidding. Two it is!'

Gianna doesn't find me funny. I imagine she'll inform her superior, tell them to keep an eye on me, you know, sensing I might get a bit rowdy, lower the tone. But she remains professional, gives me a dead-eyed smile, then pulls on a thick rope with impressive strength. I brace myself for a loud bell to sound. Instead, the back curtain sweeps up with such captivating elegance that it's like I'm transported into an old Hollywood musical. I am Dorothy stepping into Oz.

A satisfying blend of gold, rose, peach and orange dance around the room. Dimly-lit lamps sit on round tables draped with velvet and silk tablecloths, cosy booths hugging the walls. It's bustling, the waiters carrying large trays above their heads. I follow Gianna, zigzagging past huge bowls of carbonara and arrabbiata, passing floor-to-ceiling wine racks, until we arrive at my table.

I'm handed a menu complete with a gold tassel. Gianna leaves another menu opposite, at the place where Jack should be sitting.

'Would you like anything to drink while you wait?' she asks.

'Erm, Valpolicella would be lovely, thanks.'

And she's off.

So, here I am. Jack's bucket-list restaurant. It opened about two years ago, the cuisine simple but oh-so effective; Italian. The basics. Done exceptionally well, according to the reviews and framed certificates behind the bar with five gold stars. The party vibe is electric, yet sophisticated. Jack had tried to book this place for his work Christmas do, but had left it far too late, and ever since he had sought a reason to come. I surprised him on his birthday by putting the business card inside a little gift box. He told me I was magic.

'I reckon I love you, Chloe Roscoe,' he'd said.

'And I reckon I love you too, Jack Carmichael.'

We'd celebrated with takeaway pizzas and danced in the kitchen to Daft Punk.

A different waitress brings my wine, showing me the bottle first before I sample. It's perfect, but it lands in my stomach with an unpleasant slosh. I don't feel whole. I feel cut in half with a blunt knife. Everything about me being here is wrong.

Nobody is looking at me.

Except they are. The more I dart my eyes across the room, the more eyes meet with mine. They talk. Who's that girl on her own? Sat in the middle of the restaurant, of all places. Seeking attention, perhaps? Does she carry a confidence that normal people don't possess? Oh, of course, do you think she's been stood up? Yep. That'll be it.

I sip my wine and take out my phone.

I swipe, I tap. I like Beth's latest Instagram post. Her new killer nails.

Gianna walks past with a party of six, a stack of menus on her arm ready to hand out. I grab my phone, tap and put it to my ear. Antonella isn't a quiet affair: the instrumental jazz ambience isn't subtle; nor the conversations of its punters; the belly laughing; the clinking of glasses; the scraping of plates. So, I speak.

'Hey!' I say into my phone. 'God, this is weird. What am I doing?'

The last time I did anything like this was in youth drama, having to improvise being on the phone to a parent, apologising for getting caught smoking or something. Never thought I'd be testing out my skills two decades later in one of London's trendiest restaurants.

114

But there's so much I have to say. And only one person I need to say it to.

'Jack?' Saying his name makes me smile. I repeat, louder, then pretend he's saying something back. Nothing fancy. Just that he's working late.

'It's kind of embarrassing,' I tell him, 'but I went to Next after work twice last week to look at baby clothes, something I can put me hand on me heart and say I've never done before, not even when a mate's had a baby.' I take another sip of wine. The waitress is coming towards me but she backs away when she clocks I'm on the phone. 'Jack, I wanted to tell you I'm having your baby. I wanted to tell you that you're never gonna be dead, not really, 'cause you're living on in me. I wanted this so much it's been keeping me sane, I mean, I put lippy on today. Lippy! And that was before I knew me mum was coming.'

I wish he could see me, see my efforts. I'm wearing a floor-length summer dress, tiger-print. My black ankle boots aren't really appropriate for a sticky July, but they look right with the dress and besides, it was raining when I left the flat. I haven't brought a jacket; just an umbrella. My mum breathed a sigh of relief when I washed my hair and even offered to blow-dry it for me, an offer I couldn't refuse. I hate blow-drying my hair. I told her I was out tonight with some colleagues, new work pals. She was delighted. I gave my dad a number for a local Chinese.

A champagne cork pops and the table in the corner cheer.

'Look, since your funeral,' I say into the phone, 'I've found meself wondering what your relationship with Florrie was like. And then I'd tell meself how it shouldn't matter, there'll be a reason why it never worked out for you both. You'd never have met me if you'd stayed with her. But I've gotta be honest, the only thing that stopped me feeling – well, I hate to say it, but – jealous, was the sudden realisation that I might be pregnant. Like I'd won. No, no. Not won. Like I'd made me mark. With you. Like I was real.'

I play with the rose-pink napkin.

In my head, I try hard to hear Jack blurt out, 'Of course you were real!' or something poignant and rom-com worthy. I listen, I concentrate, and nothing comes. Because Jack would never say that sort of shit. How can I imagine him being anything other than what he was?

'I need to face facts, don't I? I don't want to, but I've got to, or I'm gonna drive meself mad.' I choke up; the back of my throat is dry, aching. I drink some more. 'Fuck. Why? People have unplanned babies all the time, so why didn't it just happen for us, for me, now? I thought if I can't have you, then at least – at least – I can have that. God. Sounds like a shit consolation prize, doesn't it?'

I want to hang up. This conversation is nothing like one I'd ever have had with Jack. We would finish each other's sentences or talk over each other. We disagreed and fought and laughed. Once, in a posh burger bar in Liverpool, I prodded Jack with my foot mid-chat and the next thing, we were having a thumb war. A fucking thumb war! We were every bit that annoying couple who were just having the best time in each other's company. And we didn't even need to go out to date. We had just as much fun at home, in PJs and bare feet and hair that desperately needed a wash. If there was a packet of KitKats in the cupboard, we'd devour the lot.

I've been quiet for a while, longer than I would be in a real two-way phone conversation.

'Okay . . . okay . . . That's fine . . .' I act my arse off. 'Bye bye!'

'Would you like to order a drink for . . .?' The waitress has appeared so quickly she's just missing a puff of smoke. She gestures to the empty seat opposite me.

'No,' I say, my breeziness wearing thin.

'Perhaps some water?'

'Please.'

And she pours some still bottled water out for two.

'I'll come back when you're ready,' she says, nodding to Jack's place. Ping! She's gone.

I stare at the water that won't be drunk. I'm so grateful for my wine, and for a small moment, I'm glad to not be pregnant. Oh, the power of alcohol. I order a bottle. One large glass down and one entire fake phone conversation completed, and I feel slightly better. Fewer people are looking at me; the mood has softened. The music is louder. The bottle arrives.

'Another glass?' I'm asked.

'Sure!'

So now there are two glasses of water, two glasses of wine. The room feels busier. I have to move my chair further in to allow the fella behind to get into his seat. I ask for a bread basket. Jack bloody loved a bread basket. When it arrives, the focaccia is warm, as delicate as cake. It goes down a treat with my wine. For the first time in weeks – five weeks and three days to be precise – I am tasting food in all its glory.

'I'm ready to order,' I say, catching Gianna's eye. She's on high alert, it being Saturday night and all, and she doesn't waste time turning around to check if Jack has arrived yet. She just gets her colleague to tend to me pronto. 'Buffalo mozzarella pizza please, and a carbonara. Can't come to Antonella without sampling that, eh?'

I've ordered for two. I know, I know.

117

I wouldn't be here if it wasn't for Jack having a birthday, so it's the least I can do.

And it's all I can do. There's nowhere I'd rather be.

'Whooaa!' I'm knocked forwards by the fella behind sliding backwards out of his chair and the jug of still water topples over. I save it before it rolls off the table. The bottle of wine shakes, but stays on its base. The fella is now standing, dabbing the spilt water with a pink napkin, apologising profusely. He's a large man, particularly around his middle, and while he looks as though he enjoys his food, he doesn't look enamoured by this restaurant.

'It's no problem,' I say. 'I probably should've been sitting closer to the table.'

'They know how to pack out a house here, don't they?' he says, now dabbing his brow.

The fella excuses himself to the gents' and I watch him go, struggling to get past the waiters and their huge trays, dodging Gianna on a mission, hanging back a moment as a family introduce a fancy birthday cake with about thirty lit candles. I can't help but think Jack would be feeling similar to this fella. Not because he was big. Well, he was, but in a different way. This fella is sweating, overweight. Jack was big and broad, both in physique and personality. He was the centrepiece, the one with the jokes. He brought colour to the most dismal of pubs. But in a restaurant as extravagant as this, he would be uncomfortable; he'd feel swamped. It's not his style. He mustn't have seen photos of the interior; must have simply gone on word of mouth.

I, on the other hand, bloody love it.

And I don't have to put up with Jack huffing about moving his seat in for the person behind to get in, or having to pause his story because a party of twenty are singing *Happy*

Birthday. God, this wine is fine! I throw my head back, feel the warm buzz. I'd much rather he were here, of course. Of course, of course, of course.

'Carbonara?'

The food has arrived. The five-star-rated creamy pasta is plonked down before me, swirling and bubbling in a traditional hand-painted Italian bowl. The pizza, thick with fresh dough and glistening with buffalo mozzarella, is placed down opposite. For Jack. He might have ordered something more meaty, but my thinking was that this isn't takeaway on a Friday night. This is London's top Italian and Jack would have gone classic.

I eat fast. Decadence on a plate. The pace of the restaurant keeps me moving, eating, chewing, washing it down with wine. I could be mistaken but the lights seem dimmer, the music louder. I wipe my chin with my pink napkin.

A quarter through the carbonara and two slices into the pizza and I'm done.

I head to the ladies' and reapply my lippy beside another woman, around my age, doing the same. She's bobbing to music we can hear from upstairs. The lighting is flattering: movie-star lightbulbs surround the mirrors. Through them, we catch eyes, smile. To her, I'm just another person having a night out, perhaps with my husband, my girlfriend, my entire workforce. She would never guess how painful it is for me to open my bag, fish out this lipstick and paint it on, knowing that Jack won't be smudging it with his beardy kisses during the taxi ride home.

'Love your dress,' she comments.

'It's just Zara,' I say.

She checks herself over once more and leaves. I release a long sigh. Without the circus of Antonella dancing around me, I don't feel so good any more. I grip the sink, look into my smoky eyes. I don't want to be me. I want to be that other woman. She might have pain, too; but whatever it is, let's trade. Please.

Back on the restaurant floor, the birthday boy from the large party is between the booths and tables, hugging some guests who are leaving. His arms are laden with gift bags, fancy tissue paper poking out. I'm in no hurry, so I hang back, lean against the booth. When his guests brush past, he turns around and realises he's been blocking my way. His hand slaps his forehead and he mouths, 'So sorry!'

'Happy birthday!' I shout over the noise.

'Would you like some cake?' he asks.

Before I can politely decline, he yells to someone called Eloise and she slides a slab of rainbow sponge onto a side plate for me. I say thanks and Eloise blows a kiss.

'This might sound a little strange,' I say, leaning closer to the birthday boy's ear, 'but can I borrow one of those candles, please?'

'Of course!' And on request, Eloise gets to it. She even holds up a lighter, to which I nod, and she brings the flame to life. How kind.

Careful not to blow out the candle prematurely, I creep away, baby steps. The flame dances delicately as I sit down. This is where I imagine Jack giving in. He'd bury his head into his large hands, ashamed at how stroppy he'd been all night. I'd say, *it's okay, don't be daft*. And he'd smile and he'd sway and he'd get bang into the spirit, deciding that after all, he did like this place. In fact, he loved it.

To the far left, I hear another chorus of *Happy Birthday* break out, harmonising in good tune. So I sing along, quietly.

'. . . *happy birthday, dear Ja-ack. Happy birthday to you.*'

And I make a wish, and blow.

15

My mum and dad – to my relief – are in bed.

Earlier, my dad had had some wild idea about staying in a hotel around Park Lane, finding a last-minute deal. 'When in Rome,' he'd said. I'd said, please, sleep in the bed, I was more than happy to sleep on the sofa. I didn't tell him I sleep on the sofa every night.

I'm tipsy and tired. Full from the feast.

But I'm not sad.

Wait. I'll rephrase. I'm less sad.

Now, this could be the wine.

I take my boots off by the door and tiptoe along the hallway. My mum has tidied up, even folded the tea towels into neat squares beside the sink. There's a lamp on beneath the mugs cupboard which has never worked since I moved in. My dad's fixed it. The light creates a pool of calm and makes the kitchen seem more spacious. I smile at the man sat in the shopping trolley, a great centrepiece. The image is so sharp; it's still incredible to me that it was taken – hungover – on Jack's phone. I can see us there, feel the sticky heat, the grimy city dirt between my toes in my flip-flops.

I get a pint of water, lean against the sink and down it.

Hugging the empty glass to my chest, I look at the fridge opposite, vibrant and busy. All of the should-have-beens and to-dos: ready-made plans, stuck in a time warp. I step forward, remove the Antonella business card from beneath the flip-flop magnet, hold it between my thumb and forefinger.

'We did it,' I whisper.

And instead of throwing the card away, I slide it into my purse. A keepsake.

Unlike going to the theatre with Si and paying that bloody gas bill, tonight feels like an achievement. Jack was so vivid. It was tough, but God, given the shit hand of cards I've been dealt, I'm glad I was there over any other place in the world. I had a good time. I did. A *good* time.

So what else can I do?

The estate agent's card could come in handy when Jack's brother moves in. But we missed Ross Robson's gig. And as for the skiing lesson – well, I never had any desire to do it anyway. The tiny Vietnamese bowl of noodles sparks an ache in my chest. A trip we'll never take.

'Jack?'

It's easy to imagine him here. Bloated; hiccups. He always got hiccups when we came home from fancy restaurants. He wouldn't be staring at the fridge with me. No. His focus would be past my head, towards the wall. He'd be playing his favourite silly game.

'*What's behind the picture?*' I hear him ask.

I turn around and face it myself. 'What *is* behind the picture?'

The man's eyes stare intently into Jack's camera lens.

Ronald McDonald stands behind the shopping trolley, a terrifying clown-god, a reminder of all things delicious and disgusting. I can taste the salt in my mouth; the sweet and sour tang of the dip. I can hear the buzz of the shopping mall, the bustle of the street. The man had sighed, and yet he was in no hurry to move. I'm there, too, now; I'm transported. And I want to answer Jack's final question to me. I want to find out what's going on; what's really behind the picture.

'We always said we'd go back there one day,' I say, calmly. *'And find him, Chloe. Ask him what he was doing.'*

*

I wake up on the sofa to the world's greatest smell: crispy bacon. My dad's buttering bread and hum-singing 'Hotel California'. My mum enters with her hair washed and styled and a full face of makeup on. Her clothes are ironed and she smells like the ground floor of John Lewis.

'Oh, Jesus. You didn't sleep in your mascara did you, Chloe?'

'Morning, Tilly Mint!'

I sit up, still wearing my tiger-print dress, and smile.

'I'm going to Bangkok,' I tell them.

'Y'what?' they screech in unison.

School finishes for the summer hols this Friday. I'll fly out on Saturday.

'Thailand. Bangkok.' I look past my dad and give the man in the shopping trolley a firm nod. 'Yeah. I'm gonna go.'

123

16

'And I suppose you booked two plane tickets as well, didn't you?' Beth snaps.

I'm glad she's on the other end of the phone. She can't see me giving her the finger.

She's been trying to speak to me since yesterday. But I had a sneaky plan. I've returned her call now I've checked in and I'm through passport control. When Beth wants something, she'll go to extreme measures to get it, and she doesn't want me going to Bangkok. She wants me to go with her on a yoga retreat in the Cotswolds.

'Or I could've just come with you,' Beth is saying as I browse through the paperback thrillers for some literary nicotine. 'I'm sure Jack wouldn't've minded me tagging along.'

'Beth, this is a personal trip.'

'Whatever.'

'You're being mean.'

'Hmm. You know what's mean, babes? Sending your mum and dad all the way home a day after they arrived—'

'Don't guilt trip me, they were glad to go. They hate London.'

'Everyone's mum and dad hate London.'

'Look, I didn't book two plane tickets,' I reassure her.

'Oh, phew. That's a relief. Thank fuck you realised ghosts don't need a seat and a salty ready meal—'

'I don't believe in ghosts.'

'Woop! Double relief. I'm over the moon you're only going on holiday with a figment of your imagination. Fine. I won't be offended that you'd rather do that than hang out with me, you know, someone who has skin and bones and a pulse.'

'And a big fucking mouth.'

I don't tell Beth how, amongst my loose summer clothes, flip-flops, bikini and straw hat, I packed a few of Jack's things, too. His holiday t-shirt patterned with surf boards, his khaki man-bag that predictably hasn't been used since we went to Thailand together. Inside the bag, I found five hundred baht and the hotel keycard from the resort where we'd stayed on Koh Phangan. Something practical and something sacred, patterned with his fingerprints.

'I've gotta go,' I tell Beth. 'I've found a good book. Need to pay for it.'

'If you were with me, you wouldn't need a book. I could entertain you with stories.'

'Go to the Cotswolds and have a ball.'

'On me own?'

'Take Fergus with you.'

She growls. 'Bye, babes.'

I buy the book and nip into Boots to buy a lip balm. I don't need other toiletries thanks to the lovely Body Shop set I got as a present from a pupil at school. A nice touch, really, especially since I've not exactly been Teacher of the

Year. Si walked out yesterday showered with much more end-of-term love, smelly sets and chocolates. Fair's fair. That's all you can ask for, eh? I mean, during rehearsals last week, Si worked hard to ensure the harmonies were tight and I sat on my phone and booked a Bangkok hotel on Expedia. Layla Birch (who decided to show up this time) caught me reading reviews. I looked back at her self-righteous little heart-shaped face and pulled tongues. It's a wonder I got a single end-of-term gift at all.

I don't need to go to the gate for another hour, so I head to the bar – the posh one by the designer shops. It sells caviar. Not that I've ever had caviar, or fancy trying it today. But the wine will be delicious. The good stuff. Better than the pub . . .

Oh, shit.

A memory hits me like a punch in the nose.

I've had this exact conversation before. Not in my head, though. With Jack, when we were here together on our way to Thailand. He'd been tetchy; very quiet compared to usual. I'd presumed he was one of those people who relaxes once their suitcase is all checked in. My dad's like that, you see.

'Let's just go to the Wetherspoons,' Jack said. 'I know a nice quiet corner.'

'But we can sit up on those trendy bar stools and pretend we're stinking rich,' I insisted. 'I might even pop into Chanel, you know; ponder about buying a jacket and casually inspect the handbags.'

'Chloe, can we please just go to the pub.'

'You can't see the planes taking off from that pub, though.'

He tensed up like Frankenstein with a pole up his arse.

'Fine,' he said, barely moving his lips. 'I'll go to the pub and you can get yourself a fancy glass of champers, and I'll meet you on the plane.'

126

'What?!'

'Okay, the gate. I'll meet you at the gate. But . . .'

'But what?'

'I never get to the gate early, so it might just be best to say let's meet on the plane.'

'No!'

Jack rubbed his eyes and inhaled: a slow, deep breath.

'Oh, hun,' I realised. 'Are you . . . scared of flying?'

He exhaled, kept his eyes closed.

'It's okay. There's nothing to be afraid of. Did you know you're much more likely to die in a car crash than—'

'You think I don't know all that?' he barks. 'I'm fucking terrified. Happy?'

'No. Why would that make me happy?'

'Ssh.'

'Don't shush me.'

'Chloe, I need to go and have a pint. On my own.' And he walked off.

I stood there outside the shop selling Harrods merchandise, trying not to look like a stood-up codfish. Had this come out of the blue? I thought back to the queue for check-in. I'd been pretty low key, scrolling through Instagram, WhatsApping Beth, our Kit, my mum. Then, going through passport control, I became super chatty. I told tales of family holidays, like that time in Gran Canaria when my dad was mistaken for a famous footy player. My mum totally played along to see if we'd get special treatment (we didn't). I'd thought Jack was listening to me, but was he preoccupied instead? Worried the flight we were about to board was doomed?

I didn't order a drink at the posh bar, although I did have a wander around Chanel, then Gucci, not paying much attention, just killing time, really, to give Jack some space. Rather than go looking for him in the pub, I waited for him at the gate. When the final call was announced, he stumbled up, beaming from ear to ear, flaunting his overbearing charm at the ground staff. My sober state was probably the only reason he was allowed onto the plane. Disappointed as I was not to have enjoyed an airport drink or three with him, I was glad he was buzzing, humming 'Leaving on a Jet Plane' as he slotted his hand luggage into the overhead compartment.

'I need the aisle seat,' Jack informed me; his first direct words to me since he'd left me alone in the terminal.

'No problem,' I said.

'Excuse me, darlin'?' he asked, and I thought he was addressing me, but a stunning member of the Thai Airways cabin crew came to his beck and call and he politely stumbled through his words from his seat, asking her for a double JD neat. 'I'm – a – ma – ma – v-very nervous fly – flyer.'

Between the passengers getting settled and the plane starting to taxi, Jack went to the loo about five times. Considering his size, this was, more often than not, a right hoo-hah. The cabin crew remained calm, although they were clearly agitated by him. Once we took off (which was not the hand-holding, flying off into the sunset moment I'd anticipated), he called for a crew member to give him a pep talk. And another double JD, pronto. As the crew member spoke softly about the safety of flying, I placed my hand upon his arm, but he flicked me away like he was fending off a wasp. I tried not to take it personally. When the drinks trolley came around I ordered a little bottle of white wine. A few sips helped me to relax. Three little bottles later and I was laughing my head off to a comedy starring Amy Schumer, and Jack was asleep with his head on my shoulder. He woke

128

up in a sweet, cuddly mood without a single mention of his phobia. I didn't dare bring it up, so it was forgotten. Until now.

'*Go on*,' Jack urges me as I stand alone by the caviar. '*Get yourself a glass of bubbly.*'

I pretend to be interested in the canapés displayed artfully in the glass cabinet, then order myself a glass of champagne; exactly what I'd wanted to do last time. As the golden effervescence glitters into my glass, I try to recall the flight back. Was Jack as terrified of flying then? Memory fails me. I'd been trying to meditate through a hangover conjured by the devil himself and injected straight into my bloodstream. At one point, I'd had to snooze on the floor of the departure lounge with my head on Jack's hand luggage. Jeez, we'd hit it hard on that final night. I'd thought we were in denial about going home, and making every moment count. But maybe Jack needed to block out his impending fear. Or maybe it was a bit of both.

The cold bubbles kiss my lips, sneak up my nose.

'*Are you trying to find faults in me?*' I hear Jack ask.

I almost spit out the gulp I've just taken as I see him beside me, sat up on the high stool.

'*It's clever*,' he says. '*Makes sense to get over me.*'

I want to enjoy my champagne. God knows it cost enough.

'I'm not looking for faults,' I mutter. 'I just remembered what an arsehole you were to me last time we were at this airport.'

And great. I'm talking to myself in an airport. What if I start doing this on the plane? Freaking passengers out looking like a terrorist, whispering some sort of mantra before I blow everyone up?

'*Being afraid of flying is fear of the lack of control*,' Jack says.

'Go away,' I say, trying not to move my lips.

'*And also a sign of a vivid imagination. Which I have. Oops! Had.*'

Well, yours truly also has a vivid bloody imagination and thanks to that, I'm failing at enjoying a quiet drink in my cocoon of me-time. I'm haunted and distracted, alone but not on my own. I'm lonely, but I'm with Jack. He's dead, but so alive in my mind, and I'm so fucking confused I can't see straight.

'Same again?' the barman asks.

I look to my champagne flute, dry and empty.

'I better not,' I say. 'Thank you.'

Fourteen hours later, I'm sitting in the back of a neon-pink taxi. It's a hazy, grey late afternoon in Bangkok. The rain is eager to start splashing down and it doesn't feel like five minutes since I was last here. In reality, it's been four months. I arrive at the Asia Palace Hotel, which, I know, sounds grand. It's cheap, immaculately clean and as I enter the small lobby I'm greeted with many a heartwarming *Sawasdee ka* and *Sawasdee krap* and a zesty aroma of lemongrass. The hotel is a confusing blend of corporate business and backpacker, with conference rooms and a rather soulless gym either side of a rainbow-painted cafe with plastic red chairs. The lady on the reception desk tells me about the happy hour on the rooftop, where there's also a hot tub. When she hands over my hotel keycard, I get a rush, a tickle in my tummy.

You see, I've always been a bit of a holiday junkie.

I'm the kid who was first in line to get a t-shirt for the kids' club and entered myself into every competition going, even Killer Darts, which weirdly, I was pretty good at. I'd get over excited about Fanta Lemon, something you could only get 'abroad' back then. As a teen, once I'd been initiated into a gang of others my age, we'd buy bright-coloured bottles of cheap liqueurs, amazed we got served without ID. We'd get stupidly drunk and all snog each other, swapping addresses on the last night and, through dramatic tears, promise to keep in touch forever and ever. I don't plan my holidays well, don't give myself an itinerary or pre-book trips, nothing like that. But I always want to do and try everything, all in the moment. I'll go to the club that somebody on the street is handing out flyers for; I'll eat the food on the specials board; I'll take a tuk-tuk over a taxi wherever possible.

And, oh my. Jack Carmichael was the same. The same! We were two loose cannons when we arrived in Bangkok, exploding with child-like bounce.

I put my keycard into the door, dragging my suitcase behind me.

The bed is huge. Two towels have been made into swans, but, thank God, there are no rose petals. I haven't slept in a bed since the day before Jack died. I slip off my Converse and strip off my t-shirt, my bra, my joggers. This is one hell of a first. One. Hell. Getting on the plane was one, but a mild one, thanks to the uncomfortable memory. Arriving in Bangkok was another, but I was pushed along by the speed of the taxi queue. I'm not ready to go outside and explore yet, and the only other furniture is a single wheelie chair next to a small dressing table. I can't sleep on that, can I?

I give the bed a shot.

Once I'm under the sheets, my head heavy upon the white pillows, I stare out of the window and watch the sky thicken. I don't move until it's dark. Night has fallen, and although I still can't sleep, the first of all firsts comes to me. The first time we met.

131

17

My mum was right about last Christmas. I was knocking about with a lad I went to youth theatre with. Except, being thirty-six and not sixteen, I preferred to call it 'casually sleeping with'.

His name is Dan Finnigan; once an angelic tenor with a flair for accents, and now a chartered accountant. We hooked up over the festive period, almost two decades after I first slept with him. By New Year's Eve, we'd spent every night either at his place or mine, and even went to the Philharmonic to see *Home Alone* with a live orchestra playing the score. Rather datey for a matey.

Then I made a bold move. I booked two tickets to see a new musical premiering in Liverpool at the Everyman Theatre. A mutual friend from youth theatre, Vicki Richards, had landed a starring role and plastered it all over her social media. It was impossible to ignore. This musical, *The Book of Brexit*, looked set to be her big break. I told her I'd be coming with Dan Finnigan to support her.

A-MAZING. I'll get you both into the after-show party! she replied.

Just what I'd been hoping for.

Dan didn't thank me for the ticket, or for the after-show invite. Instead, he told me his girlfriend was coming back from Japan. Now here's the thing. He'd one thousand per cent not mentioned this before in any way, shape or form. Nothing in his flat hinted at a serious attachment in his life: no framed photo, no perfume bottle beside his range of aftershaves, no spare toothbrush. And I've got to admit I was upset.

Angry.

No, upset.

Look, I didn't love Dan Finnigan. The appeal of whatever we were doing definitely stemmed from nostalgia. But he was nice. Nice enough to want more; mainly after a few drinks.

So when he told me about his mystery woman, I not only felt spectacularly dumped, but also like a dirty rag. I was the girl the fella cheated on his girlfriend with. Thank you very fucking much, Dan fucking Finnigan.

I ended up going to the theatre on my own.

And I know I could've asked our Kit to come with me, or one of my mates. Most of them would've needed to sort a babysitter, though, and well, I just couldn't be bothered with more knock-backs, more excuses – however genuine – as to why someone couldn't be my date. Still, I'd see Vicki afterwards, mingle with the cast. So I dressed up, curled my hair before attempting to stylishly mess it up, my blonde still on fantastic form from getting it bleached before Christmas. I wore knee boots, which, being on the tall side, always make my legs look longer, and a short dress with a retro zigzag pattern. Actually, the dress was more like a baggy shirt, but it's one of my all-time faves. It hangs off in the right places and – God, this'll make me sound old – it's comfy. Our Kit had bought me giant hoop earrings for Christmas and, matching them with a thick helping of red lippy, I felt fabulous. Up yours, Dan Finnigan!

The show started with huge promise; an opening number full of brilliantly observed impressions. Vicki belted out a ballad about the pain her character felt leaving 'EU'; but after that, it's safe to say the story went zooming downhill.

I took my seat for the second half and noticed a man lingering on the step in the aisle beside me. Big, but not awkward, he had his hands stuffed into trousers that matched his waistcoat and jacket, smartly paired with a blue paisley shirt open at the collar. A confident grin emerged from beneath his wild beard. His eyes were sharp like diamonds.

'Mind if I sit here?' he asked.

Ugh. If truth be told, I did mind. If I wasn't going to be here with a date, I'd prefer the extra legroom all to myself. But this fella was leaning towards me and resting his hand on the back of the empty seat.

'You see that tiny space in the middle over there?' He pointed to the block of seats opposite and I nodded. 'That's where I've been squashed during the first half of – ahem, let me lower my voice – the *shambles* that we all collectively witnessed. I can't tell you how relieved I am to find this aisle seat unoccupied.'

'Knock yourself out,' I said, with enough sarcasm to let him know I wasn't in the mood for making friends.

'I'm Jack.' He held out his hand.

I took it, shook it and said, 'Chloe Roscoe,' befuddled as to why a full intro spurted out.

He laughed, hearty and melodic.

'I reckon I love you, Chloe Roscoe,' he said, unafraid to look me in the eye.

134

I raised an eyebrow and pouted my red lips, unimpressed. 'You reckon?' I asked.

And he stretched out his large legs into the aisle, sat back and folded his arms. Releasing a long, satisfying sigh, he looked across at me again, and somehow amused by me – or perhaps my giant earrings – he grinned, so widely I spotted a dimple in his cheek. I wasn't in the mood to reciprocate.

The lights went down and the show recommenced.

Jack and I laughed at the exact same moments, many of which weren't at all funny; our laughter was subtle, and perhaps cruel. I could feel his eyes burning into me when the operatic sing-off between Boris and Jeremy kicked off. I glanced his way and scrunched up my nose, cringing. He mimicked me and I elbowed him. I didn't mind when his knee rested against mine, whether on purpose or due to lack of space. During a boring scene, the most drama being a group of audience members shuffling out of their seats and leaving, I zoned out and imagined that our legs were touching because Jack wanted them to. I was surprised by the shock of electricity it set pulsing through my body. I put my hand on his arm when the lady to my left gestured that she wanted to get out. We both twisted our bodies to the side, allowing her to leave.

'Guess you and I are Remainers, then?' Jack whispered, which tickled me.

I realised my hand was resting on his arm, and removed it to twiddle an earring.

When the show finished and us 'Remainers' did our best to give the cast a warm applause, Jack said he'd get me a drink as thanks for the seat. I met his assertiveness with a thanks, but no thanks, I was going to the after-show party. Edging our way out of the auditorium, he showed me his ticket, printed with *VIP* in the corner.

'Me too,' he grinned.

'So are you a reviewer? Or friend of the cast?' I asked.

'Neither. I have a well-connected mum.'

'What does that mean?'

'She's a journalist. She's on daytime TV a lot, arguing for the sake of arguing.' He lowered his voice and whispered right into my ear, 'She's made a fortune being the kind of woman people love to hate. Her Twitter feed is attacked by evil cretins but she doesn't care. And people are always lovely to her in real life, quite adoring.'

'Oh, my God. You're not talking about Patricia Carmichael, are you?'

'I am indeed.'

'Wow. She's your mum?'

'Guilty as charged,' he held up his hands.

'Is she here? I'd love to meet her.'

'See? People love meeting her! But no. She's not here tonight. She gets free invites all the time, and a musical about Brexit, well, that's right up her street, but she couldn't be bothered travelling all the way up to Liverpool. She'll catch it in London, if the show makes it that far.'

The private bar was in the bistro, cordoned off for the party. Jack helped himself to two glasses of bubbly from a waiter floating around with a silver tray and offered me one. Thanking him, I tried to think of encouraging words to give to Vicki Richards and now that I had company, I hoped Jack would be kind, too.

'I still don't understand why you're here,' I said, looking out for Vicki.

'You mean I don't strike you as a raving musical theatre fan?'

'Nope.'

'Correct, I'm not. I was in Liverpool for a meeting yesterday and Mum suggested I take her hotel and ticket, since she wasn't using it and it'd only go to waste. Who doesn't love a freebie?'

'I'd totally do the same.'

'Right! I've been on a couple of stag dos here in Liverpool. Great city, awesome night out. And when I realised Liverpool was playing at home to Man U – my team – well, I decided to make a weekend of it.'

'You went to the game today? How did you get a ticket so easily?'

'I just told you who my mum is.'

'Hmm. It really is cool to be famous, then?'

'Well, I get the perks without the fame. Best of both worlds.'

'Mummy's boy.'

'Oh, I am. I really am.'

'You wanna know what I am?'

'Shockingly beautiful.'

I knocked back my bubbly, not expecting that brazen compliment.

'No,' I said, my cheeks flushing. 'I'm a Blue.'

'An Everton fan?' he asked, confused. 'Why?'

'You know it's so annoying when non-Scousers ask that,' and before I could get into a petty debate about football, all five foot two of Vicki Richards bounced over and hugged me so tight I lost a few breaths.

'It's the woman with the *incredible* voice!' Jack bellowed.

'Me?' Vicki asked; hopeful, anxious.

Jack took both her little hands within his and they disappeared in his grasp.

'You're a wonderful singer,' he told her. 'I got that spine tingle. Thank you!'

And Vicki's wide doe eyes grew even larger, relief flooding through her tiny bones. It was obvious she wasn't expecting much praise, but Jack said the right thing – and in my opinion, it sounded genuine. In that moment, I could've easily said to him, 'And I reckon I love you, too, Jack Carmichael.'

Of course, I didn't.

Vicki gushed her thanks before excusing herself to go and say hello to her agent. Jack and I drank free bubbly, our bodies getting closer and closer the more we talked. When the only parts left to touch were our lips, Jack whispered, 'Come with me.'

And I did.

18

I don't rise early. It's creeping close to midday when I drag myself to the shower. I throw on a light polka-dot skirt and Rolling Stones t-shirt, keeping my bare essentials in Jack's khaki man-bag. I don't need a plan of where to go: Bangkok will take me along with it.

A tuk-tuk pulls up outside the Asia Palace Hotel and without bothering to barter a price, I hop in and simply say, 'Market.' I know from experience that anything more specific won't guarantee I'll end up where I say. I just need bustle and food.

I recognise the foot spa Jack and I ended up in once at three in the morning.

A pub called the Happy Beer Garden.

The restaurant above a t-shirt store that served the most magical green curry.

'Riverboat ride?' the tuk-tuk driver asks me.

'No. I'll jump out here, please.'

It's lunchtime.

'Table for one?' the waitress asks.

139

The place is small, neat, and each table has a map of the world beneath a pane of glass. A group of four Westerners are huddled around one table, an Asian couple on another. I recall Jack and me pointing out all the places we'd been to separately, before we'd met, and he told me about how he got all his belongings stolen from a hostel during his gap year.

I browse the menu, although I know what to order.

'Green curry with chicken and a pad thai, please,' I say. 'And a small beer.'

Eating alone on holiday is not something I've ever done before. In the life I've always been used to, you go away with the people you love to spend time with. I feel like I'm being watched, silently questioned about why I'm alone, a solo traveller. I mean, I used to sit with my family or Beth or friends from uni – God, this very restaurant not so long ago, with Jack – and wonder why that person didn't have company. And I could be so fucking judgemental, too. If a British fella in his fifties was having a bowl of noodles and a bevvie on his own, I'd mutter to Jack, 'Looking for a Thai bride?' and Jack would agree. Who were we to judge? Maybe that fella had just lost his wife of thirty years and was here in Bangkok to find his equivalent of a man sat in a shopping trolley.

The soupy curry is placed before me. It's spiky with sharp heat. My tongue frazzles. The small golden Buddha beside me on the window ledge smiles; a reminder to keep calm. Take it easy. Slow down.

But I don't want to slow down. I'm not here to enjoy meals in restaurants: I'm here to keep my relationship alive, to stretch the elastic band a little further. I need to eat and go, get on with the task. I order another beer to keep me motivated and once my belly is full and my body temperature super high, I'm ready.

I connect to the Wi-Fi and search for shopping malls close by. If I'm not mistaken, the mall I'm after wasn't far from here. My phone pings with a series of messages, all from people wanting to know if I arrived safely. I send a thumbs-up emoji to each: Beth, my mum, Kit, and – how sweet – Si. I'd sent a message to Trish a few days ago informing her I'd be away for a week, just in case she stops by the flat and wonders where I am. I get her reply now:

OK.

Google Maps has found a mall with a McDonald's and a footbridge over a dual carriageway. It's a twenty-two-minute walk from where I'm sat. That must be the one. I thank the staff and exit the restaurant, and as I walk down the steps to street level, I notice the t-shirts on display in the shop. Amongst many 'I heart Bangkok' slogans and printed poo emojis, there are lots of replica football tops and fake designer polo shirts, US army shirts and US gas station uniforms. I tap to open the photos in my phone. I find the all-important image; the one Jack had sent to me on WhatsApp moments after it he took it; the image I used to get the picture printed onto canvas for our home. I zoom in to the man and look closely at his shirt. I'd presumed it was a uniform for a hotel he worked at, and that it would be easy to find. I couldn't work out the writing on the logo, which is why I never researched for a specific hotel before I arrived. I was waiting to get here, to ask around. But shit. He could be wearing any old replica shirt bought from one of the thousands of shops in Bangkok, just like the one I'm standing outside now.

I zoom in further and see that the badge sewn to the right of his chest is yellow, with a shape embroidered in black cotton. A vehicle perhaps? Is he a taxi driver? He's not wearing matching blue trousers, either. He's wearing jeans, with the bottom all frayed. How had I not noticed this detail? I've looked at it every day, thought he was in overalls or a more formal uniform. Now what I'm seeing, in the city where I thought it would be possible to actually find him, is something rather different.

'Four hundred baht,' the fella in the shop says to me.

He's scrawny, an emoji poo t-shirt hanging off his small frame. I look at him, confused.

'Like ten dollar,' he explains. 'Same, same. Any t-shirt.'

'Thank you.'

He takes a replica Real Madrid shirt off a hanger and holds it against me.

'Oh, no,' I wave my hands. 'No, thank you.'

'Good price,' he says.

'Yes, it is—'

'Yes?' He's already rolling it into a small plastic bag.

'No!'

I show him the image on my phone to change the subject. I want to ask about the logo on the shirt. He shakes his head.

'Not here,' he says, as if he can read my mind.

'Sorry, I don't understand.'

'No. Just t-shirt here,' and he steps outside his shop and calls me to follow. Lifting his arm, he points down the main road, pointing over and over as if he's pressing an imaginary button. 'You go that way.'

'For this?' I ask, referring to the photo.

'Yes, yes.'

Does he recognise the man? Or does he know the way to the mall where this man is sitting? Unless he just wants me to get out of his shop because it's clear I'm not going to buy anything. I still want to ask him about the logo; check if it's a company here in the city, an aim for my first destination

142

in the hunt. But he's serving another customer now, a woman serious about buying something from him.

The map had told me to head this way anyway, so I start the twenty-two-minute stroll.

A man with only one arm and no other limbs passes by on a skateboard, his torso resting on the board. People push each other out of the way, or jump right over him as he whizzes past. Various women try to entice me into massage parlours. I pick up my walking pace, eager not to be an easy target. I can't remember speeding anywhere when I was here with Jack. We'd muse about how fast everybody was darting about, whereas we were like Mr and Mrs Soft, gliding through glue, in no hurry to be anywhere. Maybe we'd been easy targets together, although we'd probably wanted to stop for massages and to buy t-shirts, or at least for a bit of a chat with a local.

The main street's market stalls and tables, piled with shiny sunglasses and watches, come to an end at a busy junction. I'm one of what feels like thousands waiting to cross. The other side is more spacious: a huge golden Buddha statue rests on a tall marble slab, with tourists and locals alike sitting on the steps or surrounding grass, eating small cartons of street food from an array of vendors. A strong peanut aroma clashes with petrol fumes.

I walk on through the square city gardens. Another busy road greets me, tuk-tuks jammed beside one another, neon taxis lined up or trying to edge their way into the traffic. This is all so familiar. Although the last time I was here, I wasn't taking in every inch of my surroundings like I am today. I was meandering with Jack. I was whimsical. I was flying.

Another market engulfs me. The stalls are selling

battery-operated plastic toys, which flash and make whooping sounds. I shimmy through the tourists and slow down to glance at the fridge magnets on the next set of stalls. I don't want to buy anything, but there are so many people to push past that it's draining and, well, I'm not in any hurry. I need to breathe. The magnets seem to go on forever. They vary from Buddha to bowls of noodles to the longtail boats from the floating markets. There are flat photograph magnets of the city, the temples, the nightlife . . .

And . . .

No.

It can't be.

A line of identical rectangular magnets feature a photograph far too similar to the one close to my heart. A man in a shopping trolley. I blink, the jet lag possibly causing unreliable vision. But no. The image is as clear as the one on my phone: Ronald McDonald behind, hands in prayer and grinning. The only difference is the man. My eyes scan further along the stalls. A bonkers, eerie nightmare is starting to unfold. There are more magnets, hundreds of them, all featuring images of men in shopping trolleys. Some are smiling, some sleeping, others seriously pissed off. I look for my guy. Is he here? Will I find the exact same picture that hangs on my kitchen wall?

The selection of magnets comes to an end with something even more unexpected.

Framed photos of these men in trolleys are on sale. Plus canvas prints; t-shirts in various pastel shades with the image smack-bang in the centre; tea towels; key rings; a tea cosy. A fucking tea cosy!

'Is this a tea cosy?' I ask the lady behind the table. 'Seriously?'

'Three hundred fifty baht,' she replies.

Kids whizz past me with those plastic, flashing toys. Tourists lean across and barter with the sellers. My mission feels not only incomplete but also unnecessary; I've never felt so far away from Jack as I do right now. I'm invisible, as is he; both of us are ghosts, haunting two very different worlds.

I break free from all the merchandise and refuse to look back.

The mall is close by, across the main road.

I cross the footbridge. At the top of the steps, an older Thai woman is holding a baby, begging. Beside her sits a man cross-legged, barefoot, and the sole of his heel so worn away and infected that the bone is visible.

'Oh, God,' I gasp, trying not to gag, tears prickling instantly.

Was he here last time? Did Jack and I miss him, caught up within each other? Has this man's foot been infected all this time? When did the cuts on his heel become a hole? An actual fucking hole? Why the hell hasn't anybody helped him?

What is it the *Lonely Planet* advises? I can't remember.

So like every other tourist, shopper, worker, human . . . I don't stop. I don't help.

The guide books say not to give money.

I carry on.

The golden arches are before me. I stand on the steps to see what I'd expected, but not what I'd hoped for. Ronald McDonald's scary smile is beaming down upon a man in a shopping trolley. Only it's not the man in my picture. There's no yellow logo on his shirt. This one is brown striped, unbuttoned. He's very skinny, his dark hair long and thin, and he's lapping up the attention by flashing the peace sign, posing. A gaggle of tourists taking selfies consume the space.

This is the spot where Jack asked me to move in with him.

The exact spot.

We thought we were witnessing something unique, something that would mark the moment, so we decided to take a leap of faith. I know that's how Jack's mind worked, why he said it right here, then.

And the moment is erased now.

I erased it.

It's all my fault.

Instead of living in ignorant bliss, holding on tight to what he and I believed, I've ruined it. The moment; the memory; the answer Jack was looking for. What would I say to him if he were here? 'Ah, sorry, hun. There's nothing behind the picture.' It's tourist tat. It's a gimmick. It's, quite simply, a fella sitting in a fucking trolley.

I call out his name.

'Jack!'

I don't mean to, it just happens. I could scream and scream and nobody would notice. But in all these faces, the sea of people passing me by, I wish I could see him. Please. Let him appear. Let him frighten me.

'Jack!'

I know he's gone. I know he got hit by a van. I know he's been cremated. I know he's never coming back. I'm not crazy, I'm not delusional. But, fuck. I just want to see him again. I want proof he loved me: something solid. He 'reckoned' he loved me. That's what he always said, wasn't it? But I want to know that he wasn't an acquaintance I got carried away with. I want to know I mattered. God, how I'd love to have one massive, awful argument with him, right here and now, so I can move on from this hell I'm trapped within. I want it so bad that I've come on some sort of insane pilgrimage to, to, to . . .

. . . I honestly don't know.

God. What am I doing?

I fall to my knees, my hands landing on the ground before me. My whole body begins to convulse, so I rock, my loose hair hiding my face, my eyes shut tight.

I don't know how long I'm there before I feel a hand on my shoulder and someone gently pull me away from the selfie-takers and the mall shoppers. They get me to sit down on a concrete block. It's part of the mall's trendy outdoor landscape, fountains splashing up sporadically from grey slits in the floor design. An unopened bottle of water is thrust into my hands; a man urges me to drink it slowly.

'It's okay,' he says, in a calm, deep voice. 'Take your time.'

19

His name is Justin. He's Canadian.

I see his feet before I take in his face; sports sandals that have seen much better days, although pretty clean toes for the streets of Bangkok. He's wearing what I call traveller trousers, the sort on sale at every Southeast Asian tourist market for the equivalent of a few quid, baggy on the legs with elasticated ankles and waist. They're worn by backpackers from the moment they arrive until the moment they get home, and then demoted to pyjamas. Justin's are petrol blue, patterned with circles and grey elephants. His t-shirt is plain black, his smooth arms slim, muscular. Dark stubble covers his chin, his jawline; his deep brown eyes are squinting with concern.

'Feeling better?' he asks, crouching down to my level.

'Thanks,' I say, in a state of confusion. 'I'm not sure what just happened.'

'I don't know either. I'm sorry if I frightened you.'

'No, no, you didn't. I'm grateful.'

'Drink a little more water – it always helps.'

'I think I need to go back to me hotel,' I say, standing, although a little shaky. 'It's kind of manic out here.'

'Your first time in Bangkok?'

'First time alone.'

I'm on the verge of tears, my dignity shot. I hand the water bottle back to Justin, who pushes out his lips and declines, telling me to keep it.

'Do you wanna get a proper drink?' I ask, surprising myself with the suggestion.

Justin gives a relaxed shrug. 'Sure. Around here?'

'No, the hotel I'm staying at has a happy hour that should be called happy "any" hour. It's also got a hot tub. Not that it's cold outside, clearly; but you know, what are holidays for if you can't get drunk in a swimming cozzie?'

He laughs, although I've no clue whether he's laughing at me or with me. I'm going to take a wild guess that he finds my accent funny.

'Swimmin' cozzie!' he tries to imitate.

I guessed right.

The tuk-tuk ride to the Asia Palace Hotel is filled with pleasantries, comments about cool places either of us have already been to in this city. I mention the green curry, and of course, Justin has his own – equally as amazing if not better – recommendation. He's yet to see the Ladyboys of Bangkok and hasn't made up his mind about spending the money on it. I say it's kind of impressive, but a lot of miming to show tunes. I think I've put him off. We pass the Siam Garden Grand, a more upmarket hotel, and Justin points out that that's where he stayed for his first three nights. Fancy. He's now in more modest accommodation near the Khao San Road.

'I plan to be travelling for a long time,' he says. 'And money doesn't grow on trees.'

We squabble about who's paying for the ride. I insist, and Justin backs down.

'I'll meet you up there,' I say, showing him the signs to the rooftop bar before I disappear off to my room. For all I know, he'll be gone when I decide to go up there, and what does it matter? I'll just talk to someone else. I'm in Bangkok, and if there's one thing a city like this can do for a solo traveller, it's ensure they don't drink alone. And God knows, I need a bloody drink.

I enter my room and see Jack sprawled on the bed. His beard and hair are dripping from the shower and he's covering himself with the towel I used this morning. I focus, not wanting to lose the picture I've created of him.

'*You made a friend quick,*' he says.

'You're judging me?'

'*No. I'm jealous.*'

'Ha. That's ridiculous,' I say, taking my clothes off and rummaging through my suitcase for my swim stuff. 'You've got nothing to be jealous of, hun. I almost lost the bloody plot out there. Did you see the souvenirs? The ones that've shat all over what we thought was unique?'

I tie the halterneck of the tankini and by the time the knot is done, Jack's gone. The towel is exactly where I left it before going out earlier, thrown carelessly onto the bed. I must've forgotten to put the sign on my door for the room to be cleaned.

'I've got to stop this,' I mumble to myself.

I just had a manic meltdown in the middle of one of the world's busiest cities. I came out of it unscathed, partly thanks to a kind Canadian fella, partly due to luck. I could still be out there, vulnerable. What if I'd been robbed? Trodden on? Is that a bit too far-fetched? Is that my problem? I came all this way to search for something that doesn't exist. That's not normal, is it?

No. It's not.

But it's what Jack would've wanted. In a teeny, tiny way, I'm glad he's not here to feel this major slap in the face of disappointment. He'd be sulking now. And I mean seriously sulking. Lip out, heavy breathing, the lot. I manage a smile.

I throw on my cotton rag holiday dress and plonk my sunnies on my head.

The bar is small. A balcony overlooks the surrounding streets, although the view is made up of neighbouring hotels since the Asia Palace is only eight storeys high. The river can be seen in the distance between buildings. Justin's in the hot tub chatting away to a young couple, the girl with strands of long, adorable braids in her hair and the fella buffed up like a rugby player. The three of them sip massive cocktails, no other punters around.

'This is my friend, Chloe,' Justin says and waves me over. 'She's a Scouse.'

'Scouser,' I correct him and turn to the young couple. 'From Liverpool.'

'Cool,' they sing.

They're Jojo and Lachlan, who quit their bar jobs in Perth, Australia, six months ago to go travelling and have no plans to go back anytime soon. I feel ancient next to them, with their sparkling smiles and melodious vibe. They're also super cute, tucked into one another like koala bears. The shared love they're feeling on their journey of discovery is so apparent they might as well get it tattooed all over their beautiful, youthful skin. Justin, beside them, could be twice their age, although that's not to say he doesn't glow, too. I must look like Casper the (trying-to-be) Friendly Ghost

151

as I order a mai tai and slip into the hot tub beside them all.

'So where did you guys meet?' Lachlan asks, looking between Justin and me.

Justin smiles, throwing the opportunity at me to answer.

'Shopping,' I say. 'It was quite embarrassing, really.'

'Oh, no. Why?' Jojo asks, her concern quite convincing.

'Because I'd just tripped up, right over on me ankle,' I lie.

'No way!' Jojo squeals. 'Oh, you poor thing.'

'Tragic,' Lachlan says, and Jojo agrees.

If only they knew.

'Justin helped me get back here,' I say. 'What a gent, eh?'

Lachlan raises his hand and fist bumps Justin. Jojo gives a little round of applause.

'It's kind of romantic.' She sways beneath the bubbles as Justin and I both say something about it not being anything of the sort. 'Hey it is! You know, like Cinderella.'

'How so?' Lachlan teases, splashing her face affectionately.

'Because Cinderella was probably scrubbing the floor and the prince had to help her up to try on the glass slipper. And today, Chloe fell over and Justin had to help her up. He's like her prince.'

We all laugh and poor Jojo keeps protesting, trying to explain her notion further, digging herself into a deeper hole. She's talking about knights in shining armour now and being rescued from towers.

'I think society's moved on,' I say gently, not to sound too cynical.

'No way, Chloe. Girls still love to be swept off their feet,' Jojo states. 'Fact.'

'Or a boy might love to be swept off his feet,' I contest. 'Right, Lachlan?'

'Erm . . . Let's ask Justin? What do you think, man?'

Justin shakes his head. 'Don't ask me. Romance and the do's and don't's are so far off my radar right now, I'm almost definitely gonna say the wrong thing.'

'Ah, no,' Jojo sighs. 'Lachlan, look. He's totally heartbroken.'

'She's right,' Justin confirms. 'I got dumped.'

'You see, Lachlan? I'm always right.'

Lachlan nods, probably not out of choice. I turn around to the bar and order another round of cocktails. Justin washes his face with the hot tub water and shakes off the drips, a miniature wake-up call.

'Fuck it,' he says, flashing a toothy smile, although his dark eyes don't glisten. 'It happens to the best of us. And let's look on the bright side, folks. I wouldn't be here if she hadn't decided to end it. So . . . Cheers!'

A waiter approaches with our tray of drinks and we each take one to raise a glass for Justin's toast. Jojo tells Justin how he must take all the time he needs to heal, repeating over and over again how it's the worst thing ever, the worst thing ever, the worst thing ever, how she understands heartbreak and fuck, it really is, the worst thing ever. Lachlan is sombre. He agrees with Jojo.

'Getting dumped sucks ass,' are his precise words.

'It's cool, buddy,' Justin says. 'She wasn't anybody special.'

I pull all the generic facial expressions, pretending to join in their solidarity. It's a relief when Lachlan confesses he's so hungry he might pass out, so he and Jojo get out of the hot tub. Justin tells them the drinks are on him. Jojo gushes her thanks and Lachlan shoots out another fist bump. Their energy has drained me. I order a beer.

'Make it two,' Justin calls out.

'Well, let this be on me,' I say.

'I appreciate it. How's the ankle?'

I grimace.

'It's okay, Chloe. You don't have to tell me what really happened.'

The cold beer is a treat; better than the sugary mai tai itching my back teeth. I love the bubbles, the instant satisfaction. I spread out in the hot tub, dip my head back, wet all of my hair. In another life, I could be on a real holiday right now.

'I lied, too,' Justin tells me, a short nod of his head in the direction of the young Aussies, now gone from sight. 'A white lie, of course.'

'You weren't dumped?' I ask.

'Oh, no, that part was true. I lied when I said she wasn't anybody special. She was my wife.' Justin swigs, sighs. 'My wife of twenty-one years.'

I almost spit out my drink.

'Ah, hun. That's rough.'

'Is it bad that I didn't tell the truth to those guys? I don't even think they're twenty-one themselves yet. I didn't wanna alienate them, or make myself feel so goddamn old. Does that make me horribly vain?'

'God, no. I felt like a granny next to them two.'

'And you're still pretty young.'

'Well . . . not really. But I'll take the compliment. Ta.'

We clink bottles, drink.

'She left you after twenty-one years?' I ask, but quietly and more to reiterate the point, not expecting him to elaborate.

'Twenty-four years, actually. We were high school sweethearts: met young, married young, as soon as we'd both finished college. She was the love of my life. The only life I've ever known. Apologies for sounding, I dunno – kinda cheesy.'

'It's not cheesy at all. It's the truth, right? You basically spent your entire adult life with her. The end of your childhood, too.'

'Right. I can't be the same guy as I was before I met her, but I also don't know who I am without her. What were you like twenty years ago? Wildly different, you think? Or, do we never change? Are we actually always the same?'

'Oh, wow. I dunno. I think I was the same. Well, I was sort of the same until . . . recently.' I sink a little lower into the hot tub, enjoying the comfort of the water hugging me like a blanket. I think about myself as a teenager, spending my Saturday job wages in Miss Selfridge. I used to laugh with my mates so much. About everything, about nothing. Going to the library satisfied me. Getting a phone call enthralled me. 'I was just younger. Happier.'

'I want that again,' Justin says, unconvincingly.

'So, what happened? Did she just decide she was done? I mean, don't answer if you don't want to, Justin, I'm being a right nosy cow.'

He laughs. Again, I imagine it's my accent.

'I guess she was done, yeah. Done with me, that's for sure. Not the new guy at her work, though. She's not done with him. Oh, no. She's *doing* him! Doing him so much, she's having his goddamn baby. We never had kids. We tried, but . . .'

'Oh, Justin. And here was me thinking, oh, whatever. You got dumped. Boo fucking hoo. Goes to show, everyone's got their pain.'

'And you?'

'And me, what?'

'Your pain. It's evident. If you wanna talk about it?'

'Me fingertips've gone all wrinkly,' I say, splaying my hands out. 'How about we dry off and hit another bar. I might feel like talking about it then.'

'And if you don't, I might insist we play my favourite game?'

'Yeah, I love games. What is it?'

'Creating the most evil insults possible to describe my ex-wife.'

I don't disapprove, but that sounds like a bullshit game.

20

We go to the Happy Beer Garden.

It's a popular spot. I went there with Jack the night after we took the photograph, and I know I shouldn't be putting myself in a position to drag up old memories, but I wasn't a fan of the craziness of the Khao San Road and I didn't fancy shopping around for a decent bar with Justin. Too much pressure.

We get a little table outside, kind of a two-seater bench, facing the traffic flowing past slowly, tuk-tuks piled up. Neon strips and fairy lights hang above our heads. A young girl tries to sell us a flower and when we decline, she pulls out the wooden frogs. Justin buys two.

'For my nephews,' he says.

We order a couple of beers.

'Are they in Canada?' I ask.

'My nephews? Yeah. Toronto. God knows when I'll see them again, though.'

'Of course – you said you plan to be travelling for a long time.'

'I have to. I can't function at home.' He plays with the damp beer mat between his fingers. 'I don't know how to *be* without Sabrina. You know, the last time I remember doing anything before she became a major player in my life was when I went to the movies to see *Toy Story*. The first *Toy Story*! And even then, she was probably there, too, with her friends, because we were from the same town, went to the same elementary school. So, in the words of some terrible, mediocre philosopher, I need to go forth and well, find myself. Do I sound like an even bigger douchebag than before?'

'Absolutely,' I say, not leaving it too long before I add, 'Only messing.'

Our beers arrive and the waitress asks us where we're from and if we're married. We bypass the first question and say no regarding the second.

'Why? Why you not married?' she asks, quite offended. 'Be happy!'

'We're just friends,' I tell her.

She rolls her eyes, tuts at us.

'You want tequila?' she asks.

'Sure,' I reply. 'Why not?'

'I hate tequila,' Justin says. 'I'm too old for that stuff.'

'Fine, I'll drink both.'

I'm thinking about what he said, about finding himself. I've never met anybody in real life who's used the term seriously. Jack went on a gap year, like all the posh kids do, and he told me it was to find himself, but he was totally taking the piss. He was interrailing and getting smashed with his carefully saved allowance, his parents' credit card tucked into his wallet if things went tits-up. The only thing he found that he previously didn't know about himself was a tattoo on his left calf, of a pizza slice. But let's be serious for a second here. If I wanted to find myself – because let's face it, I'm pretty fucking lost right now – surely all I'd need to do is go home to Liverpool. Thirty-six-year-old Chloe Roscoe had been plodding along fine a matter of months ago. There was no thought of moving to the big smoke, no dead boyfriend to deal with. But would trying to erase the first half of this year be disrespectful to Jack? To what we had? Or would it be a smart move?

'Penny for your thoughts?' Justin asks.

'Sorry. I'm terrible company. It's a symptom of what happened . . . about six weeks ago.'

The waitress returns with two shots of tequila. Justin impulsively takes one and downs it, grimacing at the taste and sticking out his tongue.

'Nobody forced you to do that,' I laugh.

'So what happened about six weeks ago?'

We're in danger of having to slag off Sabrina if I don't open up.

'Okay,' I begin. 'Me boyfriend, Jack, died—'

'Oh man! Chloe—'

'Just let me unleash. You can give me sympathy later. Or more tequila. We'd only just moved in together. I met him in January and before the end of June, he was dead. Hit by a van. So the whole relationship never got a shot . . . I mean, say we were to break up – not that it was on the cards – I never got the chance to find out enough about him to dislike him, to hate him. His faults weren't as obvious as they would be further down the line. And if we were meant to be together – you know, get married, have kids, well, that's never gonna happen. Ever. So, where does that leave me? I'm not a widow, but I'm not fighting heartbreak or trying to convince myself I'm better off without him. I'm just . . . sad.'

Justin's dark eyes narrow and he cocks his head to the side, intent on listening. An older Thai lady stops at our table and tries to sell us some trinkets from a basket hanging around her neck. He reaches into his pocket and gives her one hundred baht. She leaves a small garland of white flowers – or *malai* as I recall from chatting to a local last time – beside our beers.

'Can I ask why you're in Bangkok?' Justin prompts.

'Oh, yeah! The plot thickens . . . Well, I thought it would. But I thought wrong.'

'Cryptic.'

'Sorry. Jack and I came here together in March, and . . . hang on,' I take out my phone and find the original photo to show Justin. 'You've no doubt seen this sort of thing on cheap souvenirs, yeah?'

Justin nods, perhaps unsure.

'Well, Jack took this photo, thinking he'd captured something unusual – funny.'

'It's kind of weird.'

'Right! It's so weird! And it's hanging on our kitchen wall, massive.'

'Cool.'

'Yeah, that's what we thought. Except we also thought there was more to it.'

'Like, how?'

'Like, the fella. Why was he sitting there? What made him rock up and get inside a trolley? Look – he's staring straight down the lens. Jack loved the notion that there was something more behind the picture, a story etched into his face. You know how you invent silly things or obsess over stupid stuff when you're in love?'

'Of course. Sabrina and I were obsessed with the number fifty-four.'

'Y'what?!'

'Yeah. We'd only just started dating and we were saying how much we loved each other, all goo-goo. I said I loved her twice as much as she loved me, then she said, no, she loved me ten times more . . . and I blurted out "fifty-four!" It made her laugh. Like, really, really laugh.'

'So, it became a thing?'

'For sure. Every card we sent – birthdays, anniversaries – "I love you, fifty-four" and a string of kisses. It was our number, our stupid . . . whatever.'

'I get it.'

'And your thing was this picture.'

'Yep,' I jiggle the remaining beer around the bottle and knock it back. 'I came here to find out what Jack wanted to know. And, well, the answer is nothing. It was a gimmick.'

'I'm sorry, Chloe.' He rubs his palm against his dark stubble.

'It's shit, isn't it? *I* even feel sorry for me. For Jack.'

Justin takes the garland of flowers and puts it around my neck. We drink more beer and do a bit of people-watching: it's a fantastic spot for it. It's nice to have a mate. He's easy-going and it doesn't feel strange. I mean, this is what you do on holidays, isn't it? You chat to strangers, you connect, simply because you're both there, fish out of water. If it weren't for the consistent twinge of pain running from my head to toe, the pain that's been present since my towel dropped in front of Jack's dad, I'd probably have moments here and there when I'd forget about Jack's death, sat here, a spectator of Bangkok.

'What did you hope to achieve?' Justin asks. 'By coming here.'

I heave a sigh. 'Meaning.'

'Okay . . .'

'Vague, right? I know. But – if I'm not part of Jack's future and not part of his past—'

'But of course you are—'

'Nah, you weren't at the funeral. There's no trace of me in his life; not according to everyone he's ever known. I'm just this person who occupied his spare time for five months. I somehow thought that if I could find that man, show the photo to people in the area it was taken, track him down by his work uniform, I'd get the story of his life, find out something interesting, and – oh, my God, I realise how fucking round the bend I sound. I'm from an entirely different culture from this fella. I mean, what was I expecting? Us to have a cuppa? Be invited over for Sunday lunch?'

'A good friend of mine from back home worked here in Bangkok for many years. He said his family became close with their driver, but their relationship was established over four, maybe five years. It helped that the guy was good at languages. Your guy might not speak any English, but I don't mean to patronise. I'm sure you already thought about that.'

'Me head's a mess. I haven't slept much, you know, since.'

'All is forgiven,' Justin smiles. 'Look, I can't judge. I'm backpacking like a nineteen-year-old in the hope of a new life presenting itself to me. I'm sure in reality I should go home, get my job back and move the hell on. Hurt; heal. But this – I dunno – this somehow feels easier.'

'Justin, give yourself some credit. What you're doing's brave.'

'It's also called running away.'

'Nope. A lot of people'd sit at home, get drunk and feel sorry for themselves and stalk their ex online.'

'Oh, I've stalked. I still stalk.'

'I don't blame you. But you don't need me to tell you that's pointless.'

'Sure. Why take a knife to an open wound? Human fucked-up nature.'

We cheers to that.

'And Chloe, you need to give yourself some credit, too. Who gives a shit whether you and Jack were together five months or—'

'Fifty-four years?'

'Hey, don't steal my thing!'

'Haha, sorry.'

'But, yeah. Who cares? You know what counts. You don't need to start looking for a needle in a haystack in Bangkok to prove you loved each other.'

'That's the problem, Justin. I don't know if Jack truly loved me.'

'He never said it?'

'He said he "reckoned" he loved me. Like a less serious version. He never just spat it out, said those three fucking words.'

'And did you ever say them to him?'

I shake my head, disappointed in myself. 'I copied him. Told him I "reckoned" I loved him, too. I mean, shit. He died not knowing that I was *so* in love with him, you know, as much as a grown woman can be after a few months. Tequila?'

'Ooh, I can still feel the first one about here,' he indicates his upper torso with his hand.

'Good. Two tequilas please!'

Patpong market is on the opposite side of the road. It's getting late now; the neon lights are in full glory, the haggling crowds growing by the minute. We're handed paper flyers for ping-pong shows in nearby bars, as casual as a fast food discount.

'Chloe, I think you know in your heart if Jack loved you,' Justin says, kindly.

'No, I honestly don't.'

And there lies the answer to my quest. Or maybe not the answer, but the reason. I came here to give my short-lived relationship a higher status; a deeper meaning. If I couldn't get the words out of Jack Carmichael, I was seeking reassurance elsewhere. Failing on all levels.

Naturally.

This quest is fucking bonkers.

I neck my tequila, clear my throat and put on a dreamy voice.

'What's behind the picture?' I joke, taking the piss out of myself, then snapping back to normal. 'Get a fucking grip, Chloe.'

Justin drinks his shot and for a moment, I think he might puke. Instead, he whoops.

'Okay, okay,' he says, drum-rolling his hands on the table. 'I got a game for us.'

'Oh no . . .'

'Come on, gimme a chance. I just poisoned myself with tequila for you.'

'Thanks for shifting blame, hun.'

'I think this game'll help. With our problems.'

I squint, noticing how bleary things have become. I'm drunk. And glad of it.

'You tell me one thing you loved about Jack – OR – that he loved about you,' he says. 'And then, I'll tell you one thing I hated about Sabrina – OR – that she hated about me.'

'How the fuck is this gonna help us?'

'Trust me. I'm old. Wise.'

'You're pissed as a fart.'

'Come on . . .'

'Okay, but I need wine. This beer's making me burp loads.'

Justin staggers from the bench and calls for a large glass of red. I wanted white, but what the hell. I release another burp, covering my mouth, and feel instantly much, much better. I kick off the game.

'I loved how Jack was a big, sexy bear.'

'I hated how Sabrina wouldn't let me touch her legs if she hadn't shaved them.'

'I loved how Jack'd sing all the time, any place, if a song jumped into his head.'

'Surely, you hated that?'

'No, I loved it. And he loved how I'd listen, or dance, sometimes join in.'

'Okay, well, I hated how Sabrina could never talk on the phone, not even to the bank, unless she was in a room all alone, door closed. A master of secrets.'

'I can be like that.'

'That's not the game.'

'Okay. I loved how Jack painted me toenails for me when I pulled a muscle in me back.'

'I hated how Sabrina would watch what I ate in restaurants and disapprove of my choice—'

'Justin, I think it's safe to say you're better off without her. Game over.'

'Do you feel closer to Jack?'

'No, not at all.'

I don't want tonight to turn awkward. Neither Justin nor I deserve that, so I giggle – the easy way out of a sticky situation – and call Justin a divvy for coming up with such a shit game. He admits defeat and all seems well.

'I'm flying to Vietnam tomorrow,' he tells me.

I stop giggling.

'Jack was gonna take me there in October,' I say. 'Some place called Hoi An. He said it's the most magical place, apparently.'

'So come with me? Not *with me* – I didn't mean to be so forward. But come. My flight's to Da Nang, real close to Hoi An.'

'No way!'

'Yeah. I've been to Hanoi before, so I was gonna try out the south, make my way down to Ho Chi Minh, take another flight from there further east, maybe.'

Could this be an opportunity? What if this is what I was always supposed to do? Perhaps my trip to Bangkok was to lead me to Hoi An, to a special place Jack wanted me to see. When we'd discussed this trip as a possibility for October half term, my initial reaction had been that Vietnam was too far away for a single week's holiday and that we should go somewhere closer. Jack disagreed, because he knew it'd be worth every single second.

Would it?

Is Hoi An where I can find peace? Say a proper goodbye to Jack?

'Well,' Justin yawns, stretching his lean arms above his head. 'I guess I better head to my minus-five-star hostel, shower in the en suite bathroom I'm sharing with five or six others, and hit the sack.'

I realise I haven't spoken for a while. The noise in my spinning head is making me feel quite sick.

'What time's your flight to Da Nang?' I ask.

'Noon.'

We split the bill and squeeze out of our bench. I open my arms wide to Justin and we hug it out, proper pals. God, it was good to find one of those, even for just one night.

'One night in Bangkok . . .' I start singing, in memory of Jack – the kind of thing he'd do.

'Take care of yourself, Chloe.'

Off we go, in separate tuk-tuks. I adore the feeling of the warm air from the speed of the little engine. My hair dances all around my face. I fight to keep my eyes open, not wanting to miss a minute of the madness I'm in the thick of, a feeling that there's more to this trip than sheer disappointment. When I get back to my room, I flop onto the bed and start drifting off into drunken slumber.

Maybe I will go to Vietnam tomorrow. Maybe . . .

21

The sky is the darkest shade of grey I've ever seen. It's so low, I want to touch it with my fingertips. I stare out of the round window, the rain battering against the glass. I never thought it possible for clouds to be this dramatic.

Stepping off the plane, the wind slaps my cheeks and my polka-dot skirt does a full-on Marilyn Monroe. I grip the railing, taking each step slowly, just as the passengers before and behind me must be doing. If only I could see them. My eyes are squinting, and not through choice. On the tarmac, the force of the wind almost pushes my body back onto the plane. Welcome to Da Nang, eh?

My return flight back to London is in four days – from Bangkok, of course – but like Justin reminded me, flights can be changed. Sure, it'll cost me, but so would therapy. I had no way of telling Justin I was coming, but I got to BKK in plenty of time for the noon flight, and there he was, ahead of me at check-in.

'I knew you'd come,' he shouted over.

'I like to think I'm unpredictable, but . . .'

We meet again by the baggage carousel, his elephant traveller trousers still on his bottom half, a white vest covered by an open denim shirt occupying the top. He asks me where I'm staying in Hoi An.

'Well,' I begin, feeling pretty stupid. 'I was gonna try the hostel thing. Am I wrong to think you can just rock up and get a room? Sorry, but I never went backpacking back in the day.'

'That's usually how it works,' Justin tells me. 'Presuming there's room at the inn and all, but the weather isn't gonna be on your side this afternoon, buddy.'

'God, I'm such an amateur.'

'Don't worry. I got an idea. How about you come with me to my hotel, log onto the Wi-Fi and wait for the storm to pass. By the time you find yourself a room somewhere, the sky'll be clear and we can go grab a bite. Or not. Totally your choice.'

As we approach arrivals, we notice how drenched the drivers are, awaiting their passengers. A family exit the automatic doors and are literally blown over, all four of them piling on top of one another. I turn to Justin.

'I'll take you up on that offer, hun.'

Justin spots the driver holding up a clipboard for the Golden Beach Resort, with his full name, Justin Bailey, written in black marker pen on the attached sheet of paper. He shakes the driver's hand and pats him on the back, calling him 'my friend'. We're led to a minibus, the resort's logo printed on the sliding silver door. It's a struggle against nature, but we get inside thanks to the driver's help, and wait for him to load the bags into the back as the vehicle rocks from side to side. There's nobody else on the bus.

'Fancy for a hostel,' I say, referring to our private ride.

'Oh, it's not a hostel. This place looked too good to resist, and for a great price. It has a beautiful lagoon pool and the rooms are right on the beach.'

The drive takes about thirty minutes and neither Justin nor I are particularly chatty. It's a blend of hangover, the weather and the inescapable fact that we barely know one another. I don't feel awkward, just tired and spaced out. I watch the intense rain from inside the minibus, the heavy clouds seeming rather permanent over something soon to pass. When we arrive in Hoi An, the driver crawls through some residential streets and pulls over outside a guest house called the Garden Villa.

'You stay here,' the driver says, looking at Justin through his rear-view mirror.

'I think there's been some sort of mistake,' Justin says, leaning forwards. 'I'm booked to stay at the beach resort.'

'No. You stay here.' And the driver pushes his door open against the wind.

He removes the luggage from the back, running ahead into the guest house with our bags. Justin tells me to wait here as he heaves the passenger door open, grunting as he does so. I'm not pleased about it. What if the minibus topples over into the middle of the road? The tall palm trees lining the pavements look terrified: they're no longer vertical, shaking with uncontrollable fear.

I get out.

And, whoa – I manage to get the minibus door open, but I can't close it. My hair sticks to my face; my t-shirt and skirt fly upwards. I bear down, bend my legs and, as I howl something animalistic, the door shifts and I slide it shut with a hefty slam. Keeping one hand on my skirt and another holding back my hair, I stumble down the stepping-stone footpath and into the guest house.

'No, this isn't where I'm staying.' Justin is arguing, calmly, with the receptionist.

The driver is repeating what he said before, only more firm. 'You. Stay. Here.'

'Typhoon, sir,' the receptionist is saying.

Justin shakes his head. 'But this isn't typhoon season.'

'It happens,' she laughs. 'Typhoon coming.'

The reception area is small, a polished brown wooden desk carved with intricate flowers and matching chairs with red upholstered seats; a soft, shiny fabric. Fresh flowers sit in vases beside small statues of Buddha; lush green plants with beautiful large leaves stretch to the low ceiling. The main light, covered with a red paper lantern, has been flickering, just a little. It's lovely, but it's nothing like a beach resort with a lagoon pool.

'But why can't I stay at the Golden Beach? I've already paid good money for that.'

'Oh, no. Evacuation, sir.'

'Seriously?' Justin sighs, and I join him beside the desk. 'Did you hear that?'

'Yep,' I say. 'Kind of annoying, eh?'

'Look, can you call me a taxi, please?' he asks the receptionist. 'We'll make our own way to the beach resort.'

'No taxi, sir. Typhoon coming.'

The driver waves goodbye to the receptionist and leaves, laughter in his stride. The receptionist hands Justin a key and tells him sweetly that he has a deluxe suite, the best room. I'm guessing this place is much cheaper than the Golden Beach Resort.

Another guest emerges from a room on the ground floor – a tall woman with broad shoulders and short, choppy hair. A sleepy toddler is sitting on her hip.

'The same thing happened to us,' she says. She sounds Dutch, pronouncing her 's' like a soft 'sh'. 'We made it as far as the Golden Beach Resort and we spent a wonderful day and night there yesterday. But today, after lunch, we arrived at our room to find a sun lounger upside-down on the bed. It had smashed through the glass doors. The wind is so strong down there.'

'You're best off here,' I tell Justin, who still seems sceptical.

I, however, feel like I've landed on the moon. There are rooms available for sixteen quid per night, and from the photos on the wooden desk, they look beautiful. I leave Justin standing in the doorway of the main entrance, staring into the storm and cooking up an escape plan, and check myself in for two nights as a starting point. I'm surprised to hear that this price includes a breakfast buffet and use of the swimming pool in the garden, although—

'No swimming today, Madam,' the receptionist warns.

Justin's on the phone now.

'Enjoying Vietnam?' I ask the Dutch lady.

'Oh, we love it. We've been here for one month already, travelling.'

'With a little one? That's amazing.'

'We're relaxed, so he's relaxed. He loved all the lanterns in Hoi An Ancient Town.'

'I've heard they're very special.'

'Oh, yes. We lit a lantern and made a wish, and we watched it float across the river and into the sky. So beautiful.'

Yes, yes, yes! This. This is what I want.

It's the perfect way to connect with Jack; to wish for a happy ending; to feel his presence fly away in a floating lantern. At the moment *I* seem a bit floaty, never mind the bloody lantern. Maybe this magical town is already having

172

an effect on me. Not that I've witnessed any of this supposed magic yet. But remember, Justin said the storm will pass soon. It's not typhoon season.

I make my way to my room. It's on the second level of the two-storey building, and I've got to drag myself through an outside corridor where the doors are situated. The wind hasn't calmed down, so as much as I want to peep over the balcony, take in the pool and the view, I better keep my head down and my feet forward.

The photos were accurate. The room is beautiful. Probably the best sixteen quid I've ever spent. A king-size bed with crisp white sheets invites me to bounce; it has cushions and a throw in the same material as the upholstered chairs in reception. Wooden decor creates a boho-chic feel, carved dark wood poles dividing the space between the bed and a sitting area. There's a flatscreen telly, the usual tea and coffee and a bowl with two mini bananas. The bathroom isn't much to scream about; basic, functional – and the shower doesn't look too promising. But how can I complain? Besides, there's a little round soap wrapped in mint-green paper, and a shower cap: the sort of treats I'd find in my nan's house.

There's a knock on my door. I open it carefully and the wind whips in. Justin jumps inside.

'Apologies. I wouldn't usually barge my way in—'

'Don't be soft. Did you sort out a taxi?'

'No chance.' He runs his hands across his heavy, dark stubble, irritated. 'Apparently all the beach accommodation has been evacuated. It all seems a little OTT, but maybe I'm wrong; maybe typhoons can hit this time of year.'

'I just wanna see some lanterns,' I say, like a five-year-old demanding a unicorn.

'You hungry?'

'I think so.'

'The lady on the desk told me to get food now – it might be too late soon.'

'Okay, that does sound a bit—'

'OTT?'

I purse my lips and look around my room. The wind is howling through the fan in the bathroom window. Hanging around here probably isn't the most inspiring thing to do; food is the better option.

'Let's go,' I say.

The receptionist even gives us an umbrella each, kindly requesting we remember to bring them back. It's only a fifteen-minute walk to the ancient town and that's our plan. We figure if we can get to a place where more people are milling about and restaurants aren't keen on closing for business, we'll perk up. And hopefully, the storm will pipe down.

Fat chance.

We're blown to the restaurant on the corner of the road, a stone's throw from the guest house. We never managed to get the umbrellas up. Both of us are completely drenched from the rain. I sit on the entrance step and wring out the water from my polka-dot skirt. I give my hair a shake, knowing I'll have mascara running down my cheeks. There's no door into the restaurant – it's open-fronted and currently shielded from the storm by some blankets attached to the tin veranda roof with pegs. How they haven't been blown off, I'll never know.

'Welcome!' The waitress smiles.

Her hair is pulled into a ponytail. She's wearing skinny jeans, and a red t-shirt hangs neat upon her petite physique. Her name badge reads *Linh*. She invites us to sit down and

174

hands us a menu folder, each laminated page filled with photos of various dishes, and she reads out the words printed in English on the front cover.

'You Eat, I Like,' Linh reads.

That must be the name of the restaurant. Cute.

And wow, is it cute.

Low bamboo tables are dotted around the space with bright-coloured beanbags as seats. Some red heart-shaped cushions are scattered about. A guitar hangs on a painted white wall, framed pictures of The Beatles on another. The words *All you need is love* are painted beneath the guitar. Ah, home from home. There is an open kitchen, with a man and woman doing the cooking for all to see. I notice a double bed – well, more of a mattress, really – in the corner of the restaurant, a few mismatching pillows and blankets thrown on it, a small bedside cabinet against the wall. This is a family-run business and they must live in this room, too. The first page of the menu is filled with information about their daily cookery classes.

'Beer?' Justin asks me.

I'm old enough – or wise enough, rather – to understand that hair of the dog works.

'Yep.'

It's not yet five o'clock, although it feels like the depths of night. The restaurant is bright with bulbs hanging from wires across the ceiling, and the waitress is putting out candles on each table ready to light. The Dutch lady is sat behind us with her son and, I presume, her partner. We exchange hellos. I order a special Hoi An noodle dish and some banh xeo – Vietnamese crispy pancakes. Justin is mid-order when the electricity cuts out and we're all sitting in darkness, one small flickering candle on the Dutch family's table alive.

'I guess this means we can't order from the menu now,' Justin gripes.

'Bloody hell, you are a grump today, aren't you?' I point out.

'I wasn't expecting this.'

'Ha. You're telling me?'

Linh finishes lighting all the candles and brings us ice-cold beers, asking us if we'd like food, too.

'I make?' she asks. 'We try the generator.'

In the kitchen, I can see the man trying to get the generator working. The woman is still preparing food, doing what she can with little resources.

'We'll have anything,' I say. 'You bring and we'll eat. Whatever's possible.'

'Thank you, thank you,' Linh beams.

'No, no,' Justin says, feeling like an arsehole, I hope. 'Thank *you*.'

The gentle ripple of the blankets suggests it's not too windy outside, so the storm could well be passing. It occurs to me that Jack would have been a wreck on the flight from Bangkok to Da Nang, had he known we were landing in such extreme conditions. I didn't think about it at the time, presuming the bumpy ride down was due to the plane being a small low-budget aircraft. Despite that, I wish he was here, beside me in the candlelight. He'd be best mates with Linh and her family by now, giving the little Dutch kid a shoulder ride.

'Thinking about Jack?' Justin asks.

'Always.'

I really don't want him to say anything bitchy about Sabrina. It's not the right moment.

'Everything feels a bit fuzzy,' I admit. 'Like I'm caught

between reality and a dream. I know I'm here, in Vietnam, but I'm not sure how I got here . . . metaphorically, like.'

'I know what you mean.'

'That's good. I'm not usually such an – erm – philosopher.'

'Do you feel like the decision to be here, although you ultimately made it, was out of your hands?'

I take in these words, think. 'Yeah, I do.'

What I mean is 'I hope so'.

Linh places a plate of Vietnamese spring rolls between us, a colourful-looking noodle salad and some chicken rice, plus a dish of what looks like fat, fried potatoes. One bite tells me it's not potato; it tastes cold, crumbly and rather odd. Good-odd. I try a spring roll and it's so fresh, so delicious, I'm in awe of how this was thrown together without any electricity. We tuck in.

'Sorry, sorry,' Linh says, gesturing at the food.

'Oh no, this is amazing,' I tell her as I take another potato-that's-not-a-potato. 'Even this!'

We enjoy a couple more beers and the Dutch family join us around our table. It's inevitable but I tell Linh that I'm from the birthplace of The Beatles, pointing to the quote on the wall. I'm not sure she understands what I mean, although she smiles kindly. Like a total moron, I point to the quote again and speak slower. Again, she smiles and now puts her hands to her heart, saying *yes*.

Justin stands and reaches for the guitar, asking, 'May I?'

I'm no expert, but it doesn't look particularly like a collector's item. Linh stands on her tiny tiptoes to help Justin take it down from the wall. He strums a painful chord or two before sitting back down to give the strings a much-needed tuning.

Once the guitar's in better shape, one bold strum alerts

177

everybody to the beginning of 'A Hard Day's Night'. Justin kicks off the singing and Linh claps as the Dutch couple join in. I don't think Justin is a singer, but his voice is pleasant, similar to how he speaks – low and gentle, effortless. He doesn't show off, hold notes too long or anything; he just watches his fingers move about the strings. I find myself singing along, too.

Only a handful of other customers are in the restaurant. Two pay up and leave, and the others – three young female backpackers – come and sit closer with their shared bottle of wine. 'She Loves You' is next on the list; we all sing, taking a stab at random lyrics. Justin seems able to hold the fort though: his knowledge of the correct lyrics is even better than mine. Linh brings over more bottles of beer and I order a bottle of wine, the same as the backpackers are drinking, and invite them to help themselves.

Justin leans close to me, whispers into my ear.

'What's your favourite?'

I tell him, 'In My Life'.

He spends a minute or two tuning up the guitar a little better. The backpackers tickle the toddler, who is enjoying taking the pages out of the menus, and the Dutch couple have a private moment doing their own small toast. Linh is clearing tables.

Justin plucks the opening notes of my favourite Beatles song and after repeating the sequence again, he looks up and catches my eye. Naturally, I start to sing. It's fun and rather daring, but not completely out of my comfort zone. I'm a drama graduate, remember, although I was more suited to being in the ensemble than a soloist. The fact that I'm merry, and fuzzy from a hangover that's now mellowed into a sweet haze, helps my confidence. Others sway and listen, but nobody else joins in. The round of applause at the end is both comforting and excruciating.

'You are a good singer!' the Dutch lady says.

Justin puts his arm around me and pulls me towards him with a *well done* shake. I expect him to ruffle the top of my hair like I'm a kid he's proud of, but thank God, he doesn't.

After a group effort of 'Hey Jude', we all pay up and call it a night. It's not late, but the rain is plummeting down and Linh is fixing the blankets with extra pegs to hold them in place. I give Linh a hug goodbye and tell her to stay safe tonight. She laughs this off, ever so blasé about the forceful wind outside. The toddler is wrapped up inside his sturdy buggy and a team effort ensues; we link one another in a long line to get back to the Garden Villa guest house. Nobody bothers to try their umbrella. The wind ushers us and we have no choice but to run along with it.

22

Once inside the reception area, I feel somewhat safe.

The walls are sturdy, and the noise considerably less.

The Dutch family bid us a good night and I'm reminded that I'm a good singer. I give a stupid curtsey and they respond by giving me a clap, before closing the door to their room. I wrinkle my nose, cringing at myself.

I'd never sung in front of Jack before. Not properly.

'I'm gonna check some emails,' Justin says, referring to the two desktop computers in the small lobby area behind reception. 'Hate doing that sorta shit on my phone.'

'I hear you,' I say. 'God, we sound so old!'

'Tonight was fun.'

I agree. It was.

Getting to my room, however, isn't. The wind on this side of the building is battering the doors to the rooms and I stagger, eyes closed tight, holding onto the wall. It doesn't bother me as much as earlier, whether due to the alcohol or just growing accustomed, but the pleasant warmth I was feeling moments ago has vanished, quite aptly gone with the wind. I chance a quick peek down and see the swimming pool. It's basic, rectangular and floodlit, many leaves and a couple of chairs floating on the water. The surrounding palm trees are bent double.

Once inside my room, I slouch onto a sofa and flick off my flip-flops. I try connecting to the free Wi-Fi to scroll through my phone for nothing in particular.

That's no surprise:

The WiFi cannot connect.

Could be a login error. Could be the weather. I call reception from the room phone.

No luck – the line is down. Unless I go back to reception there's no way I'll get online, and as if I'm leaving this room again tonight. As if. The front door trembles within its frame. A whistle, harsh and unfriendly, intrudes through the keyhole.

I turn on the telly.

CNN, Fox, Sky News. A French business channel, a French gameshow. A movie channel showing a film through an eighties fuzz. Michael Douglas is starring. I've seen it before, when I was little. At my nan's house, I think, when she used to allow me and our Kit to stay up way past our bedtime.

My clothes – damp during the meal and singsong – are now stuck to me like cling film. I peel off my t-shirt and polka-dot skirt, drop-kicking them in the general direction of my suitcase. My bra is also wet, and the straps are digging into my shoulders, so I get completely naked and decide to take a hot shower.

The water drips and dribbles for a while, eventually splattering enough to warrant a wash. I keep my fingers under the stream, waiting for the ice-cold water to warm up, but it doesn't. I don't actually need a hot shower, but cold won't do. I need comfort, not a shock, and just standing here waiting is making me shiver and sober up in a way I'm not ready for. Tonight was more than just fun. It was freeing. I can't believe I'm going to admit this – to think these words – but I felt like the old Chloe Roscoe in patches. Here and there. Not the ghost I've become since Jack died.

Fuck.

Since. Jack. Died.

And now all I can think about is how he's not here and how he's never going to be here and how he's not at home and how he's never going to be at home and . . .

My fingers are fucking freezing.

I turn the shower off and skulk back to my suitcase, pulling the cotton rag dress over my head. I'm not sober, but I'm not drunk like last night. I'm restless. When will the howling outside stop? Not the season, Justin? Come on. Calm down. Please, calm down.

SMASH!

I run to the double doors that lead onto a small balcony and peer behind the curtains into the storm. A plant is lying sideways, its terracotta pot smashed around it on the ground. The smashing noise was worse than the outcome and I allow myself to find it funny.

Is there a minibar in here?

A small fridge is hidden in the cabinet the telly is sitting on. Two cans of Saigon beer, two Cokes and two bottles of water are inside. Saigon will do fine. The fridge hasn't been switched on though and the can is warm. I can hear the plant pot pieces scratching around outside, jiggling in the wind. I open the beer, sip. It's better than nothing.

Interference causes Michael Douglas to fuzz and jerk about the screen.

I change channels and find the international weather

182

forecast. Bright yellow suns are plastered over most of Africa. Edging up towards the Middle East, there's the odd grey cloud. Temperatures reaching fifty. I sit on the edge of the bed, the lukewarm beer sitting on my teeth, my tongue. The map rotates and focuses on the Middle East and India, corners of Southeast Asia almost visible. I long to see white clouds or, optimistically, yellow suns. As the map rotates once more, grey fuzz fills the screen with an unpleasant buzz and the telly cuts out. My room goes black.

Is this my cue to go to bed? Dive beneath the covers?

Another smash outside, further away, tells me another plant pot has suffered the worst. I fear the broken terracotta shards are going to be swept against the windows, breaking them and shooting into my room. Shooting into me.

Oh, stop with the drama. Stop!

SMASH!!

A series of smashes continue. I want to hide; my instinct is to shelter, but there are glass windows surrounding me from two opposing angles and I don't know where to go apart from the floor. I'm being ridiculous. I can't lie on the floor.

The lights flicker back on.

The telly remains off.

The noise isn't as intrusive now that I can see again, but God, my heart is pounding. Pounding like a drum; and that's not an exaggeration or me trying to be poetic. My chest feels like a spacious cage, a heavy thudding within. I place my palm against it, calming my heart down. My knees are weak and hollow and I want to cry. I'm scared. I really am. I'm terrified. God, I'm so terrified that I can't cry. It's too much effort; too much of a decision to make; and I focus on keeping my heart pressed, secure, in fear of it exploding.

I don't want to be alone.

And nothing can comfort me. No phone, no telly. I'm far too distracted to read.

I drink more, swigging the beer until it's gone. Then I go to the door, open it and run to Justin's room. I bang on his door loudly, pounding with my fists – the only way he'll hear me against this racket. I duck down, afraid of something dangerous being blown into me.

His door opens, but only a fraction. He has the chain on.

I can't hear what he's saying – the wind is deafening – but he's struggling to open the door. Something must be stuck. I crouch down further, shielding my head with my arms. Finally, I'm pulled upwards and hauled inside. I slam the door shut with my foot and stand there, breathing heavily, my hands pushed against the back of the door.

'Did you manage to check your emails?' I ask. No idea why.

Justin's no longer in his traveller trousers, but a pair of grey joggers. Nothing on top.

'The connection was bad,' he says.

I don't think he's managed to shower, either. For such a clean, well put together man, he still looks damp with sweat, tired and dishevelled. In this moment, I like it, and I'm aware of the fact that I'm standing in his room not wearing a stitch beneath the cotton rag hanging over my body. Justin's hands are on his hips, his biceps prominent yet neat. Dark, curly hair decorates his chest, something I hadn't paid attention to when we were in the hot tub yesterday.

'I thought this wasn't the season for typhoons,' I manage.

'It happens.'

His room is bigger than mine. Almost identical, just

enlarged. I'm not sure if this makes me feel more safe, or more exposed. The lights flicker and I look up, giving it my most intense teacher's stare to stop it misbehaving. Justin leans across to the wall and turns the lights off.

'That'll give us a heart attack,' he remarks.

'Yeah. You read me mind.'

His hand is still on the wall, beside the light switch. I feel my breath lighten, getting faster. I tilt my head a little and my hair brushes his outstretched arm, my lips almost touch his skin. He takes a step closer to me, just a small one. I sense his hesitation.

I want to say it's okay. It was my choice to come here.

I want to be okay.

To have choices.

I look at him briefly in the small pool of moonlight. My eyes are beginning to adjust to the darkness. But I close them tight, hoping to disappear whilst also wanting to be present. Wanting to be wanted.

The wind is getting stronger.

Whistles rush through cracks in the door and I move a little closer to Justin, feeling my whole body draw forward, the coolness between my legs becoming warm. My breasts touch his chest, only the thin cotton of my dress separating our skin. As my nipples harden, I slide my arms around him and our lips meet.

He kisses me back with force – no, perhaps relief. He's glad I made the move, I can tell.

I let my tongue touch his and he grabs the back of my head, his hand squeezing my hair. As I push him forwards, our lips tightly locked, he guides me away from the door, until he's leaning against the outside of the bathroom wall. I tilt my pelvis close, enjoying the hard sensation coming from him. He runs his hands up my thighs, lifting my dress higher. I'm enjoying this too much – far too much.

I want him to touch me further.

But I hold out.

I wait.

And I want it more and more.

And God, I hate myself. I truly fucking hate myself. I'm a cheat, I'm a slut, I'm everything I hate. I'm a woman who's supposedly in love with somebody else. I'm having fun and I shouldn't, I shouldn't, I shouldn't.

Justin's hands move upwards beneath my dress and I don't stop him. He takes one of my breasts, massages it gently; I moan when his fingers brush my nipples.

Touch me. *Touch me!* I want to yell.

I want—

SMASH!!!

We're pulled apart by an almighty high-pitched shattering noise.

I think I scream.

I'm on the floor, my knees drawn into my chest. I want to scream again, but I can't – I'm frozen in fear. Justin puts on the light and we see that a broken plank of wood has smashed through the large balcony door. I want to cry – feel the sort of release that only crying can bring – but I'm taken over by an intense trembling.

'It'll pass soon,' Justin cries out.

'Why should I believe you?'

'Look, I know I underestimated this weather but, seriously, we're in the thick of it now. Remember a little while ago, when it felt like it was dying down? That was the calm before the storm, as they say.'

'That's actually a thing?'

'Where do you think the saying comes from?'

More crashing and smashing noises dance around us, louder now through the broken window. Justin's on his hands and knees crawling closer to the balcony.

'Justin! What the hell are you doing?'

He doesn't answer, just continues to edge closer until he can see out of the window.

'It sounds worse than it is,' he tells me. 'The crashing is only tiles falling from the roof.'

'And that's supposed to make me feel better?'

I can't be here, not for a second longer.

I find my feet and scramble to the door, open it and let it slam behind me. I don't say goodbye. I just keep on scrambling until I'm back in my own room listening to the tiles falling down around me. I heave the mattress off my bed and drag it to the floor, getting as low as possible. And I lie down, the beat of my heart so intense that I'll never sleep. I never quite realised until now, but it's impossible to think about anything when you're scared, other than what you're scared of. The moment is so enormous, the present so all-consuming.

So I wait.

Crashing subsides into scraping. Scraping becomes rustles. The noise doesn't die, but it does fade, gradually, ever so slowly. I think I drift into a light slumber, although I'm still fully aware of where I am.

There's a knock on my door.

Justin.

No. I can't. I just can't.

A dark loathing encompasses me. The wind has calmed enough for me to remember.

The knocking gets louder, faster.

Please, leave me alone . . . No! I should apologise.

He's almost banging my door down now. I mean, what the—

'Alright!' I say, pulling the door but keeping the chain locked.

'Breakfast, Madam!'

It's not Justin. It's a Vietnamese man, smiling and holding a wooden tray with a miniature banana and a croissant on a plate. A dollop of jam and a dollop of butter sit beside the croissant. A bottle of water and a glass of orange juice rattle unsteadily. The man is wearing a crash helmet.

'I don't need breakfast,' I shriek.

'Please, take breakfast.'

'No, I mean, you didn't have to bring anything! Get inside! Shelter!'

He laughs at me and leaves the tray on the floor in front of the door, waving bye-bye. I carefully open the door and pick it up. I eat the banana and the croissant, leaving the jam and butter untouched, and take the bottle of water, slotting it into the front pocket of my suitcase. I put on some under-wear, a pair of jeggings and stripy t-shirt. Slipping into my flip-flops, I leave my room and eye up the ripped-apart roof down to the swimming pool. Chairs, tables and tiles are drowning in the water.

It doesn't take long to check out. The reception is calm and quiet, not a soul around other than the receptionist, who is different from the lady yesterday. I wonder how the little Dutch boy slept, and hope he wasn't frightened.

A taxi is called and it arrives within minutes.

'Hoi An town centre?' I ask the driver as I clamber into the back seat.

If there's magic to be seen, I should try and find it;

especially now the typhoon seems to have finally passed. Opposite the Garden Villa guest house, I see a family fixing the roof of their home. Two fellas are sitting on the tin top and a woman is handing them tools. They all see me watching from the taxi and wave, smiling. Every tree on this road has been uprooted, the thin trunks sprawled in zigzags on the ground.

'Sorry, Madam,' the driver tells me. 'Too much water. River.'

I don't argue. I won't contest. This man knows more about this town than I ever will. If the town is flooded, that means the restaurants won't be open, nor the shops. Nobody will be cycling through the streets, across the bridge. There won't be any lanterns. Not today.

'No problem,' I say. 'Da Nang Airport, please.'

The magic just isn't here.

Would there have been magic if Jack was here? God, imagine how different this whole experience would've been if . . .

Imagine.

That's all I've got. And all I'll ever have now.

I must go home.

23

I ring the doorbell of the new build. It's four years old, so not exactly shiny new, but it always has that new smell, as if the paint never quite dried. Usually I'm armed with Prosecco, olives and crisps, ready for a night of board games that end dancing on the kitchen table to the Spice Girls. Today, however, it's just me and my Thailand clothes.

'Sis!' Kit beams as he opens the door.

Throwing his arms around my neck, he plants a smacker on my cheek. It's comforting that he's barefoot, wearing shorts and an old Everton football shirt, the same attire he's worn his whole life on lazy Saturdays. He swoops me up in what I've always called a 'princess carry', something he's done for the best part of thirty years despite being both younger and smaller than me. 'Gareth! Come and get Chloe's suitcase, will you?'

I'm swept into their home and accidentally kick a topless Gareth in the head in the hallway. Kit's fault, obviously. He chucks me onto the sofa and their pug, Mabel, jumps onto my lap and licks my hand. Kit chases Mabel into her basket under the stairs as I sink into the soft black cushions. The living room is all tones of grey. Splashes of bold colour spring from three similar framed posters promoting an annual music festival called Sonic on Sea. Gareth's a graphic designer.

'Coffee?' Kit asks. 'We've got a Nespresso, thanks to Gareth's ma.'

I decline, feeling jittery enough. Kit offers me a range of teas from herbal to builder's; Gareth suggests a glass of cold elderflower. I go with that. Kit's unzipped my suitcase and found some pink slouch socks. He pulls my Converse off my feet without undoing the laces and chucks them into the hall, then slips my socks onto my feet. It's one of those rainy summer days where you stay in wearing a hoody and catch up on crappy telly.

'I hope these are clean?' he asks, nodding at the socks, then at his fluffy white rug.

They are.

The downstairs of Kit and Gareth's house is always spotless. Even after a gathering, one of them is up at the crack of dawn to Dyson the spilt nibbles and take out empty bottles to the recycling. Smoking is permitted, but only on the decking in the back garden using an ashtray. The upstairs, however, is another story. They eat pizza in bed hungover on Sundays and only change their bed sheets every other month. Kit's promised my mum they're working on it.

Gareth hands me a tall glass filled with ice and elderflower.

'I'm so sorry about Jack, Chloe,' he says, although there's no need. He sent me some lovely texts when it happened. 'And I'm so sorry Thailand didn't work out for you.'

'I went to Vietnam, too,' I say.

'Oh, I love Vietnam.'

'I don't.'

'Bloody hell, Gareth,' Kit says. 'Kick her while she's down, won't you?'

Gareth blows me a kiss with both hands and then points upwards.

'I'm just gonna . . .' he says. And off he goes to the spare bedroom which is his office stroke studio stroke gym. Of course, it's Kit's too, but Kit doesn't work from home or work out at home. He works for the Liverpool tourist board and plays footy twice a week.

'How's the wedding coming along?' I ask, curling my feet beneath me.

Kit raises his eyebrows. 'Let's not talk about the wedding.'

'Why?'

''Cause we need to talk about you.'

His eyebrows return to their rightful place. They're such a perfect shape and he insists he doesn't pluck them. We share the exact same colouring except Kit doesn't bleach his hair like I do. He leaves it au naturel, mousey working so much better on him than it does on me, perhaps due to the way he styles it; neatly shaved around the back with a lovely quiff on top that he washes and blow-dries every day.

'Okay, well if you're not gonna talk, Chlo, I will.' Kit sits down cross-legged upon the white rug. 'I'm mortified I never came to see you—'

'No, Kit. Honest—'

'Sis. Please. You know I haven't got any annual leave left with the wedding and the honeymoon coming up, but I could've got the train down one weekend, stayed with you and made sure you were alright. Mum kept saying you were coming home and I shouldn't've listened, shouldn't've waited. I should've been there for you. And I'm dead sorry.'

'Honestly, I didn't want anyone coming to stay. No offence.'

'Highly offended.'

'Tough. I liked being on me own.'

'You liked it?' Kit asks, as if he's just choked on one of Mabel's dog biscuits.

I take a velvet cushion to my chest and hug it. 'No. It was awful.'

Kit leans back on his hands, sighs. 'I feel a thousand times more guilty now.'

'Don't feel guilty, hun. I'm the one who's gonna be making a show of meself at your wedding, aren't I?'

'Oh, 'cause your plus-one is . . .' and Kit pretends to slit his throat with his finger and sticks out his tongue, which I find very funny. Nobody else could ever make a joke like this, but Kit can. He always can.

'Got any chocolate?' I ask.

Kit grabs my hands, pulling me to standing.

'Don't tell Gareth,' he whispers, leading me into the kitchen by my index finger.

I sit at the table and Mabel joins us, getting herself all cosy by the washing machine. Kit takes down a large Jacob's cracker box from the tins cupboard and tells me to open it. Inside, it's full of broken chocolate, all sorts, from white to milk to dark.

'Easter eggs,' Kit says without moving his lips. 'Gareth thinks I took our eggs into work, you know, so we could kick start our wedding diet. But I lied. I bashed them all up and put them in here.'

'You do know marriage is based on trust?'

Kit wafts a hand in my face and pops a triangle of white chocolate into his mouth. Mabel jumps onto his knee and he kisses her and tickles her, whilst I dig in to the cracker box. Kit clears his throat, leans in and speaks with his mouth half full.

'Guess who's not coming the wedding?'

'I thought we weren't talking about the wedding.'

'Hush. Guess.'

'Erm. I give up.'

'You're no fun anymore.'

'Glad you noticed.' I bite into a long slab of dark chocolate. 'Come on, who?

'Gareth's dad.'

'Fuck.'

'Pulled out "officially" a few weeks ago. Work commitments, apparently.'

'What?!'

'Gareth was devastated, but he's kind of relieved now. Bastard.'

'God. I got the feeling they weren't best mates, but this.'

'I know, it's been quite the drama, sis.'

The bitter cocoa coats my back teeth and I lick it with my tongue. I had no idea about this situation. My mum hadn't mentioned it, I don't think. Kit's rubbing the back of his neck, something he does to distract himself from biting the skin around his thumb when he's anxious.

'Sorry, Kit. I must've missed this, you know, with Jack dying.'

'It was before then. Around the time you moved to London.'

'Oh,' I say, sensing the disappointment he's trying to mask. 'Ah, shit. Is this why you kept ringing me? I thought you were gonna try to persuade me not to move in with Jack.'

Kit puts the lid on the Jacob's cracker box and snatches it away from me.

'I'd never do that, sis. I've got me own life to worry about.'

I swallow, feel a burning in my cheeks. 'I honestly didn't have a clue.'

Kit rustles my already messy hair.

'No probs, sis. You were in your little Chloe bubble.'

'What's that supposed to mean?'

'Oh, come on. You've always been all or nothing when it comes to men.'

'Hardly. Jack was the first fella I'd ever moved in with. At my age!' I push my chair back a little. 'You saying Jack was just another fling?'

Kit slaps his hands over his eyes and shakes out his head.

'Jeez, Louise. This has all got a bit . . .' and he flashes his teeth, tensing the muscles in his neck, ever so Deirdre Barlow. 'And anyway, I thought we were (or were not) talking about me wedding.'

We giggle a little. Kit slides the Jacob's cracker box back towards us and flicks the lid off again. We're both keen to keep eating chocolate rather than bicker. I go for a large slab of what looks like a decapitated Lindt bunny, but Kit gets there first and my hand lands upon his.

'Snap!' I say.

Kit squeezes my hand and yanks me into him, giving me a giant hug. My throat tightens and I don't want to cry, not now, so I break away.

'I'm such a dickhead,' I say, stealing the broken bunny, 'I've always thought of meself as carefree when it came to fellas, relationships.'

'Remember the rotter who only ate Pot Noodles and smelt of soil?'

'It wasn't soil. It was weed.'

'Like *that* makes it okay.'

'You know, I thought I'd got me shit together in me

thirties, but God, I hated dating. So forced. All that anticipation, then disappointment, and oh, the inevitable drunken sex. I'm not doing it again. No way. I can't bear the thought of—'

I shut my eyes, shudder, the thought of Justin. What we did. Yeah, Kit's just taken the piss out of me for flying into flings, but in my heart, in my gut, I always knew when they were over. Some were over after the first snog: a tongue too hard, too slimy, too long. But I'd go back for more, drag it out, give that tongue the benefit of the doubt. I went out with this fella a couple of years ago who was brilliant. Kind of a real-life Tom Hardy, just taller and skinnier. He cooked a prawn curry to perfection, he loved books about the universe, he was a drummer, he went rock-climbing and he was fucking good in bed. But I couldn't laugh at his jokes. Not one. And I find most things pretty funny. Around the three-week mark, it was obvious we had no future. We called it a day about four months in. I can't call it a day with Jack. I just can't.

Kit's squinting, his arms folded, and he's sitting right back in his chair. 'I'm envisioning you still shacked up with Pot-Noodle-pothead . . . Ugh. Nah. Much prefer grieving girlfriend. It's an all-round better look for you.'

'Thanks, hun.' I put my feet up on another chair crossed at the ankles; I'm sugared out. 'Can I ask . . . Did you like Jack?'

'I only met him once, didn't I? That night you brought him here. It was boss.'

'When Gareth got his old karaoke machine out! Such a dark horse.'

'I told you then and I'll tell you now, sis: I loved Jack. Thought he was great.'

'There's a sort of sick part of me that wishes you'd hated him.'

'I can lie, if you want? I'm dead good at lying. Tara McNulty still thinks I'm straight.'

'You took her big V.'

'Eh? Don't you mean she took mine?' Kit shivers at the memory. 'Jack though.'

'Jack though.'

'I loved how I instantly felt like I knew him, five minutes after meeting him. He commanded a room, didn't he? But also made everyone in the room feel at ease. And you suited him. He wasn't your usual type and I was like, hallelujah!'

'Makes me wonder. I think a lot of people have that opinion of Jack – not to belittle what you just said, but he had that gift. Warmth, familiarity. Maybe what me and him shared wasn't so special, you know – maybe it was just that I felt special 'cause he was so capable of making me – or, people in general – feel that way. Maybe everyone felt special around him.'

'Maybe.'

'Guess I'll never know.'

Mabel starts yapping and Kit grabs some treats for her. She licks them from his palm. Gareth pops his head around the kitchen door, sweat dripping from his forehead.

'I thought you were working?' Kit asks.

'It's Saturday,' Gareth defends himself.

'Come here and gis a sweaty kiss.'

'I'm getting in the shower.'

'You came all the way downstairs to announce you're getting a shower?'

'Nope. I came *all the way* downstairs to see if you're okay.'

'I'm amazing.'

'Not you. Her.'

I'm nervous Gareth'll see the Jacob's cracker box, burn holes in its side with his gorgeous eyes. They're the sort of eyes that change colour depending on what he's wearing. Right now, they're green and mystical.

'I'm not great,' I admit.

'You're going to be, though. One day soon,' Gareth smiles.

'Have you had your teeth whitened?' I ask him.

'Thanks for noticing, Chloe. Did you hear that, Kit?'

'You got your teeth whitened?' Kit gasps. 'How much did that cost?'

Gareth runs away, his shower awaiting. Mabel gives a little bark and Kit lets her run up the stairs after him. He offers me another dip into the Jacob's cracker box, but I'm done. He sneaks a white chocolate piece out for himself and puts the box back into the tins cupboard.

'Look, sis. I know I told Gareth off for saying it earlier, but I'm really sorry the whole Thailand thing didn't work out for you.'

'Agh, well. It's brought me home, hasn't it?'

'*Erm!* A small affair called *my wedding*, I think you'll find, has brought you home.'

I give a little laugh, although Kit was expecting more. I can see he's desperate to get his sister back. I want that, too. I lean against the window, watch the rain dancing down. It's so inoffensive. It gets disliked for ruining a British summer's day, or, God forbid, a weekend. But it's not harming anybody. At least the grass will be greener tomorrow.

'Maybe I should move back . . .'

'I wanna say *yay*! I never wanted you to move to London.'

'I didn't just go to London to be with Jack, you know. He was the main reason, of course, but I knew it was the right

198

move 'cause I'd exhausted here. I love Liverpool, but I wasn't moving forward and it seemed everybody else was steaming ahead. I mean, I was still going to pubs I went to twenty years ago. And it was boss. But the people I liked and hung out with, well, they all started staying in, having kids and I tried to make new friends but it's hard to give yourself a fresh start in the same place.'

'And it didn't help that the school you were working in was fucking miles away!'

'Right! God, I don't miss that commute on the M62.'

'Builder's?' Kit asks. There are a few drops of elderflower left in my glass.

I nod and he jumps up to flick the kettle on.

'Should I come home?'

'Ah, I'm the wrong person to ask, sis. You know me answer to that.'

My heart swells and in this moment, I feel lucky. Loved. It's not the love I've lost or the love I crave, but it's still love. And I have it, in abundance.

'But,' Kit says, raising his hands as if I'm about to punch him, 'you can't stay here. I mean, you can stay here tonight, but after that, you've gotta go to Mum and Dad's.'

'That's me plan, don't worry.'

'I feel awful – I mean, you've had the whole tragic Jack thing and the whole stupid London thing and the whole sad holiday thing and now I'm turfing you out. But the blow-up bed's broke and Gareth hates anyone sleeping on the sofa, he's got this weird thing about other people's feet touching his stuff—'

'I know about the foot thing.'

'Hold on, we've got a tent. You're more than welcome to sleep in the garden?'

'Kit. Stop. I wanna go to Mum and Dad's. I wanna go home.'

'Okay. Wow. Weird. But okay.'

He hands me a boiling hot mug, teabag still in the water and enough milk for a bowl of cereal. My brother has many talents and tea-making ain't one of them. I'm reminded of nine-year-old Kit making us Roscoes a cuppa for the first time. It was Mother's Day. Bet my mum regrets biting her tongue, pretending it was the best tea she'd ever had. But I love this terrible cuppa. It's consistent, and that's just what I need.

I sip. 'Can we watch *Three Men and a Little Lady* now?'

'Thought you'd never ask.'

24

My dad insisted on picking me up from our Kit's this morning. I can't tell you how excited I am about the fact that it's Sunday, and I'm home; my mum will be cooking a roast.

'Alright, Tilly Mint,' he sings through the open window of his taxi.

'Not working today?' I ask, bending down to give him a kiss before hurling my suitcase into the boot. To avoid paying someone else double time, my dad always likes to work Sundays.

'I started early. You're me last pick-up of the day.'

'Well, I hope you're not charging me, Dad.'

'Never in a million years, my love. Your mum's booked a table at The Pheasant.'

'Who for?' I ask, pulling the seatbelt across me.

'Who'd you think? Us.'

No. I'm not going to The Pheasant. It's one of those pubs owned by a brewery chain, does a carvery, that sort of thing. Me and Beth used to work there at weekends during sixth form, and no. Not today. I'm going home, having a long bath and watching Netflix on my laptop in bed. My dad can grab me something from the chippy if my mum won't cook.

'Kit never mentioned anything about going for a meal,' I say.

'Kit's not coming,' my dad says.

'Neither am I.'

'You have to, my love. Your mum's invited your nan.'

We pull up outside the house I grew up in. There's a single balloon on the front door, a plain blue one, visible behind the glass porch. The *big* glass porch. Back in the eighties, lots of families on our street got a porch built. The houses are all identical three-bedroom semis, a little lawn in the front and a nice square garden in the back. We live on the corner, meaning once my dad's taxi business started doing alright, instead of moving to a slightly bigger house, my mum and dad just kept building on the one they already had. We've had the kitchen extended and a roof conversion, too, but it was the porch that came first. It resembles a conservatory, although don't get me started on the actual conservatory. It almost caused a divorce. Bird-poo-gate is still a touchy subject to this day.

'Welcome home!' my mum shouts from the porch.

Inside the hall, a piece of paper stuck to the banister with Sellotape has *Welcome Home Chloe* written in felt-tip pen. Mum probably found the pen in a cupboard in my old room. This confirms that the single blue balloon isn't left over from a party, but is, in fact, for me.

'I didn't wanna make a big fuss,' my mum says.

'You didn't need to make any fuss, Mum.'

'Now, go on. Up the stairs, get ready, love. We're leaving in an hour and they don't wait for latecomers in The Pheasant, you know. We'll lose the table if we don't get there on time,' my mum says. This is a fabrication conceived entirely in her own head.

'I'm not coming.'

'You bloody well are.'

'Kit's not.'

'Kit's busy.'

'No, he's not. He's eating pizza in bed with Gareth.'

'He's got a wedding to plan.'

'It's all planned.'

'Are you going to be this difficult every day, Chloe, or just today?'

My dad comes in and shuts the door. He does a stupid dance in the hall and sings about Tilly Mint coming home to the tune of the 'Three Lions' song. My nan appears from the living room, all five foot nothing of her, seething. She's had her hair set this morning, I can tell from the waft of lacquer.

'Less of the singing, Bernie,' she says. 'If anyone's gonna sing around here, it's Chloe.'

My nan thinks I'm a brilliant singer, although she hasn't heard me sing anything since I was eight. Every year, she tells me to go on *X Factor*. Every year, I have to come up with a fresh excuse as to why this will never, ever, ever happen. I get a flash of singing in Hoi An, Justin on the guitar. *No. Go away*.

'Chloe's not coming The Pheasant with us,' my mum says slowly, as if I'm a toddler and she's attempting reverse psychology.

'The Pheasant? What we going all the way there for?' my nan asks.

'Family meal,' my mum protests. 'It's Sunday.'

'Just go to Tesco and get a cooked chicken,' my nan suggests.

'We're going The Pheasant.'

'Well, Chloe's not.'

'She is.'

'I don't wanna go The Pheasant,' my nan states, hands on hips. 'Bernie, go and get a cooked chicken.'

'From Tesco?' my dad asks.

My mum unsticks my welcome home banner and starts fanning herself with it.

'I've told Carol we'd meet her there,' she says.

'Carol's not family,' I remind her.

'She's been a fabulous support since . . . you know.'

'No, Mum. Since what?'

'Since Jack died,' my mum whispers.

I roll my eyes, start heading up the stairs.

'I thought we weren't mentioning Jack?' my nan asks.

'Everyone! Ready to leave in an hour!' my mum shouts, then takes a breath, lowering her voice in fear of the neighbours hearing. 'I won't say it again.'

My dad tells her he's ready, but she tells him to change his jeans. My nan asks him to put the *Corrie* omnibus on for her and my mum tells him to do that first and change his jeans straight after. I drop down onto my old bed, head-first into an explosion of gingham. Any second now, my mum will barge in and tell me to get my shoes off the duvet, it's not a door mat. And I'll give her the finger as she walks away.

I feel like the old me. Well, the seventeen-year-old me anyway.

*

The Pheasant is on the outskirts of town, close to the motorway. If you get a seat by the right window, you get a

204

view of nice green fields with the odd horse, otherwise, it's a grey mass of traffic around Junction 7.

'I haven't been here since dropping you off for work all those years ago,' my dad says, turning into a free parking space.

'Such a liar, Bernie,' my mum accuses. 'We came here for our Val's fortieth.'

'Mum, I was the waitress that served you,' I say. 'And you never tipped me.'

'Bloody hell,' my mum ponders. 'Where does the time go?'

The brewery chain has changed since I worked here, no doubt more than once, but walking through the entrance doors really does drive home my mum's words. Where does the time go? Yeah, the decor's been updated, cool greys having replaced the nineties pink and turquoise, but it's the same. I feel as though I could charge straight through the swinging door into the kitchen, hang up my jacket and apologise for running late, hoping the chef on starters winks at me. I always fancied him, even though he had a kid with another waitress.

I message Beth.

I'm at The Pheasant!

We're taken to our reserved table, where there are fields in view, but Tesco is also clear in the distance. Carol's already waiting for us in another of her sequin tops. I can tell my mum disapproves, thinks it's too much for a Sunday afternoon – unlike my jeggings and t-shirt, which isn't enough. Carol breaks the news to us all that The Pheasant carvery no longer exists, but that the menu *is* extensive, with gluten-free options. My nan reminds us that we should've got a cooked chicken from Tesco.

'Oh, Chloe,' Carol says, coughing, clearing her throat. She holds out her arms and my mum pushes me into them.

'Come here. That's it, that's it. I'm so sorry about your fella, what an absolute tragedy. Taken too soon.'

'We're not mentioning Jack,' my nan says, shaking off her teal mac and handing it to my dad.

'Carol,' my mum says. 'I did tell you who Jack's mum is, didn't I?'

'Yeah, the one who went in the jungle last year?'

My dad corrects her. 'No. Not her. The other one.'

'Oh! I thought she was the one who went in the jungle.'

A waitress rescues my dad from hovering with my nan's coat, offering to hang it up, and he calls her a cracker. She brings over huge menus, two-foot tall and double sided. My nan says 'bloody hell' rather than thanks. A long conversation follows about what everybody's going to order. Carol could easily eat four, maybe five things off the menu; my mum's disgusted at the price of the Sunday roasts. My nan mentions chicken again, from Tesco, and my dad says he's going to the bar to order a pint. My mum tells him to sit down, he's driving, but I offer to drive home and my mum tells him to order her and Carol a double gin and tonic each.

'Is everybody getting a starter?' Carol asks.

'No,' my nan answers for us all.

As it turns out, we all order the fish and chips.

'You can't go wrong with fish and chips, can you, my love?' my dad tells the waitress.

Carol nips out for a ciggie.

'So are you gonna get one of those flats – sorry, *apartments* – in town again, like you had before you moved to London?' my dad asks.

'She can live with us as long as she likes, Bernie,' my mum snaps.

'Oh, I know that love. Goes without saying.'

'I mean, I've never known a thirty-six-year-old woman to still live at home, but hey-ho.'

'I have,' my nan says. 'Marjorie Hughes. You know, helps in the church. Never married until she was fifty-two. You've got plenty of time, Chloe.'

'Thanks, Nan.'

'You gonna contact the local schools?' my mum asks me, clearly itching for one of Carol's ciggies. 'For work?'

'Not sure yet.'

'Bernie. Speak to her.'

My dad shifts in his seat. 'Listen here, Tilly Mint. Your mum's only trying to help.'

I know what would've helped. A home-cooked roast; proper roasties, cauliflower cheese, stuffing, the lot. Even frozen Yorkshires. I could've eaten it in my pyjamas, in silence. My body aches for my bed – *my* bed – the one where I can hide and be stroppy and only nip downstairs for peanut butter on toast. Maybe even get the peanut butter on toast made for me and brought up on a tray with a glass of fresh orange and a KitKat.

'I might quit teaching,' I throw out there.

'WHY?' my mum shouts, then remembers herself and hisses. '*Why?*'

'I don't know,' I say. Because I don't.

Part of me wants as little responsibility as possible – my first step to feeling free from the hell I'm in. I'd mentioned this last night to our Kit and Gareth. At first, they both told me I was going through a process and I told them to go fuck themselves. I asked Kit what he'd do if Gareth died and he said he'd kill himself. Obviously this answer wasn't very helpful, but it shut them up; and they're now both supporting my decisions. Whatever they may be.

'You should go on that *X Factor*,' my nan suggests.

Carol returns and the food arrives. We're all overwhelmed by the size of the battered fish on each plate and my nan says she'll never eat all that, she could've done with half. I wish I hadn't offered to drive; the gin and tonics look so appealing right now, in ice-cold goldfish bowls on glass sticks. But my phone lights up and Beth has replied.

The Pheasant?! What the hell you doin there? xxx

Mum forced me.

Ah. xxx

My mum tells me to put my phone away and my dad tells her to leave me alone. I'm really enjoying the fish and chips, actually, and squeeze an extra dollop of tartare sauce onto my plate. My dad's just realised he knows the fella on the next table. They used to work on the taxis years ago, before my dad got his own business. We all say hello to him and his family, ooh and ahh at his grandson in the highchair making a right mess of a bowl of chips. For some reason, my mum thinks she needs to explain the state of me and tells this family I'm usually more chirpy, more well-dressed, but I'm grieving my boyfriend. They're extremely sympathetic and say God bless. I know this pleases my mum. A lot.

'I don't think I look *that* bad, Mum,' I say. 'If anything, I'm just hungover.'

'Oh, Chloe, don't be so childish.'

'It's the truth. And you can blame our Kit for that.'

'Where is your Kit?' Carol asks.

'Eating pizza in bed with Gareth,' my nan tells her.

I excuse myself to the loo, but walk past it and out into the beer garden. The tyre swing is still in the play area, although the springy safe floor is a recent addition. I sit down, grateful to be alone, not a single kid in sight. The motorway can't be seen from here, but I can hear the constant hum of cars not too far away. I swing, gently.

'I came here to forget about you,' I whisper. 'But even the people who never met you can't stop bringing up your bloody name.'

I stretch my legs forward and back, swinging higher.

'If you were here, this'd be more fun. Actually, it would *be* fun.'

If Jack was alive, my mum would never have brought him here. She'd be showing off, insisting we ate out in town with a view of the Liver Birds or right on the waterfront. She wouldn't be quizzing me about my future because she'd see it so clearly, like a well-constructed PowerPoint presentation. Jack would do most of the talking, which would please my dad. He's such a good listener, my dad; loves an anecdote, a childhood memory. Jack's hand would be on my back as he'd confidently spill the beans on his public-school life, his parents, his gap year. My mum would gloat at how posh all that sounded. He'd give excellent eye contact, too: engage directly with my mum, my dad and my nan, never forgetting about me either. My nan would be a bit wary of him, but that's okay. I'd be concerned if she wasn't wary about him . . .

Wait.

Jack never put his hand on my back; that wasn't one of his things. I don't think.

I let my toes touch the ground, do a little pitter-patter to bring the swing to a stop.

Oh God.

I can't remember.

Would Jack have told those stories? Would he be the life and soul around his girlfriend's family? Honestly, I don't know. Best qualities don't always shine around parents, no matter how old you are. I'm a brilliant example of that, turning into a people-pleasing mush around Patricia Carmichael and into a hormonal teenager around my own.

'Your brother, Freddie . . .' I think.

I met him with Jack at a pub on The Strand. Freddie didn't stay long, he had other plans. Jack was questioning him; who was he meeting, where was he going, did he need to lend any money. I stood there with a glass of house white and ate the entire packet of Scampi Fries that Freddie had opened out onto the bar for us to share. There was no three-way conversation. I'd been disappointed that my introduction wasn't more specific than, 'This is Chloe,' but Jack was anxious. He brushed it off once Freddie left, saying, 'Just like to look out for him.'

Was Jack anxious around his whole family? Or just his little brother?

How well did I really know my boyfriend? It's only been – what – seven weeks, and I'm starting to forget. And yet, that car park, right there, reminds me of taxis picking me and Beth up after a Friday night shift, taking us straight into town. We'd get changed in The Pheasant's loos, slap on metallic eyeshadow and wear anything with a Lipsy label, leaving our uniforms behind in the wholesale condiments cupboard. Crystal-clear memories. I can almost smell the original Jean Paul Gaultier that Beth would drown us in.

'My shoulder!' I say.

And I close my eyes, imagine Jack's fingers stroking my shoulder, lightly. That's what he did. That's what he always did. When we watched the telly. In the pub. During pillow talk.

And I'm talking to myself again, thinking of him, imagining him . . .

STOP.

My sanity is saved by a dad approaching the play area, one little girl holding his hand and a smaller one on his shoulders. I better clear away before I look like the weirdo who hangs around swings. I'm far too old to act the moody adolescent, although my mum'd probably disagree.

When I rejoin my family, they're in the depths of desserts.

'I can't say no to a sticky toffee pudding,' my dad says, tucking in.

'This tiramisu tastes nothing like tiramisu,' my nan says.

The family on the next table have gone, mashed food embossed on the carpet beneath where they'd sat, a dollop of chocolate ice cream melting on a place mat. I'm sure they only had one child with them. Carol and my mum have moved on to cocktails. I had no idea The Pheasant served cocktails, but hey, stranger things have happened.

'Where've you been?' my mum demands.

'Sue . . .' my dad tries, but she shoots him a look.

'I hope you didn't sneak off to pay the bill,' my nan says. 'I'm getting this.'

My mum's hand darts across the table. 'No, me and Bernie are getting this.'

'No, Sue. It's my treat.'

'But you don't even like the tiramisu!'

'Doesn't mean I'm incapable of paying.'

'Mother, put your purse away now.'

And so they go on, arguing. A standard occurrence at these occasions.

Although it's familiar, it belongs to a Chloe Roscoe who I can't be any more. It's when I was seven, when I was thirteen, when I was twenty-two, it was just over a year ago when we came to a similar restaurant (one with a carvery still in

211

operation) for what would've been my nan's sixtieth wedding anniversary with my grandad. I want to get involved, tell my mum and my nan to shut up, have a sneaky laugh with my dad. I want them to get a move on so I can go and meet my friends . . . or phone the boy from school I fancy . . . or hit the pub . . . or just get back to my own place and watch the telly with that massive Dairy Milk sat in my fridge. But I'm changed. I don't want to be. But I am.

Something stronger than a lime and soda in my hand would be much appreciated right now. I check my phone mindlessly, something to do. There's a notification; a message request.

It's from Justin.

No. No . . . I don't want to remember. I want to peel my skin off.

My dad does a little drum roll on the table with his hands. 'Who wants another bevvie?'

'In The Pheasant?' my nan asks, as if 'pheasant' is a swear word.

'Can we just go home?' I plead.

Problem is, I don't even know where home is any more.

25

Beth's up north this weekend and it's coincided with something I believe she will be able to help me with. Other than Jack, I can think of no better person. In fact, she'll be better.

It's to do with the small matter of learning how to ski.

I know, I know, if there was one decent thing to come out of Jack's death, it was my lucky escape from attending the lesson he'd booked as a surprise. Let's face it; it was more of a bloody shock. I'd have been more comfortable with a bungee jump. So there's no rhyme or reason as to why I'm going to the lesson he booked, other than because, well, Jack booked it. It feels right to go.

Or, more specifically, it feels wrong *not* to go.

You see, earlier in the week, I went to Matalan with my mum. She was tricking me into buying some new clothes, since I'd shown up in Liverpool with a wardrobe suitable for trekking around Southeast Asia. I've had to forfeit my personal style just to stop her going on.

'I get in from work, Chloe, and you're watching that Jessica Sarah Parker again,' she'd said, through tight lips like an amateur ventriloquist, flicking through the rails of multicoloured plain t-shirts.

'Sarah Jess—'

'And you're never dressed. It's gone five o'clock. And you're never, ever dressed.'

'So stop barging into me room.'

'You should stick to plain old-fashioned *sleeping* in your room. Oh! And that stuff you were doing in the garden. Don't. Save that for your room, too.'

'You mean yoga?' I'd motivated myself twice to do a twenty-minute YouTube workout.

'It looks a bit voodoo-witchcraft. Imagine what next door'll be making of that. Now, this is lovely. It'll show off your legs. You've always had fabulous legs.'

She hands me a little black dress with long lace sleeves.

'I can't imagine one place I'd ever go to and wear this,' I'd told her.

'You're impossible, love.'

And thus went my new norm.

So at the Matalan checkout, when I received an email reminding me of my forthcoming ski lesson, my reaction was not how I'd predicted. I suddenly had something to do this Saturday that didn't involve my mum and Carol, or our Kit's wedding, or watching my old DVDs braless. It was something planned by Jack, for me. Going keeps us alive.

'This is only going to work if you can ski,' Jack had said to me on our third date. February.

'As in, this-this?' I'd asked, referring to him and me with a pointed finger.

'Skiing's my favourite thing in all the world.'

We'd met in the middle, the Hilton in Nottingham, and we were in the pool. Outside was grey and rainy, and nobody else was in the pool except us, but we spoke low, the ambience so clinical that any echo felt like somebody might be spying on us.

'I can do basic tap dancing or a decent downward dog, but skiing? Me? Never.'

'You don't know until you try.'

'I'm thirty-six, Jack. I do know.'

'My mum learnt when she was forty.'

'Your mum's a national television star. She has spectacular blood.'

'So do you.'

'Ha. Don't flatter me onto the piste.'

'See? You already know the jargon.'

When Jack was spending his half terms in the Alps and eating fondue, I was in Pontins begging my mum for a Slush Puppy. Learning to ski felt daunting, and catapulted me into a world I wasn't comfortable with. What if I didn't take to skiing? I'd have to sit out, like the kid who was crap at sports, while Jack and his pals raced down mountains all day. What would I celebrate during the après-ski? Beth told me that's the best part, because you've survived another day on the slopes; you're drinking from sheer relief.

'I go every year,' Jack had said, opening his legs under the water and catching me between them like a shark's bite. We'd circled around, stuck to each other, kissed.

'I'm not stopping you,' I'd said. I also knew he'd been recently, meaning I had a whole year to ignore it. Maybe he'd back down, or decide against skiing next year. Maybe he'd break his leg before going. Maybe – quite possibly – we wouldn't even be together this time next year. This was only our third date.

But Jack had never backed down.

His persistence had reminded me of being ten and wanting to go to a Spice Girls concert. When I'd got Jack the canvas print of the man in the shopping trolley as a moving-in present, Jack had got me a ski lesson. An indoor slope, of course, just outside Liverpool. He'd picked a date close to our Kit's wedding so we could escape to the slopes for a day if (and when) family politics became too intense. But honestly, even with the original email confirmation stuck to the fridge, I'd never had any intention of actually going through with it. Until now.

Beth, however, has other ideas about this weekend.

'I'm not going *there*,' she says down the phone.

I'm sat hunched on the bottom stair chatting on my mum and dad's landline. We've had this thing, ever since we stopped living with our parents in our early twenties, that whenever we both happened to be back home, we would always call each other on the landline, for old times' sake.

'I'm at me niece's birthday party in the morning,' she goes on, 'and I'm taking me grandad to the botanical gardens on Sunday. Babes, don't make me spend a Saturday wearing the bowling alley equivalent of ski gear when I've brought Diane Von Furstenberg with me.'

'But we can get a hot chocolate with whipped cream and little marshmallows.'

I'm hit by that image of Florrie on Facebook.

Bet that was taken in a fancy Alpine chalet. Was Jack with her? Did he take the photo?

Stop!

'Or hot wine?' I suggest. 'What do they call it; vin chaud?'

'It's not Christmas. It's August, for fuck's sake.'

'We can go to Nando's afterwards.'

'Have you forgotten who the *fuck* I am?'

216

She wants to go to some posh place in town and have a one-to-one dinner with me where I'll be forced to eat tiny crumbs of food that cost a bomb. She'll order wine that pairs with the dishes perfectly, too. But I don't want a one-to-one with her. I don't need a therapy session or to be asked how I'm feeling about Jack. I still haven't caught up with her since the whole Thailand and Vietnam fiasco and it's not something I want to indulge in now. You see, Beth will one hundred per cent want to indulge. I'd rather not think about how wrong it went – I want to focus on what can go right. If I can get on a pair of skis, it would make Jack so proud. Who knows, maybe I'll want to book a second lesson. Or a holiday.

'Beth?' I ask. 'Please. I need this.'

She unleashes a long, deep-throated sigh. 'Fine.'

Neither of us has a car though. Beth came up to Liverpool on the train and I sold mine when I moved in with Jack – there's nowhere to park it at the flat and I don't need a car in London anyway.

'We'll Uber,' Beth says when she arrives at my mum and dad's house.

'Lalalalala!' my dad sings, his fingers in his ears.

I lean close to her and mumble, 'Don't mention the U word. Touchy subject.'

My dad's about to start a shift, otherwise he'd take us willingly. My mum offers to give us a lift instead, which is a small miracle. She can't stand driving; even gets a lift to work from Carol.

'Heard you went to Budapest last weekend?' my mum quizzes Beth. She barely waits for the answers. 'He's lovely, your Fergus. Minted, too, eh?' and she winks in her rear-view mirror to Beth, sat in the back oozing expensive scent. 'Now, you're not gonna be luring our Chloe back to London, are you, love?'

'Wouldn't dream of it, Sue,' Beth says. 'Loving your hair colour, by the way.'

'Oh, I did it meself this morning. It's called "Poppy Rust". Keeps me young. And you look stunning, Beth. Have you lost weight?'

Beth beams. 'Not by choice.'

'Lucky you,' my mum scoffs, and gives me a once-over. I'm not wearing any of my new Matalan clothes. I probably look like an ageing backpacker. 'I wish you'd give our Chloe some tips – you know, with our Kit's wedding coming up.'

I happen to be the trimmest I've been for a long time, thanks to the strange eating habits – and at times, non-eating habits – I've established since Jack died; but yeah, she has a point. I'm not toned, and I definitely look a mess next to Beth. I always have.

'Is Fergus at your mum's then?' my mum continues. 'Lurking in the shadows as usual?'

'Golf, somewhere in Surrey,' Beth says, flicking her warm caramel locks behind her shoulder. 'Middle-aged before his time, Sue.'

'It was a lovely wedding you had, Beth. Love a fella in a kilt.'

I'm bored of this. If my dad was driving we'd be listening to his CDs – The Who and Aerosmith – or he'd talk about football, something I've lost touch with over the years. He used to take me to home games when I was little, and him and our Kit still go together. The new season kicks off this weekend. Still, I appreciate the lift. We're dropped off like teens going to the local disco, my mum waving and watching us go. She's not picking us up, though. Beth has insisted we go into town later; she's booked a restaurant.

'There's children everywhere,' I say, my first impression of the indoor ski slope.

'Oh, babes,' Beth says, 'it's Saturday afternoon. What did you expect?'

I don't reply. And I definitely don't mention the funky smell in the air. A blend of bodies – particularly feet – and socks, and wet rubber floor mats. It's Beth though. She can read my mind.

'Do you honestly think I'd be able to ski if I'd started off somewhere like this?'

'It's cool,' I lie. Try. 'Honestly, this is gonna be great. And hey, you get to piss yourself laughing at me falling on me arse, don't you? Come on, when was the last time we did an actual activity together?'

'We've never done an "activity" together. We aren't "activity" people.'

'We've been to the pictures.'

'Babes That's the least active activity you can do. It's the antithesis of activity.'

At the kiosk for the ski-school, I present the email on my phone and the young lad in uniform with a man-bun asks my age.

'You joking?' I ask, not understanding. And – for fuck's sake – blushing.

'You said it's a lesson for you, yeah?'

I nod and look to Beth, who sports her most impatient frown.

The young lad swallows; scratches his head. 'It's valid for age twelve to sixteen years,' he says.

219

'She's sixteen,' Beth says, but the lad laughs. 'We both are.' He stops laughing. She's giving him that glare, the one that makes anybody do anything she bloody well wants. It's a rare talent that I've tried – and failed – to mimic over the years.

I'm handed a plastic ticket and told to gear up.

'Your instructor'll meet you by that vending machine in fifteen minutes.'

'Perfect,' Beth smiles, and it's the young lad's turn to blush now.

'Can I just ask,' I interrupt, 'it's a private lesson, yeah?'

'Erm, no. There's eight of you altogether,' I'm told, to which he adds, 'all between the ages of twelve and sixteen.'

I turn around to see kids strap their feet into huge boots, giving their parents shitloads of stuff to hold in the process. Booking the wrong lesson must have been a simple mistake, but this is so far from anything I could ever imagine myself doing with Jack. What was he thinking?

'Listen babes,' Beth says, 'forget the lesson—'

'No! I'm here and this is what Jack wanted. Just because you don't wanna—'

'Eh! Calm the fuck down. I was gonna say – forget the lesson and ski with me. I'll teach you.'

'You will? You can do that?'

'I'm a queen on the slopes, babes. I can do anything.'

Good God, to have her confidence.

Beth leads the way to get us kitted out. She sorts me with boots and skis, telling another young lad (also with a man-bun) behind the counter my sizes and experience. She lies and says I'm not a beginner. I nudge her. She says, 'Trust me.'

I've never put my foot into a ski boot before and oh, fuck me, it's weird. It's like one of those dreams where your limbs are dead weights, except the weight is cemented to my feet. Plus, when I try to walk, I look like I've shat myself. We change into the salopettes and jackets, put on our gloves. Somehow – *somehow* – Beth looks good, rocking the whole Alpine-meets-Chav look that can only be achieved with hired skiwear.

'How did Jack ever think this would be a good idea?' I say, as the escalators take us up to the slope. I'm panicking about stepping off the moving stairs in these boots.

'He's clearly only ever been skiing in the mountains,' Beth shrugs.

'God, there's so much stuff to carry,' I say. 'And it's freezing.'

'I can already see how much of a hoot you and Jack would've had, babes.'

Beth places her skis down onto the snow and I copy, mine flopping and flipping over. She shows me how to step into each ski, tells me to listen for a simple 'click, click,' and then to dig my poles into the snow so I don't lose my balance. I do exactly what she says, and immediately lose my balance anyway and fall awkwardly onto my side, one foot still attached to a ski, one not. Without fuss, Beth offers her hand to help me up; but I can't. I can't get up. I'm bulked out with an evil contraption around my ankles and quite frankly, this is fucking impossible.

'Beginner's luck, eh?' I attempt a joke.

She holds me steady as I grab her forearms to click, click into my skis. She hands me my poles and we're ready. I'm about to do this. I'm going to ski. I trail behind Beth who bends her knees, digs her poles in and gently propels herself forwards across the flat snow towards the chairlift. She's like a graceful swan. Dance music pumps across the dauntingly steep slope (which Beth has already remarked is 'tiny') and

221

the dull noise from the lift mechanisms fills me with dread. How am I going to sit down with skis on? And how the fuck am I supposed to get off when we reach the top?

'Just bend your knees, hold your centre, clench your buttocks and follow me,' Beth says. 'I'll go proper slow. Okay?'

I nod, but all my focus is on sitting down. Beth has both her poles in one hand, and guides me with the other as we shuffle along. Our skis and boots bear an uncanny resemblance to huge clown shoes. As we get into position on the line for the chair lift to sweep us up, I'm terrified. A hollow shakiness ripples through my body and I shut my eyes tight, willing myself to disappear. Then *whoosh!* We're up! I'm sitting, my skis and feet off the ground. Beth pulls the metal safety bar over us. I whoop, do a little dance to the beat and . . . drop one of my poles.

'Shit!'

Any elation is short-lived. And the weight in my ankles, hanging down with these boots and skis attached, I mean. Fuck. Me. How is Beth so calm? How?

'Don't panic, babes. To be honest, you don't need your poles when you're learning.'

'But I liked the poles!' I moan. 'They made me feel safe!'

'Look over there,' she points to a line of kids gliding at a nice pace down the slope in single formation, following the zigzag trails of the instructor. 'None of those beginners have poles. It's all in the knees. Imagine you've got little headlights on your knees – keep them facing the direction you're going in.'

'Right.'

'And keep your legs wide, point your toes in, make an upside-down V,' she holds her legs up and demonstrates. I give it a go, but she says, 'No, never cross your skis.'

Seriously, and people pay the earth to do this as a *holiday*?

The lift ascends slowly, giving me time to rehearse my 'V', think about my knees. Kids as young as four or five whizz past down the slope. If they can do this, so can I. Surely.

'In a real resort,' Beth says, 'the lifts are magical. The view; the clean air.'

'I can only imagine.'

'No need to be a sarky bitch, Chlo.'

'No need to rub it in.'

The chairlift exit is creeping up and I watch the family in front raise the safety bar and ski off, around the lift, stopping at the top of the slope. They make it look so bloody easy. A lot of people seem to wait at the top, some chatting or fixing their gloves, some psyching themselves up for the down. There are a lot of people shuffling around on snowboards.

'Okay,' Beth says, raising the safety bar, 'after three. One, two . . .'

'THREE!' I blurt, exerting all my energy into standing but keeping my knees bent, and I'm doing it, I'm off! I'm going forward, fast – so fast, too fast, still going, going, going, how the *fuck* do I stop—

I crash into a gang of teenagers.

I'm face down in the snow and have no desire to turn face up. Ever.

I hear a cacophony of 'Fucking watch it!' and 'No worries!' – both ends of the skiing spectrum unleashing their feelings. Beth's on her knees, whispering into my ear.

'Let's go and have a cocktail. Me cousin can get us on the guest list for a new member's bar off Castle Street—'

'Beth. No. I need to do this!'

'But you're miserable.'

'You reckon?'

'Yeah! This isn't you, Chloe. You weren't even the teeniest bit excited to try. You're just doing it for the sake of it and torturing yourself. Look, would Jack really want to put you through this all because *he* likes it?'

'Loves it. He loves it, pal. I mean, *loved* it.'

I haul myself up onto all fours and use Beth once again as a crutch to get into my skis.

'Jack would've understood if you didn't wanna ski.'

'Don't talk to me about Jack, Beth. Don't you ever talk to me about Jack.'

'Whoa, babes—'

'No, you don't know him. You didn't know him. *Fuck.*'

But did I? Did I know him? I know he never backed down about skiing – it was the highlight of his year, and when possible, he'd even go twice. Was this an integral part of him that I never knew, clearly never showed him a blind bit of interest in, and now, I'll never know? Had I only seen Jack's basic colours? Had the entire fucking rainbow still been out there to be discovered?

Perhaps by people who weren't like me. People more like him.

'I know you needed to get away,' Beth says, gently, still holding her arm out for me like I'm an invalid, 'but maybe going off to Thailand wasn't the brightest idea, so coming home's always good to touch base, figure out your next step—'

'Oh, what's with all the self-help clichés, Beth?'

'What's with acting like a fucking child?'

'I'm sorry. Can we just do this?'

'Fine.' Beth takes my remaining pole from me and leans forward to suss out the slope, her possible route down. 'I'll go slow. I'm not going straight down, that's not how you ski. Side to side – see? Look at those girls there, see how they're going towards one side, then almost *up* the mountain and then they slowly turn with their legs in that upside-down V? Yeah?'

'Simple. Let's do it.'

'And remember, babes, keep your legs wide. The wider they go, the slower you'll go.'

I salute, and almost fall flat on my arse.

'Steady,' Beth says, and off she goes into the snow, like Elsa in *Frozen*.

And I follow. I really do. She's true to her word, going slow and side to side. I dig deep, keep my toes pointed inwards, my legs wide. It aches; a tiring pain. I'm using muscles my body wasn't aware it had. And now, shit. It's time to turn. Beth makes a grand half circle around from left to right. She makes it look like a dance. All I have to do is copy; tread on her exact tracks.

My skis cross at the toes.

I see it happening, powerless to stop. Once they're crossed, I'm stuck. My arms start flailing around – for help; for balance; fuck knows – and I go flying down the slope at a speed I feel like I've only experienced inside a moving vehicle. I hit the floor and my skis are both gone, lost somewhere further up. I come to a bumbling, messy stop in the middle of the piste.

I sit on the slope and hang my head. Beth has skied to my side, still poised.

'I'm so useless,' I cry. 'At everything.'

'No, you're not, Chlo. You're a teacher, for fuck's sake.'

'No, I'm a failed actress who ended up in a call centre, and a teacher by absolute default.'

'Most actresses are failed ones.'

'Well, I go further,' and I attempt to count out on my

fingers, hindered by the giant gloves. 'I've failed in relationships, failed at moving away, failed at everything I've ever tried to do since I left school. I've totally failed at being an adult.' I manage to get onto my feet without Beth's help this time, which is marginally easier without skis attached to my feet.

'Come on, babes. You can't just stand in the middle of a slope without skis. It's a hazard.'

'Oh, and with skis it isn't?'

'Your attitude stinks. I wouldn't mind, but I'm doing you a favour, remember?'

'It was supposed to be fun!'

'Chlo. We need to move. You're gonna have to bum shuffle down.'

'You're fucking kidding, right?'

'No. It's the only way down, for you.'

So I go. Like a baby who's not worked out how to crawl, I shuffle. On my arse.

'Wanna try again?' Beth has the nerve to ask once I reach the bottom. My face says it all. 'Okay, that was me trying to make you laugh, babes.'

'You don't understand, pal,' I say, as Beth guides me away from a line of kids queuing for the chairlift. 'I mean, look at you. You're a success story. You move in elite circles, feel at home as a VIP.'

'You've got no clue.'

'No, I think I've got the right clue, actually.'

'That stuff means nothing and you know it. Give yourself more credit.'

'Nothing? Beth, you've got a husband and a home.'

'Look. You're not the only thirty-six-year-old who's single and childless, you know.'

226

I wish she'd stop shouting at me. We're sat right beside the speakers, taking off those God-awful boots.

'What do you want me to do, Beth? Get on Tinder? Swipe for love? To use one of your clichés, get back on the saddle?'

She scoops up her boots and wriggles her toes to let them breathe.

'I want you to listen,' she says.

'All I do is listen!'

She shakes her head slowly. 'No you don't, babes,' and looping her boots and poles onto her skis, she walks away from me. I know, from her tone of voice, that we won't be having dinner together this evening. I want to stop her, beg her to stay. We haven't had a fight since we were really young and somehow it matters more now that we're old. I feel like running to the loo, locking the door and crying, but I also want her to leave so I can try to make sense of why I'm here. Immersing myself in Jack's plans makes me feel closer to him, like we're still together. And I wish Beth could understand.

Except I don't feel closer to Jack today.

If anything, I feel further away from him than I ever thought could be possible.

26

It's arrived. The big day has finally arrived.

Our Kit stayed at home last night. We watched *My Best Friend's Wedding* and drank Prosecco with strawberries. My dad nipped out to get a Chinese takeaway for the four of us: a full-on banquet with prawn crackers and spare ribs, the lot. My mum kept spoiling the film talking on her phone. Everybody was calling her; my nan, Carol, Gareth's mum. They all kept saying the same thing: it's tomorrow, can you believe it's tomorrow, it's really tomorrow . . . I didn't complain, though. She's been easy on me since I found myself a plus-one for the wedding.

We've all woken up this morning with dry mouths from the immense quantities of MSG. We start getting ready, the Spice Girls on full blast, feeling pumped. Even my nan shows up with a smile on her face and a spring in her step.

'Ready?' Kit calls from upstairs. 'I'm coming down!'

In the hallway, my dad puts his arms around me and my mum, and my mum grabs my nan's hand. The image of Kit standing at the top of the stairs, all Paul Smith-ed and quiffed, is one to cherish. He's cheeky, he's calm, he's fucking beautiful. There's not a dry eye in the house.

'The car's here, son,' my dad says.

As much as it pains my dad, our Kit won the battle and a traditional wedding car pulls up to take us to the manor house on the Wirral where the wedding is taking place. My dad had originally wanted to pimp his taxis, but even my mum had said no. Her son's wedding isn't a business opportunity. A few neighbours stand outside their porches and wave us off. Our Kit winds down the window and gives his best Meghan Markle. My mum's never looked happier.

'You still haven't said who your plus-one is, love,' she says.

'He's just a friend,' I say, for perhaps the fifth time.

My mum nudges my nan and winks. 'That's what they all say!'

Passing a long, manicured garden, we arrive on a gravel driveway. Guests are dotted around the entrance of the manor house, milling about near the wooden double doors. I help my nan out and we leave our Kit in the car. He's planned to wait for Gareth so they can share a private moment before walking each other down the aisle.

'We're practically in Wales,' my nan says.

And she's right. There's a rural feel to the peninsula; the Welsh hills are only across the River Dee. My dress is rather country-style, too. Floaty, off the shoulder, white, and a faux daisy chain in my curled hair. I'm our Kit's best woman, rather than a groomsmaid, but he's relieved me of doing a speech later, bless him. He ordered a small bunch of fresh daisies for me to hold, knowing how much I like – well, need – something in my hands these days, and he's simply delighted I'm here with a smile on my face.

And I am. Smiling.

For our Kit.

There's nobody I want to be happier than my little brother. He's the best person I've ever had the privilege to know, and he's in love. He's loved. I might be sad inside, but it's easy to smile today.

I usher the guests having a quick ciggie inside. My mum and my nan link arms and my dad leads them to the front row. Yesterday, I spent the day here with Kit and Gareth, decorating the grand hallway where the ceremony is taking place. Ivy entwines the banisters and creates a beautiful archway at the bottom of the stairs. It was a team effort, and we only took a break when the pizzas arrived. We laid out eighty chairs, forty on each side. Now, they're almost full.

'Alright Chloe,' a man says, touching my shoulder. I don't recognise him. 'You haven't changed a bit. Must be twenty years since I last saw you.'

'I was a redhead twenty years ago,' I say with a smile and a forced singsong in my voice.

'Blondes have more fun, eh?'

I laugh, wishing I was sixteen again and experimenting with hair colour.

I wave at a few faces I do recognise, peering through a window to my past. Our Kit's school mates who I bossed around as a kid and avoided as a teenager. His uni pals I went out drinking with when I visited him during his three years in Manchester. Relatives we saw lots when me and our Kit were little, and never now we're grown up. I walk down the aisle and take a seat in the front row beside my mum and dad. I keep waving, say a few hellos. I don't want anybody's pity, anybody feeling sorry for the poor sister whose boyfriend died. Unless they don't know. Which is worse – it arouses that dark, sunken feeling that Jack never existed.

230

Jack.

My recent mission to connect with him had failed. I knew we didn't have everything in common. I mean, who does? It's where our banter lay. It made us find adorable silliness in each other. Or was that the picture I'd painted, perhaps? In what Kit had called my 'little Chloe bubble'?

I hear my name. It's our Kit's old flatmate from uni and bless her, she's so pregnant.

'Looking fabulous, Tasha!' I say. 'How long?'

'Twins,' Tasha says. 'Still got a long way to go!'

I spot Beth and Fergus. Beth's chattering away to somebody I don't know; Fergus is reading the order of service. We've been in touch since the skiing incident, but only pleasantries about today – you know, the usual logistics. I'm hoping our fight will pass by unnoticed and we'll be on the dance floor together later.

'Chloe! Yay!' a voice chirps from the seat reserved beside mine.

It's my lovely plus-one. I go straight in for a hearty hug. 'Hiya, Si.'

We tell each other how fabulous the other looks and I sit down, leaning back into my seat so I can introduce him to my family. He stretches across me to shake hands with my dad, then my mum, my nan.

'He's just a friend,' my nan confirms.

Before my mum can comment, we're all instructed to stand for the service. Des'ree starts singing through the speakers.

*

I'm cornered in between the starter and the main. In the loo.

'Of all the men you could've brought, why a gay one?' my

231

mum asks, ironically given we're at a gay wedding. There's only two cubicles, both of which we've emerged from. She's still wearing her jade-green bolero but her matching fascinator is off, unlikely to be fixed back on. I run the tap, wash my hands.

'Oh, Mum. You make it sound like I've got a catalogue of men to pick from.'

'But, why, Chlo? Why a gay one?'

'He's not gay.'

She pulls a face as if to say *don't mess with me*, like she's the godmother of all gays.

'Mum, it's really none of our business what he is, is it?'

'Well, he's having a lovely time with our Kit's friend Malcolm.'

'Good for Si. I'm glad.'

She's either getting a headache or feigning one.

'But why?' she moans again.

'Fine. You want the nice reason? Or the honest reason?'

I dig into the secret pocket of my dress and offer her my lipstick. She declines and opens her beaded clutch bag to fish out her own.

'The nice reason,' I say, 'is that Si's a lovely person. I didn't think there'd be anything wrong with having a guy who just oozes loveliness by me side on a day like today. A day which might be difficult for me.'

I hate myself for saying that last part. I didn't intend for it to sound like that. Not surprisingly, my mum rolls her eyes and puckers up to apply another coat.

The door bursts open and Tasha (having twins) enters. Me and my mum both sing, 'Hiya,' and Tasha smiles – with her mouth, not her eyes – and waddles into a cubicle. A fed-up sigh is audible from behind the door. I bet it's a drag being pregnant at a wedding.

'It's great to see Beth still so loved-up with Fergus after all these years, isn't it?' my mum says, keeping me from running off. 'She got lucky with him, didn't she, love?'

I nod, but my mum looks at me through the mirrors and mouths something at me. I have no idea what she's saying until she starts to move her hand like a puppet and I realise she wants me to talk. Keeping up appearances, as ever.

'Yeah, Beth's one lucky gal,' I say, to humour her.

Tasha emerges, says something about the more people drink, the more hands touch her bump, although I get the feeling she's talking to herself in the mirror, not wanting to open up a conversation. My mum tells her she looks stunning and Tasha leaves with a slightly better smile than the one she came in with. I'm on the spot once again.

'What's the honest reason?' my mum asks. 'Why you brought *Si*?' She whispers his name, as if he – or God forbid, somebody else, via the Grade-II-listed wall – might hear us.

'I didn't wanna get drunk and shag a random,' I tell her, giving a shrug.

The noise that escapes my mum resembles a strangled parrot.

'Chloe, you're disgusting.'

'No, I'm not. I'm grieving. And trying to stop meself from doing ridiculous things to numb the pain,' I say, quite matter-of-factly. I refuse to get upset today. I've paced myself with the booze and done bloody well (so far) to avoid heart-to-hearts with certain acquaintances. All that's left for the night ahead is a boogie and a few mini burgers.

My mum straightens her bolero and smooths down her already smooth, shimmery dress.

'Having *sex*,' she whispers the word, 'is not ridiculous. Not at your age.'

'Oh, so you'd rather I was fucking around with randoms?'

'Making love, Chloe. It's making love. Don't say the F word.'

'You can't make love to a stranger. And anyway, I'd need to get wasted.'

'Keep your voice down.'

'No. You brought up this insane conversation – it's your fault if anybody hears it.'

'Don't speak to me like that.'

'Well, it works both ways, Mum. Don't tell me to sleep with fellas just to prove that your daughter's not on the shelf. You only want me to have sex on the off chance I might get pregnant by accident, give you a bloody grandchild. Never mind who the father is—'

'How dare you—'

'No, how dare you!'

'You've put me in a horrible mood, Chloe. A horrible mood.'

'I'd say sorry, but I'm only telling the truth.'

'Even on our Kit's wedding day, you just couldn't stop yourself, could you?'

I blink, confused.

'Nothing's ever serious with you, Chloe. Ever. Whether it was your schoolwork, that degree you did, your endless stupid jobs, you never take anything seriously. Never. And now you might give up teaching? That's the last thing you said, wasn't it? You always piss all over your good fortune and act the goat—'

'What do you mean? Where's all this come from?'

'I bet Jack wasn't even that serious and you're just being a bloody drama queen.'

Thank fuck Gareth's sister shuffles in with her two little

girls, one holding each of her hands. I was making confetti cones with these kids yesterday and they light up when they see me. It makes my tummy flip.

'Oh, don't you two look beautiful!' my mum cries out and touches each little girl on the chin. They smile at her, coyly. Gareth's sister tells them to say, 'Excuse me', and awkwardly pushes the older one into a cubicle. She squeezes inside the other with the little one. She gives my mum that look that says, 'Kids, who'd have 'em?'

'See you ladies on the dance floor,' I say, and make a swift exit.

I've nothing more to say to my mum and I'm sure she's as relieved as I am about that.

27

It's about seven o'clock when I finally get a minute – the lull between the speeches and the dancing. Many people are outside, enjoying the late August warmth. Some are drinking coffee. Most are back on the ale, gearing up to get drunk for the second time around after sobering up during the meal. The chocolate mousse has put a couple of guests to sleep on various Victorian sofas. My nan's gone home. 'I've had a marvellous time, but I've had enough,' she'd said.

I'm outside in a small bandstand. It's off the beaten track, at the bottom of another manicured lawn. The only reason I know this hideout exists is because yesterday, during the decorating, Gareth's little nieces brought me here to show me what they called the fairy house.

I should be thinking about the speeches. Remembering the hilarious words from Gareth's best mate; the incredibly moving ones from my brother and his new husband. My dad nailed his jokes, surprisingly. My mum sat with her best smile fixed like the Joker, ready for a photo opportunity. When I was applauded for being Kit's sister, with the odd wolf whistle, she didn't look at me. She just kept on smiling, clapping, playing along. What she really thought of me was hidden from view, brushed beneath the top table. And it's her words that linger, that stick. They bug me on repeat.

Not serious? About anything? Is there any truth in that? Perhaps.

It's times like this I wish I smoked. Something to do with my hands. I've got a gin and tonic, but the ice has melted, making my palms cold and sticky. I wipe them on my dress, trying not to drift off into the dreamy land where Jack can sometimes still be so present. Lately, he's been popping up in my actual dreams, which – if I'm honest – is an absolute fucker. At least when I'm awake I can maintain some sort of control, but when he's there, at night, in some random mashup of Thailand and London and high school and a random clock tower, a place that doesn't exist any more than he does, I have no control. So I enjoy. I believe. I fly. I kiss him and God, I feel so aroused. Then I wake up. And for what can be minutes, maybe even an hour, I lie there part-convinced that the dream was real. Until I remember, and I don't want to wake up ever again. So I just lie there, in a heavy fog, taking as long as it takes to sit up, swing my legs out of bed and eventually stand.

'God, I wish you were here,' I say.

The bandstand creaks; the scuffle of a footstep.

'Alright, Tilly Mint!' It's my dad. He's left his jacket inside and looks smart in his waistcoat, his shirt sleeves rolled up like a bootlegger, ironically, as he's holding a cup of tea with a saucer. He's been nervous about everything running smoothly today and has hardly touched a drop of the free-flowing alcohol he offered to foot the bill for. 'Who were you talking to?'

'Jack,' I tell him.

My dad's shoulders drop a little, as does his face.

'Do you see him, my love?'

I shake my head.

''Cause I won't think you're mad, you know. I used to see me dad.'

'I know. He told you I was choking.'

'D'you remember?'

'No, I remember the story. And I've no reason not to believe you.'

He scans the gardens surrounding us, almost as if he's looking for my grandad to appear. Then he puts his cup of tea down, stuffs his hands into his pockets and sits beside me.

'Uncle Frank whispered in me ear how he was sorry for me loss,' I tell my dad. 'And I wish Jack had been here, alive. That short conversation could've been so, so bloody different.'

He doesn't say anything. He does give me a little squeeze though.

'You know what, Dad? Jack never got to see me all dressed up like this. We never made it to a wedding together. The last time he wore a suit was the night we met.'

My dad stands and holds out his hands. I accept and he pulls me up. He kisses the top of my head; hugs me tight.

'He'd tell you you're gorgeous, 'cause you are,' he says. I want to crumble, to fall into a million delicate pieces, like confetti. 'The first dance is about to start in a sec.'

'Okay.'

I lean my head into my dad's chest and we sway, side to side, slowly.

'Dad? Why's me mum so disappointed in me?'

'Oh, love. She's not disappointed *in* you. She's disappointed *for* you.'

'No, she's sick of me. She's—'

'Ssh, ssh,' my dad says, stroking my hair, still swaying. 'She wants you to have all the things you wish for. Not 'cause she wants them for herself, but 'cause she knows *you* want them. And whenever you hurt, she hurts. Christ, girl. *I* hurt. But look. I handle me hurt one way, she handles it another. Just like you do.'

'I'm so sorry for putting you both through all this, Dad. I don't want youse to hurt for me. Surely this is my problem? Not yours or me mum's.'

'It's very much our problem. It's called being a parent. And it's a lousy part of the job.'

I step away a little and look at him. If only my mum could be as kind; as honest.

'We should go back in,' I say. 'Today's about you and me mum, too.'

When we get back to the party, the photo booth is in full action. A queue is forming with lots of guests trying out different hats and accessories. My dad joins the line, rubbing his hands together. I still haven't been able to exchange more than a few words with Beth. She's still sitting at her table with Fergus and whatever they're talking about looks pretty intimate.

I find Si wandering out of the gents'.

'Sorry,' I say to him. 'I hope Malcolm wasn't boring you too much?'

'You serious? He's a Sondheim fan. Saw the original *Into the Woods*. On Broadway!'

'I still feel like I've abandoned you.'

He waves his hands around.

'Not. At. All,' he says. 'I'm having a blast, Chloe. Best. Wedding. Ever. Like, how much love is there in one room? Really? How much? It's simply marvellous.'

He's fitted right in. I'm delighted.

'Now, I hope I'm not speaking out of turn, Chloe – but your mum, she's full of shit, right?'

Now that does make me laugh.

'What's she said now?' I ask.

'Told me you're quitting teaching. And I was like, hardly, Miss Roscoe's directing the school musical. Oh, you should've seen her face. Proud as punch, she was. Why would she say you were quitting?'

I open my mouth, struggling to find words. I'd be stooping rather low if I make my mum out to be a liar, a fabricator here. Okay, so she's definitely the latter, but not always. I think my silence has answered him, though.

'You're not?' Si asks, his face dropping, the happy drama mask flipping to the sad.

'Would you judge me if I did?'

Still sad, he shakes his head. 'You need to do whatever makes you happy.'

'Problem is, I don't know the answer to that.'

'So don't be hasty.' He leans into me. 'Chloe, those kids need you.'

'You're too kind. But they don't need me. They don't even know me.'

'Look, I've heard on the old grapevine that Laura – the woman you're covering – isn't coming back. She wants to be a full-time mum. So the position is likely to be up for grabs. You should.'

'Grab it? Oh, I dunno. I'm so shit at me job.'

'You're not! You're just not committed. Yet.'

I'd never thought of it like that. I've only ever covered for maternity leave – I've never been permanent. Lack of commitment has been a running theme throughout my life. It's

240

worked both ways. People, jobs, even hobbies: they've all given up on me as much as I've given up on them. Maybe Si's right. Go where the work is. Listen to my head for once. My mum wouldn't be the only one to remind me that listening to my heart hasn't got me very far.

But going back to London means returning to the flat – to my life without Jack.

I thought I could escape all of that by coming home to Liverpool, but Jack's absence rings like a loud bell wherever I go.

Malcolm appears, taps Si on the shoulder and hands him a glass of champagne. I lose his attention, which I'm grateful for. A booze-fuelled pep-talk wasn't on my agenda for today, as sweet as Si's intentions are. A moment alone, contemplating what to drink without the pressure to speak, is nice. I give Malcolm a little wave and browse the spirits section of the drinks menu.

Nothing's ever serious with you, Chloe. Ever.

Maybe she had a point, my mum.

But what is serious, really? Why does life have to be 'serious'? Because Jack getting killed was pretty fucking serious, in my opinion, and I wouldn't wish that upon my worst enemy. Serious in the words of my seventeen-year-old self – sucks.

Seventeen. Half my lifetime ago. One of our Kit's school mates told me I haven't changed one bit. Well, other than gaining a few laughter lines and changing the colour of my hair, I can see what he means. I don't have that subtle softness from having children, I haven't transformed into a fitness guru or doubled my weight.

But I am different to who I was at seventeen. So very different.

Back then, I had hope.

Hope was bursting from the seams of my boob tube as I danced Thursday nights away at The Carwash. I was *the* 'Dancing Queen', *the* 'Brown Eyed Girl', *the* one everybody was 'Stuck in the Middle' with. And I know it's easy with youthful spirit to have a wider outlook, to dream that life can be spectacular, especially on the brink of new beginnings – like university, or even something as simple as getting into a nightclub without fake ID. Those new beginnings change with age. They become so much bigger, and most of the time, less frequent. I think about Beth wanting a baby. Once, she just wanted a Lipsy dress.

What do I want?

'Wanna dance?' Si asks.

'I need another drink first,' I attempt, but Si's already dragging me onto the dance floor. For a man of such small build, he's strong; I find myself twirling, this way and that way, and without much choice, I'm fully supported into a stylish back bend.

'Wow. You're a good dancer!' I exclaim.

'Don't sound so shocked. I've had plenty of training.'

And he thrusts me out and reins me in, until all I can do is go with the flow and enjoy myself. He's right. There's so much love in the room. It mightn't be the love my heart is aching for, but it's love all the same.

And who am I to argue with that?

28

The after-wedding blues are like returning from a holiday. Everywhere lacks colour; the pace has slowed down to a yawn. It's hard to talk about anything unrelated to the joyous event, now only a memory, a piece of history. In short, the world just feels less interesting.

I'm sat outside London Euston station amongst the smokers and vapers.

'Well, that's an excuse if ever I heard one,' I say.

I've finally managed to get Beth to answer her bloody phone and she won't meet me after work because she's viewing flats. Another one. As well as the Islington terrace, she and Fergus already own a delightful two-bed in Scotland that they rent out on Airbnb. They make a fortune during the Edinburgh Festival every August. And here I am, begging. Well, property wins.

'It's not an excuse, babes.'

'Where's the flat?'

'West Hampstead.'

Sounds expensive. I don't know the area but I know it's on the Jubilee line.

'Nice. Can I come? I can be there in half an hour. Or meet you after?'

'No, it'll look weird if you come with me. And then I'm going straight to bed.'

Great. My suitcase is in between my knees and I'm sucking on the last dregs of an iced coffee from Caffè Nero, contemplating which direction to go in. I'd banked on it being east to Islington, but Beth's having none of it.

'Babes, I've gotta go. I'm running late as it is.'

'Bye—' but she's already gone.

We still haven't mentioned our fight. I sent her a message the day after the wedding, apologising for not getting much chance to speak to her. Our cosiest moment had been at the end of the night when we found each other side by side – hand in hand – in the circle for 'New York, New York'. Our Kit had been adamant his big day wouldn't end so predictably. But it did.

I toss my iced coffee cup into the bin and open Instagram. The guests all went a bit Insta-crazy and I'm loving the captured magic, the filters, the hashtags. There's our Kit and Gareth in a selfie at the airport now, on their way to Mykonos with pints in hand, toasting. The message request from Justin remains unopened. I can't imagine it's anything more than a simple *Hi, how are you?*, but other than that being the world's most banal question – especially when you're *not* fine – I'm uncomfortable with what I did. Not only with what happened in his room in Vietnam; what had I been thinking, going to Bangkok? Trying to find that man sat in the shopping trolley? It's absurd.

I wheel my suitcase into the noodle bar. Si hasn't read the

messages I sent him two hours ago. After the wedding, he told me he 'owed me, big time', and I've politely asked if I can crash on his sofa because I couldn't get hold of Beth. I select a readymade yaki soba and pot of edamame from the self-service counter. Si will respond soon; or Beth might change her mind.

Speaking of food – my mum made my favourite tea last night; her homemade fish pie. Later, about an hour after I'd gone to bed, she barged her way into my bedroom, knowing I'd still be awake. She planted a loud, heavy kiss on my fore-head and said, 'Love you,' in the same way she'd say 'Get up' if I was having a lie-in. It's been less than a week since our Kit's wedding and neither of us has brought up *that* conver-sation in the toilets. I would've been keen to talk about it and get to the root of our problem, if my mum wasn't Sue Roscoe. Women like Sue are of a certain ilk, you see: a gener-ation who seem outspoken, but can't express what's truly going on inwardly. It comes out wrong. It's frowned upon. It's too deep. It's indulgent. It gets in the way of practical things like getting the tea on the table for six o'clock or watching *Corrie* to unwind. She'd rather just say 'Love you'. And at the very least with that, she means it.

Si still hasn't checked his messages.

I message Fergus.

Hiya! Just checking you'll be home in 30 min or so? I'm on my way to yours. Ok?

I don't mind if Beth goes straight to bed when she comes back from West Hampstead. I just need their guest room and it's always there whenever I need it. Beth's words, not mine.

Fergus replies.

Aye. Almost home.

It's lashing down when I emerge from the tube station.

245

Summer's on its last legs. My denim jacket gets soaked and sticks to my neck, my back, my elbows. When Fergus answers the door, I run inside and slip off my Converse, leaving them in the hallway with my suitcase, and hang my jacket to dry on the coat rack.

'Get the kettle on,' I say. 'I bought some biscuits from M&S. I won't tell Beth.'

He obeys my orders with a huff and I chuckle. He's so easy to wind up.

I crack out the biscuits and Fergus opens them, taking two and devouring them like a monster. The crunching echoes around the kitchen and crumbs fall onto his rather baggy t-shirt – it's unlike the usual muscle-hugging ones I'm used to seeing him wear. The kettle boils and he pours hot water into two mugs.

'Teabags?' I remind him.

'Uh? Oh. Yeah.'

He finds a box of green tea in the cupboard. Drops a bag into each mug.

'Milk?' he asks.

'With green tea?'

'Sorry.'

'You okay?'

Fergus presses his hands into the kitchen table and hangs his head down. The veins on his arms pop through his skin and he releases an animalistic growl. I was not expecting that.

'Go on, then,' he says, standing upright quite abruptly. 'Hit me.'

'Hit you with what?'

'Chloe. You've come here to have a go at me, so just get on with it.'

He takes another biscuit and eats it whole. A large crumb sits on his pale pink upper lip. Come to think of it, Fergus Douglas has never looked so dishevelled.

'I'm just waiting for Beth,' I tell him. 'I'm here to crash.'

'Crash?'

'Yeah, you know Beth's always said the guest room's mine whenever I need it.'

'But Beth doesn't live here anymore.'

I pull such a series of faces that I must look like a clown. Surely he's having me on? Although he'd need a personality transplant to attempt that.

'Don't tell me she hasn't even told you?' he yells. The table gets the brunt of it, again.

'Told me what?'

'We're getting divorced.'

'What the—'

'Yeah. Fuck. Been on the cards for a while but she finally moved out a few weeks ago.'

'Fergus, come on, hun. Stop playing with me head.'

'Why would I do that?'

'Dunno. But correct me if I'm wrong, our Kit's wedding was only last weekend. You two were like, so loved up. Gareth told youse to get a room at one point!'

He pulls a chair from beneath the table, scraping it along the tiles like nails on a chalkboard. Plonking himself down, he rubs his eyes and his neck, as if allergies have come to attack him.

'Wasn't real,' he says.

'Oh, please. You can't fake that shit,' I say and pull out a chair, more carefully than Fergus. I lean in, my elbows on my knees. 'And why would you bother?'

'Okay, look, it was real.' His voice is robotic. 'But it wasn't

247

our real, *real* life. At the wedding, we were nostalgic. We hadn't seen each other for a fortnight. We agreed to show up and have a nice time. And we used it to say a final goodbye.'

'I can't believe I'm hearing this.'

'Why not? Surely you've noticed how toxic we've been. For years, Chloe. Years!'

'Yeah, maybe. But I thought that was what made you both, I dunno, tick?'

'Nobody wants to live like that.'

''Course not, but Beth's never said anything to me about—'

'Beth's been trying to talk to you for months. Longer.'

'No she hasn't.'

Fergus stands up to get another biscuit.

'Okay,' he says, lightly, 'she hasn't.'

I don't like how his tone has changed.

Nor do I like how I never saw this coming, when it was so obvious. Oh God!

'Where's Beth living, then?' I ask.

'Staying with a friend from work, but she wants her own place.'

Ah, West Hampstead. She was telling the truth.

'Wait,' I stand up. 'You thought I was here to have a go at you. To hit you. Oh, Fergus. You didn't . . .'

'Huh? No! Fuck, no. I'd never cheat on Beth, ever.'

'So what did you mean? Did you turf her out of the house?'

He puts his head in his hands and nods.

'It's only fair, Chloe. It was my parents and my savings that bought this place – Beth's always just contributed,' he says. 'She said some hurtful things. You know how she gets.'

'But she'd never mean any harm, she's all show when it comes to arguing.'

'I know, I know, but she was cruel. She blames me through and through.'

'For what?'

'The baby. Well, lack of.'

I have to be loyal to Beth, and yet I'm compelled to reach out to Fergus. I launch forward and give him a strong hug, although he doesn't reciprocate, and he steps away throwing his shoulders back in military fashion.

'I need to find her,' I say.

Fergus gives a series of nods.

'You're more than welcome to stay, though. However long you need.'

'Thanks.'

Although I'm not sure that would be the best idea right now. I give Fergus a closed-mouth smile, which he sort-of returns, and I get my things and leave.

29

How's the viewing, hun?

She responds quickly.

Haven't seen it yet. Owner late back from work :(xxx

Okay, so I need to get to West Hampstead pronto.

It takes me about forty minutes – it's an inconvenient route on the tube. As I step off the train, I keep an eye out for Beth in case she's waiting on the platform. I know this is a long shot, but these pockets of London aren't huge; there are just so many of them. How far from the station is the flat she's been looking at? I'll wait here, on the platform – at some point, she'll come here.

It's almost eight o'clock, an hour since her last message.

I give it another ten minutes, then type.

So . . .?

And wait.

Please, Beth. I need to tell you I'm sorry.

Nah. Not worth it. Heading home. Spk tomo. xxx

Great! So she'll be on her way to this station. Now.

I lug my suitcase up the stairs to street level and wait by

the gates. It's not that busy – the rush died down a while ago. I need to keep an eye out, although it's unlikely I'll get swamped. This isn't Waterloo or Kings Cross. I should be able to spot her any minute.

But I don't.

The thing is, Beth's not going home, is she? And if I know Beth, I know what she'll be doing right now.

I go through the gate and have a decision to make. Left or right.

To my left, I see a pub on the corner. Dark wood, a lengthy food menu, serves Guinness on draught. Beth wouldn't be seen dead in a place like that on her own. So I turn right past a deli, a dry cleaners, an estate agent. Within minutes I'm surrounded by cafes, small and intimate restaurants – and bingo. A wine bar.

Beth is there, easy to find. She's sat outside the front beneath the white canopy, smoking.

'Since when did you start smoking?' I ask.

Her free hand slaps against her chest as she shudders in her seat. Her smoking hand goes to the ashtray in the centre of the circular white table and she stubs the ciggie out so ferociously she might as well be murdering it.

'I wasn't judging,' I say. 'Just asking, like.'

'You're an actual stalker,' she says.

'My intentions are good. Promise.'

'Sit down. I feel ashamed you standing over me like some sort of fucking apparition.'

She's still in her work clothes; a fitted beige dress with square neckline, the skirt touching her knee. Only Beth can make beige look bold. Her tan hasn't faltered despite her not having been on a big holiday this summer, and her lip gloss is fresh, as if she applied it seconds before I showed up. She's twirled her hair into a low bun, showing off delicate gold earrings in the shape of long leaves.

'I feel a bit underdressed for this place,' I say, referring to my jeggings, Converse and damp denim jacket. Even my pink t-shirt is sticking to my chest. My hair is like a drowned rat left out to dry.

'Nah. Go inside. Everyone in there's as scruffy as you, babes. I've just set a new standard. As always.' Beth allows herself to smile, closed-lip, one-sided. She's been crying, a gloss on her eyes that isn't due to Charlotte Tilbury.

'I saw Fergus. He told me.'

'I wanted to tell you meself—'

'I know. When we went to that bloody ski slope, you wanted to talk. Beth, I'm so sorry. I've been the worst friend.'

Her gaze falls to the drop of white wine left in her glass. She pushes it towards me.

'Look, life hasn't been kind to you either, babes.'

'No, you should've just grabbed me and blurted it out.'

'It's not that easy to admit. Remember when you couldn't tell me about Jack?'

She's right. Beth carries a wisdom I don't possess.

We became friends in high school. I spotted her on day one, her purple drawstring Benetton bag gleaming new. She was the girl every boy fancied and every bully avoided. She didn't speak to me until the Christmas disco.

'Where's your bodysuit from?' she had asked, sipping a can of Coke.

I'd agonised for weeks about what to wear, trawling through the pages of *Just Seventeen* for inspiration and finally deciding on red jeans, a floral body suit and a black chiffon shirt which I tied in a knot at the waist. When I stepped off the bus that morning, I instantly regretted the red jeans. I'd shot up in the year between eleven and turning twelve and the jeans brought too much attention to my long legs. What had I been thinking?

But Beth from Form 7G wanted to know where my bodysuit was from. Beth from 7G liked my outfit.

'Tammy Girl,' I told her. My mum had taken me shopping and treated me to a whole wardrobe of Tammy stuff for my twelfth birthday. It had been one of the best days of my life.

Beth smiled, but it was partnered with raised eyebrows and a sigh.

'Cute,' she said. 'I saw one almost identical in Topshop.'

'I love Topshop,' I blurted, although I'd never been inside.

'It's the only place I shop.' Beth took another swig of her Coke.

'Me too. Except for Tammy Girl. Obviously, duh!' I rolled my eyes and hit myself on the head, making Beth laugh. Her dangly earrings jangled and she twiddled the silver dolphin hanging from a fine black cord around her neck. Picking up her Benetton bag from beneath the table she was leaning against, she opened it and fished around inside for something. She pulled out a black velvet hat.

'You're Chloe, right?' she checked. I nodded. Then, standing on her tiptoes, she put the hat on my head, her dainty fingers positioning it as she pouted her lips. 'This looks sooo good on you. I've got a right little pin head. You can have it. Merry Chrimbo.'

In a mix of shock and delight, I struck a pose, kind of John Travolta doing 'Stayin' Alive'. Beth grabbed my hand and hauled me to the dance floor in the centre of the sports hall. Blur's 'Boys and Girls' was playing and the whole of Year Seven was jumping up and down. When the Grease Megamix came on and most of the boys decided to go and stand against the wall, I naturally took the role of Danny to Beth's Sandy. She invited me to a sleepover at her house the following Friday and now, twenty-five years later, here we are.

'Let's be flatmates,' I suggest.

'Y'what?' Beth responds, half of her upper lip rising, her nose wrinkled. Anyone would think I'd burped. Or puked.

'Well, you'd rather live with me than some stranger with a spare room, wouldn't you?'

'Babes, I'm getting me own place.'

'Oh. I just thought we could help each other out – you know, have a laugh.'

'We don't have to live together to do either of those things.'

I shift in my seat, lift Beth's wine glass and down the last drop.

'Same again?' I stand, holding the glass by its stem and giving it a little wiggle. 'Or shall I order a bottle?'

'Nope. I need to keep me head screwed on.'

I feel my shoulders slump down to my elbows. Looks like we're not going to drink and chew the fat, then. Beth's blown me out twice in the space of a few minutes. The wind has changed. I'm not familiar with this side of her. She's a million miles away in her thoughts, watching the big red bus crawl past, blocking the view of the independent bookshop and the Greek bakery. She catches me staring and I offer a quick, upbeat smile. I want my friend back. I need her.

'What you gonna do for work down here?' Beth asks. She's picking up her handbag, aptly made by Chloé, and about to sling it over her forearm to make an exit. 'Your mum said you're quit—'

'Oh, for fuck's sake, you know what me mum's like, Beth. I'm not quitting.'

Beth rests both arms on top of her bag and with widened

254

eyes, looks interested in what I'm saying for the first time since I sat down. She tells me to go on, but there's nothing to go on about. I shrug.

'But you thought about it,' she says, 'didn't you?'

I give a careless laugh. It's my turn to watch the next red bus crawl past.

'It's what? Two weeks before the schools go back? And you probably didn't even think to hand in your notice or speak to your boss, did you? You were just gonna quit. Like that?' She snaps her fingers like Mary Poppins.

'Why are you so mad at me? I've still got me job! I'm going back next week.'

'Oh, well done. Your sloppiness finally paid off.'

'Eh?'

'You got lucky, didn't you?'

'Yeah, right. So lucky, hun.'

'You talk so much shit sometimes. Quitting, but not quitting. Worrying the hell out of your mother, treating a bloody good teaching job like it's an inconvenience—'

'Hold on a mo—'

'No. This is exactly the sort of fucked-up nonsense that makes me not wanna live with you. Not because I don't like you, I hate doing this to you, babes, I love you. But you'd move in and then, what next? Get a dog and decide you don't like dogs? Move to France, then not wanna learn the language properly?'

My mouth is gaping open like a docile fish. I close it and try not to sulk, but God, Beth's being a hardened bitch. She hasn't got her fella anymore, but at least he's alive. There's a chance they *could* get back together.

'I mean, once, you desperately wanted to go to drama school,' Beth goes on. 'And all those nights I sat on your bed, helping you learn fucking Shakespeare speeches and you saying it was boring, and then you'd sing fucking *Annie*—'

'It wasn't *Annie*, it was *Miss Saigon*—'

'Same fucking thing—'

'No it fucking isn't—'

'BABES. Stop. I watched you, I cheered you on, I took you to Yates's Wine Lodge when you got rejected, I held your hair back when you puked, told you to try again. Then I sat through your uni shows, them funny sketches. Whatever became of them?'

'Oh, they were dire.'

'Nobody starts off perfect, Chlo. And now teaching isn't feeling so easy, so you might jack it in. Or not. Ooh, you might. You might not. That ski lesson was a prime example—'

'Let's not mention the ski lesson, pal.'

'Fine! But, babes, you just need to put the work in. Whatever it is.'

'And what about you? Your marriage. Aren't you gonna put the work in?'

'I did. We did. When you've tried so hard at something, it's easier to know when to call it a day.' She lets out a long sigh, as if she's been wearing a corset and the laces have been loosened. 'I'm not saying marriage – relationships – should be plain sailing, but they should never be a constant battle. If anything, the right one, it should be easy; effortless. Then you deal with the hard stuff as a team. Fergus . . . no, *we*, didn't.'

I nod. 'You know, I'm starting to think that Jack wouldn't've been so easy.'

Beth eyes fall onto mine. 'Why?'

'Just a feeling; that maybe we weren't what I thought we were.'

'You loved him, though, didn't you?'

'I did. God, Beth. I did. I've never felt that way before.'

'You need to hold onto that, babes; store it in a special place. But you're dragging it out and you know what? I think it's warping what you had . . .' then Beth puts her hand across her mouth to prevent a laugh escaping.

'What's so funny?' I ask, wondering what's brought this on.

'I've just gone on and on about how you never try hard at anything, and when it comes to Jack, fuck me, you've tried so hard. You're still trying! You've literally gone all over the fucking world. If you'd put half of that effort into being an actress you'd have won a fucking Oscar by now.'

'And I'm supposed to find this funny?'

'What else is there to do?' Her face turns serious again. 'I'm not sorry.'

'I know.'

'I want you to live your life and be happy, Chlo.'

'I want that, too! For both of us.'

'So don't drag me backwards.'

Beth straightens her skirt as she stands and hooks her bag on her arm. She shakes out both hands as if she's just washed them and the hand-dryer is broken. A shiver envelops her before she pulls herself together.

'Enough of this,' she says. 'I can't be indulging in this soft chitchat any longer, babes. I'm off. Got a ton of things to tick off me list before the morning. I'll ring you on me lunch tomoz. Okay?'

I blow her a kiss.

A single gust of wind brushes a few stray leaves around my feet. Autumn is on the horizon. The new term is imminent. Beth turns left and disappears down a residential street of Victorian terraces, where every window has white ledges and matching wooden shutters. I check my phone and enjoy the satisfaction of seeing a reply from Si.

Agggggghhhhhh. I'm in Bruges! Back on Saturday AM. X
Fan-fucking-tastic.

There are a few more messages – afterthoughts to his response: Am I back for good? How did my mum react? Have I had a change of heart about teaching? Did I want to watch the first week of *Strictly* with him this Saturday night?

This is all lovely. Truly, it is.

But it doesn't solve my current situation.

I'm going to have to take advantage of the key sitting at the bottom of my satchel.

And with an ache that could break me into jagged pieces, I head south on the tube.

30

The aroma of warm tomato sauce greets me. Onions. Garlic. Minced meat?

Nothing smells familiar.

I throw my key into the blue Marrakech dish and put my denim jacket on the coat rack. I notice instantly how it hangs tidily, with ease, with no large garments to contend with. In fact, the narrow hallway is somewhat brighter, as if a few extra inches have been added either side. There's a sense of out with the old, in with the new. Jack's coats are gone.

The floorboard creaks beneath my Converse and I freeze mid-walk, splay my fingers to keep my balance. I feel like an intruder. Tiptoeing closer to the kitchen, the smell of bolognese gets stronger.

OH! GOD!

My chest drops into my belly, like when you go down the steep part of a rollercoaster and you wonder whether you might've shat yourself. Just a bit. But you recover quickly. Relief comes as quickly as the shock did . . . I haven't shat myself.

But that hunch over the hob, stirring the sauce. That chin, cocked out in concentration.

It's Jack.

It's his brother. Freddie.

He was supposed to be moving in next week, although it looks like he's done a fine job of it already. Two new sofas have replaced the L-shaped makeshift bed I'd slept on in the weeks after Jack's death. The coffee table is littered with opened ASOS packages. Rudolf isn't anywhere to be seen. I fixate on the tealight candles on the windowsill. Some are burnt out. I wonder if they're the same ones that Jack lit months ago, or if they're new, the wick still warm. I should say hello, but the clanging of a tin lid on the kitchen floor beats me to it.

'AGH!' Freddie yells. 'HOLY MOTHERING FUCK OF . . . OH, SHIT ME. SHIT!'

I back into the wall, and echo, 'AGH!'

Freddie clambers down to pick up the lid, his hands suffering a bad bout of butterfingers. He's catching his breath whilst repeating more fucks and shits. His face is very different to Jack's, and not just because he's clean-shaven; his features are strikingly 'Irish' with those small, burning eyes and cheekbones that mean business. He's built like Jack, though, and perhaps it's the lack of hairiness that makes him look a tad overweight. I never thought of Jack as overweight, more a giant.

'I'm sorry!' I blurt out.

'You scared the shit out of me!' He's shielding himself with the lid.

'I didn't know you'd moved in.'

'I thought you'd moved out.'

'I only went to . . . erm . . .' I don't know how to explain myself. 'I'm – sorry.'

'I'm done. I'm done, done, done,' Freddie says, more to

himself than to me. His hands fly up as if he's being held at gunpoint and the lid once again crashes to the floor. We both yelp, although mine's a gasp and his is a squeal. In his frantic state, he stubs his toe on the cooker and I'm hoping he's referring to that when he calls out, 'You crazy bitch!'

He hops past me and throws himself onto a sofa. Pulling his sock off, he repeats his yelp-squeal, stretching out his toes.

'I'm not being dramatic,' he whimpers. 'I've got an ingrowing toenail.'

'Ouch,' I offer.

'I play a lot of rugby, you know.'

I nod and decide to get him a drink of water. The glasses are in the same cupboard as always; the same cups, the same beakers and tumblers. I spot a Beatles mug lurking in the back. That belongs to me. As I close the cupboard, it creaks on its hinges. Freddie lets out another yelp, but much quieter than the previous outbursts.

'It's like living in a haunted fucking house,' he says, throwing his head back into a cushion and closing his eyes. 'I've only been here for three days, but ah man, I'm done. I'm so DONE.'

'You keep saying that.'

'Because I am.'

'No need to snap.'

'I'm not snapping,' he snaps. 'I'm scared. And I'm not afraid of admitting that. I'm not, you know.'

Jeez. Freddie Carmichael has issues. But that's not for me to stick my nose in.

He takes the water I hand to him.

'Cheers . . .' he says, and falters.

'Chloe,' I remind him.

'Sorry. Chloe, yeah. Cheers.'

261

I perch on a bar stool, comfortable enough not to run away but not feeling sufficiently at ease to sit on the other sofa. Freddie drains the water in a series of fast messy gulps, then wipes his mouth with the back of his hand.

'This was such a bad idea,' he says, staring into the empty glass. 'Jack still gets post.'

Agh. I was hoping that had stopped. It's impossible to know everything he might be on a mailing list for, though. Before I went to Thailand, a catalogue for camping equipment had arrived for him.

'It's like the walls have eyes,' Freddie says. 'Everything I do, there's a thud, or an echo. That lampshade on the ceiling rattles, you know. I'm not imagining things; I'm not.'

'I know.'

I want to tell Freddie how much I believe him. The lampshade does rattle. But it's because of the fella who lives upstairs, the one who travels a lot and pulls his suitcase around the wooden floor. Now's not the time, though. I let Freddie go on.

'It's not that I don't want to remember my brother. But I don't want to be reminded of him every second of the fucking day. You think that's sick, don't you? You do, don't you?'

'No.'

'I mean, it's hard not to think about my brother and not relate it to how he died.'

I wholeheartedly get it, and I clench the stool I'm perched upon. Thanks to Freddie I can see Jack crossing the road, feet away from this flat, his heart beating with an abundance of life, his mind full and active, and I see the van come hurtling around the bend on the hill. I hate these visions, the ones I've been concocting over the past few months. God, I hate them, I hate them, I hate them.

'Are you okay?' Freddie asks.

Me? I realise I'm breathing heavily. 'I was just thinking about . . .' And I don't need to finish the sentence aloud, don't need to spell out that he's just reminded me of exactly what happened to Jack. But I don't know *exactly*. It's all guesswork.

'No one's gone down for it,' Freddie says.

'What?'

'There's literally nobody we can blame, is there?'

I'm hit with a memory, except it feels like a dream. Not a pleasant one. A disjointed conversation with Giles, the neighbour from the second-floor flat. I think I was drunk. That fog of screw-top wine I'd hibernated into during the days that followed. I was taking the recycling out. Or a bin. And I was wearing one of Jack's t-shirts with no jeans or leggings, just my bare legs, unshaven and so white they could reflect the hot London sun. Giles called my name. No; he tapped me on the shoulder. I was aware of my wine breath, my unbrushed teeth. 'Did you see it in the *Metro*?' he'd asked. His voice was calm, clipped, kind. I said, yeah. Or nodded. I can't recall. But I didn't indulge. Of course, I hadn't seen anything in the *Metro*. 'It's such a tragedy,' Giles had said. 'Nobody to blame.' I can't remember how I got back into the flat, how I said goodbye. If I said it at all.

'I blame the driver,' I say to Freddie.

He narrows his eyes and drops open his mouth, glaring at me. Without words, his whole expression tells me he's deeply offended by what I've just said. I retreat, break his gaze, but I know he's still staring at me, burning holes into my skin with his disgust. What have I done? What have I said?

'You're sick,' Freddie whispers.

'What? Why?'

'You blame the driver?'

263

'Well – erm – yeah, and why? Don't . . . you? Or, clearly not. Erm—'

'He wasn't obese! Never smoked! To all intents and purposes, he was healthy, happy, and then the Grim Reaper came along, didn't he? Ooh, decided to pick him. Eeny, meeny, miny, moe.' And Freddie turns his hand into a pistol, pointing it directly at my forehead. 'Boom!'

I jolt, intimidated.

'Boom! BOOM!' Freddie continues, spitting as he speaks. 'And that decision wiped out the driver's son, and, of course, my big brother. So yeah, I could blame him; the big fucking Grim. But no therapist is gonna help me through that shit, are they? Ha! Ha, ha. What could they tell me? That I'm in the same boat as every other living person? Pissed off at death? Death himself. Or herself. I'm not sexist, you know. I'm not. Death is as likely to be a she as a he. Unless! Unless Death is neither. Nothing. But it must be *something*. Something that's nothing couldn't make us feel so bad, could it?'

I'll be honest, Freddie lost me somewhere around 'healthy' and 'Grim Reaper'.

'Who was healthy?' I ask meekly, a croak in my throat. 'The driver?'

'BOOM!'

'Look, you've confused me and I just want to understand. Please?'

'B-b-b-boom!'

'Oh, "boom", yourself!' I say, picking up a loose tangerine from the breakfast bar and chucking it at his head. I'd like to say this was a kneejerk reaction to being shot, but maybe it was loaded with intention. Definitely maybe. Freddie breaks out into a surprised smile. He likes me challenging him. I get the feeling he rambles on like this often and perhaps nobody pulls him up on it. Trish probably thinks it's brilliant! Expressive! A stroke of genius! To me, it's plain irritating and my mum would give him a smack across the head and tell him to take a cold shower.

'What's there to understand?' Freddie asks, picking up the tangerine and holding it in his palm, examining it for damages. 'You read the papers. You were living on this road, for God's sake. Did you see it? Hear it? Maybe I'm the one who doesn't understand. Can't you give *me* some answers?'

My head is hurting. I think of that little emoji with the exploding brain.

'I didn't read the papers,' I admit.

A silence overcomes us. The pause lasts longer than I'd prefer. A bus drives past and the windows rattle. Freddie jumps up and the cushion he was leaning against falls to the floor. He picks it up and drop-kicks it carelessly, knocking the telly a little and causing a stray coaster to slip onto the carpet. With a grunt, he exits the room. I hear him thrashing around the bedroom, drawers opening and closing, zippers zipping.

I gaze at the ground in despair, unsure of what to do with myself.

The carpet is new. Cream, like before, but fluffy and immaculate, not a stain in sight. Now that I see it, I smell it; the rubbery newness. I want to take off my Converse and my socks, allow my feet to melt into the marshmallow of the soft bristles. I'm also paranoid that if there's a single mark present, it will be my fault. An effervescence grabs my attention and I see the bolognese bubbling over. I run to its rescue and turn the hob off.

'Help yourself,' Freddie says. I whip around and he's leaning against the door frame, a North Face bag weighing down one shoulder. He points to the bolognese. 'It's the family recipe, but I made it with Quorn. I'm a vegetarian.'

'Okay . . .' I realise the Quorn has contributed to the overall unfamiliar smell.

'I never read the papers,' he tells me, lowering his bag to the floor. He speaks slowly, calmly, taking deep breaths between sentences. 'I mean, I wasn't living in London then, so I didn't have access to the *Metro*. It was in our local paper, too. I refused to read it.'

I nod. He must know I understand.

'I was, however, living with my parents. When it happened. The driver of the van had a heart attack. Whilst driving. His son was in the passenger seat and apparently had tried to take over the wheel. He went straight through the windscreen from the driver's side. The driver was dead before the van even hit Jack. Case. Closed.'

My eyes close. If I keep them open, I'll see the road through the front window, the exact road where Freddie's story took place. But now, I see my own version emerging from the blackness of my eyelids. I force my eyes open; engage with Jack's brother.

'Did you know he had a day in lieu?' I say. 'It's why he was off work. If he'd gone in—'

'STOP! I'm done. Remember? I told you. I told you before. Done.'

'Sorry.'

'No. I am. Sorry. But I'm freaked, you know. Really freaked.'

Another bus hurtles past, a double decker this time. Freddie retrieves his bag.

'And THAT,' he says, any serenity in his voice gone. 'Fucking THAT!'

He's referring to the wall above the cooker, the blood draining from his round, smooth face. It's the man sat in the shopping trolley. I glance up and swear Ronald McDonald

266

blinks, bows his head a little. It's like when I went to Speke Hall in Liverpool as a kid; the eyes on the paintings followed you around the room, and we told each other stories of the Pink Lady and the Grey Lady to evoke nightmares. But I'm not scared. There's no mystery to this picture, and God, nothing to be feared. It's just Bangkok market tat.

'Anyway. Bye, Chloe. I've got to get out of here.'

'I should go, too.'

'Why?'

The new sofas and carpet are enough to remind me I don't live here any more.

'Look,' Freddie says, waving his hand, 'don't answer me. I don't want to talk any more. I'm tired, you know. I need a coffee. Like, now. A proper one – not the instant shit I found in that cupboard. Fuck. That picture is just I can't I mean . . . Chloe. Have a good life. Bye.'

The front door slams shut, and I freeze. I keep my breaths small, discreet.

Nothing creaks. No bus rattles the windows. The Quorn bolognese tickles my nostrils and whets my taste buds. The ski lesson is still Sellotaped to the fridge and for the first time, I see the funny side, imagining Jack clapping his big hands and howling at my pathetic efforts. I unpick the tape, rip the email in half, then half again, and pop it into the recycling.

'We did it,' I say. 'Kinda.'

Kit and Gareth's wedding invitation can come down, too. But I won't be throwing that away. Gareth designed it, psychedelic swirls around the date and venue, their faces camouflaged beautifully within the design. I place it on the breakfast bar. It'll look fabulous in a frame.

'We did that, too.'

The fridge looks less cluttered. I feel a strange sense of calm.

Still taking up space, though, is the flyer for Ross Robson's gig. I take it down, read the date; Jack's day in lieu. How different that day – that night – should have been. Would I have appreciated Ross's sense of humour, or would I have been on the other side of the fence? Somehow, it doesn't feel right to discard it. I put it back beside the estate agent's card.

Something is missing.

The photo of Jack on his dad's shoulders. I wonder if Freddie took it.

There's no size 13 trainer or stray stripy sock lying around anywhere, either; no parka for me to melt into. It's like the flat has been disinfected of Jack. There are, however, voices coming from the communal garden. Giles, and he's laughing at Ingrid. Or rather *with* Ingrid. The gentle lilt of her accent is musical. I walk into the bedroom and notice the window propped open on its hinge, a chill filtering in. On impulse, I close it tight. As the silence greets me, I open the wardrobe and pull one of Jack's sweatshirts off a hanger, wrapping it around my shoulders. A musty smell welcomes me, the remains of aftershave rubbed into the wool from what was once warm, warm skin.

'There you are,' I smile.

All of his clothes are right where he'd left them.

Beth was wrong. This isn't warped. This is where I'm meant to be.

I think I can finally sleep in the bed tonight.

31

Surrounded by squeaky new shoes destined to be scuffed by the end of September, I shuffle through the corridor to meet my new form class. I've been assigned a Year Nine group. God. Fucking. Help. Me. Before I became a teacher, anything I associated with Year Nine bore the fond glow of yesteryear – my first snog at Lindsey Jones' fourteenth birthday party; class detention for being rude (or witty, as we interpreted it) to the substitute maths teacher; playing Dulcie in *The Boyfriend*. Now, Year Nine is a snake pit.

But I've got this.

They're thirteen going on fourteen. I've got almost two lifetimes on them.

I perch on the desk. Echoes gradually get louder from beyond the open door. I check my phone is on silent and see two messages.

Break a leg today! Show 'em what you're made of. Love you. Mum x

Even if I'd gone into accountancy, she'd think it worthy of applause.

The next message is from Trish. We've agreed to me becoming an official tenant, but she hasn't given me a contract to sign yet. There's no time to read the message though – I must lead by example. I drop my phone to the bottom of my satchel.

'Find a space, guys,' I call out, trying too hard to sound friendly. 'Sit yourselves down.'

The kids filter in, glued to their phones, some alone and some stuck to a pal, sharing a screen. I straighten my back, elongate my neck, although my soul sinks deeper and deeper into the chair. My day is about to begin with words like 'confiscate'. Already I'm bored of myself, and I haven't even greeted them with a proper good morning yet.

I stand. Instant status.

A boy saunters past, at least a foot taller than me, with patchy facial hair.

'A'right, Miss,' he says.

'Year Nine?' I sing lightly with a warm smile, my final attempt at being on their side.

'Miss?' I hear. 'Has anyone ever told you you've got fingers like sausages?'

Baffled, I instantly make the mistake of examining my own hand and for a split second, I wonder – when it comes down to it – whether everybody has fingers like some sort of sausage; hot dog, chorizo, cocktail . . .

The whole class is laughing, and of course they're talking about actually getting fingered now. I should've known better. My drama training kicks in and I fill my lungs with air, clench my abs.

'YEAR NINE!' I bellow.

Let the battle commence.

*

'Si!' I squeal, ecstatic to see his pointed little face behind the piano in the drama hall.

He doesn't hear me though. He's tinkling away, warming up before the cast reunite for rehearsals. I pull a chair over to sit beside him and unwrap the tuna sandwich I grabbed from the Sainsbury's Local on the way to school this morning. I'll wait until he's completed the song before I give him a massive bearhug.

With a dramatic bang of chords, Si lifts his fingers and spirals around to face me. He's embracing the new term with a new goatee, trimmed and symmetrical. A distinct lack of enthusiasm oozes from him. I check the big round clock on the wall. I'm not late. I touch my chin. No crumbs.

'What?' I ask, wary. 'Not a fan of tuna?'

He sighs, his shoulders slump

'Look, Chloe. I'm over the moon to see you.'

'Hmm. Sure sounds like it, hun.'

'I'm conscious of time – the cast are arriving any minute and I need to ask—' Si stands abruptly but loses his balance and slips into the piano keys. His clumsiness causes a moment of alarm married with the plinky-plonk sound effect.

'What?' I ask.

'Are you all in, Miss Roscoe?'

'I can't tell if you're being serious or taking the piss.'

'Are you with me on this? The musical. Because I totally, totally understand if you're not feeling it, and . . .' he lowers his voice, moving his lips like a cartoon, 'I know you've been unsure about staying or going, and I fully support you. But this means a lot to me.'

'I'm in, Si. Chill out.'

'Please don't tell me to chill out. Can you prove it?'

'Prove it? Si – erm, Mr Sullivan – I thought we were mates.'

He's so jittery, I wonder if he needs the loo.

'We are mates,' he says. 'But we're also colleagues. I'm sorry, I don't like saying this, but how do I know you won't let me down? I've spent months working on this musical. I thought I might be left without a director. Gosh, I even thought you might leave the whole flipping profession!'

'I never said for sure . . .'

'I even asked! When you messaged me about being in London. I asked if you'd had a change of heart and can you remember what you replied?'

'Erm, I can't say I—'

'Because you didn't.'

'Huh?'

'You didn't reply. You just left me hanging.'

'There's no need to be so dramatic, hun.'

'Actually, *hun*, there is!'

'Calm down, Si—'

'I. Am. Calm,' he whispers loudly. 'But Chloe, I care about this musical. A. Lot. And yeah, most people won't "get it". It's not a huge football game or a die-hard rock concert, but hey, it's my passion. I love it. I created it. And I don't want it to be anything less than the absolute best that it can be.'

'I know.'

'Do you?'

I allow Si's question to digest. 'No. I don't.'

'I really do want to work with you, Chloe, but I think I need to do this . . . without you.'

'Ouch,' I say, regretting my immaturity and closing my eyes.

He's right, though. I'm not what Si needs. He's put so much of his heart and soul into this. He deserves better. Not a half-arsed director who doodles on the register, desperate for a packet of salt and vinegar crisps to soothe a hangover.

The cast arrive, running in with their hands jammed into crisp packets and swigging from water bottles. Jonah Matthews has grown about two foot taller since July. A few latecomers whizz past murmuring, 'Sorry, Miss,' and, 'Sorry, Sir.'

'In the professional world,' I project, 'being on time is considered late. So be early. And if anyone pulls a stunt like this again, you'll be replaced. Even if I have to squeeze into your costume and play the part meself. Don't snigger. I am *not* joking.'

Si starts pounding the keys for the warm-up.

'Well . . . good luck,' I say, and leave.

Instant coffee and staffroom banter will have to do.

32

Exiting the drama hall, I spot a pupil hanging out in the wrong place. Her large rucksack weighs her down, a single plait swings like a long rope from her droopy head and she seems to be playing with a stone, using the sole of her shoe to scrape on the paving. I look down and see she's managed to draw a faint heart.

'Layla?' I call out.

She jerks upright like a soldier standing to attention, a good girl worried she's been caught doing wrong. When she sees its me, she loosens a little, her eyes falling upon the heart on the floor. Like with most kids, the summer holidays has bestowed her with growth spurts in various directions. She's still petite, but more lithe, cheekbones overtaking what was recently puppy fat.

'Why aren't you in rehearsal?' I ask.

Without making eye contact, she just shrugs. I should tell her that's rude.

'I'm not doing the musical,' she mumbles.

'What?'

'Just not.'

'But you're Layla Birch. Your cast needs you. Mr Sullivan needs you!'

'No he don't.'

'Layla, I hope this isn't because you didn't get the lead because you know what Shakespeare said: "There are no small parts—"'

'Whatever, he's dead.'

I don't like her tone. Not that I say this out loud. I'm already bored of hearing myself snapping out the old teacher clichés and we're a mere three hours into the start of term. Perhaps I had Layla Birch wrong. Maybe that last term was a fluke, or her teenage hormones hadn't kicked in.

'So you think dead people don't matter?' I ask her.

She looks up at me, softens and with sincerity says, 'They're just dead, Miss.'

The tinkle of distant piano chords drifts out from behind me. There's a noticeable vamp, accompanied by the incoherent lyrics of a Kander and Ebb song, although I can't work out which one. Layla looks to the drama hall doors. I bet she knows what song this is.

'What's the matter, Layla?' I ask, softly, making the mistake of taking a step closer to her.

She jumps back. I freeze, hold out my arms, tiptoe back a little.

'Can I have permission to show you something on my phone, Miss?'

'Course.'

She drops down onto one knee, her grey school skirt covering her shoes, and takes her phone out of the inside zipper in her rucksack. A good girl. Not hiding it in her pocket to sneak a peek. God, she's even had the phone properly switched off. I wait whilst the screen lights up and comes to life. After a few taps and scrolls, she hands it over.

It's a screenshot of Layla's Instagram, reminding her of a selfie she posted two years ago. In the photo, Layla is with a woman. They're embracing each other, cheeks pressed together and pulling wide, silly smiles. A younger-looking Layla is wearing a floral headdress and the woman has a single sunflower behind her ear. It looks like they're at a music festival.

'Is this your mum?' I ask.

'Yes, Miss. She died a few months after that was taken.'

Her words crash into me.

'Oh, Layla. I'm so sorry. I had no idea.'

'She had breast cancer.'

We both pause, taking in the photograph. I notice their similar hair, long and wavy, and Layla's mum's nose, all crinkled because of the funny face she's pulling.

'I'm so pleased you showed me this, Layla. It's very personal, but lovely to see.'

'I took the screenshot last term, Miss,' Layla tells me, taking back her phone and switching it off. 'The day of the auditions. That's when it showed up on my Instagram. I'm sorry I messed up. I just, kind of, couldn't be bothered in the end. You know?'

I nod. I do know.

'I WhatsApped it to my best friend,' Layla says, speaking fast, as if she's worried she'll get caught spilling this information. 'I think I wrote something like, "Can't believe this was two years ago" and she said, "You need to stop being stuck in the past". I was like, I'm not. And she was like, you are. She said, "The past is gone".'

The harshness in Layla's interpretation of her best friend's

276

words is like venom from a snake. She blinks away tears by gazing at the sky and fluttering her lashes, a trick she seems too well-practised at.

'I thought she was wrong, Miss. So I posted the photo again, you know, as a memory. It made me happy for like, a minute or something, 'cause it was like my mum was alive again and I had the chance to post a picture of me and her together. Then, I checked my Instagram later that day and only a few people had liked it. I checked again later, and still, hardly any likes. And I'm not like a huge attention seeker or anything, Miss. I just got really confused.'

'Why's that, Layla?'

''Cause did you see how many likes the original post got? The real one? More than two years ago? Miss, look . . . It got two hundred and twenty-three likes.'

'Wow. That's a lot!'

Layla shakes her head, a cynical laugh escaping her.

'No, Miss. That's not a lot. A hundred thousand plus is a lot.'

'Did you expect to get *that* many likes?'

'Not me, Miss, no,' Layla laughs again, more genuinely. 'I'm not a celeb. I mean, two hundred likes isn't a lot in the grand scheme of things – but for me, boring old Layla Birch, it *was* a lot. I'm not even that popular or anything. I think lots of people from school were at that festival so they connected to it and liked it, or maybe they thought my hair looked good. Who knows? Then I repost two years later and 'cause my mum's dead, no one cares.'

'That's not true. You can't use *likes* to determine whether people care.'

'Yeah, Miss, I can. So many people came to her funeral, Miss. People I didn't know. It was like the whole school showed up. And everyone was so nice to me. It wasn't actually nice, though. Like, I didn't enjoy them being nice. I'd rather it'd just been a normal day, not my mum's funeral, and everyone just ignore me. But it was like, I dunno, such a big deal. For like, randoms. Kids I've never spoken to cried. But they all soon forgot, didn't they? No one cared about me reposting that photo. Like my best friend said, the past is gone. No point in going on and on about it, is there?'

I need to be careful with my words – I know I'm walking on thin ice.

'Layla, sorry but I'm a little bit, erm, confused. The school musical is in the future, not the past. Actually the rehearsals are in the present, right now—'

'There's no point, Miss. I'm not doing it.'

'Okay. Fine. But can I ask why not?'

'Yeah. 'Cause there's no point.'

'But you're talented.'

'It doesn't matter, Miss. Everyone's mum'll be watching them. Except mine.'

We freeze, the harsh truth shining on us like a spotlight.

'I used to think she was watching over me,' Layla says, almost in a whisper, as she slouches into the brick wall behind her. 'But she's gone, hasn't she? She's not watching over me at all. She's just . . . gone.'

If I'd happened to be a cocky fifteen-year-old rather than a responsible adult, I'd liked to have found this so-called best friend and shoved a spike up her tight little arse. But what would my argument be? That she's wrong? Because I don't know if she is wrong. I'm not religious, so I don't believe that Jack is in Heaven, keeping an eye on me from fluffy clouds surrounded by cherubs and harps. I'm not entirely sure I believe in the opposite, either. I struggle with thinking that we're something until we die, and then BOOM! we're suddenly nothing. And I've never found any satisfactory spiritual beliefs in the middle ground either. Never been to India. Never committed to a yoga class for more than two consecutive weeks. I'm more baffled than cynical.

'What if she's wrong?' I ask Layla, throwing it out there.

'Who?'

'Your best friend.'

'She's not my best friend any more.'

'Well, who's to say she's right?' I ask. 'Does she have hard evidence?'

'Evidence, Miss?'

'That when we die, we're gone? Because if she has, well, I'd sure like to see it.'

She straightens herself and swaps her rucksack to the opposite shoulder, considering what I've just said. Her head cocks to the side and she inhales, tense and sceptical, afraid I'm being nice to her because she's a kid, rather than being honest with her as an equal. I haven't been a teacher too long, but I've seen teenagers do this multiple times. I make the choice to be honest with her.

'Layla, me boyfriend died a few months ago. I'd like to tell you something he said to me when he was alive. He told me that being a teacher was cool. Hey, don't roll your eyes, they're his words not mine. I'm not saying *I'm cool*.' I do my best T-Birds impression, badly. Layla loosens up and forces a kind smile. 'Jack – me boyfriend – he worked in gaming. He'd oversee various projects, launch new online games and stuff, and he enjoyed it, organised events like crazy golf or paintballing and got away with calling them "team-building exercises". When we got together, I told him that sounded pretty cool. He said, "No, being a teacher is cool. You're

279

making a difference, or at least trying to." And I pulled a face. Told him, nah. In reality, it's stress, it's targets, it's listening to your colleagues saying, "Roll on half term!" And agreeing with them.'

'Really, Miss? Do you hate it?'

'No,' I say, surprising myself. 'Look, Layla. I'll never know if Jack's watching over me. There's a great possibility he's not – that yeah, he's gone. But what if he's not? What if he *is* watching me, somehow? Am I gonna be the teacher who lives for the holidays? Or am I gonna try to make a difference, even if it's the teeniest, tiniest inch?' and I hold my thumb and index finger an inch apart, scrunch up one eye and peek through the space I've created. 'In short, I want him to be proud of me—'

A long whistle from the netball court jolts me: lunchtime practice is coming to an end. I've said much more than I'd intended. With each word, I've learnt, and in a reversal of roles, Layla has stood listening to me like the non-judgemental teacher. I welcome the light breeze that washes over me, the rustle of leaves so recently fallen from the oak trees lining the street outside the school gates.

'My mum wouldn't be proud of me, would she, Miss?'

'Why's that?'

'I'm just bumming around the drama hall instead of, well, you know.'

Grateful that the focus has shifted back to Layla, I'm amazed at how our roles have reverted without me needing to click my fingers or wave a magic wand. Maybe in learning one lesson, I've managed to teach one, too.

'Mr Sullivan'll never let me back though, Miss.'

'Leave it with me.'

*

I walk back to the flat rather than get the bus. I'm hot in my cardigan, the September sun still strong when it's not hiding behind the clouds. The cusp of a new season is upon us and I pass coffee shops where customers bask in the last days of summer with an iced latte. I always walk when I'm either deep in thought or happy.

In this case, it's the latter.

I'd caught Si at the end of the rehearsal, on his knees. Split binbags of feathers, creased satin and ancient, lustreless sequins had surrounded him like a flamboyant Victorian skirt. Flustered, he'd been ticking off any items he could find from his clipboard list. I'd taken the clipboard and he'd fanned his armpits with a broken Venetian mask.

'Roaring twenties flapper dress, purple?' I'd read from the list.

'Chloe, I'm really sorry —'

'Si. Forget it. But more importantly, you need to let Layla Birch back into the show.'

'I can't do that. She dropped out. She's unreliable.'

'Trust me. She's quite the opposite. She just needs a second chance.'

'I've reassigned her part.'

'So write her another one.'

'I can't—'

'You can! It's your creation. You can do anything you want.'

He'd been holding a bowler hat in his hands and clearly couldn't resist the urge to put it on.

'You're right,' he'd said, holding back a smile. 'I *can* do anything I want.' But he'd checked his watch and started to panic-push the mounds of material back into the split bin bags. He'd sung out a high-pitched, 'Agh!'

'You look very pink,' I'd said.

'Very stressed, you mean.'

'Let me do the costumes.'

'No, you've got enough on.'

'Look, if anyone's got enough to do, it's you.'

'Well . . .'

'Si, give Layla a show-stopping role and I'll be wardrobe mistress. I've got experience, haven't I? Think of it as *my* second chance.'

I'd given Si a little shoulder shimmy and thrown a feather boa around my neck. He'd chuckled and I knew he'd give in. But deep down, I knew I wasn't giving myself a second chance. I was giving myself a final warning.

'I've got a free period now,' I'd said. 'Let me sort this utter shite out.'

'It all needs hanging up, though, and some serious TLC. But there's nowhere to do that in this joke of a school. I asked the head for a costume rail and got laughed out of her office. I mean, look at all that fringe! Tangled! Mangled! Oh—'

'Si. I'll sort it.'

I'd rolled a couple of leotards up and popped them into my satchel, planning to repair them tonight while I watch *Bake Off*. The remaining costumes are stashed in the PE cupboard under the gym horse. God knows if I'll get away with that. The head of PE is ex-marine.

I'm almost back at the flat when I decide to join in the fun and get myself an iced latte from the coffee shop by the train station. As I wait for my drink, I catch up on Trish's text from earlier.

Dear Chloe, I hope you're keeping well. It would be greatly appreciated if you could pack Jack's clothes into his suitcases and bring them to my house when you come to sign the tenancy agreement. Text me a date and time you're free over the next week or so and let's get it in the diary. I can be flexible. I'll ping you a location pin of my address. Regards, Trish.

My name's called and I'm handed an iced latte and a paper straw. I take it unwillingly; what I'd thought would be a treat is now just something else I've got to carry – it'll make my hand cold and wet, give me brain freeze and make me feel too bloated to enjoy my dinner. The evening ahead is set to be busy with a task I'm going to find unbearably difficult.

The ripped leotards will have to wait.

33

Jack's suitcases are above his wardrobe, the smaller inside the larger. I drag a stool from the kitchen to climb up and reach them. They drop onto the bed and land with a hefty, dull bounce. A puff of dust fills the room. I sneeze and rub my eyes.

'The last time we did this, we were going on holiday,' I sigh.

I haven't packed a single sock yet and already this is exhausting.

Might as well start with socks.

I toss each pair, untouched since June, into the small case: tennis balls with no bounce.

'Mermaids, clocks or buttons?' I'd said, indecisive as always. 'Jack? Oi! Jack!'

'Hmm? Oh, buttons.'

'You're not looking.' I could see the yellow bar of the BBC Sports app on his phone. I huffed, then instantly hated a part of myself. 'Fuck. We're already *that* couple.'

'What couple? Where?' Jack had asked, looking up from

his screen and over his shoulder. He still wasn't listening to me. It would've been easy to throw a passive aggressive strop, but we were in Primark. I'd been making a pig's ear out of choosing patterned socks. Not because I'd needed socks, but because they were a quid a pair. And Jack had been falling perfectly into the stereotypical bored boyfriend mould.

'This is everything I never wanted,' I'd muttered.

'What's that, darlin'?' he'd asked, but it was quickly followed by, 'YSSSS! Get in!' And of course, Man United had scored. Then he'd remembered me again, smiling with that innocent butter-wouldn't-melt look that so many fellas pull on a Saturday afternoon. We were *that* couple. Replicated everywhere a million times over. We weren't unique. We weren't even exciting. We were simply *them*. I'd put all three pairs of socks back on the hook and sulked my way through the mass of shoppers.

I'm folding Jack's boxer shorts now.

Hold on. What will Trish want with her thirty-eight-year-old son's boxer shorts? Surely I don't need to be folding them, holding them . . .

I let my fingers run across the elastic waistbands. Remember how his skin felt when I would slide my hands inside. That first time: so vivid. In the hotel after that terrible Brexit musical. Against all the self-help books' tips on finding love; against every best friend's advice: fucking at first sight. Our clumsiness was overcome with tipsy giggles. I only felt shy afterwards – that self-conscious lull as if you're covering yourself with a blanket, except the blanket is transparent, exposing what you want to hide. And why? Because it had been so good. Whoever coined the phrase 'earth-shattering' was spot on. The fumbles of two strangers who met in a bar

– well, theatre – brought together in sexual confidence by the power of booze and mood lighting, had ended in a brilliant, movie-worthy simultaneous orgasm. I did look into Jack's eyes. I did well up. I did know for damn certain that this wasn't a one-night stand. I should've just told him I loved him right then and there. Why did I break all the rules but stick to that one?

'I reckon I love you, Chloe Roscoe,' Jack had said the next morning, mid tickling me so hard I wanted to beat the shit out of him. I was gasping for air, writhing so much I could barely laugh. And why would I want to laugh? Tickling, in reality, isn't funny. It's fucking horrible. But I'd fallen in love with this man literally overnight.

NEVER tell a fella you love him after the first—

'And I reckon I love you, too, Jack Carmichael,' I'd said, angry and out of breath from his torture. 'That *is* your surname, right? Since your mum is the one and only—'

'Ugh, don't talk about my mother when you're naked.'

'Oops. Rewind.'

I start to fold Jack's t-shirts à la Marie Kondo. It's therapeutic. I come across an off-white rag with the remains of a fading print: The Mighty Boosh. It smells of musty wood, forgotten in a drawer, belonging to a person I never knew. Jack circa 2005. I think of those who knew him; the Ross Robsons and the Florries. They were a firm part of his past; his history. What am I? His end?

'I don't wanna go on any more dates,' I'd told Beth earlier this year.

We were face to face, sat at a small wooden table against an indoor brick wall, swimming in garlic oil and Rioja. She'd come up to Liverpool for her birthday and we were eating tapas at our favourite spot on Bold Street. We always treat each other to a meal for our birthdays. Rock salt and chilli had tingled my tongue as I chewed the calamari.

'Babes. How are you gonna meet someone if you don't date?'

I'd sucked the salty crumbs off my fingertips.

'I have met someone,' I'd said. 'Chloe Roscoe's dating days are done. The end.'

'Since when the fuck do you refer to yourself in the third person?'

'Since I met Jack Carmichael.'

'I like his name. Is he fit?'

'He's hairy.'

'How long you been keeping him a secret?'

'Erm, I'm not you, pal. He's no secret. I met him last week.'

Beth had rolled her eyes, mocking me with a squeaky, annoying voice, using her fingers to create inverted commas. '"Chloe Roscoe's dating days are done. The. End."'

I'd chucked a calamari ring at her nose. I don't recall us speaking of Jack again that night.

With the small suitcase full, I zip it up and move on to the larger one. Opening it out, I spot a lone, creased business card, printed with a photoshopped image of a beach.

Samui Frog Bar & Grill—'The best seafood in Koh Samui!'

Jack had had king prawns, but I didn't have seafood at this place; I'd opted for a chicken green curry. Hey, I've no regrets. It was delicious. And the setting alone was so magical, we could've been eating spaghetti hoops for all I'd cared.

We'd taken a songthaew – a pickup-truck-like taxi – to Bophut Fisherman's Village on the island of Koh Samui.

287

'Mojito?' Jack had asked as we wandered along, although it was more of an excited observation. 'Mojito!'

Like a kid to candy, I'd been drawn towards the infinite displays of beaded jewellery. When it comes to bracelets, bangles, even anklets, I can't control myself. I'd been jingle-jangling so much I was basically wearing a warning bell. Something ice cold had pressed against my upper arm.

'Mojito,' Jack had said, again. He'd bought two from a street vendor selling freshly made cocktails. The plastic glass was pint-size, the contents sweet, sour and potent. 'Cheers!'

We'd meandered through the village sipping our mojitos through straws. The bars had been open onto the streets – no walls, no doors – cosy shacks gleaming with mood lighting in oranges, pinks and yellows. Traveller trousers had hung on rails around market-style shops, rag dresses dangling by their side. I'd been distracted by every trinket, every bamboo coaster. But Jack had been hungry.

'Let's just go to the next restaurant we pass,' he'd suggested.

So we did.

Samui Frog Bar and Grill had a canteen feel to its interior; rows of square tables each with a single flower in a central vase. Mirrors decorated the main wall and a huge ornate statue of a frog stood proud by the bar. We were asked if we'd like a table inside or outside. When in Rome . . .

A waitress had led the way to a small balcony, hazardous and not well lit. I could sense the sea, that subtle cold breeze, echoes of chatter from the sand. I hadn't realised we were above sea level as the waitress started to descend, reminding us to watch our step. Obeying, I'd clutched the banister – a little rickety I recall – concentrating on my feet as the steep stairs went down, down, down. And then I looked up.

Candlelit tables sat upon the sand, each cocooned in their own glow, scattered small fires creating a magical haze. Boats in the distance glittered on the water and the stars danced above us in the clear, black sky. I felt as though I'd entered a beautiful, inviting new world. The warm air embraced me as we sat at our table, water tickling my feet as my toes had sunk deeper into the soft sand.

'It doesn't get more romantic than this, does it?' I had gasped.

Jack had leant across the table and squeezed my hand.

'And I didn't even have to try,' he'd chuckled.

I held his gaze for a second longer than should have been comfortable, and yet, it was.

The last thing to pack is Jack's suit – the one he wore the night we met. I'm pretty sure he never wore it again after that. What would've happened if I hadn't let him take that empty seat at the theatre? What if Dan Finnigan's girlfriend had stayed in Japan a little longer? What if I'd dragged our Kit along? I wouldn't be folding up a dead man's clothes, packing for a holiday with no destination, would I? I throw the trousers in without folding them; squash the jacket on top. Then I flop my body over the suitcase and zip, zip, zip; then I grab it by the handles and with a burst of sudden strength, I hurl it off the bed, across the carpet. It knocks against the Ikea drawers, making a dint in the wood, but I don't care.

A Sainsbury's carrier bag peeks out from under the bed, so I shake it open. I throw in Jack's deodorant stick and his bottles of aftershave – some in their original box, some missing the cap – and an opened tin of hair wax, not that I remember him using it. I open his bedside table drawer and empty the contents into the carrier bag, too. Old papers,

289

brown envelopes, his passport, three wire cables, God knows what for. I tie the handles in a knot. I'm on a roll now.

Several carrier bags join the two packed suitcases in the hallway. Guilt bubbles inside me, getting rid of all this stuff. Jack's stuff. From Jack's flat. I place my hands against my forehead to release the pressure building up and close my eyes.

Bang . . . Banging . . . One, two, three . . . I hear a shuffle. The door.

Knock, knock, knock.

I ruffle my hair, slap on a smile, open.

'Chloe! Hey!'

It's Giles, from the second floor. He spots the suitcases.

'Going away?'

'No,' I say. 'Quite the opposite, actually.'

'Oh, good.' Giles rubs his hands together, hunches his slender shoulders. A hint of autumn chill hangs in the air and he seems to be enjoying it. 'Because Ingrid and I would love to invite you up for dinner. At a time that's convenient for you, of course.'

From beneath his neat spectacles he's confident with eye contact, and he talks animatedly with his hands. I imagine he does a lot of presentations in work, pretends to live for the weekend but, in truth, loves his nine-to-five. His faint eyebrows stretch high as he waits for my response. How could I let him down? I don't think I could bear to see his happy face drop.

'That'd be boss,' I say. 'Just say when.'

Giles gives a tiny, enthusiastic air punch.

'Wonderful, wonderful, Chloe. We're away this weekend, so how about next Saturday at seven?'

'Next Saturday at seven.'

'And please don't bring anything except yourself. We've got it covered.'

'Pasta?' I ask, grinning; perhaps confusing poor Giles.

'In abundance! Oh – sorry, do you have any dietary requirements?'

'Not fussy at all.'

Giles and Ingrid must already know that, having seen the pizza boxes piling up in the bins out front, the microwave meal containers and the random shit. I went through a phase of eating avocados, potato waffles and pickled onions, sometimes with a knife and fork but mainly with my fingers. I can't even remember if it tasted good.

'Thank you, Giles,' I say. 'I'm looking forward to it.'

He repeats his air punch and skips away backwards. And I want to mean it; want to look forward to it. I'm touched by his kindness. Let's face it, I've been nothing more than a slob in mourning for months, and they're officially welcoming me into their home.

I put the kettle on. I'm going to watch Netflix, start something new. I text Trish with a few options for dates to meet. I think about the wardrobe in the bedroom, sitting empty. Then I message Si.

Evening hun. I'm envisioning you rocking in a dark corner, sweating over creased costumes. But fear not. I've found a solution and enough space to hang every last sequin. Now go to sleep. Night, night.

The kettle boils.

The man sat in the shopping trolley looks at me, unimpressed.

'You're nothing,' I say. 'Maybe this was all nothing.'

Yet, if it was nothing, why can't I take the picture down and put it with the rest of Jack's things?

34

Is it bad that putting on some boots, leaving the flat to walk twenty steps and ringing the doorbell to Giles and Ingrid's flat feels like a monumental effort?

Maybe I won't put boots on.

I'm not really going *out*.

This afternoon I'd bumped into Ingrid in the Sainsbury's Local. I'd only nipped in for loo roll and I was in the queue for the till when she snapped me out of a trance by singing, 'Yoo-hoo!', which was a first. I didn't think anybody said that in real life, especially below the age of seventy-five or not from the doorstep of a thatched cottage. I'd waved, of course. Said, 'Hiya!' Ingrid had waved back with an aubergine and then pointed to it and given me a thumbs up.

'For tonight!' she'd shouted with a crazed excitement, as if the aubergine was a bag of Ecstasy pills.

Beside me, the floor-to-ceiling wine fridge had buzzed. I'd grabbed a bottle.

'This too!' I'd shouted back.

'Oh, no need, Chloe. We have plenty.'

'Don't be soft. I'm not gonna come empty-handed.'

'Giles is making fresh pasta!'

God, they're making a spectacular effort. I'd lifted the bottle to see what thoughtless choice I'd made. Blossom Hill. On offer, a quid off. I should've at least swapped it for an Oyster Bay but I'd suddenly been at the front of the queue and the fella behind had been giving me a gentle nudge. I was holding everyone up.

Ugh. It feels so unnecessary to put on my boots and tie the laces just to go upstairs. I'm wearing black tights and an oversized jumper dress with a knitted leopard print; comfy and cosy, edging on smart. Slouch socks will work. Oh, come on. I can't.

When Ingrid answers the door, her makeup-free skin gleaming like a sunbeam, her natural smile straight off the billboard for a new holistic anti-ageing cream, she goes straight in for a hearty hug. A proper squeeze, in all the right places. I melt into her cashmere jumper. I want to stay here. Permanently.

'Chloe, come on, come in. Take off your boots, make yourself at home.'

I bend down to unlace my just-laced boots. Blood rushes to my head and I'm flustered with the effort. God help me if I ever find myself cooking aubergines and fresh pasta for a guest.

'White or red?' Giles calls from the kitchen.

'White, please,' I reply.

If I'm honest, I fancy red, but there's a hell of a lot of white stuff in this flat. I feel a bit like a penguin. Ingrid takes my bottle of Blossom Hill with such gratitude – as if I'm presenting her with a trophy – that I'm convinced she's possibly (hopefully) never heard of it before. As she slinks off to the kitchen to put it in the fridge, I notice how she wipes her hand on her skinny jeans, wet from the cold condensation of the bottle. Giles's head and upper body poke around the door frame and he waves, assuring me he's not being rude, he's just snowed under. He's wearing a blue and white striped apron. The aubergine is in his hand.

'Cheers!' Ingrid says, elegantly clinking her large wine glass – quarter-filled with a red I bet the Sainsbury's Local does *not* stock – with my cold, delicate glass of white. I return the cheers with a 'Woop!' and sip.

'God, that's good,' I say, a delightful tingle dancing along my tongue.

'A wedding present,' Ingrid tells me, almost apologetically. 'My cousin knows her wine.'

I think about my mum and Carol. No wonder I chose Blossom Hill.

The gentle tones of electronic jazz filter through the room from carefully positioned speakers. It's the sort of music I imagine is played by a live DJ at expensive beach bars during sundowners. Ingrid invites me to fall into a fluffy sofa and bounces herself down on the opposite one.

'Chloe! Sit, sit!'

'It's so funny to be in here,' I say.

'Why?' She looks around, startled, as if a joke might be hanging on the wall.

'Oh, no. I mean, although I live in this actual house, it's like stumbling upon a secret room, isn't it?'

'Yes, fantastic, Chloe.'

'I mean, it's practically Narnia.'

Ingrid laughs and I gulp twice in succession.

'It's gorgeous, Ingrid.'

It's much bigger than my basement. It takes over the whole second floor. At first glance, the inviting lounge is very monochrome-meets-Morocco, just the right amount of black to break up the fluffy white rug, delicious white sofas, floor-to-ceiling white bookshelves. Black Moroccan lamps stand alone, burning with cosy white candles, casting a twinkling cocktail of light and shadow in sporadic patches around the room. A grand black hanging shade matches, the light dimmed to a flicker. Wooden shutter blinds dress the double-fronted bay windows. The dining table is smooth black, set for three but with four cage-like metal chairs. They look torturously uncomfortable. I bet they're engineered to encourage the perfect posture.

From the sofa, I gush about various pretty items dotted about. Oh, the stylish singular wedding photograph; oh, the coffee-table books on fashion and feminism; oh, the silver sculpture of a slim figure running. Ingrid calmly responds to all of my comments as if I'm interviewing her for the *Sunday Times* mag.

'Yes! We got married in Dubrovnik. Popular, I know, I know.'

'Yes! Giles has a talent for picking birthday gifts.'

'Yes! My brother is an artist. He has a studio in Oslo.'

Of course he does. I'm conscious of drinking my wine too quickly so I stand and wander across the carpet to admire the bookshelves. I sway to the electronic jazz, just a little.

'I had so many good intentions of setting some time aside to do this on Jack's shelves,' I say, as I look at all the book spines arranged in colour order, red flowing into orange into yellow into green into blue into purple into black. 'But, you know, tragedy struck.' I accompany my words with a click of my fingers and a swing from my forearm, a silent, 'Darn it'. There, I've done it. Addressed the white elephant – camouflaged well in this room – in a light-hearted fashion.

She's behind me now, Ingrid. Her hand on my shoulder. She doesn't hesitate to turn me around and pull me close. I think she pecks me lightly on my cheek – or perhaps I've just imagined that – but I'm so taken aback that I try to jovially break apart from her, only to elbow the wine glass in her hand. It falls to the floor and a red pool in the shape of Africa bleeds into the white carpet.

'Shit! I'm so sorry, Ingrid. I can't believe it. Oh, shit . . .'

Giles wanders in, apron on, smiling like an innocent puppy. He's holding a glass of white wine in one hand and the bottle I presume to be the wedding present from Ingrid's cousin in the other. I'm hit with a waft of warm garlic and spices from the kitchen, and I want to die.

SPLAT!

Giles has tipped his glass of wine onto the red stain, a perfect aim.

'White gets rid of red,' he sings, merrily.

'Yes!' Ingrid agrees, snatching the whole bottle from her husband and pouring the remaining contents all over the floor. And she's laughing, as though this is a game they regularly play on a Saturday night. Giles has gone off to get 'the cloth'. Not *a* cloth. *The* cloth. The one that magically removes wine stains created by clumsy guests.

I'm apologising profusely, the sound of my voice whiney and irritating. Giles and Ingrid both tell me, 'It's nothing,' and 'It's no trouble,' and 'Really, Chloe, it's nothing.' I don't do a single thing to help. Ingrid insists that I make myself at home, again.

'I already overstepped the mark,' I cry.

Giles jumps up to standing from a crouch. He clicks and points at the pink stain followed by a thumbs up and a closed-mouth grin, then repeats his routine in reference to the kitchen. Feeling the need to explain himself, he clears this throat.

'Stain – tackled. Food – ready,' he says, slapping his hands on his hips.

Ingrid gives a 'Yay!' Then she pulls a cage-like chair out from beneath the dining table and gestures for me to sit. 'Chloe, let's eat, and you can talk to us as little or as much about Jack as you'd like. Your choice.'

I'm so shocked at this suggestion that I just say, 'Thanks.'

We get through the burrata starter with politeness, made very easy by the universal language of good food. Giles and Ingrid are equally passionate about eating well and sourcing locally. The cheese is from a deli in Dulwich they were recommended by a work colleague. According to Ingrid, it's their new favourite place on earth. Bold statement. The tomatoes are from Giles's dad's allotment. Pretending to know what the fuck I'm talking about, I ask who's responsible for the delicious homemade pesto.

'Sainsbury's!' Giles admits.

Plates are cleared and it's time for the main. Giles has made ravioli. I'm running out of improv so I thank them both for inviting me tonight.

'I'd like to say it's done me good getting out the house, but . . .'

They laugh, heartily. Kindly.

'So how are you guys?' I ask. 'Work going well?'

'I'm very lucky,' Ingrid smiles. 'My work have been incredibly supportive, under the circumstances.'

She speaks as if I'm clued up. But before I have to awkwardly ask *what* circumstances, Giles explains, with the same concise enthusiasm he used to describe his dad's tomatoes.

'We had a miscarriage,' he says. 'It was our second round of IVF.'

Ingrid shrugs, leans her head into her left shoulder. 'Maybe we'll be third time lucky.'

'At least we know we can get pregnant.'

They're saying the clichés, out loud, about themselves. I think of Beth and Fergus, how a similar situation drove them apart. In a thoughtless moment of what I'd thought to be support, I'd once told Beth she might be third time lucky. She'd told me to go fuck myself and only come back when I had something original to say. Now, as I chew this fresh homemade pasta, I wonder how Giles and Ingrid remain – or seem – so strong.

'I'm forty next year,' Ingrid says. 'Hurry up ovaries!'

'Yeah, forty's approaching fast for all of us,' I say, ashamed to bring the conversation back to me, but it seems the safest way to avoid saying the wrong thing. 'I'm thirty-seven next month . . .' and I stop talking. The rest of that sentence would be a waffling mess about how I'm unlikely to find another love of my life anytime soon, if ever, and the prospect of having a family has gone from being a big fat 'yay' to an even bigger and fatter 'nay' in less than a year now that I'm single.

Oh God. *Single.*

I haven't thought of myself as single. I guess I'd been so busy with being grief-stricken that I hadn't labelled myself. We weren't married, so I'm not a widow. Why isn't there a name for the partner left behind?

Unless it's simply 'alone'.

'Chloe, are you alright?' Giles asks. He sounds genuinely concerned.

'God, I'm dead sorry. Lost in me thoughts. I'm really sorry about your miscarriage. You're both amazing and you'll make amazing parents one day. And thanks for being so honest, you know, you didn't have to tell me that, it's so private. Me best friend's had fertility struggles, and God, she'd be so mad I told you that. Anyway, you're both strong. Positive. Stay that way. So, yeah . . .' See? Wafflehead. Waffle Queen. Where are the waffles? Chloe's mouth . . .

'Oh, no. We're not strong!' Ingrid laughs. 'We're a mess, aren't we, Giles?'

'A total mess! Monu*mental*.'

'And the arguments it's caused! Right, Giles?'

'I've raised my voice more in the last few weeks than ever in my whole life. Ingrid's been wondering who the hell she married, haven't you? Who knew I could shout like that?'

'It's made me really hate you!' She's still laughing.

'All these irrational outbursts,' Giles says, splayed hands winding around helping him to get the words off his chest. 'Blaming you, blaming me, back to blaming you. And that time I got mad about my brother posting a photo of his baby on Instagram, like he was doing it to annoy me! I broke a mug, didn't I, Ingrid? Then blamed you again. I cooled off by walking to the Sainsbury's Local and buying some super-glue. I'm just so grateful we live in such an old house with thick walls. Poor old Neil downstairs would be putting in a complaint to Neighbourhood Watch!'

I laugh. It's not funny, but Ingrid's laughter is infectious.

'Neil?' I say, catching a breath. 'I've never met him, you know. I've heard him – and the wheels on his suitcases – but never actually met him.'

'Oh, he'll be along shortly,' Giles tell me. 'He likes to pop up for a drink on a Saturday evening. Our doors are always open for our neighbours. Pudding?'

Ingrid howls.

'We've been together for almost a decade and it still makes me laugh when Giles says "pudding" for dessert. It's such a silly word! *Pud-ding, pud-ding, pud-ding!*'

Giles stands with a satisfying, 'ahhhh', as if he feels light, like a fairy in flight – although he's eaten all his pasta – and starts to clear the plates. He offers me a choice of ice cream or lemon meringue or a bit of both, apologising for not baking something from scratch. Ingrid gasps and reminds Giles of the cheeseboard.

'Blimey!' Giles says. 'Can't believe I forgot about that.'

We all agree on having the cheeseboard for *pud-ding* and Giles grabs another bottle of red from the wine rack, plonking it onto the table. He tells me just to holler if I want ice cream or lemon meringue and I'm so overwhelmed by the warm hospitality that I jump on the honesty bandwagon.

'I've been doing stuff . . . without Jack,' I blurt out. 'As in, stuff we should've been doing together. That sounds so crazy out loud. Shit.'

Giles stops spreading Camembert onto a cracker to give me direct eye contact.

'Unfinished business?' he asks; helping me, prompting me.

'I even went to Thailand. Bangkok. And then to this little town in Vietnam.'

Ingrid nods for me to go on as she stuffs her mouth with a large slice of blue cheese, sucking the tips of her fingers and then wiping her hands with the tea towel Giles left on the table.

'It wasn't long after Jack died. And it was stupid. I was convinced it'd mean something – God knows what – but I seemed to think I'd have some sort of epiphany and feel happy again. Or make sense of Jack being killed. And all it did was make everything worse.'

'Worse than Jack dying?' Ingrid asks. She really does have a knack, doesn't she?

'No. No, not worse. You're right. But it definitely never made it better.'

'There's no quick fix for grief, Chloe,' Giles says, edging the cheeseboard closer to me. 'Something broke inside me the day my mother died. I can't say it ever fixed. But now I try to accept that it's changed, rather than broken. Easier said than done, though.'

The gentle headspin created by the wine makes me speak before I think. 'You knew your mother your whole life,' I say. 'I'd only known Jack for a smidgeon of mine, except I thought I was gonna know him for the rest of it. It's made me do some really stupid things . . .' I trail off, aware that I'll sound unhinged if I mention the quest for the man sat in the shopping trolley. 'God, I'm so sorry, Giles. I was really presumptuous then, wasn't I? I hope you weren't little when your mum—'

Giles holds out his hand, gives it a shake, along with his head.

'It's okay, it's fine,' he says. 'I was seventeen.'

'Oh, bloody hell.'

'No, really. I got a whole childhood.'

Ingrid starts to clear the cheeseboard.

'What stupid things did you do, Chloe?' she asks. 'Tell us, tell us!'

'I kissed a guy.'

In the silence as Giles and Ingrid wait for me to elaborate, I remember the message request I received from Justin, still

301

unread. The thought of opening it fills me with the fear that he will mention that night and make me relive what we did. But who am I kidding? I don't need a message to remind me. I torture myself with the memory daily.

'What's considered "too soon"?' I ask.

'Don't think like that, Chloe,' Ingrid says. 'We're going to start trying for a baby again next month. Is that too soon? I don't know. But it doesn't concern anybody other than Giles and me. I would guess that the only person who cares about that kiss being "too soon" is you.'

'Because nobody in Jack's life gives a crap about me?'

'Is that true?'

'I was only with him for five months. They didn't know me.'

'Look, did kissing this guy hurt anybody?'

I frown, shake my head.

'You see? So long as you're not hurting anybody, do whatever you need to do to feel better. Kiss a guy. So what? Kiss fifty guys! There's no rules, no laws. Just get by. You're doing great.'

'Oh, I'm not. I hurt me best friend – I was so oblivious to the shit going on in her life. And I've hurt me mum. And me work colleague. 'Cause I've been selfish, or childish, or—'

'Grieving?' Giles suggests. 'Sounds like the person you're hurting most is yourself.'

Ingrid nods, standing to pick up the cheeseboard and take it into the kitchen.

'And don't you think you've been hurt enough?' she says over her shoulder, raising her voice slightly as she heads into the kitchen. 'I went out shopping and bought a new dress yesterday because the alternative was to stay in bed and cry. And you know, I bought a lipstick, too. Something I never do. I just saw it and liked the colour and thought, *yes, I'll buy this*. When I turned the lipstick upside down, its shade was called "Angel". I'm not into things like that – hidden messages – but in that moment, I felt warmth. Silly, perhaps. But it's how I felt. And it was good. Good must come from bad, Chloe. It must. Now give yourself a break. And Giles, give her some more wine.'

I'm not sure this is the best idea, but I hold the stem of my wine glass as Giles tops me up. The candlelight around the room is dancing furiously. Giles takes out his phone and after a few taps, the electronic jazz – which had built up to quite a crescendo – stops abruptly.

'Time for a bit of nineties trance?' Giles asks. 'Or Motown? Meatloaf?'

'Erm . . . Motown over Meatloaf, please. No offence to Meatloaf, like.'

'He'd take over, wouldn't he?'

'And probably overstay his welcome,' I laugh, as does Giles.

That unmistakeable sixties sound of rattling drums fills the air, and I'm glad to be here. Ingrid returns with a small cordless vacuum in her hand and zaps up the crumbs on the table like a Ghostbuster.

'How about a game of Trivial Pursuit?' Ingrid asks, leaning her weight onto one hip and resting the nozzle of the vacuum on her shoulder pretty damn stylishly. 'I'm terrible at it, but I like to try my best. I'm much better at Pictionary—'

'Oh, I *love* Pictionary,' I butt in. 'Ah, of course. We need a fourth person.'

I look to the unused chair, the cage that nobody has sat upon this evening. If Jack had gone to work that day, he'd be sitting in it now. We'd be about to play Pictionary with our charming neighbours, or perhaps be having a light-hearted debate about whether we should play Trivial Pursuit instead. Jack had a love/hate relationship with board games. When I tried to suggest a game of Scrabble in the local pub, he'd told me about how competitive his mum and his brothers were and how Christmas Day always ended in arguments. Apparently Jack and his dad would slip away from the dining table, unnoticed, and play a few rounds of poker together in the study. My heart sinks as I think about John Carmichael and what he might do this Christmas when Trish stops at nothing to get the brown Arts and Literature cheese. Where will he go?

There's a knock on the door, a friendly rat-tata-tat-tat.

'Ah, that'll be Neil,' Giles says, jumping up to answer.

Keen to put a face to the owner of the noisy suitcase, I stand and hold out my hand as Giles introduces us. Neil is so tall he ducks to enter the flat. His handshake is surprisingly warm and full of gusto. He's older than I imagined, perhaps older than my dad, with curly grey hair and a gentle but crisp clear voice. He reminds me of my old English teacher, who managed to make even *Coriolanus* interesting. Before he removes his coat, he reaches inside a pocket and removes a large Toblerone. Ingrid applauds and Giles jumps with delight.

'He never fails!' Giles adds, patting Neil on the back.

'Duty-free,' Neil tells me. 'Are you as crazy about chocolate as these two?'

'I don't know how crazy they are,' I say, 'but I'm pretty fucking crazy.'

'And we love her!' Ingrid cries. 'Now, Neil, you've arrived right on time. We're about to play Pictionary.'

And we do.

We play.

We laugh.

We disagree.

We laugh some more.

Giles draws a rocket and we all think it's a penis. The harder he tries to convince us that it isn't, drawing more lines and zigzags and buttons, the more it looks like a penis exploding.

Oh. How. We. Laugh.

It's edging up to three in the morning by the time I leave. I'm drunk, thick with red wine and heavy from chocolate. Ingrid has passed out on the sofa like Sleeping Beauty. I make some daft comment to Giles about how he has to kiss her to break the spell and I pat Ingrid's blonde hair, whispering a thank you for a lovely evening into her ear.

'Ah, Chloe, I feel like we all finally know who lives in the basement now,' Giles says. He's talking with his eyes fully closed, his hands in his pockets and unsteady on his feet. 'We invited Jack up often. He never came.'

'Shame,' Neil says, softly. 'Shame.'

'Never?' I ask. All evening, I'd presumed Jack was familiar with this flat, these people.

Giles shakes his head, eyes still closed. 'But you did, Chloe. You did.' He removes his hands from his pockets and holds out his arms like Jesus on the cross. Oh! He's inviting me for a hug. We hug it out like real mates.

'We never knew Jack,' Giles says. 'But we know you.'

'Welcome to the house!' Neil says. 'That's not inappropriate, is it?'

I shake my head, still mid-hug with Giles, and sort of mumble something about how everything and nothing is inappropriate around a woman whose fella died, and I don't know why, but we all laugh. A tired, final laugh that ends in a satisfying sigh, with a yawn thrown in for good luck. I slip my feet into my boots but I don't bother doing up the laces. Neil takes his coat and throws it over his arm, only a flight of stairs away from home. 'After you,' he says, and I trudge down the stairs carefully gripping the banister, his footsteps clomping behind me.

'Goodnight, Chloe,' Neil says, fumbling with his key.

'Night, neighbour!' I say with a salute.

35

I close the door behind me in the flat, and it feels like a window has opened.

I stumble into the bedroom and without turning the light on, flop onto the bed and tap my phone, the glow of the screen making me squint. I'm not doing anybody any favours by ignoring Justin's message any longer. Even if he's writing to tell me what a terrible mistake our horrid kiss was, I'll be on his side at least.

But by default – or habit – I open the Facebook app. Scroll. Channel 4 News clips flash by. A baby called Arthur flashing a gummy smile is six months old today. An article from the *Guardian* about the reality for 'resting' actors has been shared by three of my friends. And, like a ghost, there's Jack. His hairy face laughing, one thick arm stretched upwards and his fist punching the sky like a superhero. His other arm is around Florrie.

Florrie Ellen Tewkesbury
Missing you. You knows it. xxx

This is the Jack Carmichael who had that funeral. The one who liked Moby and The Mighty Boosh. He's podgy, out of shape from too many cheap pizzas and kebabs after pound-a-pint night at his student's union. He has a ponytail. Florrie is wearing a skirt over jeans. Both of them look pale and startled; maybe a harsh camera flash.

I don't want to see this version of Jack.

Clicking on his name, his profile appears. Unlike his real life, his Facebook life remains active. Is this what happens now? We achieve immortality thanks to Mark Zuckerberg? Will we evolve into humans who no longer grieve, knowing the digital lives of our loved ones are available at our fingertips forever?

I click into his photos. The most recent photo he posted was – of course – the man sat in the shopping trolley. I can't say I feel a sense of relief that I went to Bangkok, but there's a satisfaction in what I know. I can't play our game any more because I got the final answer. I just wish, somehow, I'd won.

What else is left unfinished?

The fridge . . . Our life . . . Slowly morphing into *my* life.

I plant my phone face down and wriggle out of my jumper dress and into bed. Once I'm cosy beneath the duvet, phone retrieved, I blink one eye open to open Justin's message.

But naturally, I bury my head into the pillow and pass out.

36

You're round the fucking bend babes xxx

At least Beth is back on text form. And she doesn't approve of what I'm doing later tonight. She'd rather me double date with her new fella and his mate.

Pal, that'd be weird.

Unlike going out alone? xxx

I never have and never will go on a blind date.

He's rich xxx

You date him then!

Nah way. My date is richer xxx

Beth, just be careful. Ok?

You too babes xxx

'Who ya texting, Miss?' Jonah Matthews asks. 'Your boyfriend, Miss?'

I don't answer, just slip my phone into my black jeans. It might be after school hours, but I'm still on duty and should be setting an example. It's Si's big night: *We Will Croon You.* Don't get me started on the other titles he came up with before deciding on that one. Anyway, it's in fine shape and

309

the kids are pumped. Ish. I've set up a makeshift wardrobe department in a maths classroom, the one closest to the drama hall. Layla Birch is in the classroom next door to that making siren noises to warm up her voice.

Other than Beth, nobody knows where I'm going tonight after the show finishes.

You see, something came in the post for Jack. An opportunity.

I haven't been reading Jack's post. He still gets letters, junk mainly, and I've been collecting them in a Sainsbury's carrier bag to give to Trish. Another month has passed without him, making it almost five months since he died; the same length of time we were together. My head can't quite understand that equation. It certainly doesn't feel equal. But anyway, a brochure arrived for Jack from an East End comedy venue. No envelope; his name and address were printed on the back page. During my uni years I went to the Edinburgh Fringe every summer, to perform in terrible student productions that played to an audience average of six. I'd spend my spare time watching stand-up. Once, in the Pleasance Dome, Michael McIntyre handed me a flyer for his gig. Goes to show – they've all got to start somewhere. I'd flicked through Jack's brochure. It's always nice to recognise a face from years ago to see who's succeeded. Or at least who's still trying. On the third page, a familiar photo caught my attention. Part fed up, part zany, one eyebrow raised high; Ross Robson. The same photo from the flyer on the fridge, but now rows of four-star reviews were printed across his curly hair. Jack and I were supposed to see his pre-Edinburgh show, testing out jokes before the big festival. Now he's performing with the critics' support.

So that's what I'm doing tonight, after the school musical.

310

I watch from the wings, arguably the best seat in the house. I get to see everything without sitting behind the fourth wall: I'm involved. The pockets of my black jeans are filled with Kirby grips. My black polo-neck is lined with safety pins. I have a needle threaded ready for me to jump into action if a leotard splits.

Some things, however, I can't fix.

The bulb on the spotlight bust during the dress rehearsal. The school budget doesn't stretch far enough to fix it – not on such short notice anyway. The painted Manhattan back-drop is slipping lower and lower as the performance progresses. The cast are doing a (moderately) good job of squatting behind it as they cross sides, except for Jonah Matthews, who is now bobbing his head up and down comically, although perfectly in time, to Si playing the famous Kander and Ebb vamp on the piano. Widening my eyes, I telepathically tell him to make himself scarce.

'*Miss!*' I hear a loud hiss beside me.

I look down to see a kid from Year Eight frantically flapping a loose piece of material hanging off her shoulder. I mime a silent 'shush', then wink. I knew the threaded needle would come in handy.

'*You're the best, Miss,*' she whispers. Right now, I'll take that.

Layla Birch's solo is up next. Si added it in at my request, and now he can't understand how it was never there in the first place. In his words, 'It'd be like *Cats* without "Memory".' Layla's long hair is swept up into a glorious bun, sparkling with glitter spray, and her elegant red dress gives her a classy maturity. It's been a month since we had our chat outside the drama hall. I've watched her take small, brave steps towards this moment. Sometimes she sang beautifully in

311

rehearsals, then sometimes she'd have a wobble, convinced she couldn't do it. I was always convinced she could, though, and told her so, spending break times working on her song and never once doodling on my costume notes.

Now, she's captivating: every member of the audience is spellbound and everybody backstage is silent, peeking through the curtains, the only part of the show they desperately need to see one more time. I know she's thinking about her mum. And I know her mum is here, too. There's no way that the woman who created this young girl has just disappeared into nothing. She's got to be somewhere, if only through her daughter.

As she sings, my own thoughts drift back to Jack. He lingers on. I wonder if he ever won't. Trish had never got back to me with a suitable date. I sent one follow-up message – you know, checking in – and when I got no reply from that, I went upstairs to see my neighbour, Neil.

'Giles and Ingrid mentioned you're going away for a while?' I'd asked as he whipped up a cappuccino for us both. 'For work.'

'When am I not going away for a while?' he sighed.

'Where to this time?'

'Cape Town.'

'Wow. Lucky you.'

'No complaints.'

I'd told him about the bulging carrier bags and two cases filled with Jack's things, still sitting in a pile beside the bookshelf in the hall. Neil had placed his hand on my shoulder mid-waffle, around when I was talking about how seeing the bags each morning churned my stomach so much that I couldn't face breakfast, and I'd shut up.

'Shall we go and get the bags now?' he'd asked.

'Now? But you're not leaving 'til Sunday.'

'I have a guest bedroom. And no guest.'

So that's where Jack's things are. I know they're there, above my head as I potter about the flat, but not physically seeing them has . . . helped. I've spent less time staring into walls and applied the energy to my job, marking work thoroughly, making lesson plans, doing whatever odd jobs have been needed for the musical. Sometimes, I catch the eye of the man sat in the shopping trolley and apologise, as if he's disappointed in me. 'Oh, don't worry,' I've said out loud, 'I can't move on. I'm just very busy.' And I'll hear a creak of the floorboards upstairs – it can't be Neil, he's thousands of miles away in South Africa – and feel hatred towards Jack for haunting me, for being right there and not being there at all.

The applause for Layla is a gentle earthquake trembling through the drama hall. I spot Si's face above the upright piano and see him flick away a tear from beneath his glasses with his thumb. As the stage lights fade to black and the audience shuffles, I'm knocked backwards by someone rushing forwards, into me. Arms are thrust around my waist, a cheek rests upon my chest, and I'm squeezed fondly.

'Layla!' I exclaim. 'You did it!'

'I loved it, Miss,' she says. 'Every second. I really loved it.'

'You weren't the only one.'

'I wanna do this for the rest of my life.'

I refrain from my typical cynical 'Oh, don't we all?' and say instead, 'And you will.'

I mean it, too.

The car park is manic within ten minutes of the final bow. Parents are yelling at their kids to get in the back seat, to stop hugging their friends, to please hurry up, they'll see them tomorrow morning for God's sake. It's impressive how quickly the place empties. I could probably leave now, but I need to speak to Si. Laden with a huge bouquet, he's man of the moment, lapping up the praise and thanks from both parents and pupils.

'It was touch and go,' I hear him say, not for the first time.

Holding the door open, I usher the last few families out of the drama hall.

'Hey, Miss Roscoe?' Layla Birch is running towards me, dress in a plastic costume bag over her shoulder, phone in hand. 'My dad wants to speak to you.'

'Okay, no problem,' and I look past her to see where he is.

'He's just moving the car, Miss. He was blocking someone.' She rolls her eyes, typical.

'Well, tell him to come and find me when he's ready. I'll be right here.'

'Thanks Miss.' Layla skips off, thanking Si, too. 'You're the best Mr S. You're wasted in this school!' And she disappears towards the main gate, embracing some of her pals along the way, grabbing a selfie.

'And dear Miss Roscoe,' Si says, once the last kid leaves. 'There's not a fallen sequin in sight.'

'Too right. I'm not risking the wrath of that PE fella.'

'He's ex-marine.'

'I know! Are you fuming? About the flowers?'

Si feigns shock. 'Never! I love them. Was this you?'

'The kids. I just sorted the collection.'

'You're going to make me cry, Chloe.'

'Please tell me you brought your car and you're not taking them home on the tube?'

314

'No, I didn't bring my car. Thought we'd be going for a drink? You always said how much you love an after-show.'

'Agh. Si, I'm so sorry. I can't tonight,' and I close my eyes, awaiting a monologue about how I've broken his showbiz heart at the final curtain.

'Don't worry!'

'What?' I don't need to feign shock. I am shocked. 'What's with the cheesy grin?'

Si hides behind the bouquet, his specs peeping over the top.

'I might have invited a certain somebody to the pub to keep me company,' he says.

'Malcolm?'

'Wah!'

'*Wah!*'

'I know!'

'Well, go. Go! Don't let me keep you!'

We air kiss and I watch Si go, holding his bouquet like he's Gene Kelly with an umbrella in *Singin' In the Rain*.

It's not raining but it's chilly, a biting wind in the autumn air. I get changed in the staff toilets; it's a swift transformation into the shirt dress, the one I wore the night I met Jack at the Brexit musical. My roots are screaming again, but it's nothing a cream beret can't hide, complemented by a bright red lip. I wrap myself up inside my burnt-orange suede coat, a second-hand gem I've had for about ten years. Yeah, this is exactly how I'd dress for a date with Jack. I'm ready.

Halfway across the car park, I hear a man's voice.

'Miss Roscoe, is that you?' It must be Layla Birch's dad.

'Ah yes, you wanted to speak to me?'

'Erm . . .' It isn't Layla's dad. Not unless he's the school caretaker and I wasn't aware. 'No I'd like to lock up, if that's alright with you?'

I blabber some apologies and make a quick exit, keeping an eye out for Layla and her dad. The road outside the school is sleepy and the houses opposite are lamplit and cosy. The buzz from the musical has gone. I'm tired, and my enthusiasm for a late-night comedy show all the way out in the East End is diminishing. I'm surprised to feel disappointed. It would've been really nice to meet Layla's dad; tell him how proud I am of his daughter.

I guess, in a strange way, I should hold onto this feeling: at the very least, it shows I care.

I dig my hands into my coat pockets and head to the station. I've already bought a ticket online for the comedy. It's date night, and it's all I've got left to stay close to Jack.

37

The gig is at a comedy club near Shoreditch High Street. Steadying myself on the banister, I walk down the narrow staircase into the bar. Guffawing laughter growls from groups huddled together holding pints carelessly, booze spilling with every jerk. There's a lot of talking. Words, words, *words*, fast-spoken, eager to be heard, nobody listening, everybody talking. More guffaws. It's like the late, late Edinburgh Fringe crowd are all in one London basement, all desperate to invent the most controversial line. And this is just the audience.

The bar is lit with blue fairy lights. The wallpaper has been stripped and I'm unsure if that's because the place is about to be refurbished or whether that's the style they're going for.

I go for a double JD and Coke. Not my usual, but one of Jack's favourites, and I want to raise a glass. We're here. We finally made it to the show.

Inside the venue, I take my suede coat off and fold it over my arm. My beret stays firm on my head. My ticket is for the standing area, which isn't all standing. There are stools, high tables and a ledge to lean on, It overlooks a seating area which is basically tables closer to the stage for double the price. Why would anybody pay to get picked on?

I lean and people-watch.

A long table dominates the centre of the seating area; it's a large party. Everybody knows each other well: the chatter is animated and intimate, personal space not a problem; touching, hugging, shoulder-to-shoulder, head-to-head. And . . . no. It can't be. It's Florrie.

I blink and lean in closer. Without that victory roll in her hair, I could be mistaken. No, it is. It's her. And I recognise a few other faces from Jack's funeral. The skinny-fat fella with – yep – there's his enormous teeth. And the girl with the baby, without the baby.

No wonder they're here. They're supporting their friend.

I should be their friend, too.

We'd all be well acquainted by now. Perhaps we'd have been to a barbecue or summer festival together. The girl with the baby looks cool; my kinda person. I imagine we'd have intense heart-to-hearts over too much wine—

The lights go down and a trumpet blasts. The show has started.

The MC gallops on and gets various groups of people whooping; those from London, those from 'UP NORF', those from far, far away. A fella in the front row gets a grilling about working in IT. It's standard amusement, but it's fun to be sharing a group experience, laughing amongst a crowd. I watch Florrie. She's unable to keep still, nosing around the whole room, perhaps looking for somebody or counting heads. Whatever she's doing, she's not listening to the jokes. Her applause lacks vigour.

'Righto, boys and girls,' the MC shouts, 'Give it up for . . . Ross Robson!'

Wearing a corduroy blazer over a creased Metallica t-shirt, Ross Robson combs back the tangled curls hanging over his eyes with his free hand, the other holding a half-drunk pint. He sports his fed-up face and a downhearted grin, dimpling at his jawline. Although he's very tall, he doesn't adjust the mic stand. Instead, he ducks.

The skinny-fat fella mouths to Florrie, 'You okay?' and she nods with a whole-body jitter, giving an equally jittery thumbs up. He gives an OK with his hand.

Ross begins. He doesn't say an awful lot, and when he does, it sounds like he's woken up with a hangover. At one point he drinks his pint and waits for a burp. He furrows his brow and releases loud sighs. Silence is padded with the odd 'fuck'. He tells a weird story about his ex-girlfriend's mum. It's really, really funny.

Florrie is sitting on the edge of her seat. She's less frantic now.

Her whole table is roaring, hanging onto Ross's every word. Jack would definitely have been here tonight. He was the first to buy tickets for the Greenwich show and promoted it like crazy on Twitter. There's no way he would've missed this one. Which means I was always coming, too. I do belong.

I clap loud at the end, wishing I knew how to whistle.

The MC returns and Ross takes an awkward bow, gives a wave-salute. Florrie is on her chair, cheering. Security wander over and tell her to get down. She's overly apologetic – bless her – and the skinny-fat fella holds up a cigarette, widens his eyes. She declines. Ross has run straight past the crowd out into the bar. The MC is introducing the next act, but I want to catch Ross, so I slip out to congratulate him.

"Ello mate,' he greets me with his deep, throaty voice. 'Chloe? I got that right, yeah?'

We kiss each other's cheeks awkwardly. He has this natural expression that's both worried and smug. It's probably his dimples, combined with his need to pull comedy out of every single situation he finds himself in: the curse of the creative.

'That was great, Ross.'

'You're from Liverpool. Aren't you supposed to say "Eh, that's boss, that!"?'

'Sure. Boss. How's it all going?'

'Not bad, mate. Yeah. Busy. On the road a lot. Did the Fringe over the summer and it's been non-stop since then, so yeah. Not bad. It's been worse, yeah. You?'

'I'm inclined to agree. Not bad. Been worse.'

Ross sips his pint and nods. Then, as if he's suddenly found something that he'd lost, he lets out an 'Oh,' and asks me if I'd like a drink. I shrug, take off my cream beret.

'Go on then.'

'Who you with?' he asks, tapping his card to pay for my next JD and Coke.

'No one,' I say, defensive, as if he's accused me of bringing a new lover. Ross is dripping with sweat and he grabs a napkin from the bar. He's pulling an odd expression and I can't be sure whether that's because he's dabbing his face or if he's weirded out by me being here, flying solo. 'I had to come and see what I missed. What Jack missed.'

Ross rolls the napkin into his fist and stuffs it into his jeans pocket.

'You're amongst friends here,' he says.

'That's kind, but not really. I don't know anyone.'

'Mmm. Yeah. Suppose you weren't given the chance, were you?'

'Nope. I appreciate you acknowledging that, Ross. It's shit, isn't it?'

'Yeah, mate. Totally shit. Then again, we're a bunch of absolute tossers so maybe you made a lucky escape.' Ross pushes his hair out the way again. 'We're not worth getting to know.'

The bar is quiet and most people are inside watching the next act. The blue lights make the basement mellow.

'Boss. I'll get a taxi now, shall I?'

'Drink up first, mate. Cost me nearly a tenner, that.'

We cheers. I want to say, 'To Jack!' but it doesn't feel organic. It was kind of Ross to buy me a drink, but he's distracted. He's clearly looking for company elsewhere. His agent, maybe. I swig and Ross lifts a single wave at somebody behind me. I turn to acknowledge whoever it is, too, but they've disappeared towards the loos. Ross continues to sweat.

'Gah,' he grimaces, flapping his Metallica t-shirt to create a breeze.

'I'm guessing that's "The Gang", then?' I ask, before he makes a getaway, referring to the table inside.

'The Gang?'

'Jack's gang. His crew, or whatever.'

'Ah, right. Yeah. The London lot. We're the ones who migrated here and – for our sins – stayed. I met Jack at uni—'

'Yeah! You shared a house in the third year and you used to cut your toenails at the kitchen table.'

'Hey. At least I cut them, rather than rip 'em off or let them grow into hooves.'

'You don't deny it then?'

Ross hangs his head low. His damp curls mask his pink cheeks.

'Ah, mate. I wish I could get my own back,' he says, his eyes falling to the floor.

He's got nothing. He's a stand-up comedian, someone used to heckles and quick comebacks, and it takes me for him to draw a blank. I'm a mystery to him, but I'm upsetting, not intriguing. I remind him of Jack, the one person not here. It's perplexing to think that minutes ago, I was belly-laughing at this man from the audience. I've single-handedly killed the comedy.

This crowd – this gang – can function without Jack here. Yeah, it's sad. But they all have history and it didn't always involve Jack Carmichael. Ross Robson will have been to parties with people sat around that table, ones that Jack didn't go to because he was working, or he was in bed with a cold, or at a family do. Ross might have been to Ibiza with them, or judging this lot, skiing. He's probably slept with one of the girls; possibly a few. That's how big groups of mates work, isn't it?

But when you throw a newbie like me in, everything shifts.

'You know what?' I say, placing my JD and Coke on the bar like a delicate ornament. 'I'm gonna go. I'm – erm – sorry. Thanks for the drink, and sorry I didn't drink – erm – I better just . . . bye, Ross.'

The narrow staircase beckons. I slip into my long suede coat and trudge upwards. Outside, two lads having a ciggie obstruct the door and before I get a chance to squeeze past them, I hear my name. My whole name.

'Chloe Roscoe,' Florrie states slowly, as if addressing an old school chum at the twenty-five-year reunion. As I turn around, I expect her to say something along the lines of, 'Well, look at you now!' or 'Who would've thought you'd become a . . .,' but she just repeats my name, even slower. 'Chloe. Roscoe.'

'I have to go,' I say, attempting a smile and hoping it sounds like I have somewhere important to be.

Florrie's bottom lip puckers and she twists from side to side. Her dress is navy blue, crushed velvet and floor length, the sleeves tight along her slim arms. Rings cover her fingers: gemstones and pagan patterns. Her eye makeup is heavy, her fiery hair loose and unstyled, as if she got out of the shower and just left it to dry. I'm into this look. It's gothic and it suits her.

'But I want to know everything!' she cries. 'After the funeral, I tried to find you on Facebook – I know, PSYCHO – but I couldn't. Are you laying low?' And she crouches down, like a cartoon cat about to pounce. She's so, so posh, it's making me want to sneeze.

'I go by Chloe Marie. Me middle name,' God knows why the fuck I told her that, ''cause I'm a teacher. Secondary. Anyway, better dash.'

I push the door a little, giving the two lads a bit of a nudge. Without any acknowledgement of my action, they flop off the step and onto the pavement in slow motion, still chatting, still smoking. The Gherkin looms in the near distance above a row of Dickensian rooftops, and the air greets me with a hint of weed from a passer-by, on a lane where Jack the Ripper supposedly once roamed.

'Chloe! Wait!'

It's Ross. He's stood in the doorway behind the two lads smoking, waving my cream beret like a flag. Florrie is on her tiptoes peering over his shoulder and beckoning me back inside with her hands.

'You forgot your hat,' Ross says.

'It's *freezing*,' Florrie calls out.

In a fatherly manner, Ross rubs his hands up and down Florrie's upper arms to give her a boost of warmth, telling her to go back inside, he'll be down in a minute. He joins me and I take back my hat, fixing it onto my head. I need to go.

'Come on,' Ross says, reaching out and punching my arm lightly. A brave move. 'Come back downstairs. I might even buy you another drink, if you're lucky.'

I raise my eyebrows.

'God, I'm a sick bastard. That just sounded like I was coming on to you, didn't it? Ah, mate. I'm sorry. I'd never. I mean, you're gorgeous. I didn't mean I wouldn't. Although I *wouldn't*. You're . . . Actually, you're probably still single, yeah?'

'Wow. Now I know what Jack meant by you being "close to the bone".'

'I'll take that as a compliment. Now can we go back inside?'

There's a twenty-minute interval before two more comedians finish up the entertainment. Ross goes straight to Florrie once we're inside at the table and I'm left without introduction or welcome. The skinny-fat fella leans across and tells me his name is Benji. Or Ben. Or Benjamin.

'Balls, call me anything!' he says, flashing his teeth. 'Everybody else does.'

'Chloe,' I remind him.

He doesn't have a fucking clue who I am.

I sit down, committing to half a seat, unsure if it's going spare. Benji-Ben-Anything yells at someone I don't recognise and a ritual ensues; fists banging on tables, thigh-slapping. A rugby chant, maybe? Was Jack into rugby? He was a Man United fan. Little old me never presumed he could be into football *and* rugby.

The girl with(out) the baby bends towards me.

'You're in my seat.'

'Oops – so sorry,' I say, standing immediately.

'Are you lost?' she asks, shuffling her seated self closer to the table, finding her question rather hilarious. I don't answer. I mean, I'm not seven years old in Tesco looking for my mum. She stares at me brazenly, amazed at – well, I don't know – something. Me? She's looking *amazed* at me. One thing's for sure – she also doesn't have a fucking clue who I am. So I hover, trying to get Ross's attention.

'You're blocking the stage,' the girl says, thinking she's made another joke.

'There's nobody on the stage,' I tell her.

'Oh, you know what I mean!' God, this one takes posh to next level. I mean, we're talking *royalty*. Clipped, Keira Knightley posh. Like, even when your family are killed in a massacre, you smile and talk through your teeth because you're bloody well English, and that's how the English bloody well deal with it, sort of posh. To think I'd thought we could be mates.

Florrie is waving me over.

'Goodbye!' I say to the girl, unable to resist putting on my best Queen's English.

'Don't talk to Minty, talk to me!' Florrie cries. Florrie and Minty. Sounds like a kids' telly programme from the seventies with sock puppets. God knows what Minty is short for. If she was from Liverpool, she'd only get called Minty if she had bad breath.

Unlike Minty, Florrie stands to talk to me. 'Was she awful to you, Chloe?'

'Who? Minty?'

'It's all a facade. She's got a heart of pure gold, that one.'

'Sure.'

'But Chloe we're all super keen to know your story. You were the first girlfriend Jack had . . . since me. And that was a long, long time ago. Like a hundred million years.'

'How long, really?'

'Erm . . .' Florrie's eyes shoot into her brain. 'Fifteen, no sixteen years. Maybe seventeen. Fuck, how old am I?'

'Dunno? Thirty-eight?'

'Eek. I'm sozzled. I was so nervous for Rossy. We heard rumours that the Beeb were in tonight. I really didn't want him to fuck up. He can be so hit-and-miss, don't you think?'

'I enjoyed it.'

'But what did you *think*?' Florrie closes one eye, pouts. The open eye flickers, the rest of her is statue-still. I should prod her, see if she tips over. 'Benji-doo! Benja-*min*! Can you talk to Chloe? I need the loo. Ah-gain!'

And whoosh. She's gone.

Benji-bloody-doo-dah makes a gross gesture for me to sit on his knee. I avoid any expression. Really, there isn't one suitable. He jumps up, apologises, plays with an unlit cigarette, puts it behind his ear. He's very sorry.

'I'm a total dick. These things give you the impression that any fucker can be funny, but well, I prove that theory wrong.'

'It's fine.'

'So, what am I supposed to be filling you in on? How can I help?'

God, I'm so tired. This is a show. An utter show. Who are these people? I wouldn't even follow them on Instagram. Even Ross, for all his depressive pleasantries and remembering to buy me a bevvie: he didn't even bother introducing me to the group.

'I'm Chloe,' I remind Ben for the third time. 'Jack's . . .' Partner? Girlfriend? Ex? What am I?

'Aha! Got it. We all thought Jack would never settle down after breaking Florrie's heart. So what was your trick? Your magic spell?'

'Wait – he broke her heart?'

'Shattered it. Told her he loved her, wanted to marry her. Slight problem, though. He was high as a kite on disco treats at a festival in Bath. Dressed as a pirate, I recall. We all were. Ah, those were the days.'

I bet.

'They were on-off childhood sweethearts,' Ben elaborates, 'and Florrie had Jack on a pedestal. Fuck, we all did. Fucker,' and he chokes up a little. 'But she really loved him. And Jack loved her, although not in the same way. I think he battled with it, if I'm honest; wished he felt the same, you know? But when the eyepatch came off and the comedown kicked in, well – he tried to put an end to it.'

'Tried?'

'Her response lacked finesse, shall we say? She refused his request. I mean, their parents used to go on holiday together; the expectations were high. So Jack went about it all in a . . . different way.'

'What did he do?'

'Started seeing somebody else.'

'Whilst continuing to see Florrie?'

'Actually, he started seeing people. Plural. Playing the field, as the saying goes.'

'Behind the poor girl's back? The fucking rat!'

'Yikes. Feels creepy speaking ill of the dead like this, don't you think? Look, we were young,' Ben reassures me. 'Jack was an idiot. But there were – and always are – two sides to the story. Florrie never did herself any favours. She refused to read the signs. Anyway, she caught him—'

'Stop. I don't need to know the ins and outs.'

'Jack never forgave himself, you know.'

'Well, you can't choose who you love,' I say, unsure of who I'm defending.

'True, true. And Jack was ever so aware of that after hurting our Flozza-belle.'

The MC interrupts us: the second half is about to commence. Ben sits, attentive; a pupil after a gold star. Since I don't have a seat, I'm able to make a French exit.

Passing through the bar, I spot Ross nursing a pint.

'Leaving, mate?' he asks. 'I sort of threw you to the lions, didn't I?'

'Yeah. Look, is Florrie alright?'

'She's fine. I'll be taking her home in a minute.'

'Oh, good. She seems—'

'I'm used to it, mate.'

'Right . . . I just wanna know, did she, erm, how can I put it? Did she ever get over Jack?'

And for the first time all night, including his performance, I witness Ross Robson break into a wide, dimpled grin.

'I fucking hope so, mate. She's been married to me for the last ten years.'

'Oh!'

'Yeah!'

'I wasn't expecting that.'

'You really didn't know?'

'Ross, I really didn't know *anything*. Did I?'

His grin drops into a bittersweet smile. 'Maybe you knew enough.'

'Maybe.'

I back away, wave.

'Not gonna stick around for the end, mate?'

'With "a bunch of absolute tossers"?' I offer. 'Your words, *mate.*'

'Don't steal my lines!'

'Ta-ra, Ross.'

And it is goodbye. These people aren't my friends; were never destined to be. I don't dislike them. They aren't bad people. Well, that Minty probably keeps puppies locked in her attic, but . . . I can't picture it. Me, hanging out with them. Imagine the bloody skiing holidays I'd have to endure. So I turn left out of the comedy club and head for Shoreditch High Street.

Back at the flat, I remove the flyer for Ross Robson's gig from the fridge and toss it into the recycling with the brochure advertising tonight's show. This isn't anger; there's no bitterness. This is simply practical. Cleansing. Another plan completed.

'We did it,' I say, removing my beret.

But – oh, Florrie. I know it was a lifetime ago, but she'd imagined a love between her and Jack that never truly existed. What if that's what I was doing, too? Ben had said it, how they all had Jack on a pedestal. What makes me so different? I'd thought Jack was the most brilliant person to walk under the sun. He *was* the fucking sun. He was the moon. He was everything.

What if I'm another Florrie?

He only ever *reckoned* he loved me.

The man in the shopping trolley catches my eye. I suppose I'll never know.

38

'You're doing so well, sis,' our Kit says, peering out from my phone screen.

'I needed to do something,' I say, tapping back into selfie mode. 'Should I text Patricia Carmichael again? I don't want her to think I'm squatting here.'

'Hold on – Gareth wants to see the flat now.'

'HI CHLOE!' Gareth smacks a kiss onto Kit's camera.

I turn the camera to show the living room again.

'It's nothing major,' I say. 'Just a few touches here and there.'

'Oh, I love the dried flowers in those empty wine bottles,' Gareth says. 'And is that us?'

He's spotted the photo of me sandwiched between the two grooms on their wedding day, in pride of place on the breakfast bar. I show Gareth the invitation he designed, sitting beside it in a matching frame.

'Did you tidy up especially?' Kit asks. 'To call us?'

'Ha. You wanna see the state of the bedroom. It's a wonder I can find me knickers.'

'A leopard never changes its spots,' Gareth chuckles.

'Is me mum still fuming?'

Kit blows out his lips. 'She never was. It's all in your head.'

I hadn't gone to visit during half term, although that had been the plan. Beth was going back to that retreat in the Cotswolds and had suggested – insisted – I went with her this time. The endless yoga did get boring, as much as I'd banked on a spiritual awakening, and the whole four days could have been more of a hoot if we'd been allowed booze, but it had been the right thing to do. Liverpool had had the potential to be a nice break. I could have caught up with mates, played Fun Aunty Chlo armed with gifts for their kids, visited my nan, but I'm not ready. I'm making progress, but I'm still worried I might once again regress to hiding in my old bedroom, emerging only for cheese toasties or to bicker with my mum. Besides, Beth asked. And she only asks when she really needs something.

'You look really good, Chloe,' Gareth says, always happy to change the subject when it concerns his mother-in-law. 'Doesn't she, babe?'

'And she's applied for the job. You know, the full-time teaching position?'

'Congratulations!'

'I've applied,' I say. 'I haven't got it.'

'*Yet*,' Gareth says. 'You haven't got it yet.'

'This is so great, sis. Do you feel like you're starting to move on?' Kit asks.

I wish we were on the phone, the old-fashioned way, so they couldn't see my face.

'Shit, what did I say?' he takes charge, walking away from Gareth.

'I'm desperate to move on, but something's stopping me. Something feels . . . incomplete.'

One plan of Jack's is outstanding, stuck to the fridge door. The estate agent's card. Jack wanted us to move out. We just never got round to discussing where or when. I've kept the card there as a potential starting point for who to call if I get kicked out.

'There's still so much I never found out.'

'You could say that about any relationship that ends abruptly.'

'Jack wasn't any relationship, though, was he?'

'You say he wasn't. And sis, I believe you. But maybe you do need to ask yourself – what if he wasn't the great love of your life? What if . . . Ah, fuck it. I'm gonna sound like me mum if I keep talking like this.'

He crosses his eyes and sticks out his tongue. We share a small, comfortable laugh.

'I'm scared, Kit. I'm so scared. Once I move on, that's it.'

'What do you mean?'

'Jack. That's it. He really will be gone.'

Kit's face softens, his voice a whisper. 'He already is, sis.'

He's aching to help me, but he can't. Just like a yoga retreat in the Cotswolds can't. With every tealight I've lit to make the living room look pretty, with every laugh I snort watching comedy panel shows at night on the telly, every lunch I share with Si, every cuppa I enjoy with Ingrid upstairs on a Sunday afternoon, I can't escape this dark cloud pressing down on my shoulders. Kit's wrong. Jack hasn't gone.

'Jack wanted us to live somewhere with a better view, you know,' I tell him.

'What's wrong with the view?'

I go to the front window.

'Ah,' says Kit, as he sees the stone stairs, a hint of daylight above tarmac. 'I see his point.'

'Dinner's ready,' Gareth shouts. He's been making risotto.

Kit throws me a 'Zig-a-zig-ah' and I quote a couple of lines from *Dirty Dancing*.

'For fuck's sake, Kit,' Gareth screams.

'He's the worst when he's hungry,' Kit whispers.

'I know. He makes Jack seem like an angel in comparison.'

'CHRISTOPHER!'

'Go! Go!' I say.

'Bye, sis!'

He hangs up. Their abrupt absence like somebody switching the main light on when you've just got into bed. I want risotto, too. But like Kit, like Gareth, I want it with my other half. Something I can't do.

There is something I *can* do, though. One last thing.

I dial the number from the business card on the fridge.

'Ashford Estates, Lorraine speaking,' says a woman, a meaty melody to her voice.

'Hiya, I'm looking for . . . erm . . .'

I haven't got a clue. Luckily, Lorraine is better at this than me.

'Rental or sales?' she asks.

'Rental.'

'What area?'

'This one, I think. It's pretty hilly around here, I bet there are some nice views—'

'Can you tell me the area? Postcode?' Lorraine doesn't show much emotion over the phone, which isn't a bad thing. She could be asking for my National Insurance number or whether I've ever had a threesome. She keeps her judgement tucked away.

'Oh God,' I say, rubbing my forehead, as if trying to remove a dirty stain. 'Your card's been on our fridge for a while. I think me partner was in touch with you or one of your colleagues, maybe late May or early June this year? He must've dropped by, unless someone he knew gave him your card.'

'Can't you just ask him?'

I gasp. That word *just* – so simple. So throwaway.

'No,' I tell her. 'He's not here.'

'Maybe give us a call back when you've had a chance to chat to him? I'm here 'til six.'

What I'd give for that chance.

I remove the card from beneath the flip-flop magnet that doubles as a bottle opener, hold it between my thumb and index finger. The last person to touch this was Jack. I bring the card to my lips and kiss it. Slipping from my grip, it flutters away, landing beneath the washing machine. I drop to my knees but my fingers can't reach to retrieve it. I grab a fork from the draining board and coax it out, my phone still pressed to my ear with my shoulder.

'Lorraine? Are you still there?' I ask.

'Yes. Can I help you with anything else?'

I'm not reading the front of the card, where the logo for Ashford Estates is printed above its address, a few metres from the Sainsbury's Local. A different address altogether is written on the back. In Jack's handwriting.

'Flat four, 68 Woodhill Road please,' I say, reading aloud. 'I'd like to view it, please.'

'Of course, Woodhill Road. Lovely. Just what you're after, on a hill. Perfect. Oh, no. Not perfect. It's no longer on the market. Never mind.'

'Oh.' I deflate. Gutted. On the verge of crying. Oh

God. Over a flat I've never fucking seen. It was on a hill. Whoop-de-doo! That would mean a steep, breathless trek from the station or the bus stop every day on the way home from school. Wonky floors. Dodgy stairs. Visitors would avoid the trip. I've saved myself the bother.

'Would you be interested in . . .' Lorraine begins, pauses. I hear the click of her mouse.

'No,' I tell her. 'It was 68 Woodhill Road or nothing.'

'68 Woodhill Road is still available. It's only flat four that's gone. You can view flat three. Same floor, flat opposite. Like a mirror image?'

'A mirror image?'

'That's what I said. Now what's your name and I'll book you in.'

On the spot, I oblige.

'Are you coming alone or should I expect your husband as well?'

'We're not married,' I say, somehow finding that marginally easier to say than 'alone'.

Lorraine releases a high-pitched, 'Oh!' and decorates her mistake with an unashamed giggle. I hear her hand banging on her desk. 'You'd think I'd learnt my lesson,' she says, catching her breath. 'Been with my other half thirty-two years. Never got round to tying the knot, though. And still, I always presume everybody else is shacked up with a ring on their finger. Oh, what am I like?!'

Lorraine from Ashford Estates has let her guard down.

Now that I'm booked in for a property viewing, Lorraine is my friend. She's telling me about a divorced couple who put their house on the market last year, how she cocked it all up – 'Oh, not the sale, just their dignity' – by putting her 'big bleeding size nine' foot in it, and well, on she goes. I might just put the phone on speaker, start tidying up, make some toast.

The man sat in the shopping trolley shares my opinion of Lorraine.

'Don't worry,' I think. 'You'll be coming with me.'

And on and on she goes.

39

Jack's problem with living in a basement flat was that this particular area of London is green and hilly. A cluster of steep parks hide behind rows of residential streets, with spectacular views of London Bridge and Canary Wharf. Jack – as grateful as he was to his parents for the low rent – always felt like he was hiding, when it suited him to be up and out. I can only hope this place is affordable.

I've got a Saturday late afternoon viewing. It's a short bus ride away. I'd walk, but the shrill wind blows sideways, smacking you in the face no matter what direction you stomp. Christmas is only six weeks away. We're in that lull before windows get their annual festive makeover; a temporary bleak darkness.

Lorraine meets me outside. She's Amazonian. She wears blue mascara. Her size nine feet sit in flat court shoes and her whole look is eighties powerhouse: pinstripe suit with pencil skirt (at least a size too small); fine black tights. She walks with a long umbrella, using it as a stick.

'So did your partner like the other flat?' she asks, jangling the keys in her hand.

Did he? I don't know. I make a comment about the weather.

She leads the way up the path towards the main entrance, unlocking the door and holding it open for me. Like the Victorian building where Jack's parents own the flat, 68 Woodhill Road is a large, double-fronted house. The exterior has been reconstructed though and the ground-floor hallway is pristine proof that the interior has been refurbished recently.

'What's his name? Your other half?' Lorraine asks. 'I remember everyone.'

'Jack. Jack Carmichael.'

I love saying his name. And I love Lorraine's question. She's innocent when it comes to the tragedy of Jack, of me. To Lorraine, Jack is still alive. Why wouldn't he be?

'Small guy, cycles everywhere?' she asks.

'Nope,' and that single word gives it away.

'Oh! I know Jack. Big bloke, beard. Laughs and the whole room shakes.'

'Spot on.'

'See? Told you I remember everyone.'

We go up six flights of stairs. The carpet is sea blue, spongey, the staircase wide.

'Keeps you fit, this place,' Lorraine says, out of breath and seemingly enjoying it.

We reach the top floor: the roof. Flat four has a tall plant outside and a faded Hello Kitty doormat. Flat three looks empty. Lorraine confirms it as she turns the key.

'Nobody's ever lived here,' she says. 'Brand, spanking new.'

It's huge, perhaps due to the lack of furniture. We're in an open-plan kitchen-diner-living area, wooden floors polished, a sloping low ceiling with beams. Three separate arched windows stretch from the floor upwards, overlooking a great distance. I press my body against the glass, taking it all in.

'You won't find any famous landmarks out there. That's the Kent countryside, a few suburbs. Still impressive though, don't you think?' Lorraine says, then points her thumb behind her back. 'That's the property with the London skyline. The one your man viewed.'

I turn around. The space between us feels vast.

'Jack viewed that flat? Opposite?'

'While ago. Early June, maybe? It was a damn sight hotter than today, anyhow. We both had to duck to stand over by the windows – bloody slopes.'

I'd thought Jack had only been into the offices of Ashford Estates; maybe looked at photos in the window. He's been here, though; actively viewed this place. Well, *that* place. Why hadn't he told me?

'Can I see the bedroom?' I ask. Ironically, I need some space.

'Plural. There's two. And three bathrooms. Go bananas.'

I have to imagine a bed, a lamp; although there's a delightful walk-in wardrobe. The slope ceiling is in here too, creating warmth within this somewhat sterile apartment. I wonder what we'd hang on the walls. Get some new prints of Thailand; frame them. A low bed, for sure. I can't imagine Jack anywhere here though. The basement flat is much smaller and yet, there, he fits. Snug. Here, he'd be banging his head and walking in zigzags.

When I return to the main space, Lorraine is inspecting the cooker.

'Thoughts?' she asks.

'Amazing. I completely love it. Out of me price range, like.'

'Probably a good thing. If you know what I mean?'

'No?'

'Oh, because your lovely man, Jack – well, it's not his style at all, is it? Said he'd rather be putting a deposit down on a place in the country, get some horses, build proper fires. He kept talking about chopping wood like his dad. What? What's wrong? Have I put my foot in it again?'

She's definitely put that bloody big foot in something; although what, I'm not sure.

'So this place is for sale? Not rent?' I ask.

'Oh! Are you guys not looking to buy any more?'

Jack and I had never discussed buying a property together. We hadn't *not* discussed it either. We'd fantasised about our future home together: a hot tub, a corner bar and pool table, a family cinema. We may as well have been planning to be a ballerina or an astronaut when we grew up. We had our dreams, but we weren't getting practical about them, scaling them down to fit reality. Not yet.

I can't tell Lorraine any of this, though. It might make her think twice, hold back. She's breaking some sort of data confidentiality, no doubt, with her stories, and I want to know more.

'We are,' I lie, 'but he's always changing his mind. Silly old Jack. One minute he wants a rooftop apartment looking over London, and the next he wants – erm – horses, like you said. No wonder it's taken us almost six months to get back in touch with you.'

'Well, what's the rush? None of us are going anywhere, are we?'

Ah. Lorraine. How little you know.

'And he really didn't like this place, did he?' I prompt.

'No, not at all. But he knew you'd love it,' and she's laughing at herself, at the memory, at Jack, at the jokes they'd shared, 'and he was saying how he was gonna have to buy you a pair of wellies filled with . . . oh, what was it . . . some chocolate bar. A Kinder egg . . . no, Bueno! Filled with Kinder Buenos! Convince you to move to the sticks.'

I turn back to face the window, let my eyes wander miles and miles past rooftops, chimneys, fields. 'Could you give me a minute, Lorraine? I need to . . .' and I swallow, steady myself on the upper window ledge.

'I'll be downstairs, there's a comfy sofa in the hallway. I've got a few calls to make.'

She leaves the door ajar and gradually, her footsteps disappear.

It's wonderful that Jack wanted to buy; that he was in a decent financial position. God knows I'm not there yet, not on my salary. I've only been a teacher for a few years. I knew he had some savings, some inheritance. I'd wondered why he hadn't already bought somewhere, but it wasn't a question I asked. And I would've asked, had the conversation come up. It just hadn't.

I sit on the polished wood floor in the centre of the room, unravel my scarf, try to feel at home. My fingers dance, creating an invisible circle of trust, sensing the vibe. It's clinical, this flat, but the potential is huge. For plants, plants and more plants, enjoying the sunlight from the long windows. How could Jack not love this place? I'd put some beanbags over in that small nook; a reading corner. The less I try to imagine Jack in this space, the more I see. A hanging rack for pots and pans; tall standing candles beside each window.

I think of Jack, banging his head. Wanting to chop wood. Did we really want such different things?

Does that matter? Or, more accurately, would that have mattered?

'Jack?' I whisper, standing up.

With everything I do, no matter how big or small, I can sense a connection to Jack. Except in here. I don't even feel like crying. Perhaps because this is beyond my means. Pure fantasy. I'm what the teacher in me would call a time-waster, viewing properties I can't afford. So I wrap myself up with my scarf, bow my head and meander out of pretty much my dream apartment.

'Miss Roscoe? Are you alright?'

I jump, dropping my satchel between flat three and flat four, startled out of my thoughts. It's a man, maybe older than me by a few years, his hair floppy – rather retro – like the hero of a Touchstone movie. His stubble is fair, his smile kind. I don't know him, but he definitely knows me. He's bent down, retrieving my bag and the pens that have rolled onto the communal sea-blue carpet.

'I didn't mean to give you a fright,' he laughs, unsure of himself.

'It's okay, I was a million miles away.'

'One too many?'

'Huh? Erm, no – not at all—'

'Whoa, I was completely joking. And I wasn't judging. Teachers are allowed to drink, I didn't—'

'It's fine. I drink all the time. Just not this afternoon. Yet.'

'Fair enough,' he says, still holding onto my satchel. Like me, he's wearing a denim jacket – although it's smarter than mine, obviously more expensive, a grey hoodie sitting comfortably beneath it. I reach out to take what's rightfully mine and get the impression he doesn't realise what he's doing. He mumbles a further apology and hands over the satchel, then the loose pens, one of them pink and fluffy, like a camp flamingo.

'A gift,' I say, defending my choice of stationery.

'Again, not judging.'

I wonder if he works at the school. He called me Miss Roscoe. I haven't been the most sociable member of staff; I'm not on first name terms with that many teachers . . . wait. Oh God. How could I be so stupid? He must be a parent.

'Congratulations on the lovely performance before half term,' he says, and now he's holding his hand out to shake mine. I accept.

'Thanks! I really can't take the praise, though. It was all Si – Mr Sullivan. Yeah, Mr Sullivan. He's boss. I mean, professional. A true pro.'

'Are you from Liverpool?'

'Yeah. How'd you guess?'

'My mum's from Southport.' He leans back into his door frame.

'Oh. Wow . . . erm . . . that's spooky. Well, not really.'

'A coincidence, maybe?'

'A mature spin on spooky. I'll go with that. Anyway, I'm glad you enjoyed the show.'

'I did. It was a very special night.'

'Well, like I said. You should tell Mr Sullivan, he'll be thrilled.'

'No, it *was* you I wanted to tell, actually. You're wrong when you say you didn't do much, Miss Roscoe. You did everything.'

I stuff the pens into my satchel and blow a raspberry to dismiss his comments. I've honestly no idea why. In a panic, I blow another raspberry, just to highlight how ridiculous I am.

'You helped my daughter,' the man says, unaware of my silliness. 'I'm Layla Birch's dad.'

'Oh my! Layla Birch's dad,' I squeal, and I shake his hand. Again.

'Oliver,' he says. 'Ollie.'

'It's so nice to meet you, Oliver . . . Ollie.'

'The pleasure's all mine.'

'You have an amazing kid.'

'You're an amazing teacher. Layla tells me you have a lovely singing voice.'

'Mediocre at best. But your daughter, well, she's gonna go far.'

'Thanks to you, Miss Roscoe.'

'Chloe! Call me Chloe. Or Chlo?'

'Okay. Chlo.'

'Unless we're in school and then you'd have to call me Miss Roscoe.'

'I'm a bit old for school, don't you think?'

And I laugh. Well, that was funny. He's funny. Oliver. Ollie. God, I'm just so made up that I helped Layla Birch; and I mean, really, really helped her, because I'm standing here with her dad, and he's genuinely grateful. And funny. He's been through hell and yet he's being funny.

'I was here to—' I feel the need to explain.

'So now you know—' Ollie says at the same time, then, 'Sorry. You first, Chlo.'

'Oh, I was just gonna say that I came here to view this flat, Number three.'

'And I was going to say – now you know where I live. I mean, where Layla lives. Should I tell her that her teacher is about to become her neighbour?'

'God no!'

344

'You didn't like it?'

'No, I loved it. I do. It's – erm – not the right time.'

'Well, if you have second thoughts and want to see how the place can look – you know, lived in, slight leak in the bathroom, clothes hanging on the radiator 'cause I never get a chance to fix the tumble dryer – honestly, drop by.'

'I will. Your flat has the better view, too. So I hear.'

'It was the deal-breaker. We needed something extra special, Layla and me.'

I nod, and desperately want to reach out, squeeze his hand.

'Well,' he says, 'shame I won't have a private tutor across the hall.'

'I don't think there's anything I could teach you—'

'I meant, for Layla. Obviously.'

'Obviously!'

'Look, I have to dash,' Ollie says and taps the NHS badge hanging on a blue cord around his neck. 'I'm on my way to work. Night shift.'

'Oh, rubbish.'

'Nah. It's fine. And anyway, I'm one proud dad. Always counting my blessings.'

Ollie Birch goes away as quickly as he showed up. I look for the shadow hanging over him, try to spot the hunch in his shoulders, the weight he must carry. But I don't see anything: just a man jogging down the stairs, on his way to work. A dad feeling proud of his little girl.

And I'm proud, too. Of myself. I did good. As a teacher. I actually did good, didn't I?

Cold air from the vacant flat tickles my neck.

It will be warmer inside Ollie and Layla's place. *Lived in.*

How I'd love a place to call my own, to paint with my colours.

Outside, I bid Lorraine farewell, tap my satchel and tell her that I'll keep her card, it's safe in there. She knows I won't call. As I watch her go, the stick of the umbrella leading her way, my own phone vibrates. Somebody is calling me.

'Chloe!' It's Trish. She's so in control of her words, so rich with authority as she speaks, that I listen to her as if it were a recorded message. 'Accept my apologies for not contacting you sooner. It's been a difficult patch. Can you bring Jack's things over tomorrow? I know it's short notice but I'm sure you're as eager to get rid of them as I am to see them. Yes, dear?'

All I can manage to say is 'Yeah.'

'And let's get that contract signed. Cheerio.'

When I get back to the flat, I remove Jack's magnets from the fridge. For all I know, they might hold meaning to Trish and John. Maybe they went to Pisa together. I take each one down and wrap them collectively in kitchen foil. Then I message Beth, asking if I can borrow her car tomorrow. I'll get Neil's spare key from Giles and Ingrid in the morning.

The fridge looks bare: an empty white space.

Or a blank canvas.

'I'm not ready,' I say, my breathing shallow. 'I'm not . . . I'm not ready.'

40

The Carmichael house is a short drive on from a quaint town in rural Berkshire.

It was like driving through a film set: thatched cottages; shops called 'Ye Olde' something; a far cry from the identical three-bed semis and shopping precincts I was used to growing up. I spotted a theatre currently home to a touring production of *Blithe Spirit*. A lot of charity shops.

I park on the road – there's ample space, this being a quiet road with just a few houses, all differing in design and era – and decide to leave Jack's things in the car for now. I can't carry everything in one go.

I'm about to release the latch on the front gate when my phone rings, the piercing tone spoiling the idyllic surroundings. Fiddling with the car key, I unlock the car and sit back behind the steering wheel. It's my mum.

'Happy birthday!' she shouts, my dad echoing the words closely behind.

'Thank you – but remember, I'm putting me birthday on hold this year,' I remind them.

'Did your cards arrive?'

'Mum, I just said——'

'I know what you said but I can't not send me daughter a card on her birthday, can I?'

'I'll check when I get back. Just out at the moment.'

'Oh my God! Chloe! You're there, aren't you? Bernie? She's there!' And my mum lowers her voice to a stage whisper. 'Patricia Carmichael's house.'

'Just got here, so I should go——'

'Oh I can't believe it, love. I just can't believe you're there. In the countryside. Patricia Carmichael's house. What's it like? Is it double-fronted? Bet it's double-fronted. And is there an annexe, you know, as if they built a pool and sauna once she got famous and the money started rolling in? Bet they never use the sauna. Who even enjoys a sauna? I'm sweating cobs just thinking about one.'

'There's no annexe, Mum. Not that I can see. It's quite modern——'

'Modern?! You mean like something on *Grand Designs*?'

'No, more like our Kit and Gareth's house but about five times bigger.'

'You mean it's got orange bricks?'

'Yeah.'

'Oh love, I wasn't expecting that. And what a shame; no pool and sauna.'

'Well, I'm not here for a spa weekend, Mum.'

'Hold on, Chloe. Shush a sec. Your dad wants to say hiya . . .'

There's a scuffle, muffled exchanges down my earpiece, a mild sort of tug-of-war; then I hear my dad's singsong phone voice, as if he's answering a call for Bernie Roscoe Taxis.

'Alright Tilly Mint! How's the birthday girl?'

348

'I'm okay, Dad. But I should go—'

'Say no more, say no more, my love. We know today's not gonna be easy for you and we just wanted to tell you that we love you. Pick a date, any date, and we'll take you for a meal, pretend it's your birthday. Or we could get a Chinese banquet . . .'

There's another scuffle; more muffled voices. I pull the phone away from my ear.

'Chloe? You still there?' It's my mum again. 'Now what car have they got?'

'Mum, I've really got to go—'

'Why? Is she there? Trish? Is she . . . Hiya Trish!'

'She's not here, Mum! I'm sat in Beth's car.'

'Well get out then, soft girl! What you doing sat in Beth's car?'

God, how I wish I could hang up.

'You know, we've been thinking about Trish a lot lately, haven't we, Bernie?' my mum says. 'She hasn't been on the telly since . . . you know.'

'I know.' Although in truth, I only realise now. I look through the driver seat window towards the house. So much sadness will have taken place in there: the loss of a son. A child. It doesn't matter that Jack was thirty-eight when he died. He was Trish and John's child. No wonder she hasn't been on the bloody telly since. I'm surprised she's left her bed.

'Anyway, give her all our love,' my mum says, and my dad reiterates it in the background.

'She'll be thrilled,' I say. 'Bye Mum, bye Dad. Love you millions.'

'Love you more,' they say in unison.

I walk up the front garden path and don't need to ring

the doorbell. John Carmichael is sitting in an armchair by the front window and gives me a cheery wave. He stands and calls out, but I can't hear what he says. He's in a warm woollen jumper, a small zip pulled up beneath his chin. He waves again and as I return the gesture, the door opens.

'Freddie – hiya!' I say. I'd presumed I'd never see this fella again.

'Hey. Come in. I can't tell you to make yourself at home, though. This isn't my house. I don't live here. Not any more,' he says, not making eye contact. He's lost weight and looks very much like he does live here. He's wearing a dressing gown and slippers. 'I'm just here for a few days. Got my own place, river view.'

'That sounds lovely, Freddie.'

John has walked into the hallway, which is vast and minimalist. It's not the cluttered interior of the country manor I envisaged at all. It's more like a show home, as if photos have been taken down from the walls, flowers taken out of vases. John is holding a mug with both hands, so he nods his head and smiles; no words. I follow suit: nod and smile. As neat as I recall him being in those few sad times last summer, he has a serene glow about him today, his hair longer and a little fuzzy around the edges, as if he's decided to boycott the barbers. He throws another smile my way before slowly returning to his armchair by the window. Freddie has sat himself upon the stairs, his elbows resting on his knees, his head hanging low.

Trish appears from the opposite side of the house: the kitchen, I presume. Her trademark earrings dangle from each ear: peacock feathers. Her glasses are hanging on the gold chain around her neck. The spikes are still in her hair, but the colour is less vibrant, the grey more prominent. Like

Freddie, she has lost weight, her beige trousers hanging off her like jogging bottoms, a knitted waistcoat cuddling her like a blanket.

'Ignore the state of the place,' she tells me straight off. 'It's got no atmosphere, I know, I know. We're leaving. Not for good. Just for a while. I refuse to spend Christmas in this damned house. This damned country.'

Freddie emits a growl and heaves himself up by pulling on the banister. He begins to flop his feet up the stairs when Trish plants her hands on her hips.

'And where do you think you're going?' she asks her son.

Trish takes my elbow and walks me forward, like a debutante being presented at a ball. Freddie's eyes burn into his mother's and I've no clue what the dynamic is between them; it doesn't feel good. I should get the bags out of the car and go.

'Freddie, put some proper shoes on and help Chloe bring Jack's things in,' Trish says, softening her tone. 'Then I'll make you some eggy bread.'

Freddie's whole body slumps and he jerks his head back, groaning, 'Fine.'

Off he goes, ducking beneath the staircase to sift through a small mountain of shoes: various types and sizes from wellies to trainers. Trish is watching his every move, analysing how he stoops, how he ties his laces, her eyes narrowed and her lips pursed. Then she opens the front door and herds both Freddie and me out like cattle. We trudge the bags into the house and leave them – as directed by Trish – by the shoe pile.

'Now go and sit with your father,' Trish tells Freddie.

He obliges, oozing reluctance. He lies flat down on the sheepskin rug beside John's chair and starts to scroll through his phone. John, who's been staring out of the window, turns his head towards us and gives a sleepy, closed-mouth smile to his wife. Trish returns it with a thumbs up.

'Follow me, Chloe,' she says. 'Coffee?'

41

I'd rather not stay. I don't see the point. I feel in the way, like I've brought back one bag too many. Trish is aware of my hesitation.

'Don't tell me you only drink tea.'

'Coffee's great.'

The kitchen is dreamy. Right out of a magazine. It's not lifeless like the hall or the sitting room. A few used mugs sit beside a half-full cafetière, the rich aroma of coffee shaking the room awake. A fresh baguette lies on a chopping board, half eaten, and crumbs are speckled onto the gleaming white island. Loose papers in a haphazard pile lie beside an open MacBook Air.

'Oh, this is beautiful,' I say, pointing at the wildflowers arranged in a basket on the table. Cornflower blues and sunny oranges poke out from the richest ruby reds; a gift, no doubt, as I can't imagine anybody would buy this for themselves. They remind me of the bouquet Giles and Ingrid bought for me all those months ago: a flash of a memory. Did I put them on display? I seem to recall hiding them in a cupboard.

'Take it when you leave,' Trish says, her glasses now on the end of her nose as she closes down tabs on the MacBook and folds it shut. 'I can't bear flowers of any sort. Not indoors, anyway.'

'Oh, me too.'

Trish dips her chin and stares at me from over the rim of her specs.

'It comes from me mum. And me nan,' I say, shaking my head at how abstractly I'm behaving. 'Sorry – I mean, I think flowers are beautiful, to look at. Especially outside, like you mentioned. But I don't like them in me own house, or flat. You see, me mum lost her dad when she was a little girl. When he died, neighbours kept buying me nan flowers. She'd leave them in the paper wrapping, slinging them on the kitchen table or by the phone in the hall, sometimes on the floor. Me nan's a proper tough cookie but she couldn't deal with the flowers, sort of like if she acknowledged them it'd cause her to wobble. She had no time for that. Tough as she was, though, she didn't have the heart to tell people to stop, they were only doing their best, being kind. Anyway, it was me mum who'd pick the flowers up, put them in a vase. They didn't have many vases – I mean, their house was dead small. So sometimes she cut the stems and put them in a tall glass or left them soaking in the sink. To this day, me mum won't go near a florist. She hates the smell and what it reminds her of. Sad, dark days. I guess it rubbed off on me.'

'Hmm.' Trish goes to the sink, rinses a couple of mugs and pours us both a coffee. She removes her glasses and chain from around her neck. 'Sounds like your mum and I have a lot in common after all.'

She lights a hob on the island cooker and takes a clean

pan out of the dishwasher, heating it up with a generous splatter of oil.

'Does your mum make eggy bread?'

'No. She's always on a diet.'

In the middle of beating two eggs with a fork, she suddenly stops what she's doing to look through the open doorway. I follow her gaze. John has moved from his armchair and crossed the hall. There's a distinct lack of background noise in this house: no telly blaring, no radio muttering, no buses hurtling past. I hear a door open, close and lock, and a minute later, a toilet flush. Trish is watching Freddie scroll through his phone. John unlocks the door and goes back to where he came from. Trish's shoulders soften. She returns to beating the eggs.

'Pills work for Johnny,' she tells me, slowly, each word clipped. 'But they don't work for Freddie.'

She adds milk to the beaten eggs and goes a bit crazy with the salt and pepper.

'I take them to sleep,' Trish continues, 'but Johnny takes them both day and night now. Doctor's orders. He's doing well. Unlike my baby. I'll never trust him on his own again. Pass me that bread knife, will you, dear?'

I oblige and Trish slices the baguette up with terrific speed before dipping each piece into the eggy mixture and tossing it into the hot pan.

'What happened?' I ask, the sizzle making me jump. 'Sorry, you don't have to—'

'Overdosed. Says it was an accident. Freddie's always needed an extra eye on him, you see: a strong arm around his shoulders. And he's had that, in abundance, his whole life. It's exhausting, Chloe. But essential. It never occurred to me that Jack would be the one I'd lose. Not for a second.'

The bitterness in her tone makes me think that somehow, she's blaming herself for Jack's death, which is ridiculous, but also achingly sad. I imagine sitting in this kitchen under different circumstances. Maybe I'd be talking to Trish about my job, or listening to tales about hers: what she really thinks about Jeremy Vine and Piers Morgan. Maybe I'd get a slice of eggy bread. Jack would be chatting to his dad in the lounge, kicking his brother jovially and telling him to get off his lazy arse, to put his phone away. I wonder what Jack and John chatted about? I want to ask Trish, but I can't. We aren't there. I can't force her to reminisce just because I'm creating a fictional scenario in my head.

'Did you keep anything?' Trish asks, flipping the eggy bread. 'Of Jack's?'

'No, I promise everything is there. Every sock, every belt.'

'Chloe, I didn't mean you couldn't keep something. I asked because I was interested to see what you'd kept, if anything. But forget it. It doesn't matter.'

'Of course it matters,' I cry. 'I would've kept a t-shirt. Any t-shirt. I've been sleeping in them, you see, since he . . . But I stopped doing that about a month or so ago. I didn't wanna stop; I wanted to sleep in them forever, just in a very different life. Sorry, that was way too much information.'

Turning the heat off, Trish slips the eggy bread onto a plate and squeezes a huge dollop of ketchup on the side. Holding up one finger tells me silently that she'll be back in a minute.

The coffee is strong; the caffeine jitter tickles my knees, my knuckles.

Breezing back into the kitchen, Trish pulls out a chair and plonks down beside me.

'How's work going?' she asks, clasping her hands together on the table and crossing her ankles. 'A teacher, yes?'

'Good. Better than ever. I've applied for a permanent post. We recently had a school production and it really lifted me spirits,' and I stop. Minutes ago, this woman confided in me how her husband and son are battling with serious depression and there's me making my life sound like a fucking episode of *Glee*. Trish gives another, 'Hmm,' a little higher pitched than last time.

'And how's your family? Do you get back to Liverpool much?'

'I try. Me brother got married in the summer.'

She nods slowly, and rocks, like she might be thinking about Kit's wedding, imagining herself there. When she stops still, she squints, searching for the words to her next question. Her eyes close briefly before pinging open and locking tight with mine.

'Thailand!' she exclaims, clicking her fingers. 'Tell me more.'

How does she know I went to Thailand? And why does she want to know what I did there? Did I tell her when I left the flat in the summer? I can't recall giving her details. It's a haze.

'Was it a backpacking sort of trip?' Trish quizzes. 'I would've thought you were a bit past it – too old for that sort of thing, yes? I can't imagine Jack splashing out on a fancy hotel, though – he was never one for lounging by a pool. I'm curious.'

'Oh!' She meant *with* Jack. 'It was just a holiday.'

'What sort of holiday?'

'Erm . . . a normal one.'

'What's normal, Chloe? Some believe a Caribbean cruise is normal, others Butlin's in Bognor. Elaborate, dear.'

'Well, we roamed.'

'Around the city? The temples? The beach?'

'Everything, everywhere. Bangkok first and last, a few islands in between. We drank loads, ate loads, didn't have much of a plan, but you know, just kept moving. Did whatever we felt like. 'Cause we could. It was amazing.'

'Why did you go?'

'Why does anyone go on holiday? To escape. Spend time with your fave people. Person.'

Trish straightens in her seat and, using her fingers, counts out what I've told her like a list.

'So . . . you and my son ate, you drank, and you had no plan.'

'Yeah. And – like I said – it was amazing.'

Trish gives a short, clipped, 'Hm,' and moves to the island to tidy up. She removes her wedding ring, placing it on the closed MacBook, and runs the tap, rinsing and scrubbing the frying pan rather than loading the dishwasher.

'I can show you some photos on me phone?' I suggest. 'But they're kind of boring. Just typical holiday snaps, you know. A few bad selfies with sweaty faces and a waterfall a bit skewwhiff in the background. And I'm sure you don't wanna see photos of me toes on a sun lounger. Or Jack's toes for that matter.'

Trish turns off the tap. 'He really did have the hairiest toes, didn't he?'

'Hahaha, oh God. Yeah!' I stand, get closer to the island, closer to Trish. 'And you know what I remember most about that holiday? Not the pad thai or the strolls along the beach at night-time, but Jack's laugh. That big, bellowing, boss howl that came from right here,' and I punch my own stomach. Trish is nodding and it steers me on. 'And I can't get this image out of me head, this annoying, excruciating image—'

'Of Jack?'

'Oh no. Of me. We were in Koh Phangan. I know, I know, it's famous – or infamous – for those full moon parties, but we weren't into that. Like you said, Trish, a bit past it. Too old for that sort of thing.'

Trish widens her eyes at me, drying the pan with a tea towel.

'Anyway,' I go on, running away with my own words, 'we stayed at this hotel. It was built on giant rocks, and all the rooms were like mini chalets, dotted around winding paths. Our room had a balcony with a hot tub – a *hot tub* – and of course, the resort offered Thai massages. So off we went, through the winding paths, towards a beach hut where two ladies were waiting with two empty mats, as if they knew we were coming. Jack and me lay on our front, heads facing towards each other, trying not to make the other one laugh. I mean, it was picture perfect, the swish of the water meeting the sand, the breeze kissing our skin . . . Then, it started to hurt. The massage. Like, really, really hurt. I tried so hard to keep a straight face, you know, not wince. But it got worse. The lady got stuck into me thighs and legs, pulling them in all sorts of directions. I was fuming. There was Jack, all zen, getting what I always imagined a Thai massage was, but for some reason, I was getting the shit beaten out of me. At one point, the lady yelled, "You tense!" And I yelled back, "You think?!" I mean, she obviously knew what she was doing, but she grabbed me leg again and hoisted it up to me ear, really going for it. I squealed and Jack opened his eyes, catching me in the most upside-down-inside-out unflattering position, rolls of flab from me hips crushed into me belly, me bikini

359

bottoms right up me bum, and as I tried to breathe through the pressure . . . I farted.'

'You farted?!'

'Yeah! And Jack. Oh! He howled. His laughter practically shook the beach hut into pieces! He was like this God of All Laughter, each chuckle causing mass vibrations, and I can hear it now, like an out-of-body experience, watching meself on the mat, and Jack just howling.'

I sit down, my cheeks hot, flushed. I didn't mean to tell the whole story.

Trish massages a little dollop of hand cream into her palms and puts her wedding ring back on. She looks deep in thought, as if she's trying to picture something. Then she laughs: a silent belly laugh, causing her to shake. She shuts her eyes and holds onto the sink, bowing her head and letting the laughter come in gentle waves.

'You farted?' she squeaks.

'I didn't mean to!'

Then she throws her head back, cackling, louder with each laugh. Just listening to her makes me feel like I'm being tickled, and it's infectious, so I slap my hand over my mouth to control myself. Trish's howling now, not too dissimilar from Jack, a trait he definitely inherited from her. My eyes are wet and I fight back the tears, laughing at my own embarrassment, but laughing with Trish – actually *with* her. She holds out her hand to me, so I stand and take it. We're crossing our legs, bent sideways, crunching each other's hands, laughing. She catches her breath and says, 'Ooooh,' before another wave sends her laughing again.

Eventually she breathes a long sigh, which I reciprocate. We're knocked for six.

Trish composes herself, re-spikes her hair, pinches her

cheekbones. Ever the professional. She taps the sink with her fingertips.

'Yes,' she whispers to herself, then looks to me. 'I get it now.'

'Get what?'

'Well, you're the reason I hardly saw my son in the last few months of his life.'

'Oh, God!'

'Chloe. I knew everything about my son. Everything. He was an open book, never had a single secret.'

'You've got Florrie to thank for that,' I say, shocking myself.

'Yes, I do have Florrie to thank for that. We only learn by making mistakes. Jack took a long hard look at himself after what he did to her. Gave him the ability to make better choices moving forward. He used to be such a people-pleaser as a child. Drove me mad. He didn't need to be anything other than his totally brilliant self.'

I smile, feel a glow of warmth.

'I didn't realise until after he died,' Trish goes on, 'that I hadn't seen that much of him during the first part of this year. Time goes so quickly – you know how it is. It's taken me a while to figure it out, but now I know he had a secret. You.'

My smile drops so spectacularly that I practically hear it smash.

'A secret?' I ask.

Trish nods.

So there it is. Confirmed. I should get Patricia Carmichael to record that on my phone, have it as clear evidence that what I thought was the biggest thing to ever happen to me was quite the opposite to Jack. How had I judged my own life so spectacularly wrong? All this grief, all this pain: what's it been for? A fantasy? God, I almost lost my best friend, my career, ruined my brother's wedding for my mum . . .

'There's more coffee,' Trish says.

'No, thanks. You don't need me hanging around.' I know now that I've lingered long enough, and I'm ashamed. 'Look, I owe you a fair amount of rent. Please don't think I'd ever rip you off. And I know I'm here to sign a tenancy, but it's probably best if I find somewhere else to live; get a clean break. Please send me your bank details. I can transfer today. All I ask is that you give me time to find—'

'Chloe?' I hear from behind me. John. He places his empty mug on the island, silently. 'You weren't a secret. Jack was just making sure you'd be ready. It wouldn't have been a picnic.' He flicks his head in the direction of where his wife is standing and on cue, she rolls her eyes.

'Jack must have loved you very much,' John adds.

Trish lets out a sigh as if John has lowered the tone, polluting the air with the 'L' word. She leaves the room, giving me a careless tatty-bye-toodle-oo wave, and heads into the lounge to join Freddie.

'I wish you were right, John,' I say, softly. 'I hope you're right.'

I say goodbye with an air of false confidence, like I can see myself out, and leave John alone with the wildflowers and coffee aroma. As I reach the front door, I hear Trish telling Freddie to mute that damn thing, and then silence crash lands.

'What was the business with the Thai man, Chloe?' Trish shouts, matter-of-fact. I can see her from the hallway, Freddie's head in her lap, stroking his hair. 'That photo. I recall you talking about it, just after he died, but I can't remember the details. Do you know about this, Freddie?'

362

Freddie doesn't respond. I think he may be asleep.

'Just a touristy photo Jack took when we were in Bangkok. Quite a common snap.'

'Oh. What a letdown.' Trish twists her head around to display her disappointment and John leans against the kitchen door, his arms folded. 'I thought you were going to tell me something magical.'

I laugh a little, kindly. 'You and Jack. Two peas in a pod.'

'What do you mean?'

'He was always saying there must be something behind the picture. I'd love there to be more of a story for you all. But there's not. I even went all the way to Bangkok to try and figure it out—'

'Wait, Chloe. Jack was always saying there was something behind the picture?'

'Always.'

Trish and John share a glance.

'Knowing Jack,' she says, 'he probably meant there was something behind the picture.'

'Huh?'

'Our darling boy was a great many things,' John says, tenderly, 'but he was not cryptic. There was nobody more transparent than Jack. He simply said what he meant. But I don't mean to patronise, love. I'm sure you knew that.'

'So you think Jack meant that there's something – an actual *something* – behind the picture?'

Trish brings her shoulder to her ears, slowly, then releases, turning back to play with Freddie's hair.

Something behind the picture?

Some . . . thing?

If so, what?

42

'Well it's obviously gonna be a ring,' Beth says, her hair and body wrapped tight with towels.

'Don't be daft, pal. Jack wouldn't put a bloody ring behind it.'

'You won't know 'til you look.'

'Beth. Please.'

'What?'

'Jack wasn't corny like that.'

'To be fair, babes, you only knew him for five minutes. Oops. I mean months.'

God, she is such a brazen little bitch, isn't she? Sitting on her throne – yes, a throne – stylishly placed beside the bay window of her new home in a building called (no word of a lie) 'Princess Mansions'.

'Watch your gobby mouth,' I tell her. 'You've only been with Paul Rudd for five minutes and he's already got a key.'

'I can always change the locks, can't I?'

The drive from the Carmichaels' back to Beth's took forever. I got every single red light. I want to be home. In my home. Our home. Whatever Jack put behind that picture is exactly what I'm ready for. I'm sure of it. Beth can see I'm itching.

'You better get going,' Beth says, unravelling the towel from her head and shaking out her wet hair. 'Paul Rudd'll be here in a mo and last time he came over, he had a rose between his teeth.'

'Gross.'

'You know I *love* that shit.'

'Do I look okay?'

'Honestly, you need your roots doing. But I'm sick of telling you. Why?'

I want to feel good when I look behind the picture. Can't pinpoint *why*. That sounds insane in my head, so imagine how Beth would react if I told her.

'Oh, babes. It's your birthday. I thought we were ignoring it, but are you feeling a bit . . .' she lowers her voice, scrunches her petite nose, 'old?'

'We're still ignoring it.'

"Cause you definitely look younger than thirty-seven. By a couple of years at least.'

'An honest compliment. Ta. Right, I'm off. Be careful with Paul Rudd.'

'Babes. I'm more than aware he's me rebound. The next fella I meet after him'll be the one I have me babies with,' Beth states, although I can hear a wobble in her voice. She's determined to get pregnant, and soon. I can only hope all her meticulous plans – Beth's version of dreams – come together. She'll be a brilliant mum one day. 'By the way, who's Paul Rudd?'

I steal a spray of her perfume.

'You know. Funny guy, handsome. The one who marries Phoebe in *Friends*.'

'Oh, him! God, you're right. He *does* look like Paul Rudd.'

I blow her a kiss and run to the tube station.

Maybe Beth's right? Maybe it is a ring.

It's a cute idea. But come on. It's cheesier than a packet of Wotsits.

Maybe Jack would've done it to gross me out. Even his dad said he was transparent. He was asking me outright to wonder what was behind the picture.

Waiting two minutes for the next train to arrive is agony. I watch the digital clock ticking, wondering if there's a fault – the seconds are passing by too slowly.

So, if it's not an engagement ring, then what *is* behind the picture?

Tickets?

And where to? What for?

I've got it. Vietnam. It was supposed to be our next big trip, wasn't it? Maybe Jack had gone ahead and booked it without telling me. The flights would have been for last month, October: wasted money, a wasted surprise. It's tragic. A holiday waiting behind the picture, never to be taken.

Nah, I don't buy it. I don't think that's what it is.

I board the tube and curse every station it stops at, and every tourist moving at the pace of a tortoise, a humungous rucksack shell, not standing clear of the doors, causing them to open and close again and again.

Come on! Get me home!

Okay. What about tickets to Vegas? Did Jack want us to elope? I vaguely recall us having a chat about that when we were drunk one night, saying how cool it would be to get it done and dusted, and even cooler to see the look on people's faces when we told them we got hitched in Vegas. When did we talk about that? Was it at our local? A pint and a pizza after work one night, an innocent idea, until three bottles of house wine later . . . God, we were absolutely hammered. I'm surprised I remember that now.

I have to switch lines, get to the Overground. I'm walking so fast that my calves burn.

Actually, I bet it's just something really sweet and simple, like a letter. A love letter. Oh, that sounds so mushy, so ancient; a gesture that belongs to a century long ago. Maybe Jack bought me a postcard, one from the stand by the till in Paperchase. You know, a unicorn with an avocado or something. The London Underground sign with a witty slogan as the station name. Maybe he wrote down how he felt, put his words into a stupid poem or changed around the lyrics of a song. That's totally Jack. He knew that sort of thing would make me tick.

But why hide it behind the picture?

Why not just give it to me before I went to work?

The train emerges from the tunnel and my 4G returns. I pass the time scrolling through birthday messages on Facebook, mostly people I haven't seen for years who aren't aware of what's happened to me this year. There's a few who've acknowledged it, some keeping it subtle. Some, not.

Si Sully

How could I not? x

. . . and a YouTube link to 'Being Alive' from Sondheim's Company.

Gareth Allen-Roscoe

HB. You deserve the world ♥

Carol Dooley
Happy Birthday dear Chloe. Your mum said you don't want to celebrate this year and that's understandable but hope you have a lovely day anyway and get spoilt rotten and enjoy a drink or three. See you soon. Your mum misses you loads. Love Carol and family. Xxxxx

Under an old photo of me as a baby:

Sue Roscoe
Can't believe I'm the mother of a thirty-seven year old. Where does the time go? Always a baby to me **Chloe Roscoe** *love you millions xxx*

There's never been a better time to delete my account.

I tap through the settings, get a bit lost in the whole app. Why's it so hard to delete? And hold on – if I do delete it, do I lose everything? Forever? Maybe I need to spend some time going through my profile, seeing what I want to keep and what I'm happy to kiss goodbye to.

I abandon Facebook – it's too complicated to think about – and switch to Instagram. I find the unread message from Justin, still there . . .

Shit! The train doors slide open and I almost miss my stop! Almost.

I run to the house and down the stairs to the basement flat. I can't get my key in the door quick enough. I don't kick off my Converse; I let my suede coat drop to the floor and it lands upon two envelopes, one pink and one lilac, Liverpool postmarks. I'll open them later. I'm not going to hesitate any longer. I'm doing it. I drag a stool to the cooker and clamber onto it, kneeling up and steadying myself with my hands against the mug cupboard. I reach over. One hand. I tap the bottom edge of the picture, lifting it gently, sliding my fingers beneath the canvas. With a little push up, it unhooks from the wall. Afraid of what might fall down from behind it, I jump down from the stool and duck, but I trip, fall, and lose my grip on the picture.

I land on my hands and knees, the kitchen tiles a cold slap to my palms.

The picture tumbles down beside me, clattering like a dull cymbal.

My eyes dart about the floor, looking for something.

What? *What?* What am I looking for?

I pull myself up on the work surface and scour the hobs, hunt behind the chopping board. Did something fall down the back of the toaster? All I find is old crumbs. How old *are* those crumbs?

I shake the picture.

Nothing falls out.

'No!' I cry out. 'There can't be nothing!'

There must be something.

I pace the flat. I need to sense him, feel him. But I can't. It's been a while since I imagined Jack, and even longer since his presence was so huge that I believed he was still here. His scent has been washed away with the candles I've burnt, the windows I've opened. His clothes are in his childhood home. His bedsheets have been washed. The bathroom is a feminine shrine to Boots, and the last male deodorant in there was Freddie's. I pick up the picture of the man sat in the shopping trolley, hold it out: just canvas on a wooden frame. I shake it again.

'No!' I cry again.

I close my eyes. Tears.

They kiss my eyelashes, stream down my cheeks.
'*No!*'

For almost six months, I've been searching for answers to questions I was never asked, holding tight onto something that was already gone. I wail, releasing long, loud sobs, desperate to be free.

And then I see it.

Through my tears, through the canvas, through the white wall that now hangs bare. I see it all. Everything that was behind the picture.

Everything.

I see my lips, intense red and puckering up to the mirror as I apply an extra coat for good luck. I see the empty seat at the Everyman Theatre, the one that Dan Finnigan should've sat in. I see Jack's suit, his hand brushing my leg, the froth from his pint that sat on the tip of his beard that I didn't have the heart to tell him about, the chips and curry sauce we ate for breakfast the morning after because it wasn't morning, it was three in the afternoon – oh yeah, we'd stayed in bed until then.

I see the trains, going north, going south, meeting in the middle; the gin in a tin and packets of M&S crisps; always meeting by the Burger King.

I see the flights and the frogs, Patpong and ping-pong, a Ladyboy winking.

I see the key.

I see the school, the double doors, the desk, the interview, the pints and pizza after I got the job, and God – that was it – the night we'd joked about Vegas – that was it.

I see Jack pulling my socks off my feet when I'm watching Netflix, squashing them into a ball and trying to throw them into an empty mug, annoying the shit out of me every time he did it, and he did it a lot. I see him missing and knocking the mug – which wasn't empty after all – onto the carpet.

I see his chest resting against mine, keeping me warm – sometimes too warm – and I'd have to wait until he fell asleep to unravel myself.

I see us brushing our teeth, elbowing each other until it became a strange little dance, bobbing and swaying in the small cabinet mirror.

I see his phone and him fixating at the footy scores.

I see us getting Belgian waffles in Covent Garden and both coming to the conclusion that they smell better than they taste.

I see us wake at four in the morning, gravitating into each other, making love that's slow and sleepy.

I see us in a beer garden, laughing about the ridiculous names people call their kids these days and losing it when we imagine a baby named Barry.

I see Jack walk in on me having a moment, playing the *Evita* soundtrack and giving it my best Eva Perón out of the bedroom window when I thought I had the flat to myself, and his disgust at either my singing or my taste, or both, but I never asked.

I see us dancing, headbanging and slow dancing, whatever took our fancy, whilst swigging from a bottle of Prosecco, 'cause it was Friday and 'cause we could, and we'd talk about how this was it, we did it, we found each other before forty.

I see us bickering, Jack making me a fried egg because he asked if I wanted eggs and I said, 'ooh yeah, fried please,' and he hated making fried eggs because he always broke the yolk, but he never told me, just muttered under his breath, passive aggression, which led to us yelling at one another, our first fight, which made us both cry, and eventually laugh.

I see Rudolf.

I see the fridge and Jack telling me he'd won a raffle.

I see my hand encased by Jack's, in a kebab shop near the flat, and we order shish taouk and chips and extra garlic sauce and as we wait, we kiss, like really kiss – snog – and the fella behind the counter mocks us, calls us a pair of lovesick teenagers, and we keep kissing – snogging – our teeth touching because we're both smiling, bashful yet brazen, a kiss that's addictive and desperate and ends with sex.

I see the pecks on the cheek, the lips, the neck; busy kisses that get us through busy weeks and that morning peck before rushing off to work. I see the Rice Krispies. I see myself opening the fridge and saying, 'we're out of milk again'.

I see Jack.

And then I go.

And I never ever see him again.

'No, no,' I sob, heaving with cries, emptying out all I have until there's nothing left.

I can't keep looking for something which isn't here.

I grab hold of the picture again, but I don't look at the man sat in the shopping trolley. Instead, I turn it around, look at the canvas stretched over the wooden frame. This picture was from the height of our happiness. I'd written him a message, short and sweet, but now faded, smudged. I'd used a pencil – the pen in my satchel had run out of ink before I got through the first letter. The message simply said, of course:

And I reckon I love you, too, Jack Carmichael.

I blink, hard. Thick, satisfying tears drip from my cheeks and splash onto the canvas. Right there, above the words I originally wrote, is another sentence, added later and written in bold capitals, in permanent black marker pen:

I RECKON I LOVE YOU, CHLOE ROSCOE.

This is what we were. What we will always be.

Not love. But almost.

I breathe in.

I breathe out.

I'm alive, and at last, I let go.

EPILOGUE

Three months later

'That's the last one,' Si says, relieved.

Lugging boxes up two flights of stairs isn't Si's forte. He takes a crumpled tissue from beneath his sleeve and dabs his brow, then checks himself from head to toe in the long mirror on the wall of my bedroom. He turns to the side, sticks out his belly and grabs it, giving the small roll of flab an angry shake.

'Malcolm!' Si exclaims. 'He puts full-fat cream in everything!'

'It's called the Relationship Stone,' I tell him. 'Everybody puts on weight when they fall in love.'

'Thanks for confirming I've let myself go, Chloe.'

'To be honest, hun, I think you look better than ever.'

Si blushes and his eyelashes genuinely flutter. It's adorable to see him so happy. He digs into his pockets again and takes out his keys. He removes the keyring and holds it out for me to take. It's a silver flip-flop with the *Mamma Mia!* logo printed on the sole.

'A reminder of our first date which wasn't a date,' he grins. 'And how far you've come.'

'How far we've both come,' I smile, dangling the flip-flop between our noses.

'I better go. You know how I can't abide being late.'

'Give Malcolm me love. Enjoy the matinee.'

'And you enjoy the party.'

I attach the flip-flop to my keys and toss them onto the king-size bed, waiting for the front door to slam shut. As it does, I release a sigh followed by taking an indulgent breath in through my nose, and out. The space is all mine to enjoy – and wow, there's a lot of it.

I moved out of the Carmichaels' basement flat this morning. I gave my official notice after Christmas, knowing wholeheartedly that in order to get on with my life, I needed to get out. Finding a new place that's affordable but suitable has been a challenge. My mum tries to entice me back up north daily; this morning it was news of a fabulous new boutique opening on Bold Street, yesterday a photo of the sun setting on the Mersey. Tempting as it is, I'm officially a permanent member of staff at the school now. Plus I love the friends I've made in London. I'll miss being so close to Giles and Ingrid, but they've put their flat on the market in the hope of finding a house in the area, and Neil travels so much, he's never there anyway. We're all going to a dim sum place in Soho next week, before he heads off to Brazil.

As of today, I'm Si's flatmate. Sounds like a step backwards, right? A regression to student life, or a refusal to grow up? I assure you, it's the opposite. You see, Si's never at home these days – he spends the majority of his time at Malcolm's mews house in Hampstead. I mean, who wouldn't? I spent a weekend there recently and as the log fire burnt bright, casting an orange haze across his immaculately kept bookshelves, I expected Emma Thompson to pop over with an apple pie or Bill Nighy to rock up and give us a well-meaning back-handed compliment. Anyway, Si's old flatmate has relocated to Scotland, so he had a spare room with an en suite bathroom to fill. I'm not joking when I say this room is bigger than that whole basement flat. My plan is to flatshare and save, so I can get a deposit together for my own place and finally get on the property ladder.

I'll unpack the boxes later. My clothes are already hanging up and I run my fingers along the garments, unsure whether to change my outfit. I'm wearing a neon-pink jumper with denim miniskirt, tights and boots. It's the neon pink I'm unsure about. I'm going to a gender reveal party. I don't want to look like I'm hoping for the baby to be a girl. Plus if the baby is a girl, doesn't neon pink scream gender stereotype? Help! I'm a gender reveal party virgin. What's the vibe? At least it's not a baby shower. They are, by far, the most difficult social events to nail. I mean, there's usually booze for all except the mama-to-be, but nobody drinks it. There's always games, and they always suck. Guessing the size of the bump? Please, somebody tell me, who the fuck thought that was a bright idea for shits and giggles? And talking of shits, the last baby shower I went to had real nappies open on the nibbles table filled with Malteasers.

Ah, fuck it. I'm sticking with the pink. It goes great with my hair. It's currently an ashy-grey silver, and honestly, I love it.

Do you know what else I love?

The picture of the man sat in the shopping trolley.

Thanks to Justin, it now has a whole new meaning.

So, yeah, I finally read his message.

During my time with Jack, we'd had the odd chat about

377

Christmas – you know, family traditions, memories of meeting Santa – but we never discussed how we'd spend the next one. We never got that far. In the end I'd enjoyed a quiet Christmas back at home, but I stayed with Kit and Gareth rather than my mum and dad. They got a sofa bed as a wedding gift from Gareth's aunt, so luckily I wasn't forced to spend Christmas Eve in a tent. I realise I've said *enjoyed*. I did. With the strength and love of my brother and brother-in-law, we embraced a different Christmas, indulged in festive activities we always said we'd do each year but never got round to doing; ice skating, going to see *It's a Wonderful Life* at the Philharmonic Hall, building a gingerbread house with Gareth's nieces. On New Year's Eve, sitting in Kit and Gareth's kitchen with Mabel nibbling my slouch socks, and before getting my creative genius into a serious game of Pictionary, I decided to read Justin's message;

Hey there Chloe, look what I did. I hope this makes you smile. Jx

Attached was a photo. Of Justin. Sat in a shopping trolley. Outside a Seven Eleven at night-time, he was giving a double thumbs up. His long legs, in purple traveller trousers patterned with tiny white elephants, were outstretched and crossed at the ankles, his calves resting on the edge of the trolley, his flip-flops flapping away from his hardened heels. Behind bushier facial hair than I'd remembered him with, his grin was goofy, his eyes dancing with a self-conscious chuckle. I imagine he'd asked another backpacker to take his picture and maybe there was a faff, or somebody walked past the pose, allowing Justin a bit too much time to feel silly, wishing he hadn't bothered with the effort.

Beneath the photo was another message, sent some days later.

I hope this picture didn't offend? That wasn't my intention at all. I just wanted you to see a guy sitting in a trolley. A real guy. Somebody you spoke to. Somebody you knew stuff about. I could print this photo a thousand times and give it away to random strangers, all of whom will just see a guy they don't know. It will mean nothing to them. But those who do know me will see something. They'll see part of my story. They might know about my marriage and wonder if I'm okay. Or it will remind them of me acting like a dork in high school. It could prompt somebody to check in on my parents, wonder if I'm still into snow-boarding (I am!), ask when I'm coming home or where I'm going next. What I'm trying to say is, I'm a real guy, with a real story. The guy in your picture isn't nobody, isn't nothing. He's just a guy who you don't know. Whether he was posing for a picture to make souvenirs or not, he will have a childhood, a family, a thought to the future of some sort. You might never know the story behind his picture, but there will be a story. Like mine. Like yours. Jx

Below this message, the following day, Justin had added two more photos.

Both images were of people I don't know sitting in the same trolley outside the Seven Eleven. One of a young Thai girl, cross-legged with her smiling head popping over the edge, giving the peace sign. The other a Western woman, plump and sweating, her hair pulled up into a high bun and her tongue sticking out. Justin included a further message;

The Thai girl is Sopa. She's seventeen and her family have a small laundry business in Bangkok. She has two sisters. Her passion is singing and she played 'Hero' by Mariah Carey on her phone and sang along to it right there on the street. She was amazing! Her dream is to go to London one day and become a student.

The other photo is Nat. She's British, from a place called Huddersfield. Do you know it? She's on her honeymoon but her new husband ate some king prawns in the hope his seafood allergy had magically disappeared, and he's room-bound, or in her words 'loo-bound'. She's a TV script writer and huge fan of Leeds United. Her mom died last year and she found her whole wedding tough to get through. I had a few drinks with her and when it comes to doing shots, you and her could be kindred spirits!

Anyway, I could have taken more photos. That happened to be a super friendly Seven Eleven! I hope you're doing great and doing whatever makes you happy. I'm heading back to Canada in the spring. If you'd ever like to visit, see the sights, don't be a stranger. Jx

When I'd finished reading Justin's messages, our Kit slid an opened Cadbury's selection box across the table. Along with Mabel, he'd sat with me as I'd read, for no other reason than to be there. The Wispa and the chocolate buttons had already mysteriously disappeared so I selected the Fudge, chewing the soft sweetness quietly. I'd passed my phone to Kit, opened the Dairy Milk and broke it into two halves to share with him as he read what Justin had to say. Mabel stopped nibbling my slouch socks; my feet were warm and heavy. I could feel her heartbeat as she slept, the gentle comforting vibrations of her snores.

'What do you think?' I'd asked.

'First impressions. Justin? Fit.'

'Oh, bloody hell, Kit!'

'No, sis. Don't bloody hell me. He's kind, considerate, eloquent, writes well and for fuck's sake, Chloe, he's absolutely gorgeous. You asked what I think. Don't ask if you don't wanna hear.'

I'd snatched my phone back, looked at the pictures again, lingered on the one of Justin.

'What do *you* think, though?' Kit had asked, taking my hand in his.

'I think . . . I'll always wonder about the man sat in the shopping trolley.'

'Even though you said he was just a bit of tourist tat?'

'I've changed me mind.'

'Thanks to Justin?'

'Yeah. You see, I'd rather wonder what he's doing. It's better than not. Makes him real.'

Kit had squeezed my hand.

'Do us a favour though, sis. Don't go gallivanting off to find him again, will you? Okay? Let's go to Jamaica and drink rum. Or fuck it. Let's go to Disneyland.'

I'd kissed his cheek.

'Deal.'

Then I'd replied to Justin.

Hiya Justin! Where in the world are you right now? Look, I could give you a shit load of excuses as to why I didn't read your messages and reply sooner, but I'd be lying. I saw your name, thought about our kiss and felt like I'd cheated on Jack. I'm sorry. What you've done with these pictures is nothing short of gorgeous. I'm so touched, over-whelmed at your kindness. I apologise for taking so long to let you know. In short, I'm okay. I've got brilliant people around me. And yes, I do (try to do!) whatever makes me happy. Sometimes that might be watching The Sound of Music *with a Meat Feast from Dominos. Don't judge!! I hope you're doing the same. And Canada, well, I've always wanted to go. It's actually second on my list after Japan. Love and hugs to you. Chloe x.*

Now, in my new bedroom, I look at the man sat in the shopping trolley resting on the carpet against an upcycled chest of drawers, and wonder where to hang him. A horn honks – my taxi is outside. I've volunteered to sort the cake – the all-important will-it-be-blue-will-it-be-pink sponge covered in thick white buttercream – and I've got to pick it up en route. This is a mammoth responsibility. There's no way I'm getting on the tube with it, not on a Saturday afternoon. Knowing my luck, it'll end up on the stairs of an escalator and a load of Spanish tourists will know the gender of the baby before its bloody parents. Currently, the only people who know are the sonographer, the admin who typed the letter and the baker in Sydenham who I hand-delivered the sealed letter to. I don't know why, but I suddenly think about Nat, the woman from Huddersfield who Justin snapped in the trolley. Will she and her new husband be trying for a baby perhaps? Is that the next part of her story?

I run down the two flights of stairs, slam the front door behind me.

The story of Jack and me has ended. Gone but not forgotten, as they say.

My story, however, will – and must – continue.

*

382

I arrive outside the redbrick Victorian house as a visitor, no longer a tenant. It's only been a few hours but already, I feel disconnected from the place, like it could be days, weeks, even months since I lived here. In a material sense, yeah, all my things are no longer in the basement. Not a single joss stick remains. If I've forgotten my purse or my red lippy, I can't nip downstairs to get it any more. The wind feels like it's blowing gently in a different direction.

Holding the white cake box with both hands, I slowly walk up the steps to the main front door. I've made it this far without a cock-up, haven't even opened the box to see the cake for fear of ripping the lid or sneezing on the icing. But I don't have a free hand to ring the doorbell. I scuffle around the open porch; attempt to lift my elbow. That's ridiculous. I rise onto my tiptoes, lightly headbutt the bell. No sound. Shit.

'Hey, Chlo! Let me get that for you,' a voice behind me calls out.

I hear the brush of footsteps coming up closer as I turn around. Peering over the top of the cake box, I'm shocked to recognise the man in front of me, although this is the first time I notice golden flecks in his brown eyes. Gasping, my knees jerk and the tense right angles in my arms break loose.

'Whoa!'

'WHOA!'

Legs bent, full squat, the man saves the cake box with one swift underarm catch.

'Layla Birch's dad!' is the best I manage.

'Miss Roscoe,' he says. 'That was almost a tragedy!'

'You literally just saved me life.'

'Best stick to teaching the drama, rather than creating it, eh?'

383

In his khaki trench coat and smart striped scarf, he straightens himself up and holds out the box for me to retrieve. Dying inside, I accept.

'Thank you . . .' I say.

'Ollie,' he reminds me.

I knew that. 'I knew that.'

'You called me "Layla Birch's dad". Which I am. But once upon a time, about fifteen and a half years ago, I was – surprisingly – a person with my own identity. I like to think he still comes out of the cupboard now and then.'

I break into a wide smile and then panic that my front teeth are stained with red lippy.

'I meant the bell, by the way,' Ollie says. 'When I said, "let me get that for you".'

'Well, you've got good instincts.'

'One of my few rare talents.'

I grip the edges of the box tight. It cannot drop again.

'Shall I?' he asks, pointing his index finger up.

'Hold on, what are you doing here?'

'I could ask you the same question.'

He smirks, coy rather than cheeky maybe, like he just answered back to the teacher. I could shoot him my best unimpressed face; give him a warning. But I'm genuinely interested. What the hell is Oliver Birch doing here, where I used to live?

'I work with Giles,' Ollie says. 'He's a good mate.'

'Wow! Really? What a small world. I used to live downstairs, in the basement flat.'

Ollie laughs. 'It's brilliant news, isn't it? Giles and Ingrid.'

'Ah, deffo. They're gonna be the cutest parents.'

'With the cutest kid.'

'Yeah, it'll be pristine. No snotty nose or food in her hair.'

'Wait – *her*? How do you know it's a girl? Isn't this a gender reveal party?'

'Oh! Shit. I dunno. Just rolled off me tongue. I meant his *or* her hair.'

'Unless, Chlo, you've got good instincts, too.'

I mean to laugh, politely, but I choke a bit, then clear my throat like a sick monster. Ollie rings the doorbell and we wait for Giles or Ingrid to buzz us up. I grip the box tighter. Ollie rocks back and forth. I can't see his shoes – the box is blinding my vision – but I bet they're smart Timberlands, or similar.

'Have you been to a gender reveal party before?' Ollie asks.

'Nope, I'm a total virgin.'

'That's something else we have in common, then.'

'Hello?' Ingrid sings through the intercom.

'Hey, it's Ollie and Chlo,' Ollie sings back.

We're buzzed in and Ollie pushes the door open wide.

'After you,' he says.

I'm being overcautious, taking my time with each step. Ollie's sniggering behind me.

'Stop it!' I snap. 'If I drop this cake, it's on you!'

'Literally.'

We make it to the top of the stairs and just before we go in, Ollie stops, his hand naturally landing upon my elbow as he looks down at the cake box.

'So, what's your prediction?' he asks.

I give a small, careful shrug, then look up.

Our eyes meet.

'Well, Ollie. I guess we're about to find out.'

Acknowledgements

This book was written during two challenging stretches; the end of my second pregnancy into the newborn phase, and a global pandemic. Without the love and support of the following wonderful people, I could never have achieved what I feared was impossible.

Thank you to the team at Avon, especially Helen Huthwaite. Your understanding for working mums is like receiving the warmest hug and I hope women all over get to experience such care. A huge thank you to my editor, Phoebe Morgan, a publishing rockstar. Your belief in this book has truly meant the world to me. And I'm so lucky to once again thank the wonderful Camilla Bolton, my agent at Darley Anderson.

To Nils Mohl and Deborah Du Preez Taylor, my kindred spirits of the storytelling world. Thank you for the early brainstorming sessions. Now, let's get that pilot written, eh?

For putting up with endless questions about teaching, a big thank you and tambourine shake goes to my three bezzie mates; Kate Benjamin, Maria Howarth and Michelle

Monaghan, I'd thank Aunty Val, too, but she never bothered to get her teaching qualification.

To Kjell and Jack Eldor-Evans, thank you for inviting me to the wedding with so much love in one room. To Rosie and Luca in Two Spoons, Honor Oak Park, thank you for supplying me with cappuccinos and scrambled eggs as I wrote a great chunk of this book with one hand and rocked a baby to sleep with the other. To my mum, for travelling between Liverpool and London to be the most loving Nannie, and to my dad, with your encouraging daily emails; thank you.

To Oli. You took that photo, we survived that typhoon; thank you for the travels before we took on the adventure to become parents. And thanks for listening to me read aloud chapters when what we both needed was trashy telly and sleep. Thank you to my son, Milo, for being the sunshine, never allowing a dull second to make an appearance. And to my daughter, Phoebe, thank you for making an appearance! You've been by my side – inside and outside – the whole time I wrote this book.

And for the luxury of sibling love, thank you Cheryl. I dedicate this book to you. My sister, my closest friend, my advisor, my mushroom, my weird person, I mean, the list is endless. I run everything – *everything* – by you, and rightly so. You're a goddess. Now, shut up and drink your gin.

Some people go looking for love.
Others crash right into it.

Zara's going one way. Jim's going the other.
But fate has other ideas...

Never
Saw
You
Coming

HAYLEY
DOYLE

Don't miss this gorgeous tale about taking risks
and living life to the full – perfect for fans of
Beth O'Leary and Josie Silver.
Out now!